MARRIAGE

ACCIDENTS

of

MARRIAGE

R.S. MEYERS

**SIMON &
SCHUSTER**

London · New York · Sydney · Toronto · New Delhi

A CBS COMPANY

First published by Atria Books, an imprint of Simon & Schuster Inc., 2014
This edition first published in Great Britain by Simon & Schuster UK Ltd, 2014
A CBS COMPANY

1 3 5 7 9 10 8 6 4 2

Simon & Schuster UK Ltd
1st Floor
222 Gray's Inn Road
London WC1X 8HB

www.simonandschuster.co.uk

Simon & Schuster Australia, Sydney
Simon & Schuster India, New Delhi

A CIP catalogue record for this book
is available from the British Library

Paperback ISBN: 978-1-4711-4044-0
EBOOK ISBN: 978-1-4711-4045-7

Printed and bound by CPI Group (UK) Ltd, Croydon, CR0 4YY

To Jeff, who makes it possible

There have been two great accidents in my life. One was the trolley, and the other was Diego. Diego was by far the worst.

—FRIDA KAHLO

Before

———

JULY

CHAPTER 1

Maddy

Maddy ran her tongue over her teeth, imagining the bitter taste of a crumbling tablet of Xanax. After a gut-wrenching day at the hospital nothing tempted her more than a chemical vacation. Nothing appealed to her less than cooking supper. Churning stomach acid—courtesy of work—coupled with anxiety that Ben might come home as frenzied as he'd left made a formidable appetite killer.

She could bottle it and make a fortune.

Each morning she spun the wheel on the Ben chart, hoping the arrow would hit *happy husband*, or at least *neutral guy*. Today his arrow landed on *total bastard*, holding her personally responsible for Caleb's tantrum, which—oh, horror!—had cost Ben twenty minutes of work.

She considered taking a pill, but the rites of family happiness demanded her attention. Gracie and Caleb sprawled on the rug, recovering from their day at camp: seven-year-old Caleb, half asleep, rubbing his cheek with his thumb; nine-year-old Gracie's glazed eyes fixed on the television. Emma, her oldest, a day camp counselor at fourteen, would be home soon.

Sluggish inertia kept Maddy stapled to the couch despite her long list of waiting tasks. Chop vegetables, pay the mortgage, and catch up on laundry before the kids ran out of socks. Find a stamp somewhere in the mess she called her desk so she could mail the electric bill. Give her children feelings of self-worth. Plus, since she and Ben had fought that morning, he'd need soothing. Fellatio came to mind.

Indestructible fabric, the sort bought by parents with children prone to transferring their sticky snacks to the upholstery, prickled against her bare arms. She lusted for air-conditioning as she'd once longed for peace, justice, and her husband. Each suffocating Boston summer in their badly wired Victorian became more hateful and Ben's warnings about global warming swayed her less. According to Ben, her environmental ethics turned situational with each drop of perspiration.

Pressing the small of her back didn't ease the permanent knot lodged deep and low, nor did shoving a small hard pillow against it. Her stomach growled despite her lack of desire for food.

Fish sticks would be easy, but she couldn't bear turning on the oven.

The back door slammed. Emma banged her backpack on the table. Her daughter's way of saying *I'm home.*

"Emma?"

"*What?*"

Maddy struggled up from the couch and headed toward the kitchen. "Just making sure it's you."

"Were you expecting someone else?" she asked.

"It could have been Daddy."

"Right." What an all-purpose word *right* had become in their family, their polite way of saying, *I am acknowledging you have spoken, but am choosing not to engage in any meaningful way.* Lately, they used it all too often.

Newspapers they'd tried to read at breakfast covered half the table. Emma stared into the refrigerator as Maddy gathered the papers, unsure whether to recycle them. Had Ben finished reading the *Boston Globe*? The *New York Times*?

"There's nothing to eat," Emma said. "In Caro's house—"

The sound of breaking glass followed by Caleb's scream interrupted before Emma could specify just how superior a shopper Caro's mother was.

"*Mom!*" Gracie yelled. "*Come here!*"

Emma followed as Maddy ran to the living room.

"Jesus, what happened?" Maddy crouched next to Caleb, her stomach dropping at the sight of blood pouring from his foot. Shards of glass surrounded him, liquid droplets of milk clinging to the pieces, a larger white puddle pooling on the wooden floor. She grabbed a wadded-up napkin to staunch the blood, crouching awkwardly to avoid cutting her knees.

Gracie's mouth trembled. "I just got up, that's all, and I knocked over his milk glass. He got mad and screamed, then he stood up and kicked the glass and it broke. He stepped on it. It wasn't my fault!"

"It's okay, Gracie." Blood soaked through the napkin, dissolving the paper as she exerted pressure. "Emma, get me a damp towel."

This was preventable, Ben would say. *This is why we have plastic glasses.*

"Make it stop, Mommy!" Tears cut through the dirt on Caleb's cheeks.

She pressed harder. Gracie mopped the spilled milk with a dirty T-shirt from her backpack.

"Here." Emma held out a dripping kitchen towel.

"You need to wring it out, Emma. Never mind, just get a clean one."

Emma stomped out with Gracie in her wake. Wet cloth slapped in the sink.

"Give this to Mom." Emma's voice from the kitchen was extra loud.

Using the hem of her black cotton skirt, Maddy covered the napkin. Gracie returned with a new towel. Emma watched from the doorway, twirling the bottom of her long brown braid.

Maddy peeled away her skirt and replaced it with the towel, Caleb whimpering. "Do I have to go to the doctor?" He squinted as she peeked under the towel.

"It doesn't look too deep, but it has to be cleaned," she said. "I don't think we need a doctor." Maddy's pulse calmed. She stopped rushing ahead in her mind: wrapping Caleb's foot safely enough to hold in the bleeding until they got to the emergency room, packing the kids in the car, calling Ben. She looked again—making sure her decision was based on wisdom and not wishful thinking. It wasn't gaping. The bleeding had slowed.

He tried to pull his foot away. "No! No cleaning. It'll hurt."

Emma squatted next to them. "You let Mom wash out the cut and I'll play Monopoly." Caleb's smile came through like a sun shower.

"That's sweet, honey." Maddy should appreciate Emma's goodness and stop losing patience with her sulks and eye rolling. "Thank you."

"Can I play?" Gracie asked.

"No," said Caleb. "Just me and Emma."

Gracie's lip quivered at her brother's words, leaving Maddy torn between soothing and yelling *Stop it*, especially when she saw Gracie make the tiny sign of the cross she'd picked up from Grandma Frances, Ben's mother, a woman given to reflexive ritual blessings. Gracie's gesture unsettled Maddy. Next thing she knew, her daughter would be genuflecting at Our Lady of the Virgins. Buying her a Jewish star or a Unitarian flaming chalice, before Grandma Frances hung a crucifix over Gracie's bed, went on her to-do list. Mixed marriage only went so far.

"Monopoly is better with more people, Caleb." Pregnant women should be required to take classes in referee and negotiation skills along with breathing and panting lessons.

"No. I only want to play with Emma."

Gracie pulled at her camp-grimy toes. "How about you and I make chocolate sauce while they play?" Maddy suggested. "We could have hot fudge sundaes for supper."

"Ice cream for supper?" Gracie raised her chin off her knees.

"Why not?" She pushed back her daughter's sweaty black curls, the only visible part of Maddy that Gracie had inherited. The kids divided their parents' parts and shared few: Skinny Caleb had Ben's thick brown hair, Maddy's long lashes and narrow shoulders. Poor Gracie, like Ben, would have to fight a tendency toward getting thick in the middle. Emma, wiry like Maddy, had her father's sharp cheekbones.

Emma rolled her eyes. "Healthy, Mom."

"Shut up, Emma," Caleb said.

"You shut up. Or I won't play with you."

"I'll play," Gracie said.

"*No*. Emma picked me. Wash my cut, Mommy."

A child leaned on either shoulder. With feet propped on the coffee table, Maddy drifted in and out of sleep. Dirty bowls decorated with blobs of hardened fudge littered the room. After cresting to a quick high of giggles over supper, they'd slumped into queasy sugar comas.

They stirred at the sound effects of Ben's nightly return: the car rolling on gravel. Scrape of heat-swollen door opening. Keys dropping on the hall table. Briefcase thudding to the floor. Sighs of relief or disgust indicated his mood level. Despite their early-morning fight, Ben sounded audibly benign. Thank God. Maybe it would be a Swiss night, with the living room their first neutral zone.

Ben entered the living room and surveyed their collapsed bodies and the scattered Monopoly pieces. Gracie pulled away and ran to him, throwing her hands around his waist. He stroked her black ringlets into a little bundle at the back of her head as she leaned into his slightly softening middle. He had the body of a forty-three-year-old man who fought gravity by playing handball twice a week, but who'd given up crunches. Not bad, but unlike Maddy, who ran and used free weights and the rowing machine in their basement, his battle against time brought fewer visible rewards.

"What happened?" he asked. "It looks like a war zone."

"We had some excitement. Our boy cut himself."

Caleb held out his bandage-swathed foot while still staring at the television.

"You okay?" Ben asked. He gave Gracie one last pat and went to the couch. "Hurt much?"

Caleb shrugged. "I guess. A little." He studied Maddy as though seeking the right answer.

Ben laid a hand on Caleb's calf. "Can you walk on it?"

"Sorta. I hop on my heel on that side."

"It's on the ball of his foot. The inside," Maddy said.

"How'd it happen?" Ben tugged on his chin—his poker tell that steam could build at any moment.

Maddy leaned over Caleb and kissed her husband, hitting the side of his mouth he offered. "Forgetting anything?" she asked. "*Hello, Maddy? How are you?*"

He exhaled. "Don't start. I've had a rough day."

Kissing was starting? *It is when you're being sarcastic,* she answered herself, using Ben's lecture voice. "He fell asleep and then got up without remembering there was a milk glass next to him. It was an accident." She knew the lie was barely plausible, but she also knew it was just enough for him to avoid being prosecutorial.

"Where was he sleeping? The recycle bin?"

"Very funny. A glass broke. End of story." There. The truth snuck in.

"Why can't the kids eat and drink at the table like they're supposed to? Why weren't they using plastic glasses?" He ran his hands through his hair. "Look at this place. It's a mess. No wonder everyone's always having accidents."

Caleb rubbed his thumb back and forth across his knee. Gracie crossed herself.

"Not now, okay? Please." She sent him a significant look.

Ben flexed his shoulders, leaned back on the couch, and stared at the ceiling. He took a deep breath, seeming to remember the anger management sheet Maddy had forced on him six months ago, after he'd thrown a shoe. *At the wall,* he insisted each time she mentioned the incident. *Not at you.* But her message had landed. For once, she'd broken through his endless rejections of her careful observations about his temper.

Good thing. She'd gritted her teeth through his rages, but she'd be damned if their house became a physical battleground. He'd scared himself when he'd thrown the shoe—just as he had years before when he'd thrown a bottle of detergent against the wall. The difference was this time he'd listened to her. He'd read the sheet despite hating it when she supposedly social-worked him. *Save it for your clients,* he'd yell when she deconstructed him. The children. Their marriage. *You're not my shrink, you're my wife.*

If he didn't want her to social-work him, then she sure wished he'd learn to manage his own moods. Maddy's sister insisted that one day it would be too late for anger prevention sheets and other tricks. Vanessa had no patience for Ben's rages, but Maddy blamed herself for the antagonism her family felt toward Ben. Maddy overshared. Everything negative, anyway. When had she last called her sister to say things were going great? To brag about Ben taking an entire day to make sure Gracie could ride her bike safely? How often did she mention that Ben took the kids to the movies while she went for a massage?

At least her mother pretended to love Ben. For which Maddy was grateful.

"We had ice cream for supper," Caleb announced.

Emma's shoulders squared. Gracie pressed into Maddy.

Ben turned to Caleb. "Ice cream?"

"With hot fudge," Caleb added.

"Nice to be rewarded for breaking a glass, huh?" Ben kicked off his shoes. "Since I haven't fallen or broken anything, what do I get for supper?"

Emma jumped up. "Should I make you eggs, Dad?"

"Thank you, honey. That would be terrific." He leaned back and closed his eyes.

Gracie tapped his forehead. He blinked and gave her a tired smile. "What is it, cupcake?"

"Want me to cut up carrots for you?"

Maddy grabbed the laundry basket from where she'd dropped it in the corner of the living room and hurried out before she had to witness the girls wait on Ben. It drove her crazy watching them being trained in the fine art of placating an angry man, but try explaining that one. What, a child couldn't feed a hungry father?

After throwing in a white wash and rummaging through the crowded shelves for fabric softener, she dragged over a small dusty step stool and climbed up, stretching to reach behind the jumble of cleaning supplies. She pulled out a dusty Baggie that held a few tablets, took out a yellow one, bit off half, and swallowed it dry. Sometimes she wondered if she could remember all of her caches. Keeping them scattered around the house gave her a convoluted sense of peace and safety. She might reach for one pill in a week; she might reach in every day. Either way, knowing that they were never more than a few steps away comforted her.

Back in the kitchen, remnants of Ben's eggs and carrots littered the countertop. She cleared the debris to one side to make sandwiches for the kids' lunch boxes. Trying to spread cold peanut butter made her hate Ben's mother. Frances had spent the past forty-six years appeasing Ben's father's neuroses by keeping a spotless house and refrigerating peanut butter, on constant guard against food poisoning, bacteria, and dust.

Because of Frances, they ate hard peanut butter.

The bread tore. She folded it around the wad of Skippy and shoved it in her mouth. Then she got a fresh slice and began making the sandwiches again: grape jelly for Caleb, blueberry for Gracie, and for Emma, Maddy's mother's homemade orange preserves.

Anger exhausted her. She waited for the kiss of Xanax to kick in, Prince Charming bearing a sheath for her nerves.

Ben hadn't cared if they ate hot mayonnaise and slept on typhus-encrusted sheets when they'd met, not while they burned off the searing heat of their early years. He'd been exciting, her Ben, a public defense lawyer demanding the world give his wrecked clients a break—a little justice, a fair shot. She could barely breathe around him, some part of her always needing to touch some part of him. Her hand on his shoulder. An ankle casually leaning against his calf.

Ben dwarfed everyone, racing through life with exclamation points coming out all sides. Poverty to the right? *Boom!* Racism? *Pow.* Dirty landlords? *Gotcha!*

Who knew all that passion and rage could be directed at a late car payment? A missing button.

Her.

CHAPTER 2

Ben

Ben hit the off button five minutes before the alarm buzzed, satisfied at beating the clock. Each weekday began with a win or loss, depending on how well his unconscious did its job.

Maddy slept curled on her side, facing away from him, her head buried in her arms. He turned off the second alarm, hers, so she could sleep another half hour, and then he crept out of bed to make coffee—he'd wake her by waving a steaming cup under her nose as he once did Monday through Friday.

Making Maddy happy was so easy, and yet he disappointed her at least once a day. It made him feel like shit. She thought he was unaware of his crimes and misdemeanors, when in actuality he only committed about a quarter of his sins without complete agency. It wasn't that he didn't know he was wrong. He was selfish. Or he chose expediency. *Why do you yell?* Maddy would ask, but he couldn't tell the truth: Saying "because it works" made him sound like a monster. He couldn't pretend shouting or screaming was kind or loving—that made him sound insane. So mostly he muttered and shuffled away.

After showering, he crept downstairs, not wanting to wake the kids, desperate for quiet so he could plan his schedule and steal time to read the paper uninterrupted. He had to get in early to meet with Elizabeth, his current favorite intern. This afternoon they'd present the motion to suppress evidence she'd prepared for B-bird, whose stand-up-guy routine had captured Elizabeth's heart, despite the client's murder charge.

Ben supposed he coddled Elizabeth, letting her spend an inordinate amount of time on that manipulative con artist. No doubt she'd lose her sympathetic glow toward clients soon, but right now, as clearly as she'd carried her Ash Wednesday smudge, she demonstrated her belief that those who grew up in the projects carried an inherent holiness.

Sweat rose on Ben's forehead as he ground the coffee. Barely six fifteen and the kitchen already felt uncomfortably warm. He snuck the radio dial from Maddy's NPR to hard rock, not that he could actually enjoy the music when it played at such low volume. He grabbed the paper from the porch. Scuffling came from the second floor, but at this hour it was probably just one of the kids peeing and then shambling back to bed.

"Dad?" Emma appeared in the doorway, brushing her long brown waves off her sleep-swollen face. "Mom needs you in Caleb's room."

"I'll be right there." He shook coffee into the filter.

"She said to come now," Emma said.

He poured in the water, turned on the pot, and then hurried up the stairs to his son's room, where he found Caleb whimpering in Maddy's arms. He knelt and rubbed Caleb's shoulder. "Hey, cowboy. What is it? Nightmare?"

Caleb winced and pointed at his foot. "It hurts."

"Let's take a look." Ben gave Maddy's knee a reassuring squeeze.

Gracie padded in as Ben unwound the white bandage. "What's wrong?"

"Caleb's foot," Emma said. Gracie moved close to her sister, transfixed as Ben revealed hot-looking pink skin puffing up around his wound.

"It could be infected." Maddy rested her cheek on top of Caleb's head, pressing soft kisses on his messy hair. "He needs to go to the doctor."

Caleb shook his head. "*Noooo.* I have to go to camp. Today's color war. I'm the green captain."

Pride surged at the thought that his son was a captain, though he was surprised they still had color wars in camp. By now, he'd figured, they'd banned all competition and had color love day. He gently turned his son's foot, checking for red streaks.

"What do you think?" Maddy asked.

Ben pressed his lips together and ran a finger along the unbroken skin next to Caleb's cut.

"*Ouch!*" Tears trickled from Caleb's eyes.

Maddy touched Caleb's head again, as though his fever might have spiked in the last ten seconds. "I don't like how this looks. I'll take him to the doctor. You drive Gracie to camp," she said.

Ben touched Caleb's arm again. It was warm, too warm, but not hot. "Can't you drop her off on the way?"

"Triage opens at seven and I want to get him right in. Camp doesn't start till eight forty-five."

Ben stood. "Then take Gracie with you. My day is packed."

"I'm scheduled back-to-back."

Maddy's tit-for-tat tone chipped at his patience. "Look," he said. "I'm sorry, but I have a prep meeting before eight."

The younger children looked from him to Maddy and back. Emma left with a small puff of disgust.

"What time is your case being heard?" Maddy took a tissue and wiped Caleb's nose, running from his tears.

Jesus. The negotiation just went on and on and on.

"When?" she asked again.

"That's not the point. I have to prepare. Take Gracie with you. Please." Why did she have to start on everything?

"Can we talk in the hall for a second?" Maddy lifted Caleb off her lap. "Gracie, get some juice for your brother, okay? And could you read to him, sweetheart?"

Ben knelt in front of his son and saw deep brown duplicates of his own eyes. "You'll be fine, cowboy," he said. "Be a tough guy, okay?"

"Mommy?" Gracie glanced at Ben before speaking. "I can go to camp, right? I'm an assistant captain."

Maddy patted her shoulder. "Don't worry, honey. We'll work it out." She didn't even give Ben the courtesy of a glance before walking out.

Terrific. Snafu time again, folks. Situation normal, all fucked up. Welcome to another morning with the Illicas. Ben followed Maddy into their bedroom, where she yanked underwear and a bra from her dresser.

"Ben, I can't take her with me. The wait might be hours." She pulled a light-pink sundress from her closet. "I can't even take a shower."

"What's the big deal?" Ben took off his robe and grabbed a pair of socks from the dresser. "Gracie only needs a book to be happy."

"Nothing in this house is a big deal to you, is it, Ben? Not like your cases, right?" She went into their bathroom and banged the door shut.

Ben slammed his palm against the closed door. "A kid's future is up for grabs," he yelled over the running faucet.

The water stopped. Maddy burst out of the bathroom, wiping her face with a towel. "My first client is a pregnant crack whore who's already lost three children. Her kids will become your precious clients if something doesn't change soon, so it actually begins here. With me. Nevertheless, I'm calling my office to reschedule. I'm just asking you to be one half hour late."

"Why can't someone watch her?" he asked.

Maddy sat on the unmade bed, red sandals dangling from her right hand. "It's six thirty in the morning. Exactly who do we leave her with?"

"I'm not suggesting auctioning her off as a child bride, just leaving her with a neighbor." Ben grabbed a pressed shirt and riffled through the closet for a matching tie. Then he frowned at his own absurdity. "Forget that idea. Stupid. I know."

Maddy brushed her hair with a few hard strokes and pulled it back into a large brown clip. "Please, can't you just drive her?"

Ben heard her hesitation and knew he'd gained the edge. "Not with a court date—I just can't wait until camp starts."

"Mom. Mommy." Gracie stood in the doorway, twisting the front of her oversized purple nightshirt. Ben could barely hear her words. "I don't have to go to camp."

"Don't worry, baby," Maddy said. "We'll get you there. Get dressed super fast, okay?"

Gracie nodded. "Do you want me to make breakfast cheese sandwiches to take?"

His daughter's false eagerness cleaved Ben in half.

"That would be great." Maddy turned to him. "Good luck today."

He took her hand and brought it to his lips. "Thank you."

She smiled too big for his small gesture.

Gracie raced over and hugged him hard around the waist. "I love you. Good luck, Daddy," Gracie said.

"I love you too, cupcake. Sorry I can't drive you." He bent over and kissed her head, smelling the baby powder Gracie had taken to sprinkling all over herself.

"That's okay. I hope you win when you go to the court."

Ben smiled briefly at Mrs. Gilman as he walked to the garage, avoiding eye contact. If he let her catch him, she'd talk for ten minutes straight about everything from the trash the postal workers dropped when they cut through their street to her wishes that they could fence off the road completely.

Their hidden road, a private way behind busy Centre Street, was only fifteen minutes from downtown Boston, but if you never left their porch, you wouldn't have a clue that they lived close to the heart of the city.

Their large house was barely in his salary range when they bought it before they married, but now it was worth more than four times what they paid. Maybe higher. Each year Jamaica Plain, which everyone called JP, became more desirable for being diverse and hip. In his estimation, when the new people moving in said *diverse*, it was code for living with people who were admirably different in skin or church while comfortably similar in bank accounts. You didn't see them screaming to diversify their way into the housing projects half a mile away. He'd grown up here in JP and hated listening to residents of two years who knew exactly what "they" needed.

Before leaving, he used an old library card to scrape off the damn bird crap that ended up on his window every morning. He kept telling Maddy to pull up so he could get out from underneath the tree that seemed to be home to every sparrow in the city. Maddy called his car his mistress—and he laughed—but she couldn't be further from the truth. Nobody would consider a V8 female. Not only was the car a guy, it reminded him of the kids he'd grown up with in Jamaica Plain, before JP became cool. His parents' house was in Moss Hill, the rich part of the neighborhood, but Ben hung out near the not-affluent Monument. He still remembered the afternoon one of his friends' brothers drove up with a brand-new 1985 Camaro IROC-Z and took them out on the expressway. Jesus. The ride felt closer to flying than driving.

Two years ago, when he came home with his own airborne car, he couldn't predict whether Maddy would scream or smile. He hadn't told her he planned to celebrate his promotion to senior attorney by buying his own flying Camaro, a 2010 SS V8. An entirely inappropriate car—one that didn't safely fit the whole family—but damn it, he could fly from zero to sixty in less than five seconds. In thirteen seconds he'd be over 110 mph. None of which he told Maddy, instead passing the Camaro off as a friendly fun car. The kids will love it! Look at how magnificent! Imagine the two of us zooming to the Cape when the kids are with your parents!

He didn't mention how those sexy looks, that long beveled hood, made the car drive a bit big, hardly perfect for twisty skinny roads, and forget checking over your shoulder or counting on the rearview mirror. Changing lanes was sometimes a point-and-go affair, but the Camaro had muscle.

He'd given Maddy his love-me-I'm-just-a-kid grin. A Jewish girl who grew up in leafy prosperous Brookline, surrounded by books and good intentions—how could she understand his Boston-boy romance with a car like this one?

When she'd smiled, he'd almost cried. "What the hell," she'd said. "Better to drive your midlife crisis than bed it."

His father's old-world scowl appeared when he saw the Camaro. Known to all as the Judge—despite being retired, the appellation had become both familial and professional—he needed few words to show displeasure, but the Judge's disapproval made Ben's ride all the sweeter.

Ben sprinted up the last flight of stairs in the Public Defender's building, opened the door marked *Level 5*, and headed toward his office, not the least bit winded. He'd bested his brother, Andrew, at their last three games of handball and intended to do the same come Friday. His office door was ajar. Elizabeth sat at his desk, hunched over a yellow legal pad, surrounded by files.

"You said you were coming in early." She took off her tortoiseshell reading glasses and smiled.

"Barely seven fifteen qualifies as early, I'd think," he said.

Elizabeth twisted her grin into mock disapproval, perhaps not completely put on—she was so young and sanctified by idealism. "But you said you'd be here before seven." She pulled a thick orange file from under a pile of standard beige folders. Color-coding hot cases was but one of the many innovations she'd managed to foist on everyone. "I got here at six."

"And that's why you're the gem of this ocean in which we drown each day."

"I've pulled together everything I thought we'd need."

He had to watch this one. Ben already found himself drawn to Elizabeth's cool blondeness, and she seemed besotted by his power as senior trial counsel for the Boston Public Defender Division. Admiration could be as addictive as cocaine.

"Unavoidable delay," he said. "Problem at home."

"Serious?" Judging from her concerned expression, she expected an enormous story. Fire! Broken limbs! Ben wanted to construct the tale well—keep that sympathetic look going.

"Caleb cut open his foot yesterday. It looked like hell this morning." Elizabeth appeared confused, unimpressed even.

"He needed to go to the doctor, and Gracie had to go to camp."

Their morning drama sounded weak. Exactly what had riled them so?

"But we wrapped it up—all's well in family world again." Ben waved his hand at Elizabeth as she started to rise—ready to return his rightful seat—gesturing for her to stay put. He settled in the worn leather guest chair he'd pulled from promotion to promotion since starting in the Public Defender's office. Before that he'd tried to work with his father, but Benedikte Illica Sr. ran his law firm as though it were the Ottoman Empire. Room for only one ruler there.

Ben leaned back. The chair gave a satisfying creak, like pulling on his knuckles and getting the snap. "Review what you have for me one more time, okay, Lissie?"

Elizabeth mock-glared. She'd told him *Lissie* was infantilizing. He grinned.

"Summary first?" she asked, shuffling through her files.

Ben pushed back a hank of hair and scribbled *haircut* into a memory Post-it, along with a reminder to call the trophy store. He wanted to give Elizabeth an engraved plaque with a quote from Oliver Wendell Holmes for her twenty-third birthday: *Young man, the secret of my success is that at an early age I discovered I was not God.*

Maddy would say he needed that plaque far more than Elizabeth. Of course, Maddy would be more interested in knowing why he was planning presents for Elizabeth's birthday. *That's why you had to rush into the office?*

He'd given birthday presents to male interns, hadn't he?

Right.

"Sure you don't want your seat back?" Elizabeth balanced her legs on the open bottom drawer she'd pulled out to use as a footrest.

Ben held his hand up in a gesture of generosity and then pointed to the papers in her lap. "Shoot."

"Okay. Nutshell. What we have, and what they'll say: Prosecution says B-bird, a.k.a. Barry Robinson, allegedly murdered Joseph Kelley last January. B-bird admits he was mad that the victim tried to pick up his girlfriend, but swears he didn't kill him . . ."

Ben laced his fingers behind his head, leaning back to make his stomach appear flatter. As Elizabeth read facts that he'd already memorized, he concentrated on the pleasure of judging her and her performance.

Finished, she folded her hands. "Did I cover it?"

"B-bird's girlfriend. What's up with her?"

"She wasn't at the scene." Elizabeth swung her legs off the desk drawer.

"The girlfriend was the reason for the fight, right? Will she be on his side? Will we see her in court?"

Elizabeth's stricken face made Ben feel almost guilty. Almost. She had to learn. "Don't worry," he said. "I spoke to her. She'll be sitting right next to B-bird's mama."

"Sorry. I thought I had it covered."

"Don't be hard on yourself. It's called learning."

Elizabeth wrung her hands, now more Oliver Twist waiting for gruel than Oliver Wendell Holmes. She gave a determined smile as she gathered her papers and then stood. "Next time, I'll ace it." Her hips strained her skirt as she stretched to place a folder in the wire basket on his desk.

Ben fought to keep from staring at her perfect backside. He'd better watch himself if he wanted to remain in the thirty percent bracket. Maddy reminded him on a regular basis, half joking, half not, that seventy percent of married men cheated. After fifteen years of marriage, they assured each other of their faithfulness in shorthand. She'd look at him and put seven fingers in the air. Ben answered by putting up three, letting her know—Scout's honor—that he still belonged to the other thirty.

Sure, he could be a supreme schmuck, but he'd never cheat—that was his inviolate line in the sand. Maybe he played the line—flirting, using a woman's admiration as an ego salve, especially during the dog days of marriage—but crossing that border? Never.

Ben felt as crumpled as his shirt when he put his key in the door at seven thirty. Traffic had sucked, as usual. Whoever said Boston became quiet in the summer didn't drive his roads. He threw his suit jacket on the chair, along with the tie he'd pulled off in the car. If he could climb straight upstairs, shower, and fall into bed, he'd be happy. The hall had to be a hundred degrees. Air-conditioning was impossible in this old house with its barely code wiring. Maddy nagged him about upgrading the electrical system, but exactly which kid's college fund did she plan to sacrifice?

Television chatter drifted into the hall. Jesus, was that all they did?

"You missed dinner," Maddy said as he walked into the living room. She kept her eyes on the screen. *The Simpsons?* Why did she let them watch that crap?

"Daddy, look!" Caleb held up his foot, showing off a thick bandage.

"What happened, champ?" Ben dropped on the floor next to his son.

"They had to sew me."

"You're going to be a pincushion pretty soon if you keep this up." He turned to Maddy. "Everything okay?"

She frowned and scratched a mosquito bite on her bare thigh, still dark from last weekend's trip to Singing Beach. Her skin, like his, ate up the sun. She'd looked good as ever at the beach—even with her curves covered in the stern-looking tank suit. Her sun-tinted skin, dense curls wild with salt air, deep brown eyes rimmed in some natural black line she must have been born with—it had kept him aroused all day. That itchy feeling he carried around for her drove him to suggest the kids sleep at their grandparents' that night.

That night, groaning in bed, Maddy hadn't been all prune-faced like she now appeared.

"The doctor threw in two stitches," Maddy finally answered.

Right. *Just the facts, ma'am.* What sin had Ben committed while not even present?

"When do they come out?" he asked.

Ah, another deep sigh from his lady of perpetual disappointment. "They're dissolvable. He should be fine; he just has to keep it very clean. Which is like asking a dog to read. That's why they put that thick bandage on. It's not infected, but they want to prevent any trouble. I should have taken him last night. Stupid. I was so stupid. We just barely hit the time period before he couldn't get stitched."

He felt like a jerk—her sighing was over displeasure with herself, not him. "Hey, we can't get it right one hundred percent of the time."

She smiled in gratitude, stood up, and gave him a tight hug. In response he ran his hands along her back.

"I won, Daddy," Gracie said. "In color war."

He smiled at his beaming daughter. "You won? Terrific, honey!"

"She didn't win." Caleb turned to Gracie. "Your team won, stupid fatso. Not you."

"Caleb, stop it," Maddy warned. "Don't ever use those words in this house."

"Do you want to be sent to your room this minute?" Ben said.

Maddy flashed him a warning look and shook her head. *What?* He'd backed her up.

Tears dribbled down Gracie's cheeks. Caleb stuck out his chin.

Maddy shook her head again. Was his wife motorized, for Christ's sake? What did she want? Handy how he could fuck up on automatic. He could do marriage on remote.

CHAPTER 3

Maddy

Why'd Ben have to ruin the hug? Just once could she be the angry parent without him upping the ante? Did he always have to follow up with his own tirade?

A rotten end to a horrible day.

At ten o'clock, she shuffled down the upstairs hall, balancing books, papers, magazines, and the shirt Ben had left draped on the couch. Using her hip, she pushed the bedroom door open and then dropped everything on the wooden chest. Ben lay in bed, one hand behind his head, the other balancing his laptop.

"Work?" she asked. "You look exhausted. I'm ready to fall over. Why don't we both close up shop for the night?"

He closed the computer and sat up, yawning. "Good idea."

Folding towels, she watched Ben pull his white T-shirt over his head. His bare chest. His thick arms and back. The olive tones of his skin. His dark hair, her dark hair. His squat wrestler's build—neither of them tall. They looked like poster children for immigrants who'd done well. Geographic cousins—his father's parents came from Romania, her father's from Hungary. Perhaps some core-of-the-earth want drove her craving to inhale his scent and nestle against his back.

He balled up the shirt and threw it toward the chair. Next, he stripped to his boxers and fell back on the bed.

Using a teasing voice, so he'd recognize she wanted détente, she asked, "Do you think you'll throw your dirty clothes in the hamper just once before I die?" She joined him on the bed, resting her head on his shoulder. "Perhaps a snowball's chance in hell?"

"Probably not even that much." Ben smiled and rolled on top of her, proof of his improved mood jutting into her stomach.

His weight, his hardness, his wanting brought on a shiver of excitement. "I have to change the wash."

"Mmm." He buried his face in her neck. "I'll do it for you in the morning."

"Right." She thought about how unlikely that was as she pushed him off and rolled off the bed, picking up the mound of books by her side, gathering them into a pile, and placing them on the built-in bookcase across from the bed.

Ben stared as she stripped off her shirt and shorts and threw them in the laundry basket—looking at her as though she were a hamburger that would satisfy a sudden hunger. In that moment he morphed from hungry lover to task. Now making love sounded about as tempting as making the bed.

But.

But.

Sometimes marriage needed to run on the *but*.

She collapsed next to Ben in her bra and underpants. "Let me take a quick shower."

"Don't bother. You're fine." Ben threw his book on the floor and pulled off his boxers. He drew a line down her stomach and then edged his body between her legs, nibbling her shoulder. Next, he would work his mouth over her body. Marital beds held few mysteries.

She wriggled a bit, aligning herself so he could slip inside.

He pulled a bit away. "What's the rush?"

She rubbed the deep furrow at the bottom of his back, already feeling the morning pressing in, mentally unloading the dishwasher and finding lost sneakers. "Wanting at least seven hours' sleep?"

Wrapping her legs around his hips, Maddy tried to wiggle him into her. He lifted himself away from her. "Can't we just have whatever we have without a plan?" he asked.

"Hon, I'm just trying to relax and push away the house stuff clogging up my head."

"Why in the world would thinking about laundry keep you from enjoying making love? That's insane, Maddy."

She felt him wilt. "You're right. Go ahead."

"*Go ahead.* Now that's sexy."

"I'm sorry. Making love would be wonderful. Of course the laundry can wait. Forgive the crabbiness; I had a crummy day."

Ben climbed off. "Never mind. I don't need a mercy screw."

Her throat tightened. She sat up and ran her hands down his chest. "Come on. Honestly, I really want to make love."

"As it turns out, now I honestly really don't." He rolled over and faced away.

She stroked him from shoulder to wrist. "Please. Stop. This is stupid."

He pulled away. "What's stupid? Me wanting to make love to my wife without a script? Christ. Sometimes our marriage just sucks." Ben grabbed a book, put on a robe, and left the bedroom without looking back.

Maddy clicked on the television, watching as a muted weatherman pointed to oncoming thundershowers. Unsaid words clogged her chest.

Ben's temper had existed before they'd had kids—fighting was nothing new. However, once they'd also taken long Sunday-morning showers together and drunk coffee laced with Jameson. Ben measured out the whiskey, swearing that if she poured it, they'd be drunk before the third sip. She'd whip heavy cream with brown sugar and swirl it into the dark liquored coffee.

Deadened, she prayed to cry, wanting the release of tears, wanting Ben to come back with a cup of creamy Irish coffee and stroke her thigh while they whispered dirty secrets.

Maddy worked a pill from a tissue hidden in her night table, rubbed off the lint, and looked at it, craving the acetic taste. She put it back and curled into a ball.

Once she'd wondered if Ben was addicted to his anger. Now she wondered if the real secret to their marriage was how she couldn't stop loving him despite it.

The sleep she'd craved eluded her. Rubbing at that spot on her chest where her heart might be, she went to the bathroom for a glass of water to help her swallow the pill.

She chanted supplications to bring Ben back to the bedroom and erase the past half hour. Everything about her would improve, she promised herself: The kids would never again have to go to school without the perfect lunch; they'd never have to grab money out of the change jar because she'd stayed in bed an extra ten minutes, or be forced to line up limp single socks on their bed to find ones that almost matched. She'd use bleach and fabric softener and static-cling-free sheets in the dryer. No more skipping steps—she'd even scrub the secret cruddy area under the cupboard when she washed the kitchen floor.

The teetering pile on her desk would be sorted, attended to, and filed.

She'd become a wizard of a mother: Gracie would get courage, Emma a loving heart, and Caleb patience. All she wanted in exchange was for Ben to come back and hold her.

Maddy met her friend Kath at six the next morning. Weather, husbands, children, and work permitting, they scheduled biweekly runs in the pristine Arnold Arboretum. Maddy needed the physical exertion. Even more, she wanted reassurance that her family wasn't a broken corporation, Illica Sucks Inc.

Kath was her rock, the best friend with whom she'd fallen into a never-ending love the moment they met at Boston University. Why couldn't husbands offer the same constancy and security as best friends? Back in Maddy's college years she'd imagined adulthood as a shining beacon—compassionate work, a passionate husband, and children who'd absorb their love and wisdom. She'd lusted for the future but hadn't expected perfection. She grew up sheltered, not naive. Balancing business, the house, and kids had exhausted her mother, and her father's blood pressure rose as he cursed clients, but each Friday they'd give thanks for their children, each other, and all the nooks and crannies that made up their daily lives. She thought she'd end up the same but better.

Maddy grew up surrounded by love. Her father sometimes exploded, but in a manner her mother could always shush away. *Jake! The children!* He'd continue to huff for a few minutes, but with her mother watching he'd catch himself. That's what Maddy had believed her home would be like when she married Ben, but instead her marriage became partitioned into spheres of influence. Competitions for time. Emotional battles about moral high grounds. Maddy learned to watch each thing she said or did—any hint that she was unhappy with him brought forth his aggressive lawyer side, ready to prove her wrong and grind the fight out of her. But Maddy wasn't able to be on guard every second, and besides, his temper wasn't parceled out in ways that were predictable. The misstep that he'd laugh at on Wednesday drove him to battle on Thursday.

But when he's good, he's so very, very good, she'd tell Kath during their daily phone conversations. They hadn't lost their college habit of comparing every mole and freckle of their relationships. Maddy knew that Kath's husband brought her lush white orchids and Viennese crunch, and rarely yelled—but that he had a problem with premature ejaculation and sometimes cried when they fought. Kath knew Ben massaged her for an hour without expecting a thing back, listened to her father's business theories without complaint—and that he shouted so loudly that Maddy had trained herself to clench every muscle so she didn't flinch.

In the beginning, Maddy had preferred Ben's faults, though she and Kath were careful to only make sour faces about their own husband's flaws. Her partiality was in the early years, when acts of contrition followed Ben's tirades. She'd trusted in his stammering apologies and believed it when he said no other woman could ever understand him. Maddy had uncovered his core! He bottled up essence of heart and gave it to her wrapped in satin bows.

And then there was the bedroom. Premature ejaculation was never Ben's problem.

These days she and Kath could skip over the familiar marital details and explanations. They knew each other's relationships well enough to speak in shorthand, and Maddy was able to detail the previous night's battle in quick strokes.

"Something about that fight made me think about the Wednesday Blues Club," Maddy panted out as they ran down Hemlock Hill Road. The Blues Club—the education and support group Maddy and her coworker friend Olivia ran for battered women—was a frequent subject of Kath and Maddy's repetitive conversations.

"How and why women stay with men who act like assholes?" Kath asked.

Maddy stopped running. Kath was a few strides up before she realized Maddy was no longer next to her.

"What was that supposed to mean?" Maddy planted her hands on her hips. "I was talking about something that happens in all relationships—not comparing Ben to my clients' husbands."

Kath walked back and tugged at Maddy's T-shirt. "Don't look at me like that. You know I like Ben—I always have. But the story you just told me—what am I supposed to do, just nod?"

"That would be nice. Come on, it's always that way in marriages— one is the parent; one is the spoiled brat. Guess which one Ben is. And what I was going to say is that men battle to win, women to be heard. Maybe not your Mr. Perfect. But most men."

"Ben has many great qualities, but he has to be put in check." Kath began running, nodding for Maddy to follow, not even panting from the effort of the incline they were on. Going up Peters Hill burned Maddy's thighs every time.

"I said it wrong," Kath said. "I didn't mean you shouldn't stay with him, just . . . What is it you want?"

Maddy was quiet—thinking as they climbed higher. All the things she didn't want flooded in. Ben so angry that he'd kicked a hole in the bedroom closet door. Looming over her. His face bright red as he yelled. About what? What was it that time?

Maddy placating him, worried about the kids being terrified.

"I just want my house to be . . . I don't know, sane?" They'd reached the summit, their reward for battling up the hill. Boston's skyline spread in front of them, puffy white clouds reflected in the mirrored surface of the John Hancock building. Living within walking distance made this bounty feel like it was Maddy's backyard. "When he's happy, the last thing I want to do is bring up this crap. And when he's being an asshole, all I want to do is get out of his way."

Kath raised her thin muscled leg onto a worn boulder and bent to tie her shoe. Leaning over, her words were faint. "You should never have to get out of anyone's way in your own house, Maddy."

Arriving early at Kelly's Landing in South Boston to pick up Emma allowed Maddy a rare pleasure of watching her daughter interact in the world. Emma worked as a counselor at a camp for disabled kids, managed by Kath, who was a high school student services director during the school year.

Exhausted from their own day at camp, both Gracie and Caleb had fallen asleep in the backseat while she drove. Maddy watched Alex McMaster being pushed in his wheelchair along the cement walkway toward Emma. His smile widened as his mother, whom Maddy had been introduced to the first week of camp, rolled him closer. When he arched in her direction, Emma jumped from the stone wall and landed next to him.

Emma knelt to Alex's height, placing a hand on his thin arm. His mother's sun-wrinkled face lit up as Alex spoke. According to Emma, camp had improved his garbled speech. From the way the woman looked at her daughter, it seemed that she thought Emma could take credit.

Maddy opened the car door and waved. "Emma! Over here, sweetie," she yelled.

"*Okay!*" Emma cut her eyes, signaling her mother to stop whatever new embarrassment she planned to inflict. Alex lifted his hand for a shaky high five.

Emma got into the car as Maddy shouted a quick hello to Alex and his mother. Gracie and Caleb, now awake, sat heat-struck limp in the back, a lumpy clay animal in Gracie's hand. Screeching neon-green designs covered Caleb's filthy bandages where they peeked out of the oversized thong he wore on his injured foot.

"Is Alex ever going to get better?" Gracie asked as Emma fastened her seat belt.

Emma rolled her eyes, showing how tired she was of Gracie's forlorn questions. "Are you ever going to get skinny?"

"Emma!" Maddy turned for a moment to glare, wondering not for the first time, and probably not the last, how her mother would have handled this bickering. Why did she barely remember fighting with her sister? God knew Vanessa could be a bitch.

"I'm pointing out that everyone has something, and not to make Alex into some sort of freak just because he's in a wheelchair. He doesn't have to walk to be acceptable."

Gracie blinked three times and then opened her worn copy of *Anne of Green Gables*.

"Oh, jeez, don't cry," Emma said. "You know everyone loves you best."

"Don't pay Emma any attention, Gracie. You're perfect, but no one loves *anyone* best." Before starting the car, she turned to Emma. "That was uncalled for. Do you hear me?"

Emma reached into her backpack and took out an almost empty pack of gum. "How could I not hear you? You don't have to scream. I didn't say anything."

"You called her fat," Caleb said. "And Mommy's not screaming. You are."

"Did not call her fat. I just asked if she was ever going to get skinny. That doesn't mean she's fat; she's just not skinny. Being different isn't bad, right?"

"Emma," Maddy warned.

Emma twisted in her seat. "Sorry, Gracie. You're not fat. Want a piece of gum?"

Gracie shrugged.

"Here." Emma drew out a stick and handed it to Gracie.

"Where's mine?" Caleb asked.

"It wasn't your feelings I hurt."

"Emma, give him a piece."

She rolled her eyes and gave Caleb the gum.

Maddy stopped for a red light. NPR droned.

"Music!" Caleb said. "Put on music, Mom. Play my CD again."

Emma whipped around to face him in the backseat. "No way. Nothing of his! I get enough of that with Dad."

Caleb had inherited Ben's love of rock, always begging for his rejected CD from years ago. Emma ejected the disc in the CD player and read the title. "Def Leppard. God, Mom, have you heard the lyrics? They hate women. I don't know how you let Dad listen to that stuff."

Remove yourself mentally.

Imagine being in a cold movie theater.

Caleb kicked the back of Emma's seat. "Daddy likes it."

"Daddy's not in the car," Emma said. "And don't kick me."

"Caleb, put on your iPod and keep it low," Maddy said.

Three blocks later Caleb was lost to his music and Gracie was deep in her book. Emma lowered the radio and spoke in the sweet voice she used when she wanted something. "Some of us are going out tonight, okay?"

"Going out? And who are 'some of us'?"

"We're going to Prudential or Copley. Just to hang out."

"You're not allowed alone on the bus at night," she said. "You know that."

"We're meeting at J.P. Licks. Do you think I'll get murdered in half a block?"

"Daddy or I will walk you over. Maybe we'll all get some ice cream—"

"Mom, please! I'll look like an idiot."

"We're walking you. And you need to call when you're ready to leave the mall. One of us will pick you up."

Emma removed her gum and held it in her hand. "God. You can be so *arbitrary*." She rolled the word out with an obvious delight in herself.

"Wrap that up and put it in the trash." Maddy understood how one could end up saying yes to everything when children became teenagers. Energy was on their side.

Emma stuck the wet gum in her T-shirt pocket. "Fine. Are you happy now?"

"No, because now I'll find it all over a shirt of mine when I do the wash. Throw it out properly. Who are these other people?"

"Just Sammi, Caro, and some boys."

"You're not going out with some boys we don't know."

"I know them."

"Very funny." Maddy pulled into the Whole Foods lot on Centre Street. "Do you have your phone?"

"Why?"

"Because I suggest you call those boys and have them meet you at the house."

Emma crossed her arms and stuck her legs out as far as they would go. Maddy reached over and grabbed her pocketbook from the floor in the back.

"I'll be right back. Watch the kids and call me if anything happens."

"I hate you sometimes," Emma said.

Maddy closed the door as quietly as possible.

CHAPTER 4

Ben

At five thirty, half a dozen other attorneys jammed into the conference room. They'd gone from bullshitting about their cases to bullshitting about the Red Sox. Debates on whether the Blue Jays or the Yankees had a chance at the wild card grew more raucous with the size of the crowd. Ben and Elizabeth were the only ones who hadn't yet voiced an opinion on the topic.

Ben put his feet up on the scarred wooden table. "Don't assume the Red Sox will make the playoffs. It's only August." He placed his hands behind his head and leaned back. Brass studs punctuating the upholstered chair felt cool and rich against his laced fingers. Other than bookcases stuffed with journals, all that decorated the room was a large oil painting of a nondescript ship navigating rocky waters.

"Point, Ben," Aaron said. He was Ben's get-it-done guy this year. "And the Yankees have stronger pitching, no matter what anyone says."

Overeager Gerry from the appeals unit stuck his head in. "Are we going for beers, or should I sit?"

They looked to Ben for a decision. They deferred to him on everything, including when and where to drink, and when to go home to their families. Ben basically owned the Boston office of the Massachusetts Public Defender Division. He liked to consider himself a benevolent despot, but after so many years atop this small mountain, the thrill was gone. Admiration wasn't enough anymore—these days only pure worship gave him a rush.

"I'm thirsty." Heads turned toward Elizabeth. The way she used her upper-class breeding and cool good looks to her advantage in this crowd amused Ben. Despite bragging about their working-class roots, the men populating the Public Defender's deferred to Boston Brahmins as though at heart they, the children of welders and bus drivers, were truly serfs of the city.

"The princess is thirsty—where shall we raise our glasses?" Gerry asked.

Lorna Kennedy, the only other woman in the room, shook her head in disgust. She was dumpy, fifty-seven, and wore flat shoes. No one raised glasses on Lorna's behalf. Ben knew he should feel indignation for her, but instead he filed it under yet another injustice he'd lost the motivation to fix.

"Let's go next door," Ben said. "But I can't stay late."

The trip anointed, they rose almost as one. Elizabeth watched Ben, her eyes hot on him—undoubtedly the alpha in the room. He stood straight to be as tall as she, rolling up his sleeves to show his handball muscles.

Ben didn't know if she had a Daddy thing, a tough-guy thing, or a smartest-guy-in-the-room thing, but he knew this: She latched on more each day.

He had two beers before calling Maddy. He should have waited on the second drink—stayed sharp. Even through the phone, he heard things slamming.

"Is it my imagination," Maddy asked, "or have you missed supper five times in a row?"

"Sorry. I couldn't help it," Ben lied.

"Where are you now?"

"I left you a message. It's that case I told you about."

"I called the office. No one answered."

"We were in the conference room," he said.

"It sounds loud. Where are you?" she repeated.

"Jesus, some of us ran out to get dinner. We were hungry." He turned toward the wall, away from the noise of the bar, pushing his cell phone closer to his ear. He should have gone outside. Water running and the sound of damp slapping muted Maddy's words. "What are you doing?"

"Cooking chicken," she said. "I'm tired of having dinner alone with the kids, Ben."

He hunched over as Elizabeth came toward him, presumably on the way to the restroom. She tapped his shoulder with two fingers as she passed. "You know how it gets at crunch time, Mad."

"Couldn't you bring work home? Then at least we could all eat together. I hate when you don't tell me what's happening in time for me to plan my night."

"What are you making? A banquet?" *Lower yourself a few notches.* He worked to rise above the beers he'd downed. Handling alcohol had never been his strength.

"Mom?" Emma's voice floated in from the background.

"Hold on," Maddy said to him. "What, hon?"

"I'm not going out tonight."

He pictured Maddy holding the phone in her right hand, just off from her mouth and ear, as she always did when interrupted.

"Caro canceled. Her—"

"Can you wait a second, Emma? Daddy's on the line," he heard Maddy say.

He exhaled through the phone. "Can I get back to my dinner?" he asked.

"When will you be home?"

"I can't say for sure." He stifled a belch, guilt and beer making a sour mix in his stomach.

"When will you know?"

"I'll call you."

"Bennie? When will we have some real time together?" He heard her sigh. "I'm tired of sounding like a bitch. I love you."

"I love you too." Mentally, he'd already hung up. "When the kids are back in school, things will get better. We'll get away, just the two of us."

"Promise?"

"Absolutely. I'll see you soon."

He walked back to the table. A fresh beer sat at his place.

Ben wondered how pissed Maddy would be. He sped toward Huntington Avenue, weighing possible excuses. Ten o'clock hardly matched "see you soon." What could he say? Life falling apart for B-bird's family? Welfare in the future for B-bird's mama if he didn't get the kid out on bail? Anything that would keep Maddy quiet.

He considered the extreme stupidity of that fourth—or was it fifth?—beer. Everyone had left except him and Elizabeth. Self-reproach crept in, even as he felt that shiver of excitement newness will bring.

Leaving had been virtually impossible with her laughing at his jokes, her eyes shining as he bragged about cases he'd won. Each self-aggrandizing word brought him closer to temptation, until finally he'd pushed himself from the table.

A large crowd milled on the outskirts of the wide sidewalk edging Copley Square. Trinity Church rose in his rearview mirror; across Dartmouth Street was the old entrance to the Boston Public Library main branch. Hell, he loved that damned building. He could have been an architect.

Copley Plaza loomed like the queen of the area—*that* was a hotel.

Why did they never get here? It was only ten minutes from the house. He should bring Maddy for a romantic dinner. Better yet, he'd have her parents sleep at their house while he and Maddy stayed over at the hotel.

He vowed he'd do it before Labor Day.

Where do all these wonderful plans go, Ben? Maddy popped into his head again. He loved her. He loved his children. Why did they always make him feel like a failure? Maybe he didn't always follow through with his intentions—but who did?

Maddy was always talking about how she should spend more time one-on-one with Emma. Jesus, she was growing up so fast. It terrified both of them. They had to stick together on this one. No bullshit.

Tattoos covering large swaths of skin fought for visual attention with skimpy T-shirts among the teenagers milling on the sidewalk. Half the buses in Boston converged here, including the number 39, which stopped one block from his house. Which, he supposed, explained seeing Emma there.

What the fuck?

Ben pulled over, turned on his flashers, and got out of the car. Emma laughed at something some skinny kid said. She looked up at the twerp as though he were a combination rock star and comedian. He snuck up behind her and clamped a hand on her shoulder. Hard.

"Hey!" the kid said, putting up a hand as though to stop Ben. "Get your hand off her."

Emma turned. Red glossy stuff covered her lips, sending a slick invitation that made him twitch for his handkerchief, dying to rub the shiny covering off. Maddy allowed that? Thick circles of black she'd drawn around her eyes made her look like a raccoon.

The kid tried to pull Emma away from Ben—point for the kid. He looked okay. At least he wasn't covered in tattoos and his ears weren't stretched out with those grotesque donut things.

"Dad!" Emma said. "What are you doing here?"

"What am *I* doing here? Hardly the question." Alcohol numbness made it difficult to feel his lips as he spoke. "Get in the car." He took care to articulate each word.

"Let me explain. Caro's here. And Sammi. It's not what you think."

"You don't have a clue what I think. Get in the car."

"Dad, could you at least let me—"

"*Get in the car.*"

She shrugged off his hand and marched away, slamming the car door after she got in. He saw Caro and Sammi trying to shrink to the size of birds.

"Need a ride, girls?"

Sammi shook her head, looking like she was about to throw up.

"My father is picking me up at the bus stop," Caro said. "Sammi too. But thanks."

Ben had never trusted Caro—he knew lying when he heard it—but he'd deal with that tomorrow. Let the kid stew in her worry about whether or not he'd call her parents for now. "Right. Be careful." He spoke slowly.

He slid behind the wheel. Emma sat as close to the door as possible.

"Where does your mother think you are?"

Emma shrugged.

"Answer me. Now." His voice rose on the *now*.

"Sleeping."

"Nice. Great stuff there, Emma. What did you do? Climb out the window? Who the hell was that boy?"

Emma sat mute, her mouth locked so tight her lips turned white.

"I asked you something."

"His name is Zach. He's friends with Caro's cousin." Emma crossed her arms. "I'm not going to talk to you when you yell. You don't scare me, you know."

"I have news for you—you *will* talk to me. I can begin and end your world."

She turned her head away and stared at the front of the Museum of Fine Arts, acting mesmerized by the Native American statue guarding the front.

"You're being an idiot," she said out the window. "And you sound drunk."

"Be smart; don't say another word until we get home." He revved the car and then took a left-hand turn so sharp the wheels squealed, turning toward Columbus Avenue.

"Guess where I found her? Come on, just guess," Ben said.

Maddy struggled up from the couch, looking groggy. A book had fallen to the floor.

"Do you have a clue where your daughter was tonight?" Ben pushed Emma forward, deeper into the living room.

"What time is it?" Maddy asked.

"Ten thirty." Emma's voice was tight. Ben suspected she was more scared than she let on.

Good.

"What's wrong?" Maddy lifted her reading glasses from her chest and sat up.

Ben loosened his grip on Emma, fearing he'd bruise her in his fury. "You didn't know she was out?" He fumed as Maddy straightened her wrinkled shirt and ran her fingers through her hair. He noticed the wineglass on the table.

"Emma? What happened?" Maddy asked. "You said you were going to bed."

"Apparently she changed her mind." Ben steered his daughter to the chair angled next to the couch and pushed her into it. "Apparently she snuck out, and did God knows what."

"Why would you do that?" Maddy asked Emma.

"*Why?* That's your first worry? *Why?*" Ben smelled his musk rising—exhaustion, court, aftershave gone flat, and beery rankness. And himself. Something indefinable, something feverish. He should shut the fuck up.

"All I did was go to the mall with kids who have normal parents, who don't get hysterical," Emma said. "Ones who let them out."

He ignored Emma and kept at Maddy. "Who's in control around here? Where the hell were you? How could you not hear her leave? What goes on around here?"

"Why don't you come home once in a while and find out?" Emma hissed under her breath. She rolled into a tight ball in the stuffed chair.

"What did you say?" Ben kicked a toy truck across the room and then forced himself to step back. Maddy moved to the corner of the couch closest to Emma's chair.

"I said, why don't you come home once in a while and find out?"

Emma repeated, pronouncing each word as though Ben were feeble-minded.

"Stop. Now. Both of you," Maddy demanded. "Emma, how did you get out without me hearing you? Did you climb out the back?"

"I climbed out my window." Emma pointed her chin at Ben. "You guessed it, Dad."

"You climbed out the window? Do you have any idea how much trouble you're in?" Ben pulled Emma up by her wrist. "Go to your room. Consider yourself grounded until further notice."

Emma wrested her arm away and turned to Maddy. "This wouldn't have happened if you'd let me go out like a regular kid instead of saying I had to bring my friends here for inspection as though they're criminals." She started to leave.

Ben grabbed her shoulder and spun her around. He stuck his finger in her face. "Don't you dare talk to your mother like that. Do you hear me? You're on thin enough ice as it is. I can make this grounding last a year."

"All you ever want is for me to take care of Gracie and Caleb," Emma screamed. "You treat me like a maid. Both of you."

"Get out of my sight. Go to your room," Ben shouted.

"*Happily.*" Emma stormed out, pushing the toy truck with her foot as she left.

Once Emma was up the stairs, Ben turned to Maddy, his rage expanding each minute. "How could you let that happen?"

"Let what happen? She snuck out."

"Because you were asleep?" He looked pointedly at her wineglass.

Maddy sat straighter on the couch. "Don't play offense. I had one glass of wine after the kids went to sleep. You reek of beer."

"Am I not allowed to have a drink to relax?"

"You're out of control," Maddy said.

Falling next to her on the sofa, Ben collapsed in on himself. At the bar, he'd been on top of his game: Elizabeth and what's-his-name clamoring for his attention. They gobbled his agency gossip spoon by spoon. Now he was "out of control."

"I feel like shit." He covered his eyes with his arm.

Maddy shifted forward on the sofa. "We need to talk about Emma."

Nausea overtook him. He sat up straight, taking shallow breaths, positive for one awful minute he'd throw up right there. "I'm done in."

"Then we need to make a date to talk," she said. "Do you think you can make it home tomorrow night?"

Maddy's voice banged through his head like the brass section of the Boston Pops. "In the morning," he said. "I promise."

"I have to leave early," she said. "I've been trying forever to get a hearing for a client, and it's on tomorrow, and Olivia and I are running an early group. You have to get the kids to camp because—"

There was no doubt: He was going to throw up. "Got it," he said as he walked out.

The bedroom door opened with a torturous squeak. Morning mouth, bitter as bile, coated his tongue and teeth.

"Daddy, don't you know how late it is? Wake up!" Gracie shook his shoulder. Caleb bounced on the bed.

"Slow down." Ben grabbed Caleb's arm. "Where's Mommy?"

"Gone." Caleb began his bouncing again.

"Quit it," Ben said. "*Now.*"

Caleb stopped.

"Mommy left," Gracie said. "She said to make sure you woke up."

"Right." Vague memories floated in. Ben turned his throbbing head and glanced at the clock. "Shit."

"You shouldn't curse."

"Right. Sorry. Daddy forgot he had a meeting in Brockton. It's a long drive."

Where were the damn papers he needed?

"Mommy squeezed orange juice for you. Do you want me to bring you some?" Gracie asked.

"Thanks, cupcake. Tell Emma to give you breakfast." He ran his fingers through his hair and caught the foul stench of the bar.

• • •

The steaming shower beat against his headache. He dumped an extra-large glob of shampoo into his hand and lathered up his head, chest, arms, and legs in one fell swoop to save time. The scent of Maddy's flowery shampoo rose with the heat and brought back his nausea. Ben flexed his shoulders, feeling the muscles complain.

Christ, what a day he faced. Senior counsel meant being senior class monitor at these case-crunching meetings. More like nut-crunching, these statewide clusterfucks. Every lawyer in the room wanted one of two things: to show they were smarter than Ben, or to show how smart they'd make him look if he brought them into the Boston office.

"*Dad!*" Emma screeched through the door.

Ben shut off the water. "*What?*"

"When are we leaving?"

Ben wrapped a large towel around his middle. He dripped over to the bathroom door and cracked it open. "Mom didn't say I was driving you. Just the kids."

"I'm not your kid?"

"You know what I mean. Watch your mouth."

Emma's eyes worked out her resentment before she spoke. "There's a camp trip this morning. Mom knew. My campers can't go on the trip without me. There won't be enough counselors." Emma crossed her arms.

Anger at Emma's attitude, pride at her responsibility, and resentment at Maddy for putting him in the position of feeling mad at Emma fought for primacy. Not that it mattered—he knew when he was beat. No way he'd be allowed in this house again if he left crippled campers swinging in the wind.

"Fine," Ben said. "Make sure everyone is ready to leave in ten minutes."

When he got downstairs, Caleb and Gracie sat on the hall bench, clutching their lunch bags. Emma stood like the family duenna, arms crossed against her chest, as Caleb swung his feet back and forth and Gracie gripped her backpack.

"Emma wouldn't let us move, Dad," Caleb complained.

"Because that's what he told me." Emma poked Caleb's foot with her sneaker.

"Here." Gracie reached for the chrome Thermos cup on the table. "Your coffee."

"Just a second. I need something." Ben dropped his briefcase on the floor.

"What happened to '*not one minute more*'?" Emma imitated Ben's clipped tone. "We have to go, Dad."

"*One minute more,*" Caleb repeated.

"Quit it, all of you." Ben went into the small bathroom off the hall. He rummaged through the medicine cabinet for a few minutes and then slammed it shut. "Jesus Christ. Is anything in this house in the right place?"

He ran up the stairs two at a time. After checking the bathrooms upstairs and the linen cabinet, he yelled out, "Where's the aspirin? Does anyone know where your mother keeps it?"

"We have to go. The trip bus will leave." Emma sounded hysterical.

"Then find the damned aspirin," he shouted as he pounded down the stairs.

Emma found and practically threw the pills at him—what the hell were they doing in the kitchen cabinet?

The moment they were buckled in, he sped out and onto Myrtle Street, getting only one short block before having to slam on the brakes and stop short at backed-up traffic.

"Damn, damn, damn." Ben hit the dashboard with the side of his hand. "I'm sunk if I don't get to the meeting."

"What will happen, Daddy?" Gracie asked. "Aren't you the boss?"

"Yes, sweet. I'm the boss. They can't start without me, but I can't have them think I screwed up."

CHAPTER 5

Maddy

Would Maddy get credit for arriving at work scarcely ten minutes late? Sure, she'd promised to be here by seven, but the hour marker had barely passed. Would Olivia appreciate the improvement from her usual half-hour-or-more tardiness?

Probably not.

The difference between Olivia, best friend at work, and Kath, best friend since college, was that Kath saw Maddy's flaws and pasted over them, while Olivia rendered them in Technicolor, asked or not, so Maddy could work on them.

Maddy's red briefcase and matching sandals provided the single bright spots in her hospital-issue, social-worker-grade office. She had time to read maybe five emails before she and Olivia left for group.

"Hey! Good of you to come in!" Olivia put down a pile of pink telephone messages, leaned back, and grabbed her hospital mug emblazoned with a blue caduceus. Oh, the perks of their job.

Maddy smiled as though Olivia was offering nothing but true gratitude. Screw her sarcasm. It was too early. "You're very welcome." She held out a small greasy bag. "Coffee cake muffin."

Olivia took the bag and then patted the roll sitting on top of her waistband. "Come on home and join your sisters."

Maddy unwrapped her bagel. "I hate when you do that."

Olivia lowered her glasses a bit and looked over them at her. "Do ya now? Well, I hate that folks in this town worship the Red Sox more than they treasure black kids. Everyone hates something."

Olivia rushed to make fun of her body before anyone else could, and she didn't give a damn if Maddy thought her Sicilian and Jamaican genes blended into Amazonian beauty. She treated herself hard—but no worse than she treated the rest of the world. If you had masochistic tendencies, then Olivia was your girl.

"Gotcha." Maddy bit into the cream-cheese-covered doughy bagel. "I hate men."

"Marriage not so good this week?"

Marriage not so good this year.

"Patience gets wearying—you know what I mean?" Maddy asked.

"Nope." Marriage had eluded Olivia. She peeled the paper cover away from her muffin. "What happened?"

"Nothing. I don't want to get into it."

Olivia must have been massively sick of hearing her complain about Ben, the kids, her life. God knows Maddy had tired of hearing her own voice.

"Later." Maddy took a notebook from her briefcase. "We'll talk about it later. I have to prepare for Sabine's hearing." Sabine and her against the DCF, the Department of Children and Families—those weren't good odds.

Sabine belonged to the Wednesday Blues Club. Some members still wore their black-and-blues; some only carried the memories of being beaten. Many had their pain doubled and tripled by having their mothering put on trial by DCF. Sabine was one of those—she was trying to regain custody of her kids.

Three children similar in age to Maddy's children—a circumstance she didn't want to imagine.

Despite the painful situations of the women of the Wednesday Blues, Maddy and Olivia loved the group. Compared to most of their hospital clients—the grieving parents, the end-stage cancer victims, the depleted spouses of Alzheimer's patients—the Blues members might be battered, but they still had juice.

Olivia and Maddy rode to Dorchester in separate cars. Usually they drove in Olivia's—she believed herself the superior driver—but Olivia would be going back to the hospital after group, and Maddy would be taking Sabine to the courthouse for the hearing.

The warm stuffy church basement where they held group smelled of long-gone parish suppers. Moira, the quietest and oldest, arrived first. Married for more than thirty years, her husband had knocked her up with a regularity that ended only at menopause. Never had hot flashes been so welcome.

Homemade oatmeal cookies sat on the pitted wood table every week; Moira's husband thought she spent Wednesdays helping at the rectory and that she made the cookies for the priest. Grateful for the sugar, desperate for any bit of comfort in their lives that they didn't have to pay or beg for, the women inhaled the treats.

"Hey, Mama," Kendra greeted Moira. The young woman bounced into the room, movement and light to Moira's stillness, with her flying braids wrapped in brightly colored clothes she'd designed and sewn, small and tight to Moira's shapelessness.

As usual, the others seemed to come in as one. Pia, the youngest, was nineteen. Beautiful as a dream, raising three children, with an assault record from when she'd stabbed a girl who'd mouthed off at her daughter, she was shy, usually silent, and always sat next to Maddy.

Olivia cleared her throat at the five women in chairs. In a group with ten on the roster, they considered that excellent attendance. "Okay, who's on first?"

"Me." Amber's stories exploded out each week. "So he's back."

"How do you feel about that?" Moira had picked up their jargon during her long tenure.

"How do I feel? That motherfucker thinks he can just walk in and start over like it never even happened? No effin' way." Amber touched her left wrist, which until last week had been in a cast. "But I gotta let him see Dion, right? A baby need his daddy."

"Didn't I hear you say you'd never, ever, till hell fucking freezes over, ever take him back?" Kendra asked. "Wasn't that you yapping last week?"

Olivia held up her hand. "Hold off. Let Amber tell her story."

Amber cut her eyes at Kendra and flipped her limp blond hair over her shoulder. "Tito was straight when he came over. And he'd bought all kinds of shit. Sneakers for Dion. A little tiny Patriots jacket and a football."

"Dion's only six months," Moira said. "Does he need a football? Or sneakers?"

"Listen, Tito's only done me up once," said Amber.

"Who are you bullshitting?" Kendra asked.

"Whoa—" Olivia warned again.

Kendra sat up straight. "Well, it's true. She's lying. Tito did her a thousand times. Unless you're only counting broken bones. Is that what you're doing, girl?"

Now Maddy held up a traffic-cop hand. "Nobody ends up here because they want to. I know I'm repeating myself, but too bad. Obviously you aren't all hearing it. You don't fall in love with a man because he's cruel; you end up in here when someone turns out to have a whole other side than you saw when you fell in love."

Like Ben. So hotly in love with her, so determined to be her hero in the beginning. Maddy shut off the thoughts with an iron fist. It was normal. Every woman who worked with victims saw bits of herself. Look at Olivia, avoiding any relationship for fear she'd end up like her parents.

"Face it, they hide it in the beginning." Olivia swallowed a bite of her cookie before her next word. "You fall in love because he's your dream. When he turns into your nightmare, you don't know what to do because it feels too late and—"

"Because he already has you hooked."

Everyone turned toward the bitter voice. Sabine spat out words as though she paid for each one. It wasn't unusual for her to intimidate the group, between her sinew-skinny body, hard as a ten-year-old boy's, arms scarred from years of drugs, and fight-scarred fists. After speaking, she ran a hand over her brown burr cut. Sabine's mother called her an ugly fish-belly half-breed and said Sabine was just like her rapist father. Maddy wondered if Sabine glanced at every white man, looking for one with her corn-green eyes and a dirty soul she believed would match her own.

"Tito's like heroin," Sabine said. "How'd you get off that?"

"I was never hooked," Amber said. "I just chipped."

Kendra snorted. Amber looked around for the right answer.

"We're all just swinging with the tides sometimes, looking to catch an anchor," Maddy said. "Waiting to find the right answer, the best path. The trick is, the problem is, you really can't just wait—"

"I just want to feel good," Amber said.

"I know." Maddy nodded and tipped her head toward Olivia. They'd worked together enough years to know exactly when it was time to pass the ball.

"The problem is this," Olivia said, looking at Amber but then directing her gaze around the entire room. "We can't be waiting for someone to hand us respect, for a man to make us feel good, as though we're puppies waiting to have our bellies patted. Happiness comes from a whole lotta different places. A man's love is just one piece of that huge cake. And even harder? You gotta bake that damn cake yourself."

Sabine's mercifully short custody hearing could have been worse—some hope for the future seemed possible. At least they gave lip service to the role domestic violence had played in Sabine's case. Still, pulling away from the Dorchester courthouse, Maddy felt as though she'd already worked an entire day. She'd offered to drive Sabine home, but was grateful she said no.

She pulled up to a stoplight and waited to make a right turn. There was heavy traffic, but she didn't care. Even worn out, she felt good—lightened. A morning without driving the kids was a gift from the gods. Leaving while Ben slept had been strange, but she assured herself everybody would be just fine. Emma would get the kids dressed and give them breakfast. She'd already packed lunches. She'd even made fresh juice. Ben simply had to shower and get himself dressed. She should be so lucky.

A siren sounded. She looked in all the mirrors, wondering from which direction the ambulance was approaching. Flashing red lights sparked close behind her. A cop car. No surprise in this neighborhood—every corner offered drug deals.

Maddy pulled over to the curb, next to an empty lot littered with garbage. Across the street were a grate-shuttered bar, a rat hole of a liquor store, a Chinese restaurant offering only a boxed window in which one could shout orders through a small hole in a plate of clouded plastic, and a series of forbidding triple-deckers.

Three young men watched her with arms crossed, cigarettes hanging from their mouths. She hit the button to lock all the windows, waiting for the cop car to pass, a shiver passing over her as she imagined what horror awaited the arrival of the police.

The men's eyes burned. The siren screeched. She was eager to be away from the unfamiliar streets, the wasteland of warehouses and empty lots.

She wanted to get closer to security. The safety of strangers was never a sure thing.

CHAPTER 6

Ben

Halfway to dropping Emma off in South Boston, Ben remembered the meeting papers sitting right where he'd left them. On the bed. He'd have to go back home, and just to make it as bad as possible, it was starting to rain.

Son of a bitch.

He'd be late for certain.

Son of a goddamn bitch.

The moment she closed the car door, he sped back home.

Forty-five long minutes later, holding the *Boston Globe* over his head, Ben ran into the house and up the stairs, leaving the door open, letting in the flies, the mosquitoes, and the jungle heat. Rain and sweat slicked his face. The bedroom was stuffy and hot; he'd closed all the windows when he'd left.

Stacks of papers and folders were scattered over, next to, and under the bed. He spread piles over the wrinkled bedcovers, throwing files one on top of another until he found what he needed. He opened the yellow folder and flipped through the pages. Yellow for administration, red for current cases, beige for closed, blue for fiscal, green for research, purple for political stuff, and brown for general crap that didn't go anywhere else. Maybe he'd tell Elizabeth to start a new category: black for nobody gives a shit.

There. He found the file. One small victory.

Three minutes later Ben barely looked in his rearview mirror as he once again slammed out of the driveway.

As he pulled onto the Jamaicaway, he turned on the radio, punching buttons until he hit "The Enemy" by Anthrax. Pounding music calmed him, something Maddy didn't understand. Rock knocked out the garbage he dealt with all day.

He passed the tired Plymouth in front of him. This traffic could make you blow your brains out. No one knew how to drive the Jamaicaway, an insane winding back road of a parkway that people drove as though it were a speedway. Ben wove in and out to get ahead, another thing that made Maddy crazy.

Some days he felt like there was just too much about him that Maddy wanted to change.

The curving road turned bumper to bumper. Ben crawled fifteen minutes to go half a mile with no way out, another reason for hating the piece of road from the dark ages.

Keeping an eye on the cars in front of him as he inched toward the rotary, Ben hit the CD button. "Jump" blasted out. Piece-of-shit song. He needed to jump this damn road. Only half an hour until the meeting started. Heavy rain slowed it all more. Moses could part the traffic like the Red Sea and he'd probably still be late.

This Elizabeth thing was playing closer to the fire than it should. After drinking two vodka tonics last night, she'd practically offered herself up in a prep school sort of way.

Cars spilled into the four-way from every direction. Some Buick Regal moron sitting like a lump of mashed potatoes blocked him. Ben tapped the horn. Regal got in first position and stopped. *You got an opening, idiot. GO.*

He could tell Lissie was interested. Not like she wanted to marry him, but the hunger of a young woman seeking a frisson of danger.

Safe danger. At her age, he seemed like power. Give her a few years and she'd consider him a hack. She'd have moved on to those in line for real power: the men who'd run for office, who'd be in line for running the biggest firms in town. Or men from New York.

Regal sat as though driving the Buddha car. In the lane to Ben's right, cars merged into the rotary on a regular basis.

Ben blasted the horn this time, joined by the growing line waiting.

Move, motherfucker!

He squeezed hard, passing in front of the Regal and cutting off a car from behind. Cars streamed around the circle. Ben forced his way in, watching the Regal in the rearview, still stuck there, the wallflower of cars, when his cell phone rang. Lissie? He glanced at the screen, where *Maddy* flashed.

For the briefest moment he considered not answering. But that was an uncrossable line. Marriage meant always answering. Marriage meant being tied by the possibility of missing a deadline.

"Maddy?"

"Ben, you have to come pick me up."

"What happened? Where are you?"

"The cops pulled me over—"

"What for?"

"Having an unregistered car. They towed away the car and left me standing on a deserted stretch of Dot Ave."

"Unregistered?" Ben drove forward three inches. "The renewal application came months ago. Are you fucking kidding me? How could you forget to do that?"

"What's the difference? Just come—this isn't a place I want to be a minute longer. Where are you?"

"On the Jamaicaway. On my way to a meeting. Late. Jesus, take a cab. You got yourself into this jam."

"No cabs will pick me up here—you know that. There's no way to walk anywhere. You're barely ten minutes away."

"Jesus, if you'd just taken care of the renewal when it came, this wouldn't have happened."

"Ben, please. I need you. Just come and drop me off at work, okay? Then I'll get my mother to help me get the car back."

He pushed out an impatient sigh and counted to three. "Give me the exact intersection. I'll be right there."

Ben barely said hello when she got in the car. He'd already called Elizabeth to cancel everything. His hands clenched the wheel so hard he thought he might be able to snap the fucking plastic in half. He couldn't even look at her.

"For God's sake, how the hell could you forget to do something so simple and so important?" He spit the words out the side of his mouth as he headed back in the same direction from which he'd come. His Groundhog Day—driving back and forth on the Jamaicaway in some version of the road to hell.

"How many times are you going to say the same thing?" Maddy stared straight ahead as she spoke.

"Until you get it through your head that you need to keep up with basic life tasks like this. I can't remind you of everything. Don't you have any type of organizational system?"

She didn't answer. Her chin jutted out. He imagined her chanting *don't engage* in her head. Just like she taught her clients.

Fuck her.

They stayed silent until he pulled past Blue Hill Avenue.

"Can we use at least this time to talk about last night and about Emma?" Maddy asked.

He glanced at her. "Seriously?"

"Is there a reason not to? We're alone and together. Pretty rare, right?"

"I'm in a crappy mood. Right now that's the last thing I want to talk about."

"We lost that privilege the day we became parents."

"What privilege?"

"The right to be in too crappy a mood to talk about our kids' problems," Maddy said. "That luxury is gone."

Ben shook his head. "I think having a teenager means you'll lose your mind if you analyze every single interaction. Face it, much as you wish for it, I am never going to turn into an angel of patience."

"I'd be glad if we could simply be people who use kindness and understanding as our first choices—angelic wasn't on my wish list."

"We? You mean me, not you. I'm the one who needs adjusting, right?"

He sensed her actions. Biting her lip. Digging her nails into her skirt.

"We need awareness of what we're doing. Both of us." He could hear her coating every word with caution. "You were too harsh last night."

"Harsh is called for when our daughter sneaks out of the house. Should I have given her a five-minute time-out? She's not a little kid anymore."

"You were practically dragging her by the scruff. You can't do that. She's fourteen. Fifteen before we know it. You can't treat her like you did, Ben," Maddy said. "Emma's at a critical stage."

"Can you stop criticizing me for one minute? Is everything wrong in your life my fault? Am I some sort of monster to you?"

"I'm worried. About Emma. About us." Tears trickled down her cheeks.

"Oh, Christ, not now. I came to get you. I'm here." He pounded on the dashboard. "Isn't that enough?"

Now she began crying in earnest. She reached over to the backseat of the car, trying to grab something.

"What do you want?" Pangs of guilt fought with irritation. He took one of those damn deep breaths she was always forcing on him. "Look. I'm sorry for yelling. Can I help you?"

She ignored him, unbuckling her seat belt and then getting on her knees to rummage around in the back of the car. The disconnected seat belt began beeping.

"Maddy, get back in your seat. That noise is driving me crazy."

"Just one second! Here, okay?" She connected the belt and went back to trying to reach for whatever it was that she wanted. Finally she hoisted up the huge suitcase of a briefcase she dragged everywhere and pulled it onto her lap. She took out a pad. "I wrote a list of all the things I'm worried about. With Emma. Things I want to prevent."

Drugs? Pregnancy? Tattoos? Did his wife have a magic social work formula to keep it all at bay? Did she think he didn't care, didn't worry? "Is this all brought on because I made the huge error of bringing our daughter home? Should I have left her on the street corner and then given her a little lecture when she snuck back in? Talked it out?"

"Please don't be sarcastic. I'm so worried about her."

"And I'm not? You haven't cornered the market on parental concern, you know."

"I don't want to fight about this. I want to be partners."

"Then stop making lists about my faults, for Christ's sake."

"It's not about you!"

A Ford Expedition barreled down the road behind them, trying to push their car out of the left lane. Humongous piece of crap. Ben sped up. A blinding force of rain pelted the windows. The rear view on this car was awful in the best weather; with sheets of water sluicing along the glass, he could barely see out the back. He set the wipers on the highest setting and then opened the window to clear the side mirror. The Expedition tailed him closer, pushing him to go faster or move over. Ben hit the accelerator, but the Expedition stayed right with him. Ben threw up his middle finger—aware the idiot probably couldn't see it but needing the satisfaction.

The air inside him expanded, pushing rational judgment out of the way and turning his moves to sheer instinct. He tapped the Camaro's traction-control button twice to turn on competitive drive control, and then sped up, pushing an Accord in front of him to move to the right lane. The Expedition stayed on top of him.

All caution gone, he rocketed. Competitive driving let him be in charge. No car computer slowed him from his fast moves. Ben might not be the athlete of the century, but he knew how to drive like a motherfucker. What did the kids say? Oh, yeah. *I got mad skills.*

The Expedition got closer, almost kissing his bumper, both of them going 45 on a road posted at 25 mph. The road opened up, and the speedometer climbed over 50, then 55, and finally hit 60, but he couldn't lose the Expedition.

"Ben, move over!" Maddy said.

"*Shut up!*"

Just at the moment the guy seemed ready to ram into him, Ben suddenly pulled into the right lane.

At the same moment the Expedition moved right to pass him.

Metal scraped metal as the oversized SVU hit them hard. As Ben tried to straighten out, he hit a slick spot, hydroplaned, and the car spun out of control.

Cars ahead and to the right squealed, maneuvering away on the twisting road, as the Camaro careened toward the tree in the curve.

Maddy screamed.

He gripped the wheel as though death chased them.

He coughed.

Where was he? His rapid breaths jabbed his left side as he tried to open the jammed door. Sharp odors from the deflated air bag burned his eyes. Someone knocked on the window and peered through the glass. An old guy stood there, grizzled, his white short-sleeved shirt soaked with rain.

Sweat and salty blood trickled. He'd bitten his lower lip. Any movement brought a stab in his chest, sharp enough to make him gasp. When he turned to look at Maddy, the searing pain worsened. Shards of jagged glass marked where the passenger window had been.

She was gone. The windshield was smashed out.

"*Maddy!*" he screamed. "*Maddy!*"

All he saw as he peered out was the rain.

He lowered his jammed window as far as he could, holding his breath each time he pressed the button.

"My wife. Help me out. I gotta find her," Ben said.

The man shook his head. "Sorry, son. Best to stay put and wait for the medics." In his peripheral vision Ben saw hazard lights flashing. "I called 911 as soon as I saw you duking it out with that other car."

"Reach in and unlock the door, okay?" Ben tried to turn his head, but a stab of pain held him still. Rain blew in from the open window.

"I don't know." The man slowly stood from his crouch. A woman leaned in.

"Don't move. You might have internal injuries." She pushed back wet hair on her forehead. As though offering a condolence prize, she held up a phone. "Do you want me to call someone for you? Do you want to make a call?"

Ben's thoughts blurred. He studied the phone and the wet woman.

Nauseated and dizzy, he hung his pounding head. Raw skin on his cheeks stung where the air bag had scraped him.

He closed his eyes. Confused.

Maddy.

Sirens sounded.

The woman was still there when he opened his eyes. Earnest. Concerned. He could see her telling the story at dinner as she served the salad: *And then I asked if I could call someone for him.*

Everything spun.

It seemed he'd just tried closing his eyes again when a husky young voice urged him to open them. A smoker's voice. Was it fashionable for young women to smoke? He'd better keep an eye on Emma.

"Sir. My name is Evanne. I'm an emergency medical worker. Can you hear me?" The light-skinned woman's beaded braids were pulled back into a thick blue elastic band.

"My wife," he said. "I need to get out of here."

"Soon. I promise. Are you allergic to latex?" When he shook his head no, she reached in and took his wrist with rubber-gloved fingers. "Can you feel that?"

Everything got hazy again.

"Yes," he whispered. "My wife?"

"Don't worry." As she questioned him, a fireman wedged a bar into the door and popped it open. By the time she'd asked what Ben weighed and what day it was, he felt faint. His legs shook so violently he worried they'd hit the steering wheel.

"Don't worry." Evanne took his arm. "The shaking is shock. Normal after a trauma.

"My wife?" he repeated.

"She's being cared for."

Was she lying? *Jesus, Maddy, where are you?* Was she dead?

Evanne and a male EMS worker brought him onto a portable cot, where he lay, arms spread on either side of the narrow slab of foam, his exhaustion profound. Still, he struggled to his elbows, working against the searing pain, then falling back.

"You should remain flat, sir," Evanne suggested. Ben found her throaty voice soothing.

"No. No. I'm all right."

"Please, sir, it would be better to lie back for now."

Lying back didn't seem like a good idea. Already it felt as though fate had simply picked him up and thrown him on the ground.

Evanne took his pulse. She held his chin and looked into his eyes. Her breath was mild peppermint, her hands lemon-scented. Maybe she wasn't a smoker. Ben pictured her life, showering with yellow soap, buying Life Savers, not knowing what each day would bring. Broken bodies. Guns. Him.

Ben slowly turned to look in every direction. Bright orange cones held cars back. A barely moving line of traffic crept around the accident scene. He turned his head to the left. Pain shot through his upper back.

The Expedition was about fifteen yards away. Even seated, the young driver seemed tall. He sat sideways, legs hanging out, one big hand cradling a phone, the other covering his free ear. Dark-black shades, despite the rain, covered his eyes. He appeared okay, but his front fender was smashed. Shards from the taillights were scattered over the asphalt. Expedition had his own EMT next to him. A white guy. Older. Probably didn't smell of lemon and peppermint.

Careful, his back stiffening, something jabbing him each time he breathed, Ben twisted his head as far as possible, searching for Maddy. Flashers from three ambulances made kaleidoscopic patterns in the growing puddles.

Wet broken glass reflected in the ambulance lights.

He forced his neck to the right. Before he even knew he'd done it, he reached for Evanne's hand.

A red briefcase, open, papers strewn over the road, had landed about twenty yards from the car. Ben felt light-headed. He squinted through the rain. Two men laid a woman on a backboard. A red sandal swayed off her right foot; her left was bare.

Dirt streaked the woman's blood-covered blouse. The men wheeled her still body toward a waiting ambulance. As they positioned the stretcher to enter the vehicle, the woman's face became visible.

Jesus, Mary, and Joseph, please, no.

Under the oxygen mask was Maddy, the gray pallor of her skin visible even through the rain.

Asleep

———

AUGUST

CHAPTER 7

Emma

More than anything, Emma wanted to leave the community center's dank locker room. She'd been on edge since the morning, when an army of water rats ran along the nearby wharf. Despite the way she'd pretended to be brave with her campers, now, with the camp day over, her stomach turned in skittish little jumps, unease growing as she waited impatiently for Caro and Sammi to finish changing their clothes.

Emma inspected herself in the wavy unbreakable mirror for the umpteenth time. Her thighs appeared bigger every day and her nose looked like a missile. Her eyes were too close together. The fact that Zach even looked at her was some sort of miracle.

Of course, she didn't have to worry about whether or why Zach liked her anymore. The way her parents were acting, it would be years before she was allowed to see him again.

Seething thoughts looped, the fury she'd put away while working with the kids returned. With camp dismissal over, she could give full rein to being angry with her idiot parents.

Emma turned to Caro. "I'll probably never be able to leave my house again this summer." Emma threw her backpack over one shoulder, her head suddenly pulled back as her braid got caught in the strap. "Help," she yelled.

Caro lifted the fastening and pulled out Emma's hair. "Doesn't it drive you crazy having it that long?"

Emma shrugged. "Not really." She couldn't admit how much she loved leaning back on her mother's legs, going into a dreamlike state as her mother slid the brush through her hair—making French braids or just bringing out the shine with a hundred strokes while they watched television.

Not that she'd ever let her do it again.

"Can you at least get ice cream with us?" Sammi pulled a tight white T-shirt over her head, muffling her tentative voice, which ended on a rising note as though questioning her own idea.

"Everyone's meeting at Kelly's—including *Zach*." Caro gave Emma an annoying smile as she singsonged Zach's name.

Emma shook her head. "My mother's picking me up."

"How long are you really grounded?" Sammi opened the wide metal doors of the community center, blinking as the wind whipped her brown hair around her face.

"I told you. Until school starts." Hatred of her parents shuddered through her.

They walked along the beach wall. Two joggers ran by, almost knocking down a toddler gripping a plastic bucket. Afternoon sun slanted over the gritty beach, blurring the trash and gray-black tones of the sand.

"Wait with me?" Emma asked as she climbed up on the wall.

"No can do." Caro said this as though Emma's idea was absurd.

"How come?" Caro shouldn't be acting so high and mighty; she should pray her mother didn't call Caro's about them sneaking out last night.

"You know why. The boys are waiting. Should we tell Zach to come see you here?"

Emma groaned. "Just what I need, my mother driving up and finding Zach. I can hear her now. *Where do you live? What do your parents do? How much did you weigh when you were born?*"

"Sooner or later she has to meet him. You've been going out since we started working," Caro said. "What are you waiting for?"

Emma wanted to keep Zach to herself a little longer. Not have her mother tell Kath, and Grandma, and Aunt Vanessa, and Olivia, and every neighbor on their street that Emma had a boyfriend. She didn't want to listen to her mother make a big deal about Zach being a sophomore, while Emma was just starting high school, or hear it become her mother's drama: *Jesus, if Emma has a boyfriend, how old does that make me?* She and Kath would talk it to death until they chewed every bit of juice from her and Zach.

Anyway, Emma wasn't exactly looking her best. Vomit traces stained her shirt from where Iggy Miller had thrown up, despite how many times she'd scrubbed the spots. "Just tell him I had to go home, okay?"

When they left, Emma rummaged in her bag until she found a pack of almonds. Her mother threw this stuff at her every morning, making sure she didn't starve to death, as though they lived in some remote Appalachian village where she'd have to trek fifty miles for food.

God, her mother was late again. Now she wished she'd let Caro send Zach. At least she'd have something to do besides stare at stupid boys showing off—battling to be the first to knock each other from the retaining wall, then looking to see if Emma was watching. The doggy smell of sand they'd kicked up mixed with the odor of throw-up from her shirt. She brought her arm up to her nose and sniffed. Vomity. She brought her braid around to her face. Dried sweat.

Where was her mother?

Salty nut dust coated Emma's mouth. She jumped off the wall and walked to the fountain in the square. Three boys about Gracie's age took turns forcing the water pressure and spraying one other.

"Excuse me," she said.

They turned to her with a *whaddya want* look.

"Do you mind?" She gestured toward the spigot.

They moved back. Slowly. She bent over the fountain, taking her time. Gross and warm, but at least the water washed the salt off her tongue.

"*Emma.*"

Emma turned, recognizing her brother's screech. She wiped her mouth with the bottom of her T-shirt, puzzled at not seeing her mother's car.

"*Come on, Emma!*"

She blocked the sun with her hand but still couldn't see her mother or the car.

"Over here, darling." Grandma Anne stepped out of her blue Volvo and waved at her over the car roof. It was her mother's mother—if it had been Grandma Frances, she'd have thought the world had come to an end.

Emma hurried over. "What are you doing here, Grandma?"

"Mommy's hurt," Gracie whispered out the window, as though it were a secret.

Emma opened the passenger door and got into the empty seat. Her grandmother slid back behind the wheel.

"What happened?" Fear hit Emma in the stomach first. A small cramp had already begun.

"Put on your seat belt," her grandmother said. "Mommy was in a car accident. Daddy also. They're in the hospital."

"Daddy only had a bruised chest." Gracie held a knuckle to her mouth, talking around it. "He's not in a room."

"She means a bruised rib. He hasn't been admitted." Grandma took a deep breath. "They're both going to be fine. Just fine."

"How did it happen? How bad is Mom hurt?"

"It's all a little confusing, darling."

"But she's all right, isn't she?"

"Everything will be okay."

Emma tugged on the whistle hanging from her lanyard. "Does she have to stay there?"

"We'll find out when we get to the hospital. I'm sure it will be okay." Grandma's voice shook. Emma didn't know what else to ask.

Her grandmother reached into the pocket of her denim skirt and gave Emma a pile of wet naps. "Wipe your face, you'll feel better. Give some to Caleb and Gracie. Everyone should cool off."

Emma handed one to each of the kids. They opened the square foil packets in unison and wiped the alcohol-saturated squares over their faces. Grandma started up the car.

Children younger than twelve weren't allowed in the surgical waiting room, so Emma had to watch Caleb and Gracie in the main lobby. For hours. At eight that night they were still huddled on a hard bench. Sick-looking people hunched against their pain kept appearing through the revolving hospital doors. Others came from the elevators, heading over toward the nearby cafeteria or going outside.

Some were too scary to look at, dragging bags of fluid hanging from poles or with faces so swollen they looked about to burst. Why were they going outside? To smoke? Get air?

Other people, healthy-looking people, carried in bright gift bags, plants, and piles of magazines, but they were also frightening, with their faces all pinched with worry.

The wooden benches and chairs afforded no comfort. Caleb's head lay in Emma's lap; Gracie leaned against Emma's other side. Daddy wanted her, Gracie, and Caleb to go home with Aunt Vanessa. When Aunt Vanessa wouldn't leave the hospital, he suggested that Kath or Olivia pick them up, but Emma refused to go anywhere.

What if her mother died?

No one told Emma what was going on.

Daddy said he was fine and it was nothing, but he'd walked all bent over when they'd seen him. Bandages wrapped his chest so thickly that he couldn't button the middle part of his shirt. How could it be nothing?

She didn't want him to make her leave, so she just stayed quiet, taking care of Caleb and Gracie and waiting for news.

"Is Mommy going to die?" Caleb's thumb in his mouth muffled his words.

"Of course not. Don't even think that." Emma smoothed his hair.

"But she could, right?" he insisted. "It's possible."

Gracie sat up. Red marks from Emma's shirt seams lined her face. "Could Mommy die?"

Hours of crying had left her sister's eyes red and swollen. Finally, frightened that Gracie's loud sobs would attract attention and their father would be called, Emma warned her that Daddy would send them home if Gracie didn't stop. The effort of not crying contorted Gracie's face until it looked as though pain twisted her features.

"She's not going to die," Emma said. "We just have to be good. And pray." Emma didn't know why she said that—praying was a foreign concept—but she had nothing else to offer.

Gracie laced her fingers and pressed her palms together. Her mouth moved silently as she clasped her hands. Caleb picked at his sad grimy bandages. None of them had received anything resembling religious training, unless you counted going to the bar mitzvahs of second cousins, or having Passover at her mother's parents' house and Easter at her father's. Christmas and Chanukah meant no more than food and presents.

Should she pray to the God of Jews or Catholics? Emma made secret little crosses on her chest, imitating Gracie, trying to make deals with God. She'd obey her parents for the rest of her life if God kept her mother alive. She'd take care of everyone and never be mean. *Baruch Atah Adonai, Eloheinu Melech Ha'Olam,* she chanted in her head. Emma didn't know what the words meant, but Grandma Anne said them each year as she lit the Chanukah candles. *Baruch Atah Adonai, Eloheinu Melech Ha'Olam, please keep my mother alive.*

"But she *could* die," Caleb repeated. "Mommy could die."

"Shut up, Caleb, or I'll send you to Aunt Vanessa's house."

"You can't do that. Aunt Vanessa's not leaving."

"Yes, I can. Uncle Sean is there. I'll put you in a cab and send you right this second."

"You're not the boss."

"Yes, I am," Emma said. "I'm the boss until Daddy or Grandma comes back. And imagine what Daddy will do if I tell him you're saying scary things about Mommy."

Caleb rose and went to a mud-colored bench away from Emma and Gracie. He crossed his arms and started kicking the wooden slats with his heels. If her father saw, he'd kill her. "Stop or they'll throw us out." Her brother looked up; his dark-brown eyes reminded Emma of war orphans in *Time*. "Come back here."

He shook his head, not looking at her, using his dirty camp T-shirt to wipe underneath his eyes.

"Come on." Emma patted the seat next to her. "I'll get you a candy bar."

Caleb shuffled back, climbed next to Emma, and put his head back on her lap. "Reese's Pieces?" He snuck his right thumb near his mouth and rubbed it against his lower lip.

"Sure. Reese's Pieces."

Baruch Atah Adonai, Eloheinu Melech Ha'Olam, please keep my mother alive.

When her father finally showed up, it seemed like they'd been waiting for a year.

"I can't stay." Daddy sat next to Gracie and kissed the top of her head. "I need to get back upstairs, baby cakes."

He handed Emma a twenty-dollar bill. "You know where the cafeteria is, right?" He pointed left. "You can see it from here."

Why wasn't he telling them more?

"Grandma already took us, but—"

"Are you hurt, Daddy?" Gracie interrupted, gently touching the blood spotting his shirt.

"Don't worry, cookie—I'm fine," he said. "And Mommy will be fine. Be good and listen to Emma. You too, Caleb." He gave them each a stiff hug, holding them away from his chest.

"What happened, Daddy?" Emma asked.

"It was an accident—just like Grandma said. I don't have time to explain now."

"Can we see Mommy?" Gracie asked.

"She's in surgery. Then she'll be in a special recovery room for a long time."

Emma put her hand on her father's arm. "Why is she being operated on?"

"She has some head injuries. It's too complicated to describe—we'll talk later, I promise, honey. Mommy will be fine," he repeated.

"Are they operating on her head?" Caleb asked her when their father left. "How do they do that?"

Emma reached over and pulled Caleb on her lap, pressing her cheek to his thin back. "Mommy will be fine. Like Daddy said."

Baruch Atah Adonai, Eloheinu Melech Ha'Olam, please keep my mother alive.

CHAPTER 8

Ben

Ben sat in the surgical waiting room, his head in his hands, elbows on his knees. The position killed him, digging the tightly wrapped tape deeper into the skin around his chest, but it kept him from having to look at his mother-in-law or sister-in-law. Pain spread with every breath and move. He didn't tell Anne, certain she'd drag him back to the emergency room. He didn't want painkillers or his mother-in-law's sympathy. Most of all, he didn't want Vanessa's suspicious looks. He drew up his shoulders and took the shallowest breaths possible.

The waiting room had to be fifty degrees, if that. Vanessa had gone to his house, his being the closest to the hospital, and grabbed a pile of sweatshirts. Anne wore Ben's gray Red Sox pullover; it hung to midthigh, her cotton skirt fanning out below. Vanessa had Maddy's orange fleece zipped up to her chin.

"Why do they keep this room so damn cold?" Vanessa asked.

"Because of the surgery, I think," Anne answered. "The temperature needs to be low when they operate."

That made no sense. They weren't operating in the fucking waiting room. The operating room had to be on a separate circuit, right?

He didn't correct her. He squeezed his eyes shut for a moment.

A wave of pain and nausea passed through him. He tucked his hands under his armpits.

"Don't you want a sweatshirt?" Anne reached for the bag.

"No. Don't." He held his hand out to stop the coming parade of clothes she'd offer. "I'm fine."

"You're shivering, for goodness' sake. Look at you."

Dirt and dried blood from Ben's torn lip streaked his white shirt. A slash on the right side of the fabric mapped a bandaged gash. "I'm fine, Anne."

"When's Daddy getting here?" Vanessa wrapped her arms around herself. "What's taking so long?"

"He's at police headquarters." Anne took Vanessa's hand. "He wanted to see what's what. What the report said. He's meeting Arnie."

Ben said nothing. His father-in-law probably had everything the cops had by now, courtesy of *Arnie*. Yet another one of his connections, no doubt. The city, the whole fucking state, was nothing but a collection of who knew whom. Photos from the scene. Close-ups of where Maddy had landed. Blowups of Ben's car. All of them were no doubt clutched in his father-in-law's fist.

"He should be here." Vanessa brought her knees up to her chest. "You shouldn't be alone."

"I'm not alone. You're here. Ben's here. Daddy would be going crazy with nothing to do. You know Daddy."

They all knew Daddy. Waiting rooms and Jake Greene weren't a match. Anne was right about her husband. He'd break in and try to oversee the operation. He'd be on the phone calling his real estate clients, seeing if one was a brain specialist or could recommend one. The best. The top guy. His daughter needed the top guy. Everyone in Jake's family needed the top guy.

"He'll have the whole thing figured out by the time he gets here," Vanessa said.

The idea that Jake could figure it all out sickened Ben. As his postaccident fog lifted degree by degree, details stood out. His speed. Pushing the traction-control button for all the wrong reasons. Overriding the car's brain to put in his own, increasing his ability to accelerate. Competitive driving functions weren't designed for idiots racing other idiots in the rain.

"Mr. Illica?" The surgeon's grizzled beard, thinning salt-and-pepper hair, and ashy skin were studies in gray. Ben had entrusted Maddy to this old man? "She's out of surgery. The operation went well. She's in intensive care now—she'll be there for quite a while."

Ben struggled to his feet, trying to stand straight, arms crossed over his taped ribs. "How is she?"

"We'll have to wait before we know much." The doctor placed a hand on Ben's arm. "These are touch-and-go hours. She came through—that's the important thing. The nurse will come in periodically and—"

Ben shook off the doctor's hand. "If it's touch-and-go, then what? The surgery went well, but my wife may not make it? What are we looking at?"

"Shh." Anne put her hand on Ben's shoulder. "Please, excuse us. You can imagine how shaken my son-in-law is. We all are. Thank you, Dr. Gordon. When can we see her?"

"The nurse will tell you the moment it's possible. Have something to eat. You're facing a long road ahead." He backed away with an expression somewhere between concern and relief, appearing grateful that his time with the family was over.

The inner-sanctum door closed behind the doctor, and Anne again touched Ben. Lightly. As though he might flame up and burn her. "Bennie."

"What, Anne?" He heard his own impatience, his search for an enemy to smack around, but he couldn't bear to apologize once more.

"Go easy, sweetheart. We're not looking to make enemies."

"Did you hear him? Maddy is just hanging on?" Ben's voice rose with each word. "He doesn't know how she is and he's telling me the operation went well? This is his idea of—"

"Enough," Vanessa interrupted. "We can't know what we can't know. All that matters now is Maddy, not us."

Ben opened his mouth to continue arguing and then sank back in his chair.

"I'm going to check on the kids," Vanessa said. She flung her bag over her shoulder. "Should I tell them anything?"

Ben looked up. "Take them home. Please."

"I can't leave; I'll call Sean and have him pick them up."

"Go with them. Maddy would want you to be with them. She'd hate thinking of them scared." Ben watched Vanessa's shoulders sag with defeat when he played his trump card.

"He's right," Anne said. "Take them to your house. They shouldn't be here. We'll call if there's any news. I promise."

Vanessa glared at Ben. She took Anne's hands in hers. She held them to her lips for a moment and then let go. "What do you need, Mom? I'll have Sean run it right back to you."

Anne smoothed back strands from Vanessa's unkempt blond ponytail. "I'm fine. Get some rest." She turned to Ben. "Do you need anything?"

He shook his head.

"A clean shirt would look better." Anne ran her hands over her chest, as though drawing his attention to the blood he wore. "For when Maddy wakes up."

"Maybe later." Fighting with Anne was like punching a down pillow. It kept coming up somewhere else, offering yet another soft spot.

"Want to come with me—say good-bye to the kids?" Vanessa cocked her head with her obvious message.

Ben bought time with a sip of cold vegetable soup. The Styrofoam cup had sat on the table for too many hours, and cold sliminess coated his tongue. Pain radiated across his chest each time he moved. "I'll see them later."

"Later when?" Vanessa took off the sweatshirt and tied it around her waist. Her arms looked overly tanned next to her yellow sundress. Her healthy skin seemed an affront to the hospital.

"Just send our love," Anne said.

Vanessa's face pinched inward. Bright cold fluorescence highlighted where her tan flaked, pink skin showing through the brown. "Fine." She stood and bent to kiss Anne on the cheek. "I love you," she said, then turned and walked out.

"Take care of them," he called after her. His eyes stung.

"How did this happen?" Flint replaced Anne's usual soft tone. "Was there a problem?"

Problem had an italicized tone. Ben stared at his mother-in-law. She gripped the edge of his sleeve, rolling the hem with such force he thought it might fray.

Ben took a shallow breath. "I feel sick. I shouldn't have had that old soup."

Anne grabbed a wastepaper bucket from the corner and held it out. "Here. Now tell me. Before Jake comes. Were you speeding when it happened?"

He straightened as best he could and looked right at Anne. "It was an accident. A horrible accident."

"You drive like a lunatic. Everyone knows. How fast were you going?"

Ben inched over to the window, tugging at the wood in a fool's errand, knowing it wouldn't open but needing to get away from her.

He turned back to face Anne. "You don't think I'd ever hurt her, do you? Jesus, I love Maddy so much."

"Of course I don't think you tried to hurt her." Anne sank back, deflated. "It's just—"

As Anne spoke, the door opened, letting a momentary wash of warmer air into the room. His father-in-law stood in the doorway.

"I saw the skid marks. Pictures," Jake said. "Did you think you were in a rocket, you fucking *putz*?"

"Jake, stay calm." Anne stood and tried to embrace him, and when that failed, she reached up to put a hand on his shoulder. Jake's chest rose and fell as though banded by a blood pressure cuff. He tore off his suit jacket, handed it to Anne, and then rolled up his sleeves.

Ben lowered his head and raked his fingers through his thick hair. "Do you think I did it on purpose?" He looked up at his father-in-law. "Don't you think I wish I were the one on that operating table?"

"I guarantee you, no one wishes that more than me." Jake shrugged off his wife's hand. At sixty-seven, he still carried the build of the amateur boxer he'd once been. He fisted his thick hands; ropes of tangled veins and muscles tensed beneath his rolled shirtsleeves. Anne kneaded the empty shoulders of her husband's suit jacket after hanging it over a chair.

"What? What was so important you had to drive like that? In the rain, for God's sake. I don't care what they find—I know it was your fault."

"The guy behind me. He jammed me up so—"

"Goddamned son of a bitch." Jake flung words like garbage at Ben's feet. *"Momzer."* Jake jutted his chin, and then translated the Yiddish for Ben. "Bastard."

CHAPTER 9

Emma

Quiet streets flew by as they made their way to Aunt Vanessa's house. No stores lined the road; nobody walked; it was just shrubs and flowers and big lawns. Aunt Vanessa made a sharp left and screeched to a stop when she reached the end of her long driveway.

She drove like Emma's father.

"We're here." Her aunt waited a moment before taking the key out of the ignition. She turned to face Caleb and Gracie, putting her hand on Emma's arm. "Mom will be okay. I just know it." She opened the car door. "Let's go."

Emma, Gracie, and Caleb scrambled to keep up as their aunt rushed down the brick path lined with pink and white hollyhocks. They followed her through the open door and a foyer that was larger than Emma's bedroom to the living room.

"Did my mother or Ben call?" Vanessa yelled as they entered the house.

"No one's called. Sorry, love," Uncle Sean answered from the couch.

Aunt Vanessa slammed her oversized shoulder bag on a leather club chair. "Jesus, Sean, couldn't you have at least picked up the house?"

Uncle Sean gave her aunt a look that managed to be both reproving and mild. "I know you're worried. But hush." Baby Melody was limp in his arms, clutching a bottle, sweaty, her hair lying in damp flat strands like an old man's. Three-year-old Ursula curled against him, sucking her thumb, wearing only flowered underpants. Yellow and red plastic blocks, stuffed animals, and dolls were strewn around the room. Cloudy glasses and blue bowls caked with spaghetti remains littered the coffee table.

"Shh. Ursula just fell asleep." He spoke softly as he tipped the bottle up so Melody could get the end of the milk.

Aunt Vanessa tiptoed over and picked up Ursula, who flopped against her mother's chest, her head hanging over her mother's shoulder. She ran her hand over Ursula's bare back. "Emma, take the kids to the kitchen," her aunt whispered. "I'll be right there to get you something to eat."

Gracie and Caleb stood as close to Emma as possible. She put an arm around Caleb's shoulders and took Gracie's hand. "I can do it."

"I was just going to scramble some eggs. Do you want to get them going?"

Emma nodded, wanting to scream *no!* What she wanted was to be alone to think and breathe. She knew she'd be sleeping in the same room with Gracie and Caleb, their night sounds sucking every thought from her head. Caleb snuffled in his sleep as though his nose were pasted shut. Anyone not used to the sound flipped out, thinking Caleb was about to expire—her family, accustomed to the seeming death rattle, only got annoyed.

Her family.

Would they have a family without her mother?

Emma steered the kids toward the kitchen.

"Take whatever you want, Em," Aunt Vanessa said. "If you don't want the eggs, have cake and ice cream. Sean hides Entenmann's and pints of Ben and Jerry's in the back of the freezer."

Permission to eat cake for supper worsened Emma's cramping fear. Aunt Vanessa never did stuff like that—her family nickname was the Nutrition Czarina. How badly hurt was her mother for her aunt to let them overdose on sugar? She led her brother and sister to the kitchen table, where Gracie and Caleb dropped into chairs like boneless dolls. Gracie made a circle of her arms and put her head in the center.

"I want Ben and Jerry's," Caleb said.

"First you have to eat eggs." Emma opened and closed cabinets until she found a frying pan.

"Are you crying?" Gracie asked.

Emma wiped her eyes with a dish towel. The cloth felt stiff and smelled oniony. She took a paper towel, ran it under the faucet, and held it to her face. "I'm okay. Don't worry."

Caleb put his arms around Emma's waist. "It's okay," he murmured, sounding like Grandma Anne. "Shah, shah."

Gracie stood next to Caleb, patting and rubbing Emma's back.

Their tiny touches calmed her. She took a deep breath and hugged her brother and sister. "Let's see what's in the freezer."

Aunt Vanessa came back, her eyes puffy from crying and black from runny mascara. "You okay?"

"Did my father call?" Emma asked.

Her aunt's face twisted as if she'd tasted something rotten. "No. No calls. You all set here?"

Emma nodded and continued scooping out ice cream into three red polka-dot bowls. The dishes seemed oddly happy in the gloomy atmosphere. "We're fine. I'll put the kids to bed."

Vanessa came over and planted a kiss on each of them, giving Emma an extra squeeze. "Thanks, honey."

You don't have to thank me for taking care of my own brother and sister. That's what she wanted to say. But she was terrified it would come out mean and she'd end up sounding like her father.

The silent house felt foreign when Emma woke. The clock showed five a.m. She climbed out of bed, careful not to make a sound.

Violet-pink streaks flamed across the sky as she slipped outside. Sharply delineated flowerbeds outlined the large backyard. Emma's family had flowers, but not in perfect patterns like Aunt Vanessa's. Her father called the suburban area where her aunt and uncle lived "city-light," emphasizing *light* so no one missed his opinion on the whole thing. Each time her mother rolled her eyes.

Her mother wouldn't mind living out here with Aunt Vanessa, having what her mother called "guaranteed schools" available. She'd heard her and Kath talking about it, all *oh, marriage is so hard* and *husbands drive you nuts* as they drank wine coolers as though they were still in college or something. *I'm sick of having to research schools. Why can't I just send them to school, like Vanessa will do with her kids? Why does everything in Ben's life have to prove something?*

Emma learned plenty listening to their conversations. Like maybe getting married wasn't such a good idea. When they saw her listening, her mother and Kath would shut up, but Emma knew how to hover in the background.

She leaned back in a green straw chair, her thighs poking through the sagging weave. It wasn't comfortable, but she was too tired to get up and move to the cushioned chaise.

Were wires and junk hanging out of her mother, like the patients on TV? What did it mean when they said "tube her"? Was her mother tubed? Emma slipped her hands under her thighs, letting the cross-hatching cut into her palms, questions and horrible images endlessly running.

When the sun rose, Emma tiptoed to the back door and slipped inside. She crept upstairs to grab her backpack from the guest room. The air-conditioned bedroom was stale. Gracie and Caleb were in one twin bed, facing away from each other, their feet and butts pressed together. An old patchwork cover outlined them, a quilt made by Emma's great-grandmother, the blue and white squares shredded in spots. Her mother and aunt had fought over that blanket when Grandma Anne offered it up last year. During the argument Aunt Vanessa had ticked off three things that had already gone to Emma's mother: *one, Grandma Bessie's mortar and pestle,* as though her aunt would ever use it; *two, Mom's locket,* which Emma thought especially stupid because Aunt Vanessa only wore big ugly chunky jewelry and the locket was a delicate filigreed piece; and *three, you have Grandma Greene's old silverware from Daddy's parents.*

She got back to the porch without waking anyone, and then dug through her backpack until she found her phone and large silvery barrette. Heavy humidity had turned her unbraided hair into an itchy cape. She gathered it at the back of her neck, clipped it up, and called her father.

He answered as though the phone were already in his hand.

"Daddy?"

"Emma? What's wrong?"

"Nothing." Emma crossed her legs on the sagging chair. "Why didn't you call us?" She couldn't bring herself to ask the real question—*Is Mom alive?*—convinced her father hadn't called because her mother had died in the night. She couldn't remember the last thing she'd said to Mom, but the likelihood that it had been bitchy and mean haunted her.

"Mom is out of surgery. She's in the intensive care unit. I'm still at the hospital."

Alive!

Still, Emma listened to her father's lawyer words carefully. *Mom is out of surgery.* What did that mean? "Is she okay?" Her father didn't answer. "Is she?"

"The doctor says she's holding her own." His words were slow and measured.

"What does that mean, Daddy? Did you talk to her?" Emma leaned her chin on her knees, gripping the sweaty phone.

"She's still unconscious. They had to give her a lot of anesthesia, honey. Later we'll know more—I promise. Are you okay? How are the kids?"

"Fine. What happened? Is her brain . . ." What was the right word?

"I told you, we'll know more later. Go back to bed, honey."

"Daddy, call me as soon as she wakes up. Promise?"

"I promise."

After hanging up, Emma realized he hadn't told her what to do. Was she supposed to go to work, or should she stay with Caleb and Gracie? They could be here with Aunt Vanessa, but Emma thought they'd be happier if she stayed too. Anyway, she didn't want to go to work.

She'd call Kath.

Oh, God, had anyone thought to call Kath? Maybe her father hadn't. And how about Olivia?

If they knew, at least there'd be people to ask questions.

She went back into the house, poured a glass of orange juice, and carried it to the study. The computer was already on. She guessed they never turned it off. Her father would kill Emma for doing that.

She logged in on Aunt Vanessa's icon. Weight Watchers came up as the home page. God, her aunt was such an obsessive. Emma paused, and then typed *brain surgery* in the search box, immediately over-whelmed by an endless list:

ABC's of brain tumors
Aneurysm
AVM
Arteriovenous Malformation: formed during fetal development
Aneurysms of the Brain. Meningioma
Surviving brain injury in the family: depression, frustration, speech loss

Emma clicked on the last one.

Family members in the hospital setting: Patients may not know where they are. Be careful to speak in short simple sentences.

Emma tried to speed-read about keeping the hospital room simple and helping patients adjust gradually, until she gave up and printed it. Before leaving the site, she emailed herself the URL.

Clicking back, she scanned a list of types of brain surgeries until she saw the one she'd heard Grandma Anne say to Daddy, *craniotomy*. She dug deeper, looking for something, somewhere that would tell her that her mother would be okay.

Craniotomy (krā' • nē' • ä' • tə • mē): Surgery performed on the skull where a portion of bone is removed to gain access to the brain, and the bone is put back in its place. Craniectomy (krā'• nē • ek'• tə • mē): Surgery performed on the skull where pieces of bone are removed to gain access to the brain, and the bone pieces are not replaced.

Baruch Atah Adonai, Eloheinu Melech Ha'Olam, please keep my mother alive.

In a craniotomy, the skull is opened to relieve the causes of increased pressure inside the skull. Causes may be fractured bones, blood clots, or swollen brain tissues.

Emma visited a virtual hospital and landed inside a brain, watching a virtual operation in full color, skin and bone pulled aside to reveal photos titled "obliterating an aneurysm." Did her mother have that?

"What are you doing?"

Emma leapt up as though she'd been caught surfing porn.

Aunt Vanessa's hair hung in ragged clumps. An edge of faded red underwear showed beneath her oversized white T-shirt. Without makeup, Aunt Vanessa looked plain and worn. Melody laid placidly in her arms, chewing a corner of her blanket, her bright green eyes so similar to Uncle Sean's that it seemed as though Aunt Vanessa held a tiny version of her husband.

"Nothing." Emma hit the X in the corner of the screen, making it all go away. "I was just checking my email."

"I guess at your age it gets checked even when your mother's in the hospital, huh?" She planted an absentminded kiss on Melody's forehead.

As though anyone uses email. Sometimes the ease with which you could fool adults pained her. She crossed her arms and gripped her elbows.

"I didn't mean that as an insult, hon. Honest. I'd probably do the same thing if I could," Aunt Vanessa said.

She swung Melody around, switching hips. Her shirt rode up, revealing more of the red underwear, more of her ropy muscled thighs.

Aunt Vanessa seemed exaggerated to Emma, especially her blue eyes, just like Grandma's, but so sharp on her aunt that they reminded Emma of a doll's. Her mother's warm dark ones were better. People referred to Aunt Vanessa as a knockout, but Emma thought people were more comfortable around her mother. She didn't have to paint herself pretty.

"Here, help me out." Aunt Vanessa held out Melody as though she were a UPS delivery. "I'm desperate for coffee."

Breakfast was a bleak affair that held no reason to rush, as nobody was going to work or school. She'd never seen Uncle Sean in pajamas before, and it made her feel shy, despite the fact that he had more flesh showing when he wore shorts and a T-shirt.

"Shouldn't we call Kath?" Emma asked for the second time. She placed bowls in front of the kids. Melody alternated pounding a foam hammer against her high chair tray and throwing it on the floor for her never-tiring cousin Caleb to retrieve.

"Your father called her already." Her aunt's answer scared Emma. Calling Kath last night made it sound too serious—like notifying people about a funeral.

"Shouldn't I tell her I'm not going to be at camp? What if she needs me? Maybe I should go." Now Emma wanted nothing so much as getting dressed and walking the fifteen minutes to the train, just to be someplace where her mother wasn't sick.

Uncle Sean put a plate of cut grapefruit in front of Aunt Vanessa, who seemed increasingly frustrated at trying to coax mashed banana into Melody's mouth.

"Caleb," he said. "Don't be picking up the hammer for Melody now. You're getting her all excited and she won't want to eat."

Bran Flakes was the only cereal Emma found in the cabinet. Aunt Vanessa offered to make French toast, but the offer sounded pro forma—Emma's current favorite word from the legal vocabulary her father taught them. Emma could have made the French toast, but she didn't want to cook while her aunt watched—her movements became stiff and jerky every time her aunt eyed her. Instead, Emma cut up bananas and put them in Caleb and Gracie's cereal, topping the mixture with heaping tablespoons of brown sugar.

"Are we going to the hospital to see Mommy?" Gracie asked.

Emma tipped the milk carton back up, stopping midstream, and waited. She'd been afraid to ask, not wanting to hear no.

"Pour," Caleb said. Emma drenched the sugary cereal with milk until it threatened to spill over and her uncle quietly urged the carton upright.

"I'm going over right after breakfast. Uncle Sean will stay with you."

"Why can't we go?" Gracie asked.

Thank you, Gracie, thank you, thank you, thank you.

"Your poor mum hasn't woken up yet," Uncle Sean said. "You'll be better off here with me, and anyway, you can help me entertain Miss Sourpuss." He made a face at Ursula, who wrinkled her nose.

"Why is she still sleeping?" Caleb asked. "Don't people wake up from operations?"

"Of course they wake up, son. However, they do it at different times. Everyone's body reacts differently."

Emma peeked at the clock. It was seven thirty. Her mother's operation had been hours ago. Even if all her medical information did come from watching television shows, Emma was sure they should be upset if Mom hadn't woken by now. It couldn't be a good sign.

"Don't worry," Emma told her brother and sister. "I spoke to Daddy, and he said everything would be okay." Lying seemed the kindest way to go. Mom would do that, right?

"You spoke to your father?" Aunt Vanessa asked.

The question made her feel strangely squirmy and defensive. "Yes."

"Did he say anything to you?"

"About what?" Emma put the spoon down.

Uncle Sean put a hand on her aunt's arm, as though stopping her. Her aunt pursed her mouth and shook her head. "Never mind."

"It's about Grandpa, right?" Gracie said. "I heard you talking to Uncle Sean."

"Didn't anyone teach you not to sneak around eavesdropping?" Aunt Vanessa asked.

Gracie's lips trembled. "I wasn't sneaking! I went to the bathroom and heard you."

"Heard what?" Emma took Gracie's chin and turned her so that they were face-to-face. "What about Grandpa?"

Gracie squirmed out of Emma's hold and turned to Uncle Sean, seeming to seek permission.

"We have to tell them now, Sean." Vanessa laced her fingers on top of the table.

Sean shook his head and placed his hands in the air as if giving up.

Emma, Gracie, and Caleb stayed silent—an unspoken message zipped between them as happened so often with her siblings. *Stay quiet; we'll learn more.*

After a few too-quiet moments Aunt Vanessa twisted up her ratty hair and then let it fall back. "Kids, you know how crazy your father drives. That's what's bothering Grandpa."

"We don't know how it happened, Vanessa." Uncle Sean frowned at her aunt. "Another car was involved. The driver was tailgating. And speeding."

"Did that car make it happen?" Gracie asked. "The speeding one?"

"Probably, honey." Her uncle took Gracie's hand.

"But what about Daddy's crazy driving?" Gracie's sweetness confused people. They didn't realize you could be sweet as pie and still dig, dig, dig until you got the truth.

"It was an accident," Uncle Sean said. "Sometimes terrible things just happen."

Caleb pushed away from the table hard enough so that his chair fell over as he ran to the living room and switched on the television.

"And sometimes they're preventable," Aunt Vanessa said.

CHAPTER 10

Ben

"Wake up, son."

Ben opened his eyes. He prayed the sight of his father standing over him was some fucked-up dream. Look at him. Wearing a suit in August as though he were at Maddy's wake. Ben's mother stood beside his father, twisting her wedding band around a thin finger. Seeing her shake her head, Ben straightened up and made an impotent attempt to smooth his wrinkled shirt.

After giving him an unreadable look, his mother turned to his mother-in-law, all stiff and sorrowful. "Anne. I'm so sorry. I'm sure she'll be fine."

The Judge, as Ben always thought of him, sat next to Anne and kissed her cheek. "Where's Jake?"

"Getting something to eat," Anne said. "I'm so glad you're here. Please, talk to Ben. I'm worried. I'm positive he's hurting more than he's letting on."

His mother turned her head. "Oh, no! Were you hurt?"

"Just some bruised ribs."

"The doctor said they were fractured." Anne laced her fingers. "I think he should go home and get a few hours of sleep."

"I slept in the chair." Ben lifted his arm and checked his watch, trying not to wince. Bright sun poured into the room through the bank
of windows. It was nine thirty. Without the frigid air-conditioning,
the place would be a sauna. "Anne, really. I think you're the one who
should go home and take a break."

"No. I can't leave." She held Maddy's jacket that Vanessa had left,
patting the fleece as though it were her daughter.

"You can't stay forever," Ben's father said in his slow measured tone.
"We'll take this shift."

"Nobody needs to take a shift. Maddy won't be alone." Ben ran a
hand over his scratchy chin, surrounded by his own rankness. "I'm here."

"Of course," his father said. "But you must clean up. And you need
to check on the children."

"The kids are fine. They're with Vanessa and Sean. And I already
spoke to Emma."

"Then you and I must go somewhere. Away from this waiting
room. We need to talk."

"About what?"

The Judge glanced over at Anne and stood. Even at seventy-six
Ben's father appeared taller than his actual height. Somehow the Judge
always appeared patrician, despite his immigrant roots, while Ben
carried the mark of their Roma ancestors in every feature. "There are
issues to discuss."

"My only issue at this moment is Maddy."

His mother tapped his wrist with two fingers. "Don't be difficult."

Ben pulled away, exhaustion and hunger battling inside him. He
looked around to see if his parents had brought anything practical: a
donut, a muffin, even a glass of juice. Nothing. Just the Judge's counsel.

Ben followed his father into the hall. The moment they separated
from Anne and Ben's mother, his father's demeanor went from man-
nered and concerned to controlled vehemence. "I spoke to your
brother. He made some calls. He thinks you could be charged with
reckless driving. Driving to endanger."

Between Jake using his connections to indict Ben and his father calling on his brother Andrew's second-rate legal skills to help him, he'd be squashed like a bug.

"Under what auspices did you have Andrew speak for me?" When he spoke to his father, Ben became a ridiculous imitation of to-the-manor-born, matching the Judge haughty word for haughty word.

"He's simply your temporary counsel."

"If I needed counsel, I would have arranged it."

Before his father could respond, Jake came toward them, carrying a cardboard box divided into four spaces. Giant white cups took up three of the notches; a grease-stained bag was balanced on top of the fourth. Ben opened the door and followed his father-in-law and father back into the waiting room.

Jake placed the overstuffed box on one of the side tables, then pecked Ben's mother's cheek and shook hands with the Judge.

"I am sorry that you must go through this terrible time, Jake," the Judge said. "Whatever you need, we're here."

"Sure, sure. Sorry I didn't know you were here. I'll go back and get you both a coffee. Wait. No. Frances, you take mine."

"We're fine." Ben's mother pressed her hand to her chest—the nervous gesture familiar. "We already reached our limit."

Anne lifted the cups from the cardboard box. "You didn't go to the cafeteria?"

"I know you like the Dunkin's. I figured you'd want a bagel, even if it was from there. I brought Ben an egg-and-cheese." He turned to his son-in-law. "You didn't eat last night, right?"

"Thanks, but I'm not really hungry."

He was famished.

Anne ripped open the bag and made a flat paper surface for the food. "Eat." She put three napkins under the egg sandwich and brought it to Ben. "I'll get your coffee."

"He can get his own coffee, Anne." Jake reached over and grabbed a cup, ripping the lid off with a pop. Anne placed a coffee next to Ben.

Gloom regained control of the room. Anne ignored her bagel. "Oh, God. What are we going to do?"

In answer, Jake put an arm around her. No one else picked up the question.

At the moment when Ben thought he'd suffocate from the stuffy quiet, when the likelihood of his bashing his fist into the wall simply so he could feel the pain seemed imminent, a sober-faced man in his early fifties walked in, carrying charts and authority. Probably Jake's top doctor. The neurologist.

"Mr. Greene?" The man looked around the room.

Jake stood. "Dr. Kaplan?" The sought-after specialist had pink scrubbed skin. Thick white hair, combed a little long in the back, gave him the look of a symphony conductor.

"How is she?" Jake asked. "Sid told you that nothing should be spared? Nothing?"

Ben put his hand out. "I'm Maddy's husband. Have you seen her?"

"I spoke to the surgeon," the doctor began. "Dr. Gordon."

Anne joined the tight circle. "I'm Maddy's mother."

The doctor backed away from the three of them and moved to a center chair, where he commanded the small room. "Everything I say is preliminary. We can't be sure of anything yet."

Anne twisted a napkin until paper knots popped. "What do you know?"

"Mrs. Illica's head trauma caused brain swelling." Dr. Kaplan opened the chart, ran his fingers along the pages, read some, stopped, and then looked up. "The surgeon removed a blood clot and repaired the damaged blood vessels. She shouldn't have further bleeding. He inserted a pressure-monitoring device to let us know if her brain starts to swell again. This will look intimidating, but it tells the ICU team if there's a problem." He looked around. "Stop me if you have a question."

"What happens now?" Ben asked.

"We wait." He paused, perhaps to let them catch up with him, to take it all in. "We won't know the extent of her injury until she wakes up, which isn't waking up as you and I know it. Waking from a brain injury is a slow process; we call it emerging. At this stage, I can't tell you when, or if, that will happen."

Ben looked at the doctor's face closely. "Maddy's in a coma?"

"Your wife had an injury to the temporal lobe. The left side. Right now, yes, she is in a state of coma."

"State of coma. Coma. Is there a difference?" Panic crept in one limb at a time.

"It means that it's early and there's hope."

Hope. The doctor's words, meant to be reassuring, terrified Ben. Why did he feel the need to tell them there was hope? Analyzing those words told him that some would say there wasn't hope. One only said "there is hope" when perhaps there wasn't. When one possibility was "hopeless."

"You can see her now, Mr. Illica," the doctor said.

He couldn't take in the whole picture when he finally saw Maddy. For many minutes, Ben could only look at one part of her at a time.

Had they drained too much blood during the operation? Her skin was the color of oatmeal. Tubes snaked in and out of her; machinery surrounded her. There was no place to touch her. Thick elastic stockings and white plastic boots hissing in and out with air covered her feet. Finally, Ben touched the end of her pinkie. How could he let Anne come in? Or, God forbid, Emma? Maddy's head wrapped in gauze—Jesus, had they shaved her head?

Her hair was so fucking beautiful, even though she always complained about it. Too frizzy. Too curly. But Ben loved her hair. Had he told her? In the last ten years, had he even mentioned it?

He sensed someone behind him and turned. "I'm Bernadette," said the woman. "Your wife's nurse." She wore pink scrubs. "Do you have any questions?"

Ben searched for the right words, wanting her to know that this woman, this object lying here in the bed, held his vivid Maddy. That she had people, family all around her who would ask questions, who cared, who'd pummel the staff with questions until they answered. Did Ben have a question? How could he possibly pick one out of an entire Bible of hopeless queries?

"Is she okay?" Ben made a half circle over the machines around Maddy. "I mean . . . I know she isn't okay. But is she comfortable? Is she in pain?"

"She seems peaceful, Mr. Illica."

"Ben. Please. Call me Ben," he said. To his shame, a tear leaked out. Bernadette put her hand on his back.

"Please . . ." He couldn't speak. He wanted to tell her not to be nice, certain that her kindness would bring on more tears.

"It's okay, Ben. When you can't cry, that's when you have a problem."

He had no idea if that was true or just some sort of nurse bullshit, but it soothed him. Each time he looked at Maddy, he noticed another horrifying piece of equipment attached to her that struck him cold. "What's that?" He pointed at a cuplike disc attached to Maddy's head, thick tubes coming out the top.

"That's the one that always scares people. It looks terrible, I know, but at the moment it's your wife's best friend. It's an intracranial pressure monitor."

Ben nodded, vaguely remembering the doctor's words. Pressure monitor. Sweet Jesus, look at her. He held the tip of her pinkie again, rolling his fingers over the rubbery flesh. What were his last words to Maddy? He'd been so angry with her. Jake had hit it on the head: Ben was a fucking putz. A perfect definition of someone who paid more attention to his clients than he did his family: a fucking putz.

". . . it will beep if that happens. She's intubated to guarantee an airway until we know she's breathing on her own."

Ben nodded. "Right." *Sharpen up!* He hadn't heard a goddamned word.

"I'm afraid I'm going to have to ask you to leave now." She touched him again—they must learn that, the soft touch, the nod. "It's only ten minutes to each visitor."

Right.

"And Ben, here's a little advice from someone who has worked in ICU for fifteen years."

Ben, wary of her words, eager for her help, leaned in. In the last ten minutes Bernadette had become his world.

"Go home." Bernadette placed a hand on his arm. "Take a shower. Sleep. This isn't going to be an overnight crisis. You're in shock. You're hurt yourself; you were also in an accident—"

"Caused an accident," he said, spilling to this nurse confessor.

Bernadette took his hand. "Never assume she can't hear. She may be taking in every word you say. So don't raise your voice. Don't speak without thinking. She's here to heal. Now say good-bye, let your in-laws in, go home, and get rest so you can be strong for Madeline."

"Maddy."

"Thank you." She placed a hand on Maddy's thigh. "Maddy. I'll let the other nurses and doctors know."

Ben couldn't handle any more caffeine; his stomach already felt as though it had been corroded by sulfuric acid. He glanced at the cafeteria offerings, wondering how sick people were supposed to get healthy while being offered this shit: donuts, cookies, greasy pressed mystery-meat sandwiches. Finally, he grabbed a carton of milk, paid, and looked for his father.

The Judge sat at a corner table, sipping his own carton. The Judge had ulcers. No doubt Ben's were waiting twenty years from now. Ben sat at the none-too-clean plastic table.

"You'd think they'd keep a hospital cafeteria cleaner." Ben brushed away crumbs with a napkin. Conversations with his father came in fits and starts, if at all.

"Look at this." The Judge shook a copy of the *Boston Herald* in his face. No wonder his father had dragged him to the cafeteria. A photo of the accident scene took up a quarter of the page. Reading the headline made him want to flip over the table.

Accident on Jamaicaway: Senior Public Defender Driving to Endanger?

"Jesus fucking Christ. Bastards." Ben pushed the paper away and slammed back in the cafeteria chair. "What if the kids see this?"

"Are you surprised?" the Judge asked. "It's August. Slow news month. Didn't you realize this would happen? Do you think that your actions have no consequences?"

Ben wanted to belt his father in the chin. "You think lectures will help me? Maddy? Or the kids?"

His father sat up even straighter. "Can we deal with realities and duties? Leave the drama for later?"

"Listen, Dad. I need—"

His father placed his hand hard on the table. "Enough. It doesn't matter what we need. We need to keep you from a court case. That's what we need."

Ben's house was just as he'd left it twenty-seven hours ago. Hot. Airless. Windows shut against rain, Gracie's book on the hallway bench. Breakfast dishes littered the kitchen table. An inch of cold coffee sat on the bottom of the carafe. Ben picked up a crumpled napkin, stepped on the garbage can lever, balled up the paper, and threw it in. Hunger gnawed, and he grabbed the peanut butter out of the refrigerator. The fucking bread tore when he tried to make a sandwich. He took only a few bites of the cold peanut butter spread on stale bread before he tossed it on the table.

An individual pack of chips Maddy used for the kids' lunches caught his eye, no doubt left on the counter during the morning rush. Yesterday. A thousand years ago. Had one of the kids' lunches been short a snack?

He ripped open the small package and ate the greasy chips in three handfuls. Then he put his mouth under the faucet, drank, washed days of filmy residue from his mouth, and went upstairs.

Files were scattered across the unmade bed where he'd left them. He pushed everything over and forced his shoes off with his toes. As he fell across the bed, he tore a loose page, a file escapee.

Visions of the accident looped. He probed for every mistake he'd made, where he should have gone faster, slower, moved up, back. Headline: *Husband Puts Wife in Coma.*

Lying on his stomach wasn't tolerable. He rolled over. The number 23 blinked on the base of the phone unit. Twenty-three messages. He struggled up to get the phone and then fell back. Screw it. The hospital had his cell. The kids had his cell. He took it out of his pocket, flipped it open, and ran through the calls. No hospital. Kath. He'd call her later. Emma twice. He listened to the last one. She wanted to talk to him, but she was okay. He'd call her soon.

His head was killing him. His ribs were killing him. Visions were killing him. He'd just close his eyes for a minute. *Please live, Maddy. Please be okay. Oh, dear Jesus up above, please, please, please, please, please.*

CHAPTER 11

Emma

Emma called her father. Again. She slouched at the table, picking at a dried cereal flake stuck to Melody's high chair, listening to her father's cell phone ringing in her ear until his voicemail picked up for the tenth time.

"Daddy. Call me back. Where are you?" She closed her phone and held it, not wanting to let go of her only connection.

The kids were watching television.

There was no one to talk to, no one to answer her questions. Uncle Sean went to work after all, needing to cover for Grandpa, who was at the hospital with Grandma and Aunt Vanessa, who'd dropped Ursula at nursery school. Some old-lady babysitter was here, but just for baby Melody—Emma was in charge of Gracie and Caleb.

She opened the phone, hating to do it, and dialed her aunt.

"Aunt Vanessa? It's Emma."

"What's wrong?" Aunt Vanessa asked. "Do you need anything?"

"Is Dad there?"

"No."

"Can I talk to Grandma?"

"Who is it?" Emma heard her grandmother in the background.

"Just Emma."

"Give me the phone," Grandma said.

"Hold on, hon." Aunt Vanessa sounded tired.

Emma put her feet up and leaned her head on her knees. The small pink mark where she'd picked off a scab, the one her mother had told her to leave alone, was turning silvery.

"Emma, it's Grandma."

"Grandma, where's my father?" Emma choked out the words around her tears. "He didn't answer the phone."

"It's okay. Daddy went home to sleep. He's exhausted."

"Is Mom awake?"

"Not yet."

"Is she going to wake up?"

Emma heard an intake of breath, but her grandmother didn't answer.

"Is she in a coma?" Emma looked over at the notebook she'd placed on the kitchen table. "Did they do a Glasgow score yet?"

"A what? Tell me."

Emma cleared her throat and read her notes aloud: "Listen. *The simplest bedside clinical exam performed in TBI*—that means traumatic brain injury—*is the Glasgow coma score, evaluating eye opening ability, vocal or verbal ability, and best movement ability.* Do you want me to read the rest?"

"How long is it? Shush, Vanessa. Sorry, darling."

"There are only a few more lines."

"Go ahead."

Emma blew her nose, cleared her throat, and continued. "*The scores range from 3, which indicates no detectable function, to 15, which indicates fully alert. A score of 8 or less indicates coma. A single score cannot predict an outcome or prognosis, but a series of scores over a period of time indicates a trend.* That's it."

"And that's called what?"

"Glasgow coma score."

"Glasgow like in Scotland?"

"I don't know. I guess. But it says it's the main test."

"Glasgow. Okay, Grandpa and I will ask. Did you find it on the computer?"

"I want to come to the hospital. I can take the train. I know how to get there."

"Daddy doesn't want you to come here, sweetheart. It's not a good place for you."

Now Grandma wasn't even trying to hide her tears.

"It's okay," Emma said. "I just got scared for a minute. But I'm okay." She stood and walked in circles, running her hand over the stove, the counter, picking up the fresh box of Oreos that Uncle Sean had put out for them and then putting it down.

Grandpa's voice replaced Grandma's. "Emma, Grandma is upset, baby. She can't talk anymore."

"I'm sorry, Grandpa."

"No, no, it's not you, darling." Emma heard his slow deep sigh. "She's just worried about Mommy. You need to be a brave girl and take care of Caleb and Gracie. We're counting on you, darling."

"Okay. I'm okay, Grandpa. Don't worry."

"I know. I don't have to worry about you, kiddo. You're my spunky monkey, remember?"

Grandpa had a name for each of them. Emma had been Spunky Monkey from the time she'd been old enough to walk, spinning around the house, a determined little dervish, Grandpa said. Gracie was Grandpa's Sugar Cookie. When Caleb was born and announced his presence—*Gottenyu, what a set of lungs!*—Grandpa christened him the *Gonster Macher*, which Grandma explained meant "big shot" but different, which it seemed was always the case with Yiddish.

Emma made a plan. She rushed into the living room, where Gracie curled in a chair reading. Caleb rhythmically swung Ursula's Raggedy Ann against his shins. Melody lay asleep in the playpen, her plump bare legs on the naked sweaty plastic. The old-lady babysitter snored in the stuffed chair in front of the blaring television.

Emma tapped Caleb on his shoulder, putting her index finger to her lips, and then motioned for him to come with her, nodding at Gracie, *You too.*

"Shh," she said when they'd left the room, and pulled Caleb to the guest bedroom, Gracie following. "Get dressed. And get me all your stuff." Grabbing things at random, she threw underwear and socks at them and shoved their books and Caleb's small electronic game into their backpacks.

"I didn't take a shower. Mommy would hate that." Gracie turned her back and pulled off Uncle Sean's T-shirt. "Where are we going?"

"We're all dirty, Gracie. It doesn't matter. Do you have any money?" Emma opened Gracie's backpack, pawing until she found a small plastic pouch. She unzipped it and pulled out a twenty-dollar bill.

"That's my emergency money!" Gracie grabbed for it. "Mommy said never to touch it."

"Don't you think this is an emergency?" Emma turned to her brother. "Where's yours?"

"I'm saving it. Mommy said if we never touch it the whole summer we get to keep it."

"You're not touching it, I am." Emma rummaged through Caleb's pack and found the bill folded into a small tight square in a zippered compartment.

Gracie pulled on her wrinkled blue shorts. "What are we doing?"

"Going home," Emma said.

The cab pulled up at the corner of Myrtle and Centre. "This is close enough," Emma told the driver. She'd watched the fare click since they'd left Newton. When the meter hit thirty-five dollars, they got out.

They trudged the quarter block to their unpaved private way, backpacks dangling from their shoulders and hands. Emma saw the empty driveway, and for a moment she thought no one was home. Then she remembered about the car and the accident, though she didn't know where Mom's car was. She dug her key from the pocket of her tight jeans shorts and opened the door.

The quiet house smelled hot and dirty. Her father's half-empty mug from yesterday still sat on the hall table. The mail was kicked to the side of the entry from where the mailman had dropped it through the slot.

They dumped their backpacks in the hall and went to the kitchen. Dishes from yesterday's breakfast were in the sink; half a peanut butter sandwich lay on the counter. Mom hated when someone put food on the table without a plate or a napkin underneath it.

"Is anyone home?" Caleb asked.

"Only Daddy could be here, right?" Gracie looked at the sandwich fearfully. "Do you think he's here, Emma?"

They looked at each other. Emma took their hands and led them to the stairs. The three of them stood at the bottom, staring up.

"It's quiet." Gracie gave a little shiver.

"He's probably sleeping," Emma said. "Grandma said he was up all night."

"Maybe we shouldn't wake him," Gracie said.

Her sister made sense, but Emma needed to know—anything, something; she needed news about Mommy.

"Let's go."

They climbed the stairs, avoiding the squeaky step. They peeked in before they entered their parents' bedroom. Their father lay sprawled horizontally across the bed on his back, papers and files and rumpled covers under him, his hand clutching a pillow. Caleb reached for Emma's hand.

Gracie pulled off her sneakers and padded toward the bed. Carefully stepping over the files on the floor, she lay next to their father as best she could. Curled on her side, facing him, her chin touched his outstretched elbow.

"Daddy?" Gracie tapped his forearm with two fingers. "Daddy, are you awake?"

His breathing changed; he opened his eyes, looking confused. "Gracie?" As he raised his head, his eyes met Emma's. "What are you doing here?"

"I wanted to come home," Emma said.

"Me too," Gracie said. "We all did."

"Does Aunt Vanessa know you're here?"

Emma avoided the question. "She wasn't there when we left."

Caleb patted his father's leg insistently. "Where's Mommy?" His voice clutched on the words. "Were you driving crazy? Was it your fault?"

Her father rose on his elbows, grimacing. Emma's stomach flipped. "Are you okay?" Gracie asked.

He inched into a sitting position, hanging his feet over the side of the bed. "One question at a time, okay, guys? Caleb, who said that? Emma?"

He looked at her.

"No one said anything about it being your fault. Caleb heard it wrong." Emma turned to her brother. "Aunt Vanessa didn't mean Daddy made it happen on purpose. She said the accident might have been Daddy's fault, but that doesn't mean it's not an accident."

"Sorry." Caleb sounded not at all sorry, but confused. "But why did you hurt her?"

The three of them looked at their father, waiting for him to explain everything. He took air in and pushed it out, slowly. "Nothing was on purpose. It was a big horrible accident."

"Can we go see Mommy now?" Gracie asked.

"I need a shower. Emma, could you hold down the fort?" Her father groaned as he stood.

"Are you okay?" she asked.

He shook his head; she couldn't tell if that meant yes or no. He stumbled toward the dresser as though his legs didn't bend anymore and he were a thousand years old.

Emma straightened the kitchen while her father showered. Rancid odors came off the soaked sponge when Emma squeezed it. "Gracie, get a new sponge from the drawer." She ran her hands under water and then pumped out a large dollop of lemon-scented hand soap from the jar on the counter. "You shouldn't leave the sponge sitting on the counter without wringing it out." Emma took the new fresh sponge from Gracie.

"Who said I did it?" Gracie asked.

"Who said you didn't?" Caleb spoke through a mouthful of chocolate bits from the Nestlé bag he held.

"Where did you get those?" Emma asked.

He shrugged and shoved in more chocolate.

"Those are Mommy's baking bits. They're not for eating. Do you want me to tell Daddy?"

"He won't care." He flung the bag on the table and spread the chocolate bits around, coating them with bits of cereal and toast crumbs, mashing them into his hand.

"Stop it, Caleb," Emma said. "What's wrong with you?"

"What do you think Mommy is doing right now?" Gracie put a few chocolate chips in her mouth and then began clearing the table of the crusted breakfast dishes. Caleb began eating the abandoned peanut butter sandwich.

"Everyone says she's sleeping. That she's been sleeping since her operation."

"Is she in a coma?" Gracie asked.

"What's that?" Caleb asked.

"It means like a dream place that you can't wake up from." Gracie turned to Emma. "Like Sleeping Beauty, do you think?"

Emma pictured her mother, eyes closed, silent, her rosy cheeks and dark curly hair. "I guess, sort of."

"Maybe Daddy should kiss her to wake her up," Caleb said. "Should we tell him?"

"Don't be stupid," Gracie said.

"But what if it worked?" Caleb started to cry. "He should try, right? I want Mommy."

Emma put her arms out, and he ran to her. "I want Mommy," he repeated, crying and gulping for air.

Gracie fell into the chair Caleb had left. "Me too."

"I know, Gracie. Me too."

Gracie slid her chair close to Emma. "I'm going to pray. Like you said." She genuflected and lifted the tiny cross Grandma Frances had given her and kissed it. Closing her eyes, she held Emma's hand as she moved her lips in a soundless prayer. Emma closed her eyes.

The three of them were locked together when the bell rang. Emma opened her eyes. "I'll see who it is. You guys start cleaning up in here, okay?"

"I want to see who's there," Gracie said. She stood and followed Emma.

"I'm coming too." Caleb lined up behind Gracie. The bell rang again in three short bursts before they got there. "Hold your horses," Caleb said, imitating his father.

Emma moved the door curtain aside. A man in a suit stood on the porch. When he saw Emma peeking out, he nodded.

"I'm Detective Perez. With the police," he said, loud enough to be heard through the door. "Is your father home?"

CHAPTER 12

Ben

"*Dad!*" Emma screeched through the closed bedroom door. "A policeman's here."

"Hold on." Ben fumbled as he buttoned his jeans and then opened the door. "Tell him I'll be right down. One second."

"Are you in trouble because of the accident?" Alarm colored Emma's face.

"It's just normal procedure, honey." He gave her a one-armed hug, cautious of his aching ribs. "No big deal. Promise. Go be with Gracie and Caleb. I'll be right there."

"I love you, Daddy." She hugged him hard around his middle.

Ben's throat closed, realizing how grateful she was for a crumb of attention. He kissed her on the forehead. "I'll be right there," he repeated. It struck Ben in a great wave of sadness how alone his children had been since the accident.

After he'd closed the door behind her, he picked up his dirty clothes from the middle of the room and added them to a growing pile on the chair. The clean blue T-shirt he pulled from the drawer and jerked over his head muffled the harsh sound of the phone ringing. He tugged the fabric down and looked at the caller ID. His private office line number.

"Ben Illica."

"It's Elizabeth."

Her tentative tone was unfamiliar and probably a portent of days ahead. For a moment, he was breathless with a lack of desire to speak with her.

"How are you?" she asked. "Sorry. Stupid question. I called to see if I could help."

"Thanks. I can't think of anything."

"Do you need someone to handle the papers? Did you read them?"

He pictured the rolled-up *Boston Globe*, still bound by a rubber band, on the hall table where he'd thrown it. He hadn't read it—seeing the headline and photo in the *Herald* had been enough.

"Not really. Tell me. Quickly, please. I have a policeman waiting."

"The police are there? Maybe I should come over—or someone else from the office?"

"I'm fine."

"You should consider having someone there when they talk to you."

"I'm not being grilled in the box. He just came for a statement. Tell me what's in the *Globe*. Quickly." He put the phone on speaker and pressed his fingertips to his temples, working to stave off his rising anxiety. Rustling paper sounds mixed with Elizabeth's nervous breathing.

"It's inside the Metro section. The headline is 'Crash on Jamaicaway. Investigation Under Way.'"

Ben closed his eyes in thanks for there being no headline about speed or road rage.

"It could be worse, Ben," Elizabeth assured him. "They don't name you in the headline."

"I'm not famous. And it is worse," he said.

"I mean . . . I just meant in terms of this coverage."

Shame nipped. Why had he pitched that ugly retort at Elizabeth?

There was no reason for it except that in some awful way it soothed him.

"I thought it would be hard on you and the kids," she continued. "It's probably good school hasn't started. This will probably be a one-day story."

"I have to go, Elizabeth."

"Reporters have been calling. Do you want me to say anything?"

"No comment."

"Is that meant for me, or are you telling me to say that to the reporters?"

Was she serious? Elizabeth was no joker. Perhaps this was his first taste of people's caution around tragedy, tiptoeing around him and his family, worrying they'd shatter with the first off-target word.

"No comment to the reporters, Elizabeth. And thanks for calling." Now, being kind felt soothing. Conferring onto others, not receiving emotional handouts.

The police officer stood as Ben entered the living room. He was a detective; Ben knew because the man wore a suit, not a uniform. He looked older than Ben, but not by much. Like Ben, he was built wide and powerfully. They must look like bulls facing each other.

"I'm Detective Perez." He put out his hand. "Sorry about having to come at this time. How is your wife?"

"Not good." Ben needed to keep it brief and never sound self-pitying. Better to have the stiff upper lip had been his experience with cops. "We'll deal with whatever comes our way."

"Mr. Illica, I have to take your statement. Actually, your brother—your attorney, correct—led us to believe you'd be at the station this morning."

"I was at the hospital all night and most of this morning. Then I had to be with my children, of course." Ben waved his arm toward the sofa. "Have a seat, Detective."

The detective chose the chair, leaving Ben to sink into the couch.

"Could you tell me everything you remember about the accident?"

Detective Perez took a cheap-looking black notebook from his jacket pocket.

Direct and simple.

"I was on the Jamaicaway, heading toward the bridge going over Huntington Avenue. A car was right behind me, tailgating in a dangerous manner. Practically kissing my bumper. A Ford Expedition." Ben didn't hesitate for a moment. "Slick roads played into the accident, but it was the Expedition. Pushing me, trying to get me to speed up or move over—which, as you know, is not easy at that hour on that road. When I finally had an opportunity to move to the right, he sped up and tried to go around me at that same moment. Cutting me off. He crashed into me when he tried to pass me. As I said, the rain was an accelerant. I gave a blood sample at the hospital."

Ben stopped himself. Less was always more.

"How fast would you say you were going, sir?"

"I'd be hard-pressed to estimate."

"Within the posted speed limit?" Every scratch of Perez's pen on the lined pad added to Ben's nervous irritation.

"Certainly."

"What happened next?" Perez kept his pen poised above the pad.

"Next thing I know some old guy is looking at me. And a woman. I guess they stopped. Good Samaritans. Then the EMT." Ben paused so the scratching pen could catch up.

"Right. Go on."

Ben kept his eyes looking up. He knew facial detectors—he used them in his work. Looking up meant retrieving information and looking down signified searching for a decent lie. He struggled to keep his mind linear. "Then I saw my wife."

"Do you know what happened to her? Was she wearing her seat belt?"

"I don't recall."

"Do you usually wear a seat belt?"

"Me?"

"Anyone in your car?"

"Always."

"And was your wife?"

"I would think so."

"Can you swear she was?"

"I don't recall. So swearing would be impossible."

"Do you remember your speed?"

"I don't recall."

"What do you recall?" the detective asked.

"The pain. The deflated air bag. Trying to get out. Looking for my wife." His voice got lower. "Seeing her on the stretcher. I saw her brief-case—it's red. I saw her shoes—they're red. And the blood."

Detective Perez tapped the pen on his paper a few times. "Do you think speed and recklessness played a role in the accident?"

Ben nodded. "No doubt. The Ford was being driven in a reckless manner. Tailgating too close. Speeding."

"And you?"

Gracie charged into the room. "It was our fault! He had to drive us to camp, so he was already late. And then he had to get Mommy. It wasn't his fault." Emma and Caleb stood in the doorway. "Tell them, Daddy."

"Honey, of course it wasn't your fault. Or Mommy's. And I wasn't that late."

"Were you in a rush because you were late, sir?"

"I was not late in any extraordinary sense. Nothing of note. And I was not rushing."

"Were you disturbed?"

"I was not disturbed," Ben said.

"I'm sorry, Daddy. I was trying to help." Gracie sat next to Ben on the couch. Her tears seemed to come from some unlimited source. He folded his shaking hands into fists. He needed to get back to the hospital.

"It's all right, baby."

Emma sat staring at the *Boston Globe*, with Caleb looking over her shoulder. A fuzzy photograph of the accident scene was juxtaposed with a file photo of Ben taken at the famous Franker rape trial he'd won. No one could believe he'd gotten the kid off. It had been a huge win.

"Listen to me, all of you. Honey, put that away."

Emma's hand remained on the newspaper as she looked at her father.

"This is going to be a difficult time." Ben paused, trying to think of a stronger way to word it without terrifying them. "A very difficult time."

"Did you do something wrong?" Caleb asked. "Is that why the police came?"

"No, of course not. It's just . . . It's just . . ." His children looked at him, expectant, waiting for the father who always had the answers, who never said I don't know. Ben prided himself on being that sort of father—if he didn't know the facts, he'd look them up. He relied on facts. "It's just a procedure the police have to go through whenever there's a crash where someone gets hurt."

"To find out if someone committed a crime?" Gracie asked.

Someone mowed their lawn nearby. The whining vibration sliced into his brain like a buzz saw. "Sort of. Like driving while intoxicated—drunk—that's a crime. But there was no crime here."

All three children stared at him.

"What happened?" Caleb asked.

Ben tried to be a good father. An honest father. Always.

But not a stupid father.

"Were you playing a CD too loud?" Gracie asked in a tentative voice.

"That would be a good example of something wrong, honey, if it took away your concentration. But it's not a crime. And no, I didn't have the music too loud."

"But sometimes you do play the music loud. Could that make a car crash?" Caleb asked.

"No. And I didn't have the music on."

Ben remembered being angry.

Late.

Hungover.

But he hadn't hurt Maddy. "It's exactly as I told the police officer; it was the Expedition. He cut me off illegally, he hit me, and that made our car crash into the tree."

"So did *he* do a crime? The other guy? Will he go to jail?" Caleb asked.

Ben wanted to go back to bed, go back to the hospital, be alone, be alone with Maddy, sit by her side and touch her finger. "It's too early to know anything yet."

"When is Mommy going to wake up?" Caleb asked. "Will it be today?"

Ben closed his eyes. "Maybe not today, cowboy."

"Tomorrow?" Caleb joined Ben and Gracie on the couch. "She'll definitely wake up tomorrow, right?"

Ben kept his eyes shut. Caleb shook his upper arm. "Daddy. Daddy. *Answer!* Tomorrow?"

Ben heard the newspaper being folded and felt Emma move toward them. The couch settled as she sat next to Gracie.

"When, Daddy?" Caleb sounded panicky.

Ben squeezed his eyes shut tighter and tipped his head back. "Soon," he answered without opening his eyes. "Soon."

CHAPTER 13

Emma

Five days passed like a year. Emma was stuck watching the kids every minute, but complaining about it even one bit—even to herself—seemed like the worst thing she could do.

Even as she pulled on her jeans, she wondered if she should wear something more respectable. She'd begged and begged to visit her mother until her grandmother gave in and helped Emma talk her father into saying yes. Now Kath would be there in a few minutes to take her, and all Emma wanted was to stay home.

She combed her still-damp hair back and braided it. Her mother loved when Emma wore her braid hanging down her back. And her mother adored the electric-blue T-shirt that she wore, the one her mother had bought for her last month. Emma thought it embarrassingly bright, but Maddy thought the contrast with her hair incredible. *Stunning!* That was her mother, always speaking in giant exaggerations. Emma had *the most gorgeous* hair, and Gracie was *the smartest* nine-year-old ever, and *no other child* could draw as well as Caleb. She did it about Emma's dad also. When her mother thought Emma wasn't listening, she'd told Kath he had the biggest balls in the world.

Emma knew what she'd meant, even though the implication made her want to throw up. Daddy never seemed afraid of anything. Sometimes Emma liked that, and sometimes she wished he would hold back. Two years ago, when he went with her to register for Saturday gymnastics, she'd cringed as he'd performed his lawyer tricks.

"Mr. Illica, there's simply no more room in the class. It's limited to ten girls and we're filled," the instructor had said. The teacher had been new at the community center, a college student, and Emma had thought she was trying hard to sound like a teacher.

"Will one more girl, just one, actually make a difference?" he'd asked.

"Never mind, Dad," Emma had said, standing behind him. "I don't care."

Ben had held his palm out toward Emma, efficiently shutting her out as he pled their case. "It's likely—practically a given—that a minimum of one girl will drop out or not show up each week. Moreover, when you say ten, is it a *hard* number, or is it more of a general guide? How large is the gym?" he'd asked, knowing exactly how large it was. Emma had been taking classes there since she was six. "Why don't we walk over and take a look?"

Emma had died a little with each word her father had spoken. He'd leaned across the counter, his wide hand flat on the wood, getting close enough to the instructor so the scent of his woodsy aftershave had to be drifting over.

"Listen," he'd said, lowering his voice. "I wouldn't make such a fuss about this, but it's so important to my daughter."

"Sir, I know that. It's a popular class, but—"

"Excuse me for one moment." He took out his wallet. Oh, God, was he going to bribe the teacher? Her father handed Emma a five-dollar bill. "Honey, would you mind running across the street to Dunkin' and getting me a coffee? I'll meet you at the car."

He didn't have to ask twice. She'd sprinted out of the building, down the steps, and over to the car, certain he didn't need coffee—his car cup would still be steaming hot since she'd filled it for him like two minutes before. They wouldn't have been going through this scene if her mother had remembered she had to register for class by the fifteenth, but as usual, she'd forgotten.

When her father came out, Emma was lying on the hood of the car, stretching her legs, pointing them straight up to the sky.

"Practicing for class?" her father had said.

Torn between happiness at knowing she'd gotten in and fear of what method he'd used to do it, she'd asked, "What did you say to her?"

"How about saying, 'Thanks, Dad'?"

"When you tell me what you said." Emma sat up and crossed her legs. "I should know if you said I have like one year to live or something."

He'd reached over and tweaked her nose. She'd pulled back.

"Dad, stop. What did you say?" She'd hated how being Machiavellian put him in a good mood. *Machiavellian*. She'd looked the word up after hearing her mother use it to describe her father in one of her and Kath's let's-talk-on-the-phone-while-we-make-dinner conversations.

"You know the old saying: What you don't know can't hurt you."

"Dad, tell me." She didn't know what she hated more—when he relished his own creepy side or when he got into his pounding anger, throwing words as if they were knives and hammers.

"No worries. Get in the car, I'll tell you while I drive."

As he'd recounted how he'd portrayed Emma as a victim of some mean-girl conspiracy, with gymnastics the only place she healed, Emma thought she'd puke at his pride at fooling the teacher, even though she'd loved that she'd be back in gymnastics.

It ended up being the last time she took gymnastics class.

Now, as Emma sat at her desk clicking through photo files on the computer, searching for the perfect one to blow up and bring to her mother's hospital room, she realized how often her father left her grateful and angry all at the same time.

"Kath's here." Gracie came over to Emma's desk after her announcement from the doorway. "What are you doing?"

Genius Gracie inspected the goofy picture coming out of the printer, showing Gracie, Caleb, and Emma's heads meeting at the crown, the picture taken from above while they lay on a blanket at the beach, all of them squinting against the sun. "I thought you hated that picture," she said. "You said you looked fat. Why are you printing it?"

"Mommy likes it. I'm bringing it to her room."

"*She woke up?*" Gracie took it off the printer tray and held it out to Emma, practically leaping in the air.

"No. But I thought if she opened her eyes . . ." Emma took the picture from Gracie and stared at it. She carried it over to her bed and sat at the edge. "But maybe I shouldn't. I printed out a family guide thing that says to reduce stimulation."

Gracie sat next to her on the bed. "What else does it say?"

Emma grabbed her backpack and took out the pages she'd printed. "I highlighted some parts." Even as she wondered if her sister was too young for this, she handed the sheets to Gracie with gratitude at being able to share it—even if it was only with her nine-year-old sister.

Gracie analyzed the material in front of her. "I think you should bring the picture, but maybe make it a little smaller so it doesn't jump out at her."

Emma nodded. "Good idea. I'll bring one of each and see what's right when I get there. Want to do it for me? The file is still on my desktop."

Gracie hurried over to sit in Emma's chair. "You're so lucky you have your own computer. I don't want to wait till I'm in high school, like Mommy says." A stricken expression came over Gracie. "But I don't care—whatever Mommy says, I'll do." She turned to the screen and began shrinking the picture.

Riding in Kath's car, Emma pressed her legs back and forth together, as though she were a six-year-old needing to go to the bathroom. Embarrassed at how she was fidgeting, Emma pressed her thighs together, despite knowing that Kath wouldn't mind and, even if she did, she'd never say anything.

Funny how little Kath's appearance matched her personality—her mother's best friend almost looked as though she'd be mean. Emma loved her, she was nicer than any other adult Emma knew, but she looked sort of cheap. It didn't seem fair that Kath's outer self was so at odds with her spirit.

Emma said that to her mother. Rather than being angry with Emma for practically saying that her best friend looked slutty, she explained how sometimes people got such a strong sense of what beauty was from their youth and the neighborhood where they grew up that they just couldn't erase the imprint. Kath grew up in a part of Boston where thick lines of black encircling your eyes and hair dyed the color of tar was considered gorgeous. According to Emma's mother, some women froze at a certain point in their lives, never moving past that particular moment when they thought they looked their best.

"Why don't you tell her to change?" Emma had asked. "Don't you think she'd look much prettier if she wasn't so, um . . . ?"

Her mother had smiled at her. "If she wasn't so what?"

"I don't know, Mom. Kinda cheesy-looking?"

Her mother had shaken her head. "The important thing, Em, is that she feels pretty. Just the way she is. Why would I want to take that away from her?"

"What are you thinking, hon?" Kath asked now. "Stupid question. You're worried. How are you holding up? Are they throwing everything on top of you?"

Emma didn't have to ask who *they* were. She shrugged, not wanting to trash her father, not wanting Kath to think that she'd hurt Emma's feelings. "Kath, how's my mother? Really how is she? Please. Tell me the truth. No one tells me anything."

"No one knows, honey." Kath reached over and patted Emma's shoulder as she pulled into the hospital's parking garage. "That's the truth. There's a hard road ahead of you. I want you to know you can always come to me."

Emma nodded. Tears stung. She needed to swallow them before she saw her mother.

Her grandmother, her grandfather, and Olivia, who worked with her mother, were in the waiting room when Emma came in. She felt their need to touch her. Unsure who to embrace first, she lingered just inside the doorway.

Olivia's solid arms folded around her. With the scent of roses enveloping her along with Olivia's arms, Emma relaxed for a moment. Then she pulled away and turned to her grandmother. Grandma Anne's eyes looked sore. She seemed smaller, with her face washed of makeup and her hair flat—Grandma and Grandpa both looked shrunken, as though they'd collapsed in on themselves. Emma hugged them hard, trying to give them her energy, wanting to send her youth into their bloodstreams. Her grandmother's tears fell on Emma as she kissed her.

"Oh, you smell so sweet. Like a peach."

"Give her to me," her grandfather said, his gruff voice breaking. "I need to hug my spunky monkey." His eyes were also red, though not as swollen as Grandma's.

Emma looked at Olivia. "Did you see her?"

"Yes." Olivia put her arm around Emma's shoulders and pulled her close. "Sit for a second, honey? We'll talk before you go in."

Olivia led Emma to the couch and sat on her right; Grandma took the left. Emma was being patted from all sides. Oh, God! Mommy had died, and that's why Grandma and Grandpa were crying.

Emma braced herself when Olivia took her hand. "Emma, you have to be prepared," Olivia said.

This was it. Grandma took Emma's other hand, holding tightly.

Please don't let her be dead, please, please, please.

Her grandmother took a crumpled tissue from her sweatshirt pocket—Dad's sweatshirt pocket—and wiped the tears dripping from Emma's eyes. Emma leaned her head on her grandmother's shoulder, smelling her father's aftershave mixed with Grandma's soft Cashmere Bouquet scent.

"Your mother is going to look terrible," Olivia said.

"She's alive?" Emma lifted her head from Grandma and turned to Olivia. "She's okay?"

Olivia looked surprised. "Of course she's alive, baby. Why else would we be here with you?"

Emma's stomach twisted. "I thought maybe something happened while Kath and I drove over."

Grandma made the spitting motion to ward off the evil eye. "*Puh.* God forbid."

"We just want you to know that Mommy looks . . . scary," Grandpa said.

"They had to shave her hair and put in tubes. Including a special thing on her head which measures the pressure inside," Olivia said.

"Can I go in alone? Is that okay?" Emma fingered the folded picture in her pocket.

Grandpa frowned. "I'm not sure that's a good idea."

"But I need to talk to her by myself." Emma saw her grandparents exchange glances. She sent a begging look to Kath. "Please."

Kath turned to Emma's grandfather. "It'll be okay, Jake. Maddy would want it."

Emma couldn't take it all in: the skeins of tubing, the monitors beeping, the hissing machines, and the plastic boots expanding and contracting on her mother's feet. Tiny spots of gray mixed with the brown stubble on her mother's scalp—the parts that peeked out from the helmet of white tape. God, her mother would hate that so much. Why had they tied her arms? Emma wanted to touch her, but she was afraid. There didn't seem to be anywhere Emma couldn't accidentally dislodge something keeping her mother alive.

"Is this your momma? Do you have any questions?"

Emma felt a presence behind her. She turned. The woman's light-blue scrubs were a stark contrast with her dark-brown skin. "Yes."

Yes, this was her mother. And yes, she had questions.

"I'm Angela—Mrs. Illica's nurse. I can help you understand your mom's condition."

"Do you think she can hear me?"

"I've been working here for a long, long time, and I still can't vote yes or no," the nurse said. She spoke with a pretty lilt Emma couldn't place. "But if you ask me, better go with yes. Speak as though she hears you."

Emma nodded.

"You can talk to her. It's okay. It might help."

"Is she cold?" Emma asked.

The nurse shook her head. "The temperature is fine for her. Just right."

Couldn't her mother just collapse, sleeping under all these machines? Was she dreaming? Did she know Emma was here? "Thank you."

The nurse nodded and walked to the next bed. Emma couldn't look at her mother's roommate; he resembled a monster with his yellow and purple bruised skin.

"Mom," she whispered. "Mommy, I bet you can hear me. You'll be okay soon."

She tried to remember what the family guide said. *Keep it simple.* That was for after she woke up though, right? Emma couldn't remember what they said to do with unconscious people. Touch could be bad for some reason. Or was it good? She was frightened to ask the nurse. Placing her fingertip on her mother's knee seemed safe until she worried that maybe her mother's knee was broken. Emma jerked her hand away.

"Mommy, we're all okay. Daddy, Caleb, Gracie, we're all okay. We miss you. We love you. But we're okay." Had she said the wrong thing? She didn't want her mother to think they could be okay without her. "We need you. I need you, Mommy."

Emma took a deep breath for courage and then, in a rush of words, spilled out the fears pressing on her. "I'm sorry about what I did by going out without telling you and about being mean to you. I love you. I'll take care of everything until you come home. I promise." She looked for some sign. "Blink if you can hear me, Mom."

Her mother didn't blink. She remained a broken Snow White in a glass coffin. How had Snow White breathed? Was one of these machines breathing for her mother? There was a tube going down her throat. Shouldn't someone wipe around her mouth, all icky and shiny like that? Would she get in trouble? She looked around. No one watched. Emma reached into her pocket, pulled out a tissue, and wiped her mother's mouth. Then she worried maybe she had given her mother germs.

Oh, God, what did her mother need? *Baruch Atah Adonai, Eloheinu Melech Ha'Olam. Please tell me what to do, God.*

CHAPTER 14

Ben

Bits of toilet paper covered the nick Ben had razored from his upper lip. When had he last changed the blade? As he left the bathroom, he noticed the towels looked gray. Garbage pails overflowed in every room. He couldn't tell if the kitchen or bathroom chaos was worse.

The house had begun to reek in the days since the accident. Could decay spread in nine days? Caleb stunk—he refused to shower unless Emma bribed him with two candy bars. Gracie's filthy red robe wasn't helping the cause either. She wouldn't wash it because Maddy had given it to her last February as a Valentine present. Red was Maddy's favorite color, and Gracie had attached herself to the robe as though it were her wire monkey mother.

"*She's not dead!*" Emma screamed.

Ben tightened his cotton robe and headed down the hall.

"*I know, I know, I know,*" Gracie shrieked. "*I'm making sure she knows I'm thinking about her.*"

Ben rushed in and saw Gracie blocking Emma from a group of photos arranged on Gracie's purple rug. A quick glance showed they were shots of Maddy, photos Maddy had carefully arranged in year-by-year albums until life had overwhelmed all her good intentions.

Ben didn't have a clue whether he should stop Gracie from pillaging pictures from the family albums. If it calmed her, who cared?

"What's going on?" Ben stood with his arms crossed, but his stance didn't stop Emma's shower of verbal fury.

"She's in a coma, Gracie," Emma continued to shout. "That doesn't mean she has some kind of superpower and knows what you're thinking or doing. Stop being so frigging creepy. Put all of them back where they belong!"

Emma pointed an anger-stiff finger at the pictures leaning against books piled on the carpet, semicircled around a red candle leaning in a red mug. Gracie had arranged them as symmetrically as possible, placing them in age order, starting with Maddy as a baby, her giant smile stretched like a rubber band across her face, and ending with a recent beach picture. Maddy squinted against the sun, her hair stiff with salt, her smile still broad.

"You can't have a candle in your room," Ben said.

"I'd never light it, Daddy. Promise."

Why have them, then? Ben didn't want to hear the answer. Gracie had probably Googled *voodoo.* Yesterday he'd found a Christian prayer site bookmarked, one where you entered names for prayers. Maddy would have a fit when she came home, but Ben wouldn't do anything to stop his daughter. His mother's son, he'd considered logging on and adding an entry of his own.

"Aren't you hot?" Ben asked. Gracie was wrapped in her red flannel robe, the belt tied tightly around her plump belly. He looked a little closer and saw a tiny angel on the collar. "Who gave you that?" he asked, pointing to the gold pin.

She covered it as though he were about to take it away. "Grandma Frances."

Wonderful. A perfect match for the crucifix and rosary his mother had already given his daughter. Leave it to Saint Frances to use tragedy as an occasion to turn Gracie into a little novitiate.

"Honey, you don't need to do all this," Ben said.

"But I want to," Gracie said.

"Dad, do something." Emma bent and picked up a stray sock, using her thumb and forefinger as pincers.

"What do you want me to do? Forbid your sister to have pictures of her mother in her room?"

Emma exhaled like an old woman. "Fine. Let her build her crazy pyramid. Don't worry; I'll clean around it. When it catches fire, I'll call the fire department. And then when they call the Department of Children and Families to take us to foster homes, I'll call Olivia."

Ben picked up two dirty bowls from Gracie's dresser. "Come downstairs for breakfast. Kath and Olivia will be here soon."

Emma lit up as though the Queen of England were arriving. "We should clean up."

"They're coming to talk to me about Mom. This isn't a party. Anyway, the three of us are going out—you need to watch the kids so I can talk to them. Until Aunt Vanessa comes. She's taking you all to her house."

"Even if you go out, they're still coming here first. Mom *always* cleans up when people come over." Emma threw her chin in the air, grabbed the full laundry basket, and walked out of the room.

Gracie trailed after Emma, rubbing her collar angel. Ben, in third place, walked behind them one dirgelike step at a time. When he reached the entry, he opened the door to get the paper. Yesterday was the third day in a row there hadn't been a piece on the accident. Thank God. Ben suspected it might be one more favor he'd owe his father, but for once, he didn't give a shit. Small things like fewer stares would be a great help for *the man who put his wife in a coma*. Whispers assaulted him everywhere from the local Whole Foods to the CVS where he waited on line to get his prescription for the pain from his ribs.

"Morning, cowboy," Ben greeted Caleb as he walked into the kitchen.

Caleb grunted, staring at the comic book on the table.

A light scent of urine and the peppery odor of unwashed jeans rose from his son. Ben reminded himself to check Caleb's closet for another set of wet pajamas and underwear before the smell permeated the closet forever. The Glade strips or wicks, or whatever it was Anne had stuck to the closet walls when she visited, weren't doing much good.

Ben bent to give his son a kiss.

Caleb pulled away, his face twisted in disgust. "You're scratchy. And you smell funny."

And you're violets and roses. He placed a hand on Caleb's head, rubbing his son's too-long hair. "Guess we both need a shower, buddy?"

Caleb shrugged and dragged a chair to the counter.

"What are you doing?" Emma asked.

"Making toast." He climbed on the chair and jammed a frozen bagel, crystals clinging to the outside crust, in the toaster.

"Daddy is making pancakes," Gracie said.

Caleb shrugged again. "I don't want pancakes."

"I'm making them from scratch, just like Grandma Anne," Ben said. "She gave me the recipe." Unasked for. Some kind of hint, he guessed, to wake him from the steady diet of frozen food and pizza he'd been feeding them. Like the world spun on whether or not they ate some goddamned vegetables.

Emma snorted. She sat with her feet up on Maddy's empty chair, turning the pages of the *Boston Globe*.

"Is that so unlikely?" He went to get the flour canister. Gracie was on her knees, rummaging through the low shelves of the pantry closet.

"What are you doing?" he asked.

"This is what Mommy uses." Gracie held up a package of Aunt Jemima. "She says it's easier than Grandma's and just as good."

Ben took the box. "You want me to make this kind?"

Now it was Gracie's turn to shrug.

Oh, God, Maddy, the kids are doing nothing but shrugging and peeing. Wake up, baby.

He grabbed a pair of reading glasses—Maddy's—filmed with grime and dust from sitting on the kitchen counter, and held the box up to eye level. *Add 1 egg and 1 cup water.* Sure looked a hell of a lot easier than Anne's page-long instructions.

"What do you think, Em?"

"Pancakes are too fattening. I'm just going to have a hard-boiled egg."

Come on, Emma; help me out here. I'm drowning. "If anything, you're too skinny. Have the pancakes with us."

"I'm only skinny because I don't eat pancakes."

Ben threw the box on the counter. "Jesus, you ate a pint of ice cream last night."

"I don't want the pancakes." She kept her eyes focused on the paper as she said it.

"Fine. Forget it. I'll just make them for Gracie and me. Don't ask for any when they're all done either."

He reached for a mixing bowl.

"I don't need them either." Gracie's tentative voice came from behind him. "I'll eat a boiled egg like Emma."

Ben came up too fast, bumping into Gracie and dropping the blue plastic bowl, which looked chewed on one side. They lived like paupers, surrounded by mangled bowls and freezer-burned bagels.

"I said I'm making pancakes, and I'm making pancakes. *Everyone* is having pancakes. Do you hear me?"

No one answered. Emma gave him a disgusted look and sucked her teeth.

Ben clanged a large metal stirring spoon and ladle on the counter. He opened the drawer at the bottom of the stove, pulling the screeching metal out far enough to find the griddle. "What a mess," he muttered, feeling his children's disapproval the moment he finished speaking. "Well, it is a bloody mess."

"Do you know that's a swear word in England?" Gracie asked.

Ben ignored the question as he lifted pots and skillets from deep in the drawer, trying to reach the flat pan at the bottom. When he finally had it in hand, he wanted to make pancakes like he wanted to go food shopping, or fold laundry, or pay the bills, or any of a thousand other goddamned tasks. He kicked away the pots he'd flung and banged the Teflon griddle on the front burner. The toaster protested as Caleb jammed the bagel a second time. "I said we're having pancakes, Caleb. All of us."

"So? I can have a bagel too. And you can't make me eat them, anyway."

"Don't think I can't," Ben said.

Caleb ignored him, kicking the cabinet door from his perch on the chair.

"Stop that. Do you want to dent it?"

"You can't dent wood." Caleb kicked the cupboard again, a little softer this time.

Ben took two deep breaths. "You can gouge it. Which is basically a dent." Ben opened the refrigerator and took out an egg. He reached into the cabinet for a measuring cup, went to the sink, and poured a cup of water. Using a tired plastic whisk, he beat the batter until it only had a few lumps, and then dropped a chunk of butter on the skillet.

"You don't need butter." Emma's voice was rich with resentment. "It's Teflon. Mommy doesn't use butter."

"Well, Mommy isn't here to cook these, is she?" He felt them lock up like wooden dolls. "Anyway, this is how *my* mother used to make them."

"I thought you said Grandma Frances hardly ever cooked," Emma said. He saw her in his peripheral vision, pointedly ignoring him.

God help him, he'd like to muzzle all of them. "*Hardly* is the operative word," he said. Calmly. He ladled pancake batter into the sizzling butter, trying to make a *G*, *C*, and *E* like Maddy did, but ending up with misshapen globs. When he tried to smear them together to make circles, he succeeded only in dragging the half-cooked batter around, making a goddamned lumpy mess. He grabbed the spatula to scrape them off and start again.

"You're supposed to use a plastic scraper on that pot," Emma said. "And you didn't let the pot get hot enough."

"Do you want to do this, perhaps?" he asked.

"Forget it, Dad. I was just trying to help. Excuse me."

"Cut the crap, Emma."

"You're just unwilling to control your anger, Dad. You could if you chose to."

"Watch it."

"Why? Isn't it the truth?" Emma asked. "That's why Mommy's in a coma, right? Because of you. You were probably so mad you were speeding like Evel Knievel."

First he had to hear Maddy's words coming out of Emma's mouth, and now Jake's words assaulted him. He closed his eyes for a moment. He took a page from the advice Maddy gave him—advice he'd mocked even as he stored it up for emergencies.

Self-talk, Ben. Use self-talk. You can't have two thoughts going simultaneously. Replace the ugly thoughts with good ones. Replace "She's a fucking idiot" with "Do I really want to hurt the woman I love?" It works.

Ugly thought: *I want to muzzle my children.*

Self-talk: *My children are going through a hard time. They need me.*

He would not yell anymore this morning. He would not.

Self-talk: *Be cool and unruffled. Do I want to hurt my children's feelings?*

"It wasn't my fault, Emma. We've spoken about this."

"Not according to the police, right? Because they're building a case, right?" Emma stood, using the sides of her fingers to wipe off her tears. "And Grandpa's going to try to pull strings, right?"

For God's sake, was Jake inside his daughter's brain?

"Grandpa can't get charges dropped against a guilty man. That would be corruption. He's not getting involved anyway. He's just helping the lawyer." The lawyer who was the Judge's old law partner.

"He could twist the law to your advantage. That's what Grandpa Jake said. And if you hadn't had road rage, you wouldn't have crashed. It *was* your fault."

"*Road rage?* Grandpa said I had road rage? Listen, the next time you want an answer, you come to me. I'm your father, not Grandpa Jake. It was the other car who caused this accident." He shook his finger at Emma. "Who do you think is holding this family together right now? It sure as hell isn't Grandpa Jake."

A burning smell and screeching noise came from the toaster. Ben turned around to see Caleb sticking a fork into the metal appliance.

"*What are you doing? Take out the fork!*" Ben shouted as he ran over to Caleb.

"The bagel's stuck."

"Are you nuts, Caleb?" Ben grabbed his son's arm, swinging him off the chair in one motion. He unplugged the toaster, bent it on the side, and pulled out the bagel with tongs. "Are you trying to kill yourself?"

Caleb ignored him, giving another annoying shrug using only one shoulder.

"Well, are you?" Ben screamed.

"Maybe you want me to die. Just like Mommy."

He sat on the floor, next to where he'd tossed his son. "Oh, Jesus, Caleb." He pulled him on his lap, trying to hug the stiff boy. "Mommy's not going to die. And I love you. I love all of you."

Caleb remained rigid. Ben felt as though he were trying to comfort Pinocchio before he became a real boy. His son's little-boy legs and arms stuck out like wood sticks, resisting Ben's comfort as though by a force of will. Ben pulled him closer, and at that moment, as though blinders were removed from his eyes, he saw the filthy bandages covering Caleb's foot.

One long hour later, Vanessa arrived to take Caleb to the doctor to check on his bandages. Ben should have gone. He should have canceled this date with Kath and Olivia, who stood on the porch now. They terrified him as a couple. He assumed that between them Kath and Olivia knew his every foible and habit, from whether he wore boxers or briefs to the sounds he made at orgasm.

Kath hugged him, holding him a moment longer than usual. It was a sympathy hug, acknowledging troubles. Olivia pecked him on the cheek.

And that was the mark of a woman who blamed him.

"Kath! Olivia!" Emma ran over to the women, who each took one of Emma's hands as though following stage directions.

"Baby girl, how are you?" Olivia kissed Emma's forehead. "Mmm, you smell good. Like oranges. What is it?"

Emma glanced at Ben before answering. "Some body lotion of Mom's."

"She'd be happy you were using it," Kath said.

"Finish it. We'll buy her another bottle." Olivia looked over at Ben, who didn't have a clue what message he was supposed to be getting.

"Right. Sure," he said. "I'll get some just in case. We won't upset Mom."

Ben saw the look of complicity pass between Olivia and Kath. They were sending some secret *stupid man* message. Because he didn't know some ultimate connection that lay between lotion, marriage, and love.

Sometimes women just drove him crazy.

"She'd never be upset, Ben," Olivia said. "She'd love to know Emma was using her lotion."

He didn't have a clue.

"Let's get going," he said.

Students filled J.P. Licks, drawn in by the free wireless and a staff who didn't care if you stayed from the moment the door opened until the time they closed the gates.

Olivia put on oversized blue reading glasses and cleared her throat. She shuffled through the blue file folder she'd removed from her briefcase, making three piles of papers. "I made three sets of the report. Thanks for the permission to talk to Maddy's doctor, Ben. Summary's in front."

She handed a stapled packet to each of them, saving one for herself. "Read it, and later we'll make action plans. I stopped at the hospital and gave one to Anne and Jake."

Ben started to say thank you, but his throat closed as he saw the packet label:

Madeline Greene Illica: Postaccident update.

"Remember, these are my translated layman's notes," Olivia said. "This is for us."

Kath dumped three sugar packets in her tea. "Thank God you

could do this. I can't wrap my brain around the dense medical stuff."

Olivia shook the papers at her. "Read so we can talk."

Kath wound her long black hair around her fingers as she looked at the papers. "This is so horrible."

"Right. It's horrible. Now move on and read, okay?" Olivia squeezed Kath's hand. How did women do it? Ben thought of his father, his brother. Even with blood between them, they'd never build up enough closeness to show their bellies. He didn't even know if Olivia and Kath had met before the accident—yet here they were, soul-sisters.

What we know: Left temporal lobe closed head injury. Impact caused her brain to bump the opposite side of her skull. Blood clot required surgery. Possible damage at site of impact and opposite side (don't know yet!).

Maddy is in a coma. A coma rarely lasts more than 2 to 4 weeks. A persistent vegetative state sometimes follows a coma. Maddy is not presently in this state and may never be.

Some patients may regain a degree of awareness even after persistent vegetative state. Others may remain in that state for years or even decades. The most common cause of death for someone in a persistent vegetative state is infection, such as pneumonia.

"Right back," Ben said. He left Olivia's packet on the table and headed to the bathroom, where he locked the stall, put down the toilet cover, and sat, head in hands. He inhaled Lysol, soap, and human waste particles. He concentrated on the graffiti on the wall. *Janelle DiRosa sucks.*

Maddy was the love of his life. She knew that, right? Their roots tangled around each other's so densely he didn't know how to separate them. He'd have no family without her.

The cold water Ben splashed on his face soaked the collar of his golf shirt. He pressed his fingers into his forehead until his face ached. He looked too damned normal in the mirror. Shattering the glass would work—his face would look as fractured as he felt.

What if Maddy didn't wake up?

What if they charged him? Found him guilty?

For God's sake, driving to endanger was a criminal offense. He'd be facing anything from probation to jail time. At the very least, he'd have to report it to the bar, and God knew he had enough enemies there.

What if he lost his fucking job?

When he returned to the table, Olivia and Kath wore matching maternal looks of concern, though Olivia's face managed to infuse impatience into the caring. She held out the sheaf of papers. "Are you okay? Do you think you can finish?"

He couldn't determine if she was being sarcastic or solicitous, but he took the high road and chose solicitous.

Postcoma Outlook: Difficulties can be expected with memory, fatigue, anger, judgment, concentration, disinhibition, dizziness, seizures, and depression.

Taking care of yourself: Signs of stress: inability to sleep, nightmares, poor self-care, poor appetite, guilt or self-blaming, feelings of loneliness and worthlessness, excessive use of alcohol and/or medication.

This he didn't care about. He skipped the rest of the sympathy until he got to:

Family Members, what you can do: Read to get information, don't hold vigil 24-7, and be prepared for a marathon, not a sprint . . . Remember, patients may hear what you say while in coma . . . Expect they may strike out when they wake up . . . Take comfort that 99% eventually get out of agitated state . . . Family burnout is common. Reduce stimulation. Physical touch can be upsetting. Test the waters. Don't talk down.

Signs of Improvement: Following simple commands. Localized response . . . Agitated and confused . . . Higher-level responses: The patient may seem more like herself . . . However, there may be personality changes.

"Are you okay?" Kath asked.

Ben tapped his fingers on the report. "I'm fine."

Olivia nodded. "You have to make plans. Get the house ready for when Maddy comes home. It's paramount to create the right environment."

"You might think it's too early, but it's important for so many reasons." Kath put her hand lightly on his forearm. "For the kids—for everyone—we have to believe in her coming home. Create a positive atmosphere. I don't care if it sounds hokey. It might work, and it sure won't hurt. Do it for the kids, if nothing else."

"Right. Got it. Positive. The right environment. Okay. We should." Contrary to Olivia's findings, stress wasn't inducing agitation in Ben, but rather a narcotized feel of total collapse. Falling asleep at the table seemed possible. He shuffled ahead a few pages.

How does TBI affect sexual functioning?

The following changes in sexuality *can* happen after TBI: *Decreased Desire:* Many have less desire or interest in sex. *Increased Desire:* Some find their sexual desire increases after TBI and may want to have sex more often than usual. Others may have difficulty controlling their sexual behavior. They might make sexual advances in unsuitable situations or make unsuitable comments of a sexual nature.

He closed the report.

Olivia leaned forward, pressing her breasts on the tabletop. "Are you listening, Ben?"

"Of course. Let me take in all this information, and I'll come up with a plan."

"We. I think *we* should come up with a plan. I've spoken to Anne. To Jake. We all need to help."

A fatigue headache built steam. The medical words had blurred into word soup. "I said I'll take care of it, Olivia."

"Like you took care of Maddy?"

His jaw tightened. "You want to go there?"

Kath switched to holding Olivia's arm. "Leave it be. Okay?"

Ben watched her hand tighten. "Okay?" Kath repeated, her voice toughening.

"Fine." Olivia looked disgusted.

"Ben?" Kath asked.

"Right. Got it." He stood and walked out.

Once home, Ben threw himself on the couch. His eyes burned from sweat and lack of sleep. He got up and wandered from hot room to hot room. Finally, he poured a glass of cold water and brought it into the dining room.

They rarely ate in there. Dust covered the top of the table, except where Ben dropped daily piles of mail and magazines. He swept it all aside and placed the sweaty glass on the wood. Seeing the ring of moisture forming, he lifted it, wiped it with his arm, and put a weeks-old *Atlantic* underneath.

Sitting, staring at nothing, he took small swallows of water while rubbing his tight chest. The collection of fifteen years of marriage surrounded him. Charcoal-black china with three blood-red circles lined up straight in the buffet, waiting for a special occasion. Maddy had found the pattern so exciting she'd almost killed him when she leapt on him to tell him she'd found *the perfect plates*.

Framed photos stared at him. Emma holding Gracie, who held infant Caleb. Ben's arms enveloping a hugely pregnant Maddy from behind, her smile crinkling her puffy face. Ben's father appeared stiff yet quietly happy, standing with Emma at her recent eighth-grade graduation.

Where was his family going to end up?

Maddy's grandmother wearing fox furs around her neck, proud and sophisticated—probably years younger than Ben's present age, but looking older than he thought he and Maddy appeared.

Cobalt-blue wedding goblets glinted from a glass shelf—the cups they'd used for their first sip as a married couple. A Jewish tradition. The glasses were not so much expensive as precious, and thus behind glass, taken out each anniversary. Last year Gracie spent an hour getting the room just right for them. Candles. The table cleared of clutter. Two pressed white napkins.

What the hell am I supposed to do, God?

Ben walked to the cabinet, opened the door, and took out the deep-blue glasses, leaving two clean circles in the dust. He carried them to the table. The faceted crystal shimmered in the sun. He lifted the glasses high and tapped them together. Music. Glass music, Gracie called it the last time he and Maddy toasted.

He clinked them again and again. He clinked them until the music was no longer sweet. He clinked them until the glasses ground against each other. He slammed them harder and harder until finally he threw one against the wall and watched it shatter.

CHAPTER 15

Emma

Emma perched at the edge of her mother's hospital bed, reading aloud from *The Family Nobody Wanted*, one of her favorite childhood books. An old-fashioned sketch of happy parents holding up a happy baby illustrated the cover. When her mom gave Emma the small worn paperback years before, Emma remembered turning it over to read the large brown letters on the back cover. *They had very little money—but a great deal of love to share.* The story was about parents who'd adopted children others had rejected.

Exactly the kind of book her mom adored: happy misery.

Emma was almost at her favorite part, where the mother, desperate to feed the family, opened a can of rattlesnake meat she'd previously kept on the shelf as decoration. She cleared her throat and began reading.

"*Rattlesnake is supposed to taste like a cross between chicken and tuna fish,*" she read. "*Any resemblance ours might once have had to either certainly had been lost in the long passage of years since it had been canned. It turned out to be something closer to cotton strings in a curdled cream sauce. We ate it because, after all, it had calories.*"

As always, Emma loved the description—imagining strings in sauce.

"*The minister dropped by that night for a visit. When he went to the kitchen for a drink of water, he reached for the can, which was back in its usual place on the window shelf.*

" '*When are you two going to eat this rattle—*' *he began, and then broke off in surprise when the can came up light in his hand. He turned it over and stared. Carl had reamed it open from the bottom, washed it out, and replaced it on the shelf . . .*"

As she read on, through the part where the minister laid ten dollars on the sink, Emma's throat clogged. That family was so lucky. Would her father ever think to wash out a can because her mother thought it was pretty? More likely, he'd yell at her because it was spreading germs, or because tin cans were ruining the environment.

Emma studied her mother's eyelids. She put a finger to one cheek and then the other, touching the slack muscles. Was it her imagination, or was her mother becoming faker-looking every day? Like a rubber doll.

"I have to go now, Mommy." Antiseptic and medical odors filled the area, smells her mother would despise. Reaching into her jeans pocket, she slid out a tiny plastic travel jar she'd bought at CVS. She scooped out a bit of almond-perfumed cream, one her mother used to moisturize her hands. Not the one Emma had borrowed—she'd already tried that one.

I love the smell, but it never lasts, her mother said when she used this one. *Still, it's so good while I'm putting it on.* Emma took her mother's hand and rubbed the lotion in, the short-lived scent sweetening the air around them.

"Smells good, right, Mom? Tomorrow I'm going to bring something different. I don't know what—I'll go to Sephora, okay?"

What could wake her mother? Strong sexy perfume like Aunt Vanessa wore? Something soothing and familiar, same as the cozy sun-warmed fragrances her mother chose? Perhaps the known would remind her mother of life and draw her back like a Gypsy spell. Romanian, like on Grandpa Benedikte's side. Maybe something new would penetrate. Emma wished Nurse Bernadette were there, instead of Nurse Angela, so she could ask.

She took gentle hold of her mother's thinning wrist. "Wake up, Mom. School is starting soon. Gracie wants you to take her shopping. Daddy will be terrible at the mall, and I can't drive. We need you."

Emma rushed upstairs to her bedroom after supper. No one had said a word during the entire meal—they just watched television as they ate their Mrs. Budd's Chicken Pot Pie. Three days before, her father had carried the portable TV from the guest room to the kitchen. Now it played during every meal. Her mother would hate that. Mealtime television was only allowed when her mother had been so tired that she'd brought pizza in and they ate it in the living room. Or the time they had ice cream for supper.

Or once in a while just because she'd been mad that Daddy hadn't shown up.

Baruch Atah Adonai, Eloheinu Melech Ha'Olam, please make Mommy wake up.

Emma drifted along with Rihanna, trying to not-feel. When she opened her eyes, Gracie stood in front of the bed.

"You're supposed to knock," Emma yelled.

"I did. You didn't hear me. Daddy wants you downstairs. *Now.*"

"Is he mad?" Emma asked.

"I don't think so. But maybe. He said he wants to talk to us."

Emma got a sick feeling in her stomach. "Did he look upset?"

"He said Mommy was the same," Gracie answered.

Emma and Gracie walked downstairs. Caleb sat on the floor by the television, twisting an ancient Rubik's Cube he'd latched on to after finding it in their mother's desk last week. Or was it longer ago? She knew it was after.

Time had a new meaning—before and after. When she'd looked at a calendar that morning, it didn't seem possible it was only two weeks since the accident. It seemed like forever.

"We need to talk about when Mommy wakes up," her father said after she and Gracie settled side by side on the couch.

"She woke up?" Gracie's giant grin split her face in half. "Mommy's awake?"

"No, no," her father said, fast. "I'm sorry, kids. I didn't mean to raise your hopes so high. But she could be coming up a little at a time. Maybe. That's what the doctor says. So we can hope. We can be positive. Kath says being positive is important."

"Hope?" Emma said. Kath and Olivia must have drugged her father or something, but still, weird as it was, hearing her father talking about being positive lifted her spirits an inch. She almost laughed, wanting to joke with him as she might have a year ago. *Hey, Dad—why don't we wear matching prayer bracelets?*

"Not just hope, honey. Her eyes fluttered. She responds a little more to pain."

"Pain!" Caleb bit at the edge of his thumb. "Why are they making her hurt?"

"It's just tiny tests, Caleb. A little tiny prick. Like this." Her father leaned forward and pinched Caleb on his knee. "Just to test her response."

"What's response?" Caleb asked.

"It's how much her body, um, shows it knows that it got pinched."

"How does she show it?" Gracie asked.

Her father leaned back in the soft chair and closed his eyes for a moment, then opened them and slapped his hands on his knees. "They have a special, safe way of measuring it, but—"

"How?" Gracie asked.

"Let me finish, Gracie. I want to talk about—"

"Just tell her, Dad." Emma also wanted to know. How did they measure her mother's pain?

"I think it's the nerve endings or something." He stopped speaking.

Emma stared at him just as intently as her sister and brother. *Tell us!*

"Actually, in truth, I don't have a clue. But it's okay—I promise." He looked at Gracie. "Cross my heart." Her father made the sign Emma was used to seeing from her sister and Grandma Frances.

"When did the doctor tell you all this?" Emma was suspicious of this rush of happy talk.

Her father stared at each of them in turn. "This is what he's been telling me all along. And today I asked about her pain response—and it's getting better. And yes, that really is a good thing. Ask Grandma; she was there when he said it."

Gracie nodded. Emma guessed that her sister's little computer brain had decided if Grandma thought it was good, it was good.

"Listen, guys." Her father's voice had switched gears. He sounded less worshipful-prayer father and more deal-maker dad. "I'm asking you to be as wise—that means truly smart, Caleb—as possible. Grandma and Grandpa and I talked about something important today. Something for Mommy."

"What?" Emma sat up straight, alert.

"When Mommy is, um, better, when she wakes up, she won't be all the way better right away—after she wakes up, she's going to go through stages. Like the hospital counselor told us. Do you remember?"

"Like a butterfly?" Gracie suggested. "How it changes from a caterpillar?"

"Sort of—but in her head, not just in her body. So she'll talk slower and not understand everything for a while. Some things she'll have to learn again."

"Like what?" Caleb crossed his legs and rocked on his butt.

"We won't know until it happens—but things like reading. Or how to tie her shoe."

"I can help, right?" Caleb asked.

"Sure, buddy."

"How long?" Gracie asked.

"I'm not sure. No one knows until it happens."

"But what if she never wakes up?" Caleb asked.

"She's going to wake up." Emma squeezed her brother's arm.

Her father put up his hand, signaling them to stop. "Listen. When Mommy wakes up, she's going to need plenty of help and lots of love, and we have to treat her special. One way is going to be making sure she doesn't have to worry. It's very, very, very important. Do you understand?" His voice raised just enough so that Emma knew they were meant to nod—even Caleb got the message.

"When she comes home, we're not going to talk about the details of the accident," her father continued. "Otherwise she'd get upset."

"You mean how you went too fast?" Caleb asked.

"None of the details need to be . . . shared with Mommy right away. I mean that it doesn't matter how it happened. The important thing is that she gets well."

"We're lying about it?" Gracie's forehead wrinkled until she looked like Grandma Frances.

Her father tapped his foot against the table. "We're not lying. We're just making the beginning easier for Mommy."

"How?" Gracie asked.

"By explaining the important part, how it was raining and there was a car too close to us that tried to pass. We have to keep it simple."

Her father looked at Emma, appearing grateful when she didn't say anything.

"She's going to have to get used to a lot of things that will be difficult for her," he continued. "And she'll need all her energy for getting better."

"Are we ever going to tell her?" Gracie fingered her cross.

"We'll see, cupcake. If the right time comes, we'll tell her everything."

"How will we know when it's the right time?" she asked.

"Because I'll tell you," her father said.

Right. Because you're so wise, smart, and know how to handle family matters so well. Emma thought she should say something—speak up for her mother, for truth, for doing the right thing. Still, how would her mother feel coming home to the news that it might be Daddy's fault? That without Grandpa Benedikte he might be in jail right now? That's what she heard Aunt Vanessa say. Her aunt was probably exaggerating like always, but it was true that they were deciding whether to charge him with driving to endanger. They were investigating. Emma wasn't exactly sure what that meant, but she knew it had to be very bad. And that he could be in lots of trouble.

He drove too fast. Like a maniac. End of story. Maybe Grandpa Bene-dikte's lawyer will get him off, but he'll always be guilty to me.

Last time she was at Grandma and Grandpa's house, she'd heard Grandpa Jake say that. They thought she was upstairs, but she'd been right in the next room, listening to them.

Does it really matter in the end? Grandma's words were so teary it was hard to understand everything. *Isn't what is, is? Let's just get her better. Now she'll need Ben more than ever.*

What was Emma's responsibility here? Weighing one bad option after another left her queasy and in need of someone who wasn't in-sane, crying, or angry.

CHAPTER 16

Ben

The hospital corridor had become all too familiar, a perfect lane for considering crimes and misdemeanors. What new sin had Ben committed the night before, asking his children to lie? He tried to recall his childhood, his catechism classes, and knew, at the very least, he'd forced them into a sin of omission by forbidding them to reveal the details of the accident. For him it was a sure sin of commission.

Big pat on the shoulder for only sending his kids to purgatory.

Jesus, his sins piled up so fast he could barely sort them. Sometimes shutdown was the only way he could function; otherwise looking at Maddy, thinking of her, knowing he'd put her there stopped him dead. Piling up barriers against his self-loathing was a constant job.

His life had become a perpetual loop. Wake. Get kids up. Drive to hospital. Quick kiss to Maddy. Check with nurse. Check in at work. Lean on Elizabeth. Barely know which end is up. Motions, briefs, court appearances—all on automatic. Call kids. Thank Anne for being there. Ask for news on Maddy. Go back to hospital. Hold Maddy's hand. Talk about anything and nothing in another one-sided conversation. Go home, stopping for pizza, Chinese, bagels, Thai, if no Anne dinner waited. Homework. Laundry. Clean. Read to Caleb. Fall asleep.

How had Maddy ever done it?

When he reached Maddy's bedside, Ben took out a crayoned picture of Caleb's. Should he tape it to the side of the pressure monitor? The heart monitor? Finally, he folded it until only a crooked pink rose on a lily pad showed. Using the small roll of tape Gracie had given him, he fastened it to the side of a compression box and then gave it a quiet little pat for luck.

"Ben." Bernadette gave him a caretaker pat when she came over to Maddy's bed, her touch conveying compassion with a wee bit of *buck up, buddy*, and then she placed a hand on his wife's.

"Maddy, my sweet—how are you? Could I borrow your husband if I send him right back? First, I'll give you two a moment."

Agitation hit him in the gut. She couldn't possibly be bringing good news, right? Hospitals were citadels of horror, with nurses bearing the early warnings. Compassionate canaries in the health mine— that's what they were.

"I put up another work of art from Caleb, Maddy. That kid is an incredible artist—just like you always said . . . say." No past tense. One of Ben's many coma rules. He kissed Maddy's forehead. "I'll be right back, beautiful."

Bernadette looked concerned when he caught up with her at the nurses' station. "What's wrong?" he asked.

Before answering, she pressed her lips as though physically holding her words inside. "There's something I'm keeping an eye on, though I probably shouldn't be telling you this. Really, it's just instinct."

"Did you see something?" His chest contracted. "What happened?"

"It's not really that anything happened. But I watch you and Emma, and the pictures you bring in from the little ones—the way you come in to kiss her good night every night." She stopped, shook her head, her soft blond dandelion-fuzz hair moving under the thin hairnet she wore. Bernadette was one of those semi-ugly women who wrenched at Ben's heart—made him wish he were a better man. Someone who would date her because she was so fucking nice and then marry her because she was so fucking good.

"It's okay, Bernadette," he said. "I'm not going to hold you to anything."

"She opened her eyes today."

"And nobody called me?" Ben's heart pulsed.

"Shh!" Bernadette glanced at the Haitian nurse, the one who frightened Emma. "I saw it only once, and just for a second. No one else saw it. I put it in the chart, but I wanted to tell you myself."

"This is good, right?" Ben wanted to hug her, find a kind and gentle man to marry her. "Terrific?"

"I think so." Caution coated each of her words. "I think so. But the doctors will say it's that the absence of more instances of eye opening that's a bad sign, than opening her eyes one time is a good one. More to the point, to regain consciousness, Maddy must both react *and* respond."

His hopes sank to where they'd been before as he lost his brief dance with optimism. "So what does this actually mean?"

"The doctor won't want to raise your expectations—not simply on one eye opening—but I felt her presence, Ben. Truly. It's like a baby quickening." Bernadette placed her hands on her belly as though remembering a mound of pregnancy.

He knew nothing about this woman. Was she married? Children? Maddy would have known all that and much more. She'd have brought brownies and taken her out to dinner. No wonder Maddy yelled at him for complaining about their neighbor, Mrs. Gilman, who exasperated Ben each time she buttonholed people for conversations first thing in the morning.

"You have to open your eyes and see people who aren't your clients," Maddy had told him. "It doesn't take much. It's not as though I talk to Mrs. Gilman for hours on end, but I know she treats her Pekinese like her baby and collects china ballerinas. You could have a thousand suppers with her, and you'd know no more about her than you do today."

He'd probably screwed up ten thousand suppers with Maddy and the kids just by being an asshole.

"Maybe I shouldn't have said anything, but it's something I feel. As though her soul's come back." Bernadette stared as though seeking his soul. "I know this much is true. There's a spiritual light that's there or not there. Something indescribable. Maddy's in there, but you have to pull her back. I think this is the moment to put out your hand and pray she catches it."

Ben noticed the twisted rope crucifix she wore, with tiny Jesus writhing upon it.

"Thank you," he said.

Nothing happened.

Ben sat by Maddy's bedside each day, waiting. Her eyes didn't flicker. Her hand didn't twitch, but based on Bernadette's report, they held vigil all weekend: Anne, Jake, Vanessa, Olivia, Kath—one of them was always there.

Nurse Bernadette avoided him. She probably knew she'd made a huge mistake with her voodoo I-see-into-the-soul shit. Or maybe she was just crazy. Still, Ben didn't take any chances. He talked to Maddy about anything he thought would reach her—from his memories of holding her shoulders as Emma slipped into the world, to how they'd snuck into the bathroom to make love when they'd gone away for that week with her parents and all the kids. He played her favorite music— even the shaky-achy country stuff she had a weakness for—using the tiny and wildly expensive CD player Jake had bought for her room.

And he did all this while staring at machines hissing in and out, as he monitored Maddy's pale, inert body.

Monday he was dying to get to the office. They'd slowed the vigil. He drove to the hospital on his way to work—back to the loop, back to an eternal round of checking items off a daily schedule that he'd never imagined. This morning he'd left earlier, hoping to buttonhole the doctor making early rounds.

He caught up with a flunky from the big cheese's office just in time. Dr. Flynn was full of himself and his white coat.

"How's it looking?" Ben asked.

Flynn looked at his chart, as though he needed to consult the record about someone he'd examined three minutes ago. "Mmm. Hmm."

Ben self-talked himself out of punching words from the doctor's girlish pink lips.

"I don't need a full medical lecture. Just tell me how she's doing. Any changes? Where's the hope level?"

Ben watched Flynn's eyes for truth, more than he'd ever get from the guy's words. Every bit of hope he'd had—fluttering eyelids, the fucking wonder of pain response—sunk as he watched the doctor's eyes hesitate, saw him grasp for the right words.

"We never discourage anyone from hoping. The world is full of miracles."

He pulled into the Boston Common Garage, sorry he'd let Vanessa pick up the kids to take them back-to-school shopping. Wanting to be at work had dissipated. Right at that moment he wanted to be with Emma, Gracie, and Caleb. He wanted to break up fights and pick out socks and dresses. Anything not to be hearing the word *miracle* looping through his mind.

He walked first to Elizabeth's office, unready for his first full day back, but needing to catch up on everything she'd been taking care of for him.

"Hey," Ben called as he entered. He sat in her guest chair and reached for the coffee she had waiting. He couldn't have been more grateful if she'd handed him a hundred-dollar bill. The first sip, hot, black, and bitter, shot straight to his heart.

"Thanks," he said.

"Least I can do." Elizabeth tilted her head and gave a sad smile. "How are you?"

He shrugged and grunted. "Not great."

She shook her head. "Poor Ben. How are the children?"

"Wretched." He tipped his cup toward her as a mini toast. "Let's talk about something else." At least she hadn't asked about his case.

He felt like a ten-year-old the way he'd left the legal decisions in his father's and the lawyer's hands. Was he being a fool? The lawyer side of him knew they couldn't truly come up with a case against him. He hadn't been drunk. All he'd done was move over to the right; the Ford had rammed into him.

But. There was always a but.

How about turning on the setting for competitive driving control? How smart was that?

They wouldn't know. It reset back to the normal driving mode after stopping. And anyway, it wasn't illegal.

Just stupid and wrong.

But he'd been driving recklessly. His wife was in a coma. They could find a way to charge him if they wanted. And Ben, as the Judge was fond of saying, wasn't a popular guy in the DA's office.

Stop. It will be fine. Ben knocked twice on Elizabeth's desk. "What do you have for me?"

She nodded as though husbands coping with wives in comas were part of her protocol. "The Barry Robinson case file is ready for you. Problem: B-bird's mother keeps calling. She thinks there must be some way to lower the bail. What do you want me to tell her?"

"Why don't you tell her the truth? That she should give up and let her kid do some time. Tell her that for once he shouldn't get away with something." Ben put his coffee down and rubbed his temples. Another monster headache was building to a crescendo. "B-bird needs more cooking. Tell mama to keep her son in the pan and turn him when he's done."

Elizabeth flinched. Still tender to the bone as she was, she hadn't perfected the art of joking at a client's expense. He missed Maddy. He could fucking die from missing her at this moment.

When his desk phone rang at five, Ben's stomach cramped. He didn't want to pick it up; he didn't want to talk to B-bird's mother or some piece-of-shit client or his piece-of-shit brother, Andrew, making one of his twice-a-week duty calls. Too bad ignoring the phone was no longer one of Ben's luxuries.

"Illica," he said.

"Bennie?"

Since the accident, his mother-in-law had taken to calling him Bennie. As though he were a fucking dog.

It wasn't that.

Maddy called him that once in a while. He didn't want to hear it from Anne.

"Is everything okay? The kids?"

"Everything is okay." They never used the word *fine* these days—things were never fine. "How about the kids sleep over at our house tonight? After shopping for school clothes all day with Vanessa, they're ready for a home-cooked meal."

"Are you sure? They're not so easy at night. Caleb, um—"

"I know, I know. He's wetting the bed. Big deal. A little pee. You think Maddy and Vanessa never peed?"

Ben avoided thinking about exactly how Maddy was peeing these days.

"If you're sure," he said.

"I'm sure, I'm sure. Jake and I need a little life in the house. Pick them up after work tomorrow. We'll all have supper together."

If by having "a little life in the house," she meant Emma glaring, Caleb screeching, and Gracie worshipping Jesus, then he was happy to oblige by offering up his children.

Maddy and the kids stared from the picture on his desk. Her smile flew right at him—she'd directed love eyes to the camera as he snapped the shot of her building a snowman with the kids. The snow had been so high it covered the steps to the porch. They'd leapt straight into the pile of cold puffy flakes.

Her cheeks were bright red. He could imagine the taste of her cold lips.

So many times he hadn't kissed her.

He didn't know how to keep containing the pain. Missing her was a rusty blade, but no matter how it sliced, he had to keep going. Somehow he had to contain the damn pain.

Ben and Elizabeth went out to dinner. Then back to her place.

She lived in the Fenway, smack in the middle of the student ghetto, but her building had been remodeled to appeal to young professionals. Her condo appeared as spare as Elizabeth. Pale walls, glossy oak floors, furnished with minimal pieces and maximum money. Certainly not paid for by her meager intern stipend. Those sleek ebony vases and lamps weren't the T.J. Maxx variety Maddy brought home.

He should leave this shiny place right fucking now.

"Wine?" She held up a bottle of white. "Or an after-dinner drink?"

"Wine," he said.

She filled an oversized goblet halfway and then settled next to him on the couch. "Thanks for dinner." She leaned over and lifted a chrome fruit bowl—holding it toward him. Purple grapes and plums overflowed. "Dessert?"

He shook his head. "No, thanks."

She bit into a plum and curled her legs underneath her. "Everything was wonderful."

Really? What did she think was so much fun? That he'd had too much to drink and ranted about politics? She'd gazed at him with overserious eyes. "Glad you liked it."

"I love the North End. Italian food's my favorite."

The first time he'd taken Maddy on a date they'd gone to the North End. How had he forgotten that?

What was wrong with him? How had he let his life end up like this?

He drank half the wine, letting the alcohol pile on top of the full-strength martinis he'd had at the restaurant.

Elizabeth slid closer. She brushed her fingertips over his cheek. "Heavy-bearded guy. Do you need to shave twice a day?"

"Need?" He shrugged. "I don't."

"Actually," Elizabeth said, "it feels good."

Ben finished his wine. Her skin, her skin was so damn clear and perfect. She glowed. From what he could see, there wasn't a trace of makeup, just her rich vanilla complexion. He reached out, put a hand around the back of her neck, and drew her close, tasting plums and wine and health. She wound herself around him, swung a leg over him, and pressed hard against him. Feeling the heat of her, he thought he might lose control. He laid her on the couch. She allowed him to put her flat, laying her arms to either side. Slowly, he unbuttoned her silky gray blouse.

Seventy percent. He didn't want to join the seventy percent.

Maddy. Wild hair framing her grimace of joy when he touched her, the deep hollow of her lower back where his fingers met when she rode him.

Pale ashy legs covered by bleach-smelling sheets, tubing trailing from her as though she were a medical Medusa.

Elizabeth's bra clasped in the front. The two cups fell away when he unfastened it. The first time with Maddy. Licking along the line where a thin locket chain traced her collarbone. His fingers finding home in every curve. He'd wanted to live his life breathing in Maddy.

Elizabeth drew up her skirt and tugged off his pants, and then urged him inside. He closed his eyes.

"Where are you going?" Elizabeth lifted herself on one elbow. Faint light slid through the blinds. It was four thirty.

Ben was dressed and ready to go.

"Home. It's almost six in the morning."

Elizabeth sat up, surprising him by not being a sheet clutcher. The thin cotton blanket puddled around her waist. Her bare breasts looked casual and ready.

"Are you coming back?"

Did she mean ever? Tonight? "I have to get home. Before the children wake."

Weak lie. Maddy's voice. *However, of course, you've never been an especially good liar.*

"Aren't they with their grandmother?"

"Yes. With Maddy's mother. But I need to get things ready before they come home."

Ben considered going to church. Heading straight to confession. *Bless me, Father, for I have sinned. It's been thirty years since my last confession. In that time, I took the Lord's name in vain. I was arrogant and mean to my wife. I pulled my son in anger. I screamed at my daughters. I drove like a madman, causing my wife to fly from the car and strike her head. I put her in a coma. Then I slept with another woman. Am I evil, Father?*

"Will you be back?" Elizabeth asked again.

Every night since the accident, he'd been at the hospital to kiss Maddy good night. Last night he'd missed it.

"I don't know if I can," he said, meaning *No. Not ever. Never.*

"Look, Daddy!" Gracie grabbed his hand, pulling him toward an end table the moment he walked into his in-laws' hallway. The smell of fresh-baked bread mingled with the aroma of simmering meat. Gracie held a small stained glass upright box edged with bright copper, a small slot on top. "Put in a dollar, Daddy."

"Grandma and Grandpa charging admission these days?" he asked.

"Daddy, you need to. It's important."

"Okay, okay." He stuffed two singles through the opening. "See? Now what is it?"

"It's a seduction box."

"A what?" Ben stepped back and looked askance at the box. His mother-in-law walked in laughing.

"It's a *tsedakah* box, Gracie." Anne knelt to Gracie's level. "You pronounce it like this: *suh-dock-ah.*"

"Sah-dock-a," Gracie repeated. "Sahdocka."

"Close enough," Anne said, and hugged her. "It's a charity box, Ben. I took Gracie to Harvard Street today, to Kolbo, the Israeli art store, and bought this for her."

Ben picked up the box, turned it over, and saw the price tag—sixty dollars. "Couldn't she have decorated a little milk carton? Given the sixty dollars to charity?"

"Was it wrong, Daddy?" Gracie got a quivery look. "Should we bring it back?"

"Absolutely not, sweetheart." Anne caressed Gracie's cheek. "We spent an hour picking out just the right box. This will last the rest of your life; it's an investment." She shot a look at Ben over Gracie's head.

"I was joking, hon. Here, I'll prove it." Ben fed another dollar in the box. "And tell Grandpa I'll match anything he puts in. Double it. What are you going to do with the money? Who gets it?"

"Emma said I should give it to a head injury place. We're going to find one on the Internet." Gracie's face became serious. "And to the New England Little Wanderers. That's a place for children without parents. Mommy worked there."

"Volunteered, Gracie," Anne said. "During high school. As a tutor."

Gracie clutched the box as though it were a doll. "How old do you have to be for that?"

"Older than you, pumpkin," Ben said. Between his mother, Maddy, and Anne, Gracie had a great future saving crippled orphans in a Christian leper colony.

"Did you stop at the hospital?" Anne asked.

Ben pulled Gracie to him. "Not today. I got really busy."

"Too busy to visit your wife?" Anne asked.

Gracie stiffened under his hold.

"It's the first time."

"Lower your voice. I don't want to upset Jake."

"Listen, I haven't neglected her at *all*. I resent—"

"She's not *her*, she's Maddy—your wife."

"I know she's my wife, damn it."

Gracie wiggled from Ben's hold. "Grandma said not to shout, Daddy."

"Then treat her like your wife," Anne said.

"Wait a minute—"

"No. I'm not waiting one second," she interrupted. "You listen to me. Step up. Learn grace under pressure. What's wrong with you?"

"What did I do?" he asked.

Anne pressed the heels of her hands to her eyes for a moment. "You should be at Maddy's side every day, Ben. Every day. I shouldn't have to tell you this. There's no such thing as a busy day. Your priority is taking care of Maddy."

What could he say that wouldn't send him deeper into hell? Nothing came to mind. He opened his mouth, closed it, and then simply nodded.

"Gracie," Anne said, "I'm sorry for yelling. Run to the kitchen and check that the brownies aren't burning. Please."

Ben nodded assent. Seeming both reluctant and relieved, Gracie ran out. Ben waited for the sound of Jake charging down the stairs. He looked up but saw only the familiar Oriental runner in shades of blue, bracketed by mahogany wood.

"I don't know where you were last night. I called your house," Anne said. "And you weren't at the hospital. I called." She pointed her finger at him like a gun. "I'm not asking anything—I'm assuming you were out having a drink. But don't try to bully your way out of anything with me."

"I love your daughter," Ben said.

"Love isn't an excuse for anything but treating someone well."

CHAPTER 17

Emma

Emma and Zach walked along the secluded Riverway path, a stretch where the fenced-off trolley line and thick trees hid it from prying eyes. Not that many people were there at ten on a Thursday morning anyway.

Boston Latin, her high school, was closed for a teachers' in-service day, despite it being only five days into the school year. Not that her father knew. Emma hadn't mentioned it, and her father hadn't bothered finding out.

Her mother marked everything on a giant UNICEF calendar hanging in the kitchen. Emma's first day of high school was written in big purple letters—because purple and white were Boston Latin's school colors, her mom said—followed by about a hundred exclamation marks. You had to take a test to get into Latin. Emma's mother acted as though she'd won the Nobel Prize when she was accepted; the purple notation had been on the calendar for months: *Emma Starts Boston Latin!!!!*

It sort of embarrassed Emma, especially since some kids started Boston Latin in seventh grade, so beginning in ninth didn't seem like such a huge accomplishment. Still, her mother's pride had been nice at the time. Her father hadn't even mentioned it when she went to her first day of high school.

Emma almost noted the day of her mother's accident on the calendar, but she thought it would send Gracie into full prayer-meeting mode. The accident had been twenty-two days ago. Emma dreaded counting in months.

Autumn edged the air despite the summery warmth. Zach grabbed her hand and squeezed as they walked toward the echo tunnel.

"Want to go to my house?" Zach asked.

Emma shrugged, uncertain. "Let's just walk around for a while."

"Race you to the tunnel." Zach's hair blew back as he took off. Emma let him run, not even pretending to speed up. When she reached the entrance, Zach was already leaning against the tunnel wall. Thin to the point that his chest looked sort of caved-in, he was still handsome. His coppery skin didn't have a single blemish. A tiny diamond stud glinted in his left ear—his big rebellion. Otherwise he was pure Jewish good boy from his starched oxford shirts to the chinos his father insisted he wear to school.

Zach pulled Emma close, reversing their positions so that she leaned against the tunnel. Rough cool concrete chafed Emma's bare skin where her shirt rode up. He pressed into her as they kissed. He ran his hand over her hips and up under her shirt.

She pushed him away.

"What's wrong?" Zach asked.

She leaned her head onto his thin chest. How could she explain that when his touch excited her, she didn't know how to get back to ground? "It's just. Just too much feeling."

Zach wrapped her braid around his hand. "When I touch you, I can't think of anything else I ever want to do." He intertwined their fingers.

The hospital was just a few blocks away. "What do you do when you feel awful?" she asked. "So awful that there's no place to put your mind?"

Zach was so still Emma wished she hadn't asked. Was his life so wonderful that he never felt awful? His parents who watched him so carefully, did they make his entire existence perfect?

"Sometimes I pray," he said.

She squinted as they walked out of the dim tunnel. Did he mean pray like *Please, God, let me pass the physics test*? Get on your knees by your bed like in old movies?

"How?"

"Stuff I learned in Hebrew School. What my parents taught me. You know."

"I don't know." Her religious ignorance could fill a Bible. *Ha ha.* "Tell me."

They sat on a bench, facing the stagnant water of the unofficially well-named Muddy River. Thick reeds grew from the banks. Birds pecked around, searching for food. Zach put on his lecture face.

"According to my rabbi, 'Even in hard times, we should seek to pursue happiness,'" he said and put a hand around her shoulders. "I think that means you should let me kiss you more."

Emma shrugged him off. She wanted someone caring—not clutching at her. Was this what her father had warned her about in that ride home from when he'd found her in Copley Square? *They only want one thing at your age.* "Tell me about praying."

"Prayer helps you get a good attitude and connects you to the world in the right way."

"I don't understand." Emma felt her heart speed. "What does it mean? How does it make you feel better?"

"Maybe it's not about making you feel better. My father says God judges us on how we behave—it's not always about how others treat us, Emma."

Emma picked up Caleb and Gracie from school, gave them bowls of Froot Loops, went up to her room, and shut the door. She stared at the computer screen: How could she find a temple? What words should she use? Was she a bad Jew to worry about herself more than she worried about others? Could being Jewish help her family?

Entering *Jewish* in the search bar brought up everything in the world, including a confusing menu of Jewish subtypes she'd heard of, but never before considered. Conservative. Reform. Hasidic. Orthodox. It took two hours just to learn *Reform* meant more liberal. That's probably where her mother would tell her to go. In the liberal direction.

When she was twelve, Emma had asked to go to Hebrew School, just like her classmate, Gillian, who was preparing for her bat mitzvah. Emma had imagined it being like an Israeli Girl Scout. *The Diary of Anne Frank* had haunted her; after reading it, she'd gone online and read all the horrifying possibilities of being Jewish. Going to Hebrew School seemed a way to prevent being sent to a concentration camp and having to run around naked in front of laughing soldiers. Dying in an oven. Somehow she'd believed that Hebrew School taught you to fight like a Sabra.

Emma's mother had said she'd look into it, but she never had. By the following year, Emma had moved on to wanting to go to dance class.

Googling led Emma down twisted roads; she found "Ms. Brisket cooking class" and the "Rock My Mensch Soul Band," but nothing about finding a temple where she could pray. Finally, she found worship services listed at a temple in Cambridge, but had no idea how to proceed next. Did you just show up and walk in?

Emma extended her cramped arms and flung herself on the bed. What kind of an idiot couldn't just figure out how to go to some stupid temple? She grabbed the stuffed sock monkey she kept on her pillow, stretched it over her feet, and pulled. Then she threw the monkey against the wall.

Her brother pushed open her door and walked in. "I'm hungry."

"You just had cereal. Have some peanut butter. Leave me alone."

"I'm *still* hungry. Peanut butter is all you ever say. I want something different."

"Goody for you. Tell Daddy when he comes home."

Caleb's voice rose. "But I'm hungry now!"

Emma grabbed a stuffed zebra from the floor and threw it at

him. "Just shut up for one second," she said, and turned back to her computer. "*Contact us*," she read on the top of Temple Beth Tikvah's screen.

Dear Rabbi, Emma wrote. *I want to come to services at your temple. Is it okay to come alone? I am fourteen and just want to watch. How do I do this?*

She sounded ten years old.

"A second's over." Caleb kicked the wall with each word.

How much worse could it get?

She clicked send.

"Do you want to come or not?" Emma screamed up to her brother the following Saturday morning. "We're going to be late."

"Don't. Want. To. Go," Caleb yelled down the stairs.

Gracie tugged at Emma's sleeve. "Why don't we just leave him with Kath?"

Emma shook her head. "Daddy will think I'm irresponsible, and anyway I don't want him to know where we're going."

"Why not?" Gracie asked.

She wasn't sure how to answer. Her father looked beaten when he placed folded dollar bills in Gracie's *tsedakah* box each night. Somehow, Emma knew the knowledge of their going to temple would burden her father.

"Just don't tell him. Trust me." Emma looked up the stairs. "Caleb, get your behind here now or I'll tell Daddy about the lamp."

Caleb pounded down the stairs. Three nights before, he'd thrown a ceramic lamp against the wall because Emma wouldn't change the TV channel. She'd told her father it had fallen when she vacuumed, but in the end taking the bullet for her brother didn't matter. Her father barely seemed to care, which made everything worse. She'd rather he found out and screamed his head off.

Blistering sun seared their shoulders as they walked to the bus stop. A September heat wave suffocated the city.

"I'm thirsty," Caleb whined.

"We'll get soda when we get to Park Street." Emma kept moving.

"Mommy wouldn't like that. We can't have soda in the morning." Gracie held her thick hair off her neck. Emma should have told Gracie to put it in a ponytail. Why did her father have to work on a Saturday?

"But Mommy's not here, is she?" Emma said. "So I say what we drink."

"I don't want soda. I want water." Caleb's voice quivered. "Mommy packs water before we leave."

"We'll get water at the Store 24 while we wait for the bus."

"What if the bus is coming when we get there?" Gracie asked.

Emma grabbed her brother and sister by their shoulders, keeping them from walking. "You're hurting me," Caleb said as he tried to squirm away.

"Shut up, both of you. Maybe if you stop being spoiled brats and come with me to pray, Mommy will wake up, okay. Don't you want that? You have to be good, or we can't go. It's up to you. Will you behave?"

They nodded, Gracie biting her bottom lip.

Emma grabbed Caleb's hand. "Okay, c'mon."

After walking silently for a few moments, Caleb tugged on Emma's hand. "What?" She choked out the word through her closed throat.

"How do you pray?"

Emma walked faster, forcing them to keep up with her. "We just try to do what other people do. And if we can't figure it out, we'll just pray in our heads."

Gracie skipped ahead to face Emma. "I know prayers from Grandma Frances. Should I use those?"

"As long as you don't say them out loud." All she needed was her sister chanting to Jesus as they sat in a synagogue. She led them across Centre Street to the bus stop in front of Goodwill.

"What do I say in my brain?" Caleb's voice rose with each word.

Emma saw the bus coming. "I'll teach you on the bus." She reached into her pocket and touched the prayer she'd printed from the Internet: *You will serve G-d your Lord, and He will bless your bread and your water. I will banish sickness from among you.*

• • •

They walked up the wide stone stairs and entered a cool vestibule. Three open copper doors revealed a large room beyond the entry.

Small clumps of people stood at an inner door, the men taking yarmulkes—small caps like Emma's grandfather wore at Passover—from a basket. Women pinned lace squares to their hair, using bobby pins from a separate pile. Gracie tapped Emma's arm.

"What?" Emma whispered.

Gracie motioned for Emma to come closer. "All the boys and men are putting them on," she said softly in Emma's ear. "Only some of the girls are. I don't know why." Leave it to her sister to crack the code in one minute.

The doors closed behind the last person. They stood alone in the air-conditioned vestibule. Emma's sweat had dried to chilled stiffness.

"What do you think we should do?" Emma asked her sister.

Gracie took a black yarmulke from the basket and handed it to Caleb. "Put it on."

He did, tipping his head as the slippery material slipped off. Emma fastened it with a bobby pin and then, imitating Gracie, pinned a lace kerchief on her own head.

The room beyond the doors surprised Emma. When she'd gone to church with Grandma Frances, everything had been wooden and dark. Purple, green, and red stained glass scenes filled with Jesus and Mary had blocked the sun. Here, the walls were bright white. The windows opened to the sun except for one cobalt and yellow stained glass window with golden Jewish stars. Twisted metal sculptures hung from the ceiling. Instead of an altar, a lectern covered with a velvet curtain sat on the stage.

Most men wore suits; the women, summer dresses or silky tops. Thin red books and thicker leather-bound blue ones fit in small holders in front of them.

Emma imitated the nearby people and took out a blue book. Caleb and Gracie copied her. Five people circled the lectern; a girl who looked about Emma's age sat on a bench toward the back of the stage.

"Page one fifty-four," said a woman onstage. "We will read from a

Psalm of David when he changed his behavior before Abimelech, who drove him away, and he departed."

Emma riffled the soft thin pages, confused when she saw page one at the back until she remembered the Haggadahs Grandpa Jake passed out at Seders. Hebrew was on the right side of the book, English on the left.

The redheaded girl onstage walked to the podium, an ice-blue dress floating around her. She placed two hands on the lectern and began reading in Hebrew.

"Who's that?" Caleb whispered.

"Shh." Emma cut her eyes hard and mean.

"Why is a kid up there?" he persisted.

"I don't know," Emma hissed.

"What is she saying?"

An old woman turned around in front of them.

Emma got ready to be thrown out.

"That's my great-grandniece," the woman said. "She's having her bat mitzvah."

Perhaps Emma's brother looked as ignorant as he was because she whispered a few more words. "Because she's turning thirteen." The woman's thickly lipsticked mouth stretched into a broad red smile. She reached over and patted Caleb's hand. "Thanks for coming."

"Were we invited?" Caleb asked.

"You don't have to be invited to a bat mitzvah service. Everyone's welcome." She looked at the three of them, her face friendly. "Come say hello at the kiddush. Have some cake."

Emma squeezed Caleb's hand. *Keep quiet or else.*

"Can we go? To the kiddush?" Gracie whispered. Caleb looked at Emma.

"If you both shut up for the rest of the time."

Caleb pressed his lips together in an exaggerated show of compliance, and Gracie brought her hand to her mouth.

• • •

"Why can't I ask what kind of cookies these are? They taste horrible."
Caleb held up a flaky spiral of browned dough.

"Then don't eat them," Emma said. "You can't ask because we'll
look retarded." They were sitting at a small table in the corner. Everywhere people hugged and kissed.

"Don't say *retarded*," Gracie said. "It's disrespectful."

"That's right. Mommy says it's disrespectful," Caleb repeated.

Emma's eyes filled. She hoped everyone stayed near the tables
piled with bagels and bowls of cream cheese and didn't come near
them.

"Don't cry." Caleb sounded panicked. "I'll eat the cookie."

Gracie took Emma's hand. "You can say *retarded*. It doesn't matter.
We know you're good." Gracie's eyes welled. "Why are you crying?"

Emma blinked until her tears disappeared. "I'm okay," she whispered. "Let's go."

"But that woman said we could talk to her."

"Please, Caleb. We don't belong here."

"Because we're only half?" Gracie asked.

"*We just don't belong.*" Emma emphasized each word.

People greeted one another with shrieks of delight. The woman
who'd sat in front of them put her hands on the bat mitzvah girl's
shoulders, holding her at arm's length, smiling. Emma smoothed her
denim skirt.

"I thought we were going to pray for Mommy." Caleb laced his
hands in a prayerful position. "What happens if we don't?"

Emma shrugged. "Maybe it doesn't matter."

"Yes, it does. You said so. It has to matter." His voice rose. "Mommy
will die otherwise. *You said!*"

The rabbi walked toward them from across the room. Emma pulled
her brother close. "Caleb, you need to stop right now. Mommy will be
okay. This was just like . . . This was just like going to a prayer store."

The rabbi got closer. A little throw-up came to her throat.

"Emma?" Despite his gray hair, he had a young face.

"Who are you?" Caleb asked.

The rabbi placed a hand on Caleb's shoulder. "I'm Rabbi Berger. And you?"

"Caleb." His voice shook. "Are you in charge? Are we in trouble?"

The rabbi smiled and knelt to Caleb's level. "Yes, I'm in charge. Moreover, no, you are not in trouble. I'm the one who answered your sister's email. We're happy to have you here, though it's unusual to have young people come without a parent or grandparent."

"Our Jewish parent is our mother, and she's in the hospital," Gracie said.

"I'm so sorry." The rabbi wrinkled his forehead and then stood. "Why don't you three come to my office?"

Emma shrugged and nodded to her brother and sister. They followed him to a cozier-looking part of the building, the rabbi speaking about nothing in particular as he pointed out this painting and that sculpture, as though they were in a museum.

"Ah, home at last." He stopped in front of a glass door, which he opened with a key. "Welcome."

His office had a desk area and a section with a leather couch and soft chairs. Piled next to the tightly packed bookshelves were stacks of more books. Chairs were lined up in front of his desk, and he gestured for them to sit.

The rabbi folded his hands on his desk. "Perhaps you can tell me what brings you here today."

Gracie covered the tiny angel pinned to her shirt. "We're praying for our mother to wake up. She's in a coma."

"I'm so very sorry," he said again. He reached over and gently touched Gracie's hand. "Does the angel provide comfort?"

Gracie uncovered the angel. "My grandmother gave it to me."

"The Catholic one," Caleb said.

"Seems like you have all bases covered," the rabbi said. "It's okay— it's not as though we're competing baseball teams."

He sounded like Emma's crappy teachers did when they shared some joke that only they knew.

"They never make us, um, take sides," Emma said.

The rabbi shook his head. "I'm just teasing a little. Many of our families are of mixed faith. So—it's your mother that brings you here today. Are you seeking solace from God?"

"What's solace?" Caleb asked.

"It means comfort," the rabbi said.

"Is that what a synagogue offers? Comfort?" Emma asked.

"What do you think?" the rabbi asked. "What do you expect?"

Emma looked to the ceiling, uncomfortable with the rabbi's intense stare. How much could he care what she thought? He was playing a game with her. She shrugged. "I don't know."

"Why did you come?" he asked.

Emma crossed her arms, tired of the rabbi's quizzing. *Just tell us what to do.* "People always talk about God. *Thanks, God. God forbid. God only knows. Leave it in the hands of God.*" She took a deep breath. "Or they get mad. *God damn it.*"

"*God damn it to hell,*" Caleb said in a perfect imitation of their father.

Gracie smiled and held tight to the angel. "*Holy Mary, Mother of God,*" she said in imitation of Grandma Frances's high voice.

"Sounds like you children get quite a few voices of God." The rabbi placed an ankle on one knee and tapped it as though summoning wisdom. "People search for God when they're in pain. Sometimes when they're seeking joy. It sounds like you're searching for a healing."

"Will God hear us better if we pray from here?" Gracie gripped the edge of the rabbi's desk.

The rabbi placed his hand on his heart. "God will hear you wherever you speak." He turned to Emma. "Sometimes, in the act of seeking God, we learn what else we are looking for. Like love. Do we seek God when we are actually seeking love? On the other hand, do we seek love when we are really seeking God? It is also like that with prayer and help."

"Right." Emma nodded, understanding nothing except her sudden hatred of this man.

The rabbi smiled. "There are no fast answers. It's a question of what we want from our faith. And how we find faith. And in whom we place our trust."

"My father almost killed my mother," Caleb blurted.

"What?" The rabbi straightened from his know-it-all lecture position.

"It's not what you think!" Emma said quickly, imagining the rabbi calling the police. "It was an accident. They had a car accident. It was raining."

"My grandfather thinks my father was driving too fast. And maybe he was mad," Caleb said.

Gracie, who sat closest to the rabbi, leaned over and placed her hand on his. "Don't worry—it was just a terrible accident. Everyone knows that."

"Perhaps I should call someone," the rabbi said. "Do you feel safe at home? You sound troubled. We have a wonderful, kind social worker on staff here who I'm certain can help you all. I'd like you to speak with her."

A social worker? Her mother was a social worker—Emma knew the message he was sending with his prayerful words. They'd come home to someone questioning their father. She had to get them out of there. "We're fine. Our father is at work. We just came here to pray for our mother to get better. That's all we wanted. We have a large family. Everyone's pitching in."

Complications came no matter what Emma tried to do. She couldn't fix anything. "We better get home." She stood and then reached out a hand for her brother and another for her sister, squeezing hard the moment they touched, sending them the message to keep their mouths shut. "And we already have someone—a social worker from the hospital that we speak to. Her name is Olivia."

Later that day, Emma sat on the floor behind her mother's desk, opening up drawers, looking through files, reading old bills and bank statements. Emma found a blue folder with pictures of her sixth birthday party. After spreading them on the floor, she got on her knees and studied them. Her mother looked a little fat; she must have been pregnant with Caleb—not like now: bones sticking out, pinched and taped, wires slithering all over her.

That rabbi had let her and Gracie and Caleb simply walk out after hearing their story. She'd fooled him just fine. Her mother would never do that if three kids wandered into her office.

Emma pushed the pictures away and grabbed books from the bottom shelves until she found *The Merck Manual*—the book her mother consulted when anyone in the family showed signs of illness. She opened to the index and scanned the Cs for *coma. Diabetic coma. Hepatic coma. Myxedema coma.* Nothing fit; nothing made sense. She threw the book on the floor on top of an old copy of *The Joy of Cooking* she'd pulled out. Yeah. Big joy. If she made one more sandwich she'd scream her head off.

Emma began stacking books back on the shelves. As she put back *The Family of Man*, a letter fell out of the book, a long passage in her father's writing.

Dear Maddy,

In one month, we'll become a family of three (and then maybe four, or five?).

I know, I know. You don't want to talk about it yet. Get this one out first, right?

(See, I do listen sometimes!)

Happy Anniversary, sweetheart. The bracelet's to complement your beauty (which I should compliment more—I know, I know), and the book is to complement your heart. (And compliment it.) I want you to know that I don't ever forget for one day how big it is. (Bigger even than your belly. ☺) You complement me. Forgive me the days it seems I forget. Perhaps at those times, you can bring out this book, read this, and remember . . .

"Emma?"

She looked up. Her father stood in the doorway. She shoved the book back in the case and kicked the files and photographs under the desk.

"What're you doing, honey? How were the kids?" He sank into the leather club chair and let his head fall back. "Sorry about being so late.

I spent a little extra time with Mommy. How about I take us out for Chinese food? Or maybe order in?"

Emma scrambled up from behind the desk. "You never do what you're supposed to. Never. Not Mommy either. And you never do what you promise."

"What are you talking about? What's wrong?" Her father's voice sounded scratchy. His suit was crumpled, and there was a big stain on his tie. Part of her wanted to shut up and hug him, but instead a hot stream of angry words poured out.

"I didn't even get a bat mitzvah. Nothing. You and Mommy just . . . You . . ." Emma began screaming so loud her throat hurt. "*You probably drove like an asshole and you were probably yelling at her. Right? How could you do that, Daddy? How could you be so stupid?*"

"Emma, it wasn't—"

"I hate everything. I hate this house the way it is. I hate having to do everything. I hate you both." She slammed out of the study, tears streaming, shaking, and wanting nothing else in the world so much as for her mother to be upstairs, ready to ask her what was wrong.

CHAPTER 18

Maddy

She blinked.

Sticky eyes.

Turning her head, bending iron.

"Do you think she's awake?"

Voices cut through the murk, but weights tied her arms and legs. Gulliver on his travels.

"Maddy, wake up. Wake up."

She tried to pry her pasted eyes apart. They obeyed for an instant. A woman's face came over her. Too close.

"Buh." Her mouth wouldn't obey.

"Maddy, can you hear me?"

Who are you? Where's Ben?

"She opened her eyes."

"Maddy? Maddy? Can you hear me?"

"I think she tried to talk. Did she appear sentient when her eyes opened?"

"It looked that way to me. Her blood pressure's up. Brain activity measures higher."

"Call her husband."

Ben. Ben. Ben. Where's Ben?

Something tugged at the top of her mind. Her brain pulled up and then pushed down. Like the taffy machine in Provincetown. The kids shouldn't eat taffy. They'd get cavities.

Need sleep. Tired.

"Take my hand, Maddy. Here."

Skin against skin. Scraping.

Stop.

She wanted to shake it off, but her arm wouldn't comply.

"Is she squeezing?"

"No. Nothing."

"Should we page her neurologist?"

"Jesus, yes."

"He'll kill us if it's nothing. He's such a bastard."

"Her father will kill us if we don't."

Kill a neurologist? Daddy? Neurologist? The word *neurologist* haunted her. She chewed, almost tasted the meaning, and then it disappeared. Sleep.

"Squeeze, Maddy, squeeze. Squeeze."

Push, Maddy, push, push, push. Come on. You can do it. Oh, my God. Look. She's here! Maddy, look. Our baby. Oh, I love you.

"Is she smiling? It looks like she's smiling."

The light went out. Blocked. Someone leaned over. Face almost kissing hers, smothering her.

Go away.

CHAPTER 19

Ben

Ben shuffled through the piles of papers on his desk, not caring about any of them. Add it to his list of fuckups: ignoring work.

A fuckup? Elizabeth is on your list of "fuckups"? Try sin, buddy boy.

He could list both his fuckups and his sins all too quickly. Ben Illica, master of sin. Venial. Mortal. Get 'em here.

Sin: Throwing a bottle of Tide against the wall. Watching the viscous fluid run down the gray basement wall. Maddy cowering. Why had he been so angry?

Sin: Refusing to accompany Maddy to her fifteenth high school reunion because she'd bought five-year-old Emma an expensive doll.

Sin: Grabbing Caleb and shaking him until Maddy tackled him from behind.

Sin: Driving like a fucking lunatic.

And now.

There wasn't a help sheet in the world Maddy could give him now. He'd broken their vows.

His membership in the thirty percent club was over.

On the computer screen, an endless email from Aaron Manning scrolled, looking for help with some of the trial work with which

Ben had stuck him. Aaron could plead out B-bird's case, but B-bird's mother insisted on a trial. *Could you talk to her?* Aaron wrote.

What Ben wanted to write was: *Dear Aaron: Who gives a fuck? Lock him up. Protect the city. Thanks! Good work, buddy.*

But what he actually typed was: *Aaron, I am confident of your ability to handle the conversation. Too overloaded to speak to mother. Appreciate you handling this.* He pressed send. Being the boss made it easier not to give a damn.

According to the catechism drummed in and chanted back at Our Lady of Life Sucks, mortal sin *must be of a grave matter*. It must be committed with full knowledge that it is a mortal sin. It must be committed with full consent. Thus, sleeping with Elizabeth constituted a worse sin than almost killing Maddy.

No wonder he hated church.

He dug out a Maddy folder and opened it at random, praying that pretending it would all be okay would bring that miracle. Masses of information had been cited, categorized, and then underlined where Olivia thought he had the greatest chances of screwing up.

> Stages of Recovery: Fatigue is a primary problem. Insight is v.v. poor. Maddy might deny there are problems and rebel against her need for rehabilitation. She may endanger others with her actions. You must be vigilant at all times and enlist "minders" when you're not there.

Finding "minders" for Maddy would be Christmas compared to his nightly hospital visit. He skimmed paragraphs, stopping at *Amnesia*.

> At the moment of injury, the brain stops storing memories. This is why it's pointless for the patient to waste energy trying to remember the accident. You don't need to worry about the accident's emotional effects if she does not get this memory back. Things that happened immediately before and at the time of the impact did not have time to be changed into memories, so they can never be remembered.

Ben studied the words until a knock on his half-open door interrupted.

"What are you up to?" Elizabeth leaned against the doorjamb in a manner designed to seem casual. She twirled a strand of loose hair.

"Just clearing the decks before lunch," Ben answered.

Elizabeth sat across from him. She reached over the desk and briefly touched the dark hair above his wrist. "Are we okay?"

Captured. He'd managed to avoid being alone with her during the ten days since they'd slept together. *Were they okay?* Sure. As long as she knew there was no "we." Elizabeth looked at him with the soft melting eyes women had in the early throes of crushes—before rage and pain joined the party.

When he didn't answer, she walked behind him and leaned ever so lightly against the back of his chair. Ben felt her long white fingers brush his neck, so swiftly he could have imagined it, smelled her understated perfume. Some combination of low-pressure flowers.

"Are we? Okay?" she asked. "Are you?"

"For Christ's sake, Elizabeth." He reached up and removed her hands from his shoulders. "The door is open."

She walked over, shut it, and returned. She stared at him with all those questions in her eyes.

The first time he'd seen Maddy, she'd burned his eyes right out of his head. Orange stained glass windows made the sun flare outside the old courtroom where they met. Her skin, her eyes, her hair, all shades of drowning black and gold, outlined by light as though God had created her just for him. A month later, when Ben brought Maddy to his office Christmas party, she'd worn blackberry velvet, the soft fabric cut low in the back. As they danced, her bare flesh warmed his hand.

"Don't," he told Elizabeth, now in his guest chair.

"Don't what?" Elizabeth twined her fingers into a tight ball.

"Don't anything." Ben held up his left hand, visible proof of why not. The nurses had removed Maddy's rings. To avoid germs. And comas made fluid settle—Maddy's fingers had swollen.

"It meant something to me. Our night together."

Ben stifled a sigh. "I'm sorry about . . . about confusing you."

"You felt something, right?" She leaned toward him. "It wasn't just . . . a thing?"

Jesus, go away. "You're an incredible woman. But you know we can't have anything." What he wanted to say was *Pretend this never happened, rewind, erase, delete.*

Elizabeth squared her shoulders. "I just wonder if you care about me at all."

Do I care about you?

I will go from here to visit my unconscious wife.

Do I care about you?

I want you to disappear.

An hour later Ben read a trial transcript as he ate lunch. He took another tired bite of the turkey sandwich Anne had made him. He turned a page by pushing it with his clean pinkie. One pile of paper had lowered by a few inches.

Ben startled at the ringing phone. He'd asked to have his calls held. "Illica," he answered.

"Ben? It's Nurse Bernadette. From the hospital."

"What's wrong?"

"It's not wrong, it's good."

"What's good?"

"We think she's waking up, Ben."

His chest pounded. "Did you call her parents?"

"Not yet. We were just about to."

"Let me," he said. "I'm on my way."

"Maddy?" Ben ran a finger down her arm. He outlined the rough red skin around her mouth where they'd removed the tape when she began breathing on her own. That's when they'd moved her from intensive care. Jake had insisted on a private room with a private nurse when they took the tube out. *The minute it's out,* he'd demanded. *A private room with around-the-clock nursing. I don't care what it costs.* He'd glared at Ben, his hands stiffening into fists, as though Ben would argue against his wife's comfort.

"Maddy. Sweetheart. I'm here." Ben pulled the chair closer to the bed. He'd sent the nurse out. He and Maddy were truly alone for the first time since the accident.

He put his mouth close to her ear. "Can you hear me, Mad?" He tried willing her awake, awkwardly following Bernadette's instructions to envision Maddy opening her eyes and smiling. "Press my hand if you hear me."

The clock on the wall ticked forward one more second. A truck beeped. Midday sun splattered patterns on the bright quilt folded on the chair. Anne put it across Maddy each time she came, despite knowing the nurses would remove it as soon as she left, concerned about temperature control—not believing that Anne's mother's instinct trumped their medical wisdom.

"Please wake up." Ben put his head lightly on her breast, listening to her blood pulse, speaking straight into her heart. "I'm spinning out, baby."

Anne rushed in. "Is she awake?"

Ben sat up, holding Maddy's limp hand in his. "I haven't seen anything."

"Why didn't they call me right away?"

"They phoned my office. I called you as soon as I got here."

"So why didn't you call me from the office?" Anne approached the bed, the lines on her face emphasized by harsh hospital light. "Maddy, sweetie, baby, I'm here." Anne enunciated each word. "Daddy's on his way. With Gracie and Caleb. Vanessa's picking up Emma."

She edged him away, stroking Maddy's cheek as though she were a baby. "You had a car accident, darling."

Ben looked for a reaction, a sign that Maddy heard. Anne lifted her eyebrows, commanding him to talk. He cleared his throat. "You're going to be okay, honey. I promise." His wife's fingers felt papery, like onionskin.

"The children started school," Anne said. "Guess what? I offered to make them all sorts of fancy things to take to school, but they chose peanut butter and jelly. Like Mommy makes, they said."

"Guess what else," Ben's stomach cramped in fear. Where was she? "I've been taking sandwiches to work also. Your mother is spoiling me—you better get out of bed fast."

Anne gave a theatrical chuckle. "He wants you to get up so you can work? You wake up, and I'll take you to a spa like you wouldn't believe."

She inclined her head at Ben's hand holding Maddy's, where he caressed her knuckles—the part of her that seemed hardiest at the moment. "Move your fingers, Ben. You'll wear away the skin going over and over the same spot. Right, sweetheart?" Anne lifted her voice on the last two words, including Maddy in the conversation as though some unseen expert whispered in Anne's ears on how to handle the situation.

Ben heard running footsteps, then his father-in-law's voice. "Slower, kids. *Stop!* You'll break your neck!"

"Mommy?" Gracie's anxious question preceded her entrance.

"Mommy, are you awake?" Caleb's words exploded from him as he ran in. "Mommy! *You're alive!*"

Ben caught Caleb before his son jumped onto the bed. "Calm down, cowboy." Neither Gracie nor Caleb had seen Maddy since the accident. Maybe they hadn't even believed she was alive.

"Where's Emma?" Gracie asked.

"Aunt Vanessa's bringing her, darling." Jake pressed Gracie toward the bed. "Talk to Mommy, honey. Like we said in the car—to bring her back."

"Maybe," Ben emphasized. "Maybe to bring her back."

Anne glared at him. She smoothed Maddy's uneven hair, avoiding the shiny skin rising around the scar on her left temple.

Jake scowled. "Be positive. We're bringing Maddy to the light on the surface." Hearing Jake repeat Anne's words felt like watching his father-in-law drape chiffon scarves around his razor-scraped neck.

"The kids shouldn't think that they're responsible for Maddy waking up," Ben said.

"Oh, my God," Anne whispered. "Were we making them think that?"

Gracie wrapped her arms around her grandmother. "Don't worry, Grandma. Daddy's not mad at you."

Vanessa swept into the room, leaving Emma in her wake. "Why are you crying, Mom? What happened? Ben?"

"Daddy didn't do anything," Gracie said. "He just wants us to be careful."

"Nobody's blaming Daddy." Jake smoothed the quilt Anne had placed over Maddy. "Why don't I go get some soda for everyone? The kids must be hungry and thirsty after school."

"No soda," Vanessa said. "They'll just get a sugar high. Look at Caleb."

Caleb perched so precariously at the edge of Maddy's bed he could barely stay on without falling.

"Be careful, don't hurt Mommy," Vanessa said.

"I'm not." Caleb's voice was muffled, his head buried in Maddy's white hospital blanket. "She likes it. I can tell."

"We have to be calm. And quiet," Emma whispered. "Like it says in the book."

Ben felt as though he'd lost his chance. He'd wanted to be alone with Maddy, to be the first one she saw.

"*Daddy, look!*" Gracie tugged his jacket sleeve.

Ben looked. Maddy's thumb swept a slow arc through their son's hair. Gracie and Emma came to him, one on each side. Holding hands, they walked to the side of the bed next to Caleb and stood.

CHAPTER 20

Maddy

"Want . . . home." Words weighed so much.

Ben nodded. "I know, baby. I want you to come home, but first, you need the rehabilitation center. Remember?"

Maddy squeezed her eyes.

She tried to concentrate.

"Laigh ning?" she asked.

Everyone kept telling her she was . . . what? Lighting? Lighting up? Hit by lightning? She was lightening?

"Lightening, Maddy," Ben said. "It's what you're going through . . . coming up a little at a time. It feels like coming up from underwater, right?"

She tried to repeat the word. "Laight. Nnnng." Words, so clear in her head, slipped out soft and slurry. Mercury words.

"Do you remember, Maddy?" her father's voice boomed.

DO YOU? DO YOU? DO YOU, MADDY?

"We just told you this five minutes ago, honey," her father insisted. "Remember?"

REMEMBER? REMEMBER? REMEMBER?

"She needs to hear things repeatedly." Ben put a whisper-soft hand on her knee. "Her memory is shaky."

"I know, I know." Maddy's father paced back and forth at the end of her bed. "Where's Annie, for God's sake? How long could it take to drive over from Coolidge Corner?"

When she or Vanessa made their father mad, he'd huff and turn to their mother with bullet eyes. *Annie, take care of this.* This she remembered.

"She'll be here soon," Ben told her father.

"Why the hell is it taking so long?" Her father walked to the window.

Her eyes closed. She opened them again, trying to speak, wondering why her hands were fluttering in slow circles. "Mom? Loost?"

Her father went to the foot of her bed. "Of course she's not lost, baby." He grabbed her toes, holding a foot in each of his calloused hands.

"Stoh . . . stoh." Maddy tried to pull away from his firm grip.

"What's wrong?"

Why couldn't she pull her legs away?

Finally. Her feet were free. She could wiggle her toes. "Hat. Hat . . . that."

"You love having your feet massaged," he insisted.

"Haaaat," she tried to scream. She hated it, and she hated her father for not knowing she didn't like it. Words roared inside and came out as little whispers. "Foook." Her breath caught with each labored sob. "Foook . . . foook. Foook."

Her father rubbed her arm until it felt like the Indian burns she and Vanessa gave each other as kids. *Up burn. Down burn.* Her huffy sobs came faster. "Staa. Staaaa."

"What, Maddy? What?" Her father gripped her arm until she moaned, and Ben peeled his hands away.

"She's saying stop," Ben said. "She doesn't want you to touch her."

Salt stung her eyes. Mucus clogged her nose. "Stah."

"I'm sorry, baby." Her father spoke too loud. He hurt her ears. *I'M SORRY, BABY.*

"It's not you, Jake," Ben said. "Maddy feels overstimulated. Remember what Dr. Paulo told us? Physical touch overwhelms her—we have to gauge everything through her reactions."

Ben's words were soft. Running word rivers. She floated in Ben River. Sun poured . . . Ben-words were cushions for floating.

"We love you," her father said.

Too loud! "Staaaa."

"What's she saying?"

"She's still trying to say stop," Ben said. "Why don't you give us a minute?"

"You want me to leave?" her father asked.

"Just give us a moment alone, okay? I have to get her ready for the transfer. When she gets upset, it's even harder for her to talk."

"Noo. Staa." *Quiet, please, please, please, quiet.*

"See, she doesn't want me to go."

"That's not why she's saying no," Ben said.

She opened her eyes. Trying to focus. Like squeezing a muscle. Concentrating. Pushing baby carriage up a hill. Trying to get a word out. Lost her breath.

"Ben. Waaaaant. Ben. Peeease." Slop speech. Cement. Last stage before hardening.

Her father backed away from her bed, putting his hands up in front of him. "I'll call your mother—see what's keeping her."

Her breathing slowed. Her father started to bend, looming over her, and then stopped. "I love you, Maddy."

"La. Lo, Daaa." He walked away. The door whooshed shut. Ben's hand soft, soft, teensy touch landed on her cheek. She turned into it. His hand cupped her face. She caught his hand between her face and shoulder. Her tears wet his hand and then came back on her. "La lo, Ben."

"Shh, shh. I love you too." Ben reached into his pocket and brought out his folded white handkerchief. After wiping her eyes, he held the white cloth to her nose. "Blow. Can you blow, Mad?"

She tried to blow but didn't have the power. Panicked, she rocked forward. Tried to clear her nose, her throat. Ben put his broad arm behind her, lifted her forward, stuffed pillows behind her, and traced soft circles. "It's okay. Breathe out. Breathe slowly. It will come back."

She tried to breathe through her mouth. In and out. One. Two. One. Two. In time to the circles. Ben put the handkerchief back to her nose. Maddy blew until her nose cleared and then fell back into the pillows. Exhausted. Closed her eyes.

"I'm going to wash your face, Mad. Just shake your head if it doesn't feel good, hon."

Ben swept the hot moist cloth over her skin. Over her temples, her cheeks, around her neck. Another little towel. He patted the wet from her face, and then took her hands, one at a time, and wiped each one with the damp cloth. Cleaned each finger separately. Like she'd cleaned Caleb's hands. Caleb was her sloppy eater.

"Than . . . than."

"Shh. No thanking needed, honey."

"I . . . I . . ." She aimed all the power she had into her throat. "Nee tahk."

"It's temporary, it will just take time. Remember?"

"Wha ha?"

"You were in a car accident. Remember?"

Remember. Remember. Remember.

"Caah?"

"You hurt your brain." Ben crouched next to the bed so they were eye to eye. "And the muscles around your mouth have been affected. It's called dysarthria. *Dis-ahr-three-uh.* The muscles are slowed. It's hard for you to move them. It will heal, Mad. I know it's frustrating. Your speech can't keep up with your thoughts, and you can't hear everything right—the processing button is off."

She stared at him. Processing button! Like their oil burner's red button. Restart. She needed to push restart. "So . . . so . . ." How to say *tired*? Exhaustion bore down like a thousand-year flu. "Tar . . . ed."

"I know. You're tired. You've been sleeping," he said. "A long time. Weeks."

"Wex? Many?"

How many weeks had she been sleeping? She remembered nothing. Were the kids in the car? Were the kids hurt? Dead? Did she kill her children? Her breath sped up. Fast jerky catches hurt her chest. "Chil . . . ren. Eem? Grazee. Clab?"

Ben kissed her hand. "The kids are fine. They weren't in the car. Just us. It's been three weeks. Well, four now—you woke up a week ago. Shh. It's okay. You're going to be just fine, baby. You'll be in the rehab just for a little while. We're lucky—your body is okay."

She tried to shake her head from side to side. More tears leaked out. Ben wiped them. He rubbed her curls back. Where she had hair. His hand brushed the bad spot. She pulled away.

"Sorry. Let me fix you up a little. For the ride. In the ambulance. I'll be with you."

She sagged into the bed as Ben opened the drawer in the nightstand. "Here we are." He took out a little pink brush. "I'm going to crank up the bed a little." He pushed the pillows to the small of her back. With soft hands, he stroked the baby brush over the outer layer of her thick hair. He brushed it into a lopsided ponytail, looping a red scrunchie around it twice. "I won't be replacing Lola, that's for certain." He smoothed back the hair that escaped.

Lola? She wrinkled her face, trying to remember. "Lo?"

"Your hairdresser," Ben said.

Hairdresser. Dressed her hair. Put on a little hair shirt and hair skirt. She laughed. Ben tried to tuck in her stray curls, smoothing and touching her as though she were Gracie.

"I love you," he said. "I missed you. I need you." He leaned on her shoulder for a moment with a weight she couldn't bear. She tried to shift, slide him off, and succeeded in moving only millimeters.

"Sorry. I forgot. I know. You're all raw skin now. That's what Bernadette said."

She forced a hand over to his. Tapped his knuckle with a finger.

"Bernadette. She's the nurse you like. The one who keeps coming in, remember?"

Remember, remember, remember.

No, she didn't remember. She wanted to go to sleep.

"That's okay. Close your eyes. Rest. I'll read to you." She heard Ben reaching. Cotton shirt rubbed against plastic chair—a soft slidey sound. She felt him put his feet up on the bed railing. Safe.

After

———

OCTOBER

CHAPTER 21

Maddy

Rehab—ha!

Prison.

All of them said it, all the prisoners. After group therapy, they said it. Eating the horrible food, they said it. Begging for snacks, they said it. Playing sadistic brain games, they said it.

Maddy sat on the scratchy orange couch in the rehab lounge room. Lounge room! Ha.

Grunge room. That's what it was. Lavender scent rose from her arm as she reached into her shirt pocket. Vanessa buried her in perfumes, giving her reasons for every one. *Lavender soothes. Cinnamon . . .* What did cinnamon do? She took out the little notebook they made her carry everywhere, opened it to the last page, and found her morning entry written in her shaky hand: *Day 20 rehab hospitl. Thersday October 2. Meat Jack at one. Then do with Zelda.*

Ick, Jack the puzzle man. She hated the puzzle man. She went to the Jack puzzle room. Went to the puzzle table where Jack sat.

"You're late."

Nice way to say hello—fuck Jack.

"You need to remember to get here on time. It's part of your rehab. Now, time to get to work. Sit."

Blah, blah, blah—that's what he sounded like in her head. Jack made her stare at wooden words that made no sense until she squeezed, squeezed, and squeezed her brain. Her head, crystal clear one moment, tangled like twisted chains the next. No one cared. She'd remember, and then, like a snow globe shaken by an evil god, white layers covered her thoughts.

It's the drugs, the rehab counselors said.

Sleep, the rehab nurses said. *You need lots of sleep.*

Your brain is healing, the brain doctor said.

Zelda said that was just the way it was. Up and down. Genius to blockhead and back again. Zelda was her good person helper, the nice one.

"Come on, now, Maddy. You can do it. You did it yesterday," the puzzle man said.

Puzzle Man was her worst jailer. She hated, hated, hated him. What was his name?

Jerry? Joseph? The puzzle man had a *J* name. She knew it. Every day stupid puzzles from the *J* man. The curved plastic chair made her squirm. Never a comfortable spot. Green too. Everything had turned putrid green. Mental-institution green. Green was the color of crazy, though she didn't know why she remembered that. Or if she were correct. But she knew that she hated this place.

Chipped Formica tables were scattered around the puzzle room. They reminded her of the cafeteria in Gracie and Caleb's school. She still hadn't seen them—Gracie and Caleb. Either of them could do the stupid puzzle in three seconds. She missed them. They couldn't come here, Ben said. Too scary.

"One piece at a time," Puzzle Man yelled.

ONE PIECE.

ONE PEACE.

NO PEACE.

"Match it. You have to exercise the memory."

She shook her head, whipping it for him to get the point.

"Nooooo. *She* said no. No exercise. Won't help." Maddy's words huffed and puffed out, slow and wooden. She had to take a breath between every other word. The nice one said it was just a matter of time. *No over and over and over.* Waiting. For healing.

Jack rolled his eyes to show he hated her. "Zelda meant that trying to perform exercise for talking wouldn't help yet. She's right about that."

Zelda. That was the name. Right. She took Zelda breaths to speak right.

"But for memory, you have to practice. Come on, now. I'm waiting." He tapped the puzzle three times. Tap, tap, tap, he rapped her brain.

She tucked her lower lip under her front teeth and concentrated on the wooden puzzle. Black words, stark against green, read *French. Library. Train. Orange.* Below each word, an empty space waited. Four wooden rectangles, each with a little wooden handle sticking out, sat on the table, waiting for her to fill the proper empty puzzle spots. *Station. Juice. Fry. Card.*

"Come on, Maddy. You can match them. Start with one. Which one do you know right away? All you have to do is put it in the right hole."

I know what I'm supposed to do, stupid jerk!

"Fuck."

"Swearing isn't appropriate." He tapped the puzzle again. "You can do this."

She touched the stem of *Juice*, lifted it, and held it, swaying, over the words. *French. Library. Train. Orange.* She mouthed each word. Was there a French juice? There was orange juice. Right? But was there also French juice? There were French fries. Was it a trick question? Banging her knee against the leg of the table, she shook the piece back and forth, finally putting it down. She picked up *Train.* Wasn't there a train card you used to get on the train? She held the puzzle piece over the slot under *Card* and tried to fit it in, finding it impossible to line up the edges. Sweat pooled between her shoulder blades. She was hot and cold, cold and hot, hot, hot.

"Hot."

"Yes, I know. I told you yesterday, remember?"

Remember, remember, remember.

"You'll be hot and cold for a period of time. It's normal for you. Your internal thermostat is adjusting. Remember?"

Remember, remember, remember.

Again, she tried to fit *Card* under *Train.*

"Are you sure that's where you want to put it? Think, Maddy."

Think, Maddy, think, Maddy, think, Maddy.

"Fuck." She banged a wooden card on the edge of the table.

"No swearing! No hitting. Concentrate. Think!"

HATE YOU SO MUCH!

She picked up the puzzle and smashed it on the table.

"Stop it now, Maddy. Right now!"

"Stop . . . it . . . Maddy," she mimicked as she swept the loose pieces to the floor in one satisfying motion.

Puzzle Man leaned over and put his hands, with big fat ugly sausage fingers, on her shoulders. "I said stop."

"Stop. Stop. *You stop!*" She tried to shake off his heavy hands. "*Noooo!*" When he held her, she couldn't catch her breath. She would suffocate and die. She kicked the table legs in rhythm to her words.

"Calm yourself, or I'll be forced to do it for you. Quiet down. You can do it."

"Home . . . home. Go . . . now." She twisted and jerked, trying to get away from him, kicking out, thrusting her legs until she connected with his thigh.

"That's it. Now you'll stop." He went behind the chair and imprisoned her from behind. Cigarette sweat smells overwhelmed her.

"What's going on here?" Boss Nurse appeared like magic. "Jack, what are you doing?"

Jack! His name was Jack.

Back, Jack.

His arms loosened. Maddy shook, angry tears smeared over her face. "*Ben! Want Ben. Call!*"

"She was out of control," Fuck Jack said. "She needed to be restrained."

The nurse put a light hand on her shoulder. "It's okay, Maddy. Jack, why don't you take a break?"

Maddy wrapped her arms around herself, looking at her feet. White sneakers. Her mother brought? Kath?

"I'm fine," she heard Jack say.

"Take a break," Boss Nurse said. "Now."

"But—"

"Now."

Fuck Jack's feet and legs headed toward the doorway. The nurse knelt before Maddy. Muscular thighs stretched white pants. Nurse Sandra. That was her name. *Never Sandy. Sandra. Never Sandy.*

"It's okay, honey." Nurse Sandra, never Sandy, put a large hand on Maddy's forehead and pushed back her sweaty hair. Maddy saw Sandy's thin mustache hairs. "Let's go back to your room. I'm sorry about him."

"No, no. No . . . more. No more."

"No more, hon. I promise." She pushed herself up and held a hand out. "Come on, let's get you freshened up. Soon your handsome husband will be here. Every day at six. What a good man."

Ben joined her for supper every night. Where were the children? Ben had told her, but she couldn't remember. Alone? Children couldn't come to this smelly jail. Emma could come, but only once.

Who was with the children? She shook her head.

Did mustache nurse know?

"Look who's here!" Mustache said.

"Maddy? Are you all right?" Kath! Tears again overwhelmed her. Crybaby. Kath knelt where the nurse had been moments before. She put out her arms, and Maddy fell into the circle.

"He hurt." She had to stop and breathe. "Me. Hurt me."

"Who hurt you?" Kath asked.

"Your friend had an altercation with one of the occupational therapists." Nurse Sandra-never-Sandy Mustache stood with her arms folded. "He had to restrain her."

"Maddy had an *altercation*? What in the world happened?"

"To be honest, I don't yet know." The nurse again put her hand out. "Why don't we sit and talk about this? Someone else will be using this room in a minute."

"Want. Kath." She held her best friend's hand as though Sandra-never-Sandy might pull her away.

"Of course I'm coming with you," Kath said. "Do you want me to call Ben?"

"Yes. Call. Yes, yes, yes. Want Ben."

Dr. Paulo came out from behind his desk when they came into his office. He was a special doctor. For broken brains. Fizziest?

"Maddy." Dr. Paulo patted her upper arm. "Are you okay?"

She frowned as meanly as possible, turning her lips down and making squinty eyes.

"Mr. Illica, good to see you again." He offered Ben his hand. "How are you?"

"I'll be better when I find out why your employee terrified my wife." Ben looked stern. Maddy put her hand out. He held it, squeezing lightly a few times. *It's okay! I'm just scaring him!*

She could read Ben-hand!

"Please, sit. Both of you." Dr. Paulo gestured toward the long brown leather couch. This room looked pretty. When she had her exams with him, they met in a cramped room with two chairs and an examining table. Good chair for him. Bad chair for her.

Ben led her to the couch. "What happened?" he asked.

"First, let me assure you that if Maddy was ill-treated in any way, that staff person will be held accountable. Our patients are our first and only concern."

Ben leaned forward. "Dr. Paulo, if this person—whose name I want immediately—has ill-treated my wife in any way, he will not be accountable. He will be dismissed."

Fitz-a-trist?

Dr. Paulo folded his hands on his big brown desk. "Mr. Illica, you're a lawyer. You know our employees have rights. Due process. Employee confidentiality is at play."

Her chest tightened as she tried to follow the flying words. Ben again placed his hand over Maddy's.

"Maddy is incapable of lying in her condition. Right?" Ben asked.

"Believe me, Mr. Illica; I will not keep an employee who is hurting patients, but I must proceed legally. Trusting in your confidentiality, I will tell you that the man in question is temporarily suspended."

"Still—"

"Please. Let us speak about your wife." He turned his dark sad eyes to Maddy. Dr. Paulo reminded her of a dog. What kind? Floppy long ears. Droopy eyes. What? What kind?

"Are you still scared, Maddy?" the doctor asked.

"Basset!" she shouted, excited by remembering the name.

"Basset?" Ben asked.

"He's a basset," she said.

"Do you mean he's a bastard?" Ben asked.

"*No!* Basset."

Ben shook his head. "I don't understand."

"Basset," she insisted and began crying. Why didn't he understand?

Dr. Paulo handed her a tissue. "Mr. Illica, we all need infinite patience. Including you and me. And most especially the staff. If Maddy gets upset in any way, speech skills become even less accessible. Though she still has complex thoughts, she can't express them. Imagine her frustration!"

She scrunched the tissue. Zelda made more sense. She looked at her fingers. Stretch up. Stretch down. Up. Down. Up—she was happy. Down—she was sad.

Ben punched his fist into his hand. Maddy flinched.

"Look, I will not let my wife be hurt. Emotionally or otherwise. I worry that she'll say the wrong thing and get her feelings hurt and then—"

The doctor held up his hand to stop Ben. She sounded out the words on his jacket pin. *Dr. Paulo. MD. Physiatrist.* Fizziest. "Even when Maddy can't express herself, even when she seems incoherent, she may be able to understand most of what is said. You must always include her and act in ways that honor her comprehension. This will prevent you and others from making hurtful comments to which she cannot respond. She is quite vulnerable to you, Mr. Illica."

He looked at Ben and then at her. With basset eyes. Dr. Paulo never scared her. He clasped his hands and pressed them to his lips for a moment. "The language used to express emotion resides in special sections of the brain. Different from those usually used for speech. Sections used for emotional expression are often less damaged than those used for speech. Can you both follow me? Maddy?"

She shook her head. "No. Zelda says better."

Zelda had a blackboard. She drew the brain. She made circles inside the brain. She labeled the circles. *Emotional Word Place. Regular Word Place.* She made roads to each. The road to the regular word place squiggled in and out. There were secret doors. The road to the emotional word place was smooth and clear.

Dr. Paulo smiled at her. "I agree. Zelda says it better. Mr. Illica, you should make an appointment with her. I know she told you this is why, at this stage, Maddy will reach into the section used to express emotion more often. At times, inappropriately. Swearing and aggressive words will come out at unfortunate times—"

Ben clapped his hands. "Yes. How can I ensure—"

"Mr. Illica," Dr. Paulo interrupted. "I know that this distresses you, your family. And others. However, this inability to express herself properly is far more disturbing to Maddy than it is to you. She *knows* she is floundering. Awareness of one's deficits makes it all the more difficult. It is Maddy's high level of frustration that is evoking these inappropriate words. The calmer the environment, the better for Maddy's recovery."

"Exactly. This is why this incident upsets me. I think it's time to talk about bringing Maddy home and continuing her therapy outpatient," Ben said.

"We can discuss that," the fizziest basset said.

She laid her head on Ben's shoulder and cried once more. Until then, she'd thought they might leave her there forever.

• • •

Ben took her out a few nights later. All night. For the first time. Just the two of them. To ease her, Ben said. Prepare. First this. A hotel. A date? Then, home.

She wore a soft yellow dress Ben had brought to rehab prison. The hotel scared her. Too fancy. Veiny marble. Gold swirling all over the ceiling. They were eating in the hotel restaurant. Her hands shook on the Important White Tablecloth. She might spill everything. But the food made her swoony. Butter thick as she wanted, spread on bread that didn't taste like Communion wafers.

Once she took Communion just to see what the wafer tasted like. Ben joked that she was going to hell, but she ate it anyway. Now she knew a Communion wafer tasted like rehab.

Ben ordered for her. Ravioli. Easy-to-eat creamy meat wrapped in buttery rubber-silk dough. Food could be so good!

"You'll be out in just a few days," Ben said. "I know it's been a long three weeks."

He reached across the table, using his fork to break her apple pie into smaller wedges. The nurses told her how lucky she was to have Ben. That she was lucky she could walk. Pee in the toilet. And make number two.

Lucky! She could poop in the toilet!

Lucky! Just the right part of her brain was jangled and mangled so she could do *all the large motor skills*. Nurses said that like she'd won a giant prize.

Her hair was gone. The whirls and curls were now a little bowl on her head. *We had to even it,* they'd said. Why? Wouldn't the gone side grow to meet the long side? She could have waited. Where was she going?

She took Zelda-type thinking breaths before every move she made, not wanting to end up wearing salad dressing. Ben talked while she tried to be good. Finally, they had dessert. When she picked up the apple pie with two fingers, Ben cleared his throat. She dropped it.

"Sorry." Tears began spilling.

"Shh!! Don't worry about it," he said. "Look at the beautiful sunset."

She looked out the window and watched the sun fall into the water, the airport, and the tiny distant skyline. Everything and nothing seemed familiar.

On Sunday, Ben would take her home. For good. On Sunday. Today was . . . She took out her notebook and peeked at the morning entry. *Day 24. Fryday.*

"You're not going to have to worry about anything ever again, sweetheart. No one will hurt you." He shook his head and reached for her hand. "Ever. If that hospital is lucky, I won't haul them into court. Are you okay?"

"Puzzle Man is. A fuck. Man."

Ben peeked at the next table. "One good thing about your not being able to speak loudly," he said. "Whispering takes the edge off the cursing."

She tried to smile back but instead hiccuped a small sob. "Sorry. Fuck, fuck, fuck. Sorry."

She rested her head on her arms. Her cheek squashed the apple pie. Ben came around the booth and slid in next to her, helping her off the table. She rested her face on his shoulder. Apple pie face. Pat, pat, pat, he touched.

"It's okay. I was just teasing. Please, don't cry. I know you can't help the swearing, honey." He lifted an arm and swirled it in the air at the waiter. "Come on. Let's go upstairs."

She leaned on him as they went out the restaurant door, through the lobby—slow, slow, with Maddy planning each step to show Ben that she was good. That he should take her home and not leave her in the rehab.

He murmured soft words as she might have done with Gracie.

She would disappear without him.

"Here we go," he said when the elevator came, his hand tucked in the small of her back.

The elevator doors closed, and she grabbed him. "I. Love." She pulled him close. She needed him. Now. Two floors up the elevator stopped. An elderly couple entered, and Ben gently pushed her a bit away. She threw her arms tighter around him and pressed her lips deep into the hollow of his neck, pushing aside his starched collar. Stabbing hard desire for him hit her deep inside.

"I want. I want . . . f—"

Ben pressed his lips to hers.

They got off at the seventh floor. Ben turned to the elderly couple. "Good night."

Zelda had warned Maddy that she'd have little control. Sexual need will pierce you with a ferocity that seems uncontrollable. Maddy saw the truth of her counselor's words. At supper she'd almost kissed the handsome waiter. To thank him. For being handsome. She had to pinch hard on wanting that handsome-waiter-kiss or she'd have jumped right on him.

Ben opened room 719. Subdued light fell over ivory walls. An ocean of cream-colored carpet lay in front of them. Abstracts dotted the walls. Bags covered the bed.

"What's. What's that?" she asked.

"Presents. Remember, I told you that you didn't need to pack a thing, right?"

Remember, remember, remember.

"Your mother did it all. I called her and told her to buy a few things and have them sent."

Bags were everywhere. She touched a corner of a glossy brown one. Burying her, was that her plan? She looked up at Ben to share the joke but didn't know how.

She pushed all the bags off the bed.

"Are you okay, Maddy?" Ben came toward her. She held out her hand. They laced their fingers. She pulled him on the bed.

"Lie . . . next. To me."

"Maddy. I'm not sure—"

"I'm sure. Married. Right?" She kissed every bare piece of Ben's skin within reach of her lips. His cheeks, his neck, his forehead. "Please, Ben. Want normal."

He put his hands to her shoulders. Gentle. Like she'd shatter.

"Won't break, Ben." She climbed on top, hungry to have every part of her touch some part of him. She pressed her breasts into his chest, matched their legs bone for bone until her feet touched his ankles. Starving, needing his skin against her lips, she buried her face in his neck. Too many barriers. She ripped his shirt apart, yanking it away from his chest. Heat rose from the white cotton. She yanked off her dress. And pressed her body to his, only her bra between them.

After unbuckling his belt, he stripped off his pants. Then everything. Holding her hand, he pulled down the bedcovers, exposing the expanse of white linens and pillows.

They fell back onto the bed. She pulled him until he covered her, stretched out her arms, took her hands, and matched their limbs again. He breathed into her ear. Hair on his chest rubbed against her breasts. She turned her head to his neck. Wanting him to be the only part of the world that she could see.

CHAPTER 22

Emma

"Put on your jacket," Emma said.

"I don't need a jacket." Caleb twisted the knob on the front door back and forth until Emma was ready to smack him.

"It's freezing out."

Weeks of school had gone by, and not one person in her family had a clue that Emma had become the family slave. Clean clothes for school? Emma. Buying school supplies for everyone? Emma. Checking Caleb's reading list and washing his pissy sheets? Emma.

Emma had entered ninth grade as an entirely different person— not almost fifteen, more like almost thirty. And though her father treated her like a grown-up when he needed her, the moment he wanted to shut her up, he demoted her back to kid.

In two days, her mother returned home. A queasy awful feeling came over her at the thought. She should be jumping for joy. Instead, all she could think about was what her mother would be like when she came home. The stammering, scared woman she'd seen at the hospital—was that now her mother?

Emma could fall asleep right now. Washed out—that's how she

felt. As though all the color had leached out of her. Her hair would be transparent soon, and her eyes would look like quartz.

"Wait right here." She squeezed her brother's shoulder to emphasize her words. Before he could yap at her, she slipped into the hall bathroom. The pile of Dixie cups on the counter looked gross. Caleb, their in-house ecoterrorist, kept putting back his used ones. Emma slipped a clean cup out from the bottom of the stack and filled it with cold water.

After a moment's hesitation, she pulled a small plastic bag from her pocket. She rattled the ten pills for a moment, then reached in, popped one in her mouth, chased it with water, and swallowed.

With one scowl in the mirror, she jammed the Baggie back next to her hip bone.

"I didn't move," Caleb said when she came out.

"You're a miracle child." Emma reached into the closet and pulled out Caleb's green fleece jacket.

"Here. Put it on." Emma held out the jacket for Caleb, who struggled to get his arms in.

"It's too small," he whined.

He was right. "Dad!" she called upstairs.

"What?" Her father's disembodied voice sounded annoyed. Snafu. Just like good old Dad always said: Situation Normal. All Fucked Up.

"Caleb's coat is too small," she yelled.

"So find him one that fits."

No problem, Dad. I'll reach into my invisible department store.

"Try one of Gracie's," her father added.

"I'm not wearing a girl coat," Caleb screamed.

"She has the denim one. That's for girls or boys," Ben yelled back.

Gracie appeared at the top of the stairs. "Don't take my jacket!"

Her father's voice got louder. "Emma, all of you, figure something out. I'll be there in a minute, and when I get there, you'd better be ready to leave."

Caleb wrestled his arms into his coat. Gracie ran downstairs, grabbed her own denim jacket from the closet, and ran back upstairs with it.

"Emma, help!" The too-small jacket had imprisoned Caleb's arms. "Get me out."

She grabbed the jacket, yanked it off her brother, and threw it on the hall bench. "That's it. No more. I'm leaving. Tell Dad I'm taking the bus."

She walked out before her father appeared, before Caleb could ask a million questions: *Why are you leaving; which jacket should I wear; when is Mommy coming home; what did Grandma make for lunch, for supper, for snack; what's on TV tonight; can I have a cookie?*

Emma ran to the bus stop. When she didn't see one coming, she continued walking. Who cared? She'd catch one, or one would catch her, or she'd just walk to school. Nobody would worry about her.

Emma found Zach in the school library, reading at a table. She came up behind him, waiting for him to sense her. He turned around, grinned, and pretended to clutch his heart like an old man. "You're early. I'm shocked."

Emma sat across from Zach and put her feet on the edge of his chair—looking around first to see if the librarian was watching. "I hate my house. I hate living there. I hate my father."

"Bad morning?"

"Caleb was a brat." That sounded so nothing, as though Emma herself were the brat for complaining about a minor scuffle. She could hear her father: *That's because you were being reductionist, Emma*. And she could hear her mother: *Whah wrung?*

"What was he doing?"

"Nothing. Just being himself." Emma picked up *Calculus in Action* and put it back on the table. "I walked out without telling my father," she confessed. "Let him take care of the kids for a change."

"You shouldn't have done that, Em. He needs you, you know."

"Don't I need someone?"

"Your father is probably fried."

"Trust me. He didn't exactly appreciate my mother before the accident." She shuffled the pile of books in front of him. "You don't understand; your family is so perfect."

"Just because my family doesn't scream and yell at each other doesn't make them unflawed. Anyway, would you feel better if my family was as screwed up as yours?"

"I didn't say my family was screwed up." As she spoke, she imagined Caleb and Gracie shrinking back from her father as he screamed and yelled when he discovered Emma had left.

"Sorry. I meant 'screwed up' as in bad things happening to them. To you." He touched his fingertips to hers.

Emma knew he was lying, but who cared. He was just trying to please her. She wished she were with Caro. At least she could be a bitch to her without feeling bad.

"Let's cut school. I can't stand being in one place right now." Words flew out as though she were manufacturing them at hyperspeed. "Wouldn't that be a good thing? You and I spending the day together? I mean you and me? Right?"

Zach laughed as though she'd told a joke.

"No, really." Caro had been right about the pills. Powerful. That's how she felt. Caro had a prescription for them, so they couldn't be bad, right? She said it was just to improve concentration, that's all. And it helped when you were tired. She made Ritalin sound like a vitamin when she offered them to Emma.

"No way, really. My father would kill me," Zach said.

"How would your father know?" she asked.

Zach clicked his pen until Emma was ready to grab it and throw it at him. "He knows everything. Besides, don't they send something home?"

For someone bound for medical school, Zach was an idiot. "They don't send home a letter for being absent for one day."

"Someone could see us," he said.

Emma tapped her feet against the chair. "Come on, Zach. We can go to my house." She paused and added, "No one's there."

"Are you sure this is okay?" Zach asked as they walked up the stone path to her front door.

"I already said yes a million times." Emma pulled her keys out of her jeans pocket. After opening the door, she turned to him. "Everything's a mess."

"Who cares?" Once they were inside, Zach seemed more self-assured, while Emma wished she were in English class where she was supposed to be at that moment. The burst of pill energy had become a screeching in her head. It seemed wrong, so wrong, being in the empty house with Zach. He hadn't even met her parents—unless you counted the time her father snatched her off the street.

"Are you hungry?" she asked. Had Gracie and Caleb finished the cookies Grandma made? "Want one of my grandmother's cookies? They're good. Peanut butter with a Hershey's Kiss."

"How about an Emma kiss?" Zach put his arms around her and pulled her close.

Until now, their touching had been outside, hidden only by trees. They couldn't go very far in public. Now what?

He pressed in close. Now her fear and confusion mixed with a thick longing tangled in her stomach, her throat—everywhere. Her father's stupid words rang in her head. *Once you go forward, there's no rolling it back.* She heard her mother: *Emma, remember this—it's important. Engrave this on your brain. Don't ever, ever, ever do anything with your body if it doesn't feel one hundred percent right. Do you hear, Emma? One Hundred Percent,* her mother would repeat, capitalizing each word.

How was Emma supposed to know if something felt one hundred percent? Zach pulled Emma in until they were face-to-face. She only needed to tilt her head a bit to meet his spicy-sweet lips—like the cinnamon gum they'd been chewing. She must taste the same.

He took her hand and led her toward the steps, making a little bobbing question with his head. *Is it all right?* She bobbed back: *I guess so.*

Embarrassed by her unmade bed, she began to pull the covers up, but Zach stopped her, pulling her next to him. Brushing her bangs away, he kissed her forehead, gentle and sweet.

"You're so pretty." He touched his mouth to hers, his lips closed. His hands trembled on her waist. Finally, they kissed hard enough to topple to the bed. They'd never kissed like that before. Prone. She'd never even kissed any boy but Zach.

Zach pulled up her T-shirt, uncovering her bra. She tried to pull the shirt back, but he put a hand over hers. "Just one minute? Over the bra?" he asked.

Do I want this one hundred percent?

"Please, Emma. You're so beautiful. You know I love you."

Need roughened his pretty face—tightening his jaw, narrowing his eyes. His soft lips were puffy from their kisses. Emma's neck burned from where he'd rubbed his chin. Her stomach ached with pain and pleasure.

He held himself over her, all his weight on his arms. "Please." He kissed her again. Soft. "You're so special. So beautiful. Like a princess."

Boys will say anything when they want something. Her father's words stung.

Listen to your heart, but obey your intellect. Her mother.

Zach's mouth touched the bare skin of her neck.

Pure pleasure shot through Emma until she thought she might die. His mouth moved down. He rolled to his side and touched her breast—first soft and whispery, then firmer, then as though he'd squeeze the secrets of the world from her. She wanted him to press deep, lie on top of her, and help her go away.

One hundred percent. Baruch Atah Adonai, Eloheinu Melech Ha'Olam, tell me what to do.

Her mother in the hospital appeared before her. Sad and rumpled. Always looking like she might cry. And behind her towered an angry apparition of her father. *What the hell are you doing? Get the hell out of that bed. Now!*

She pushed Zach away. Hard.

"What? What is it?"

Shut up, Zach!

Emma rolled into a ball, hugging her knees to her chest. She rocked back and forth. She wanted to call Caro and Sammi so they could tell Emma what she would feel if she didn't have the weight of her broken mother taking over her brain. Taking over everything. Without her father making her into his housekeeper.

She wanted her parents out of her head.

Emma removed the last dinner plate from the dishwasher. No one knew she'd stayed home all day yesterday watching television. That Zach had been here until she'd thrown him out. Which seemed to make him happy. Relieved. Probably snuck right back into school.

After, she'd scrubbed the tub until the whiteness could hurt you if you looked at it too long.

Tomorrow her mother would be home.

"Can I hang up the welcome sign?" Gracie skidded into the kitchen in her white-turned-gray socks. Her father never thought to buy bleach, and Emma never bothered to remind him.

Whiten up! That's the stupid joke her mother used to make every time she put bleach in with their underwear and socks.

"Just don't make a mess, or Daddy will go nuts. And have Caleb help."

"*Caleb!*" Gracie screamed as she ran out. Neither Gracie nor Caleb had seen their mother since the day she'd woken up in the hospital. They were too young to visit the rehab. When her father talked about getting an exception, Emma had shrieked that it would be stupid and mean to make them go there, and for once her father listened. If the place scared Emma, what would happen to them? People drooled and wheeled themselves along the halls as though they were living corpses. The place smelled like rotting things covered up with flowered chemicals.

Caleb collided into Emma as she swept the floor. "Gracie needs the tape. Where is it?" He hopped from leg to leg.

Emma reached into the junk drawer and rummaged until she found an almost empty roll. "This should be enough, right?" As answer, Caleb threw his arms around her waist and squeezed hard.

"I love you."

"I love you too, stink. Bring the tape to Gracie."

In truth, the people and smells didn't bother Emma that much; she just told her father that. She could volunteer to read to all those broken people and be happy doing it. Just like her mother would have been. Content taking care of the wrecked.

Seeing her mother had been the problem. Choking out words, slow, halting. Everyone told her it would get better, but no one knew for sure. She looked it up. Dysarthria. Hearing her mother speak slashed Emma's ears. *Eem.* Pause. Breathe. Wait . . . *Aah.* Wait . . . Pause, *Ahh. Eem. Ahh, where . . . is . . . Dad?*

He went to the bathroom, Mom.

Emma had answered the same question a minute ago, and then a minute before that, and before that. Her mother gave her a sad stare and said, *Oh. Oh.* She'd look at Emma, waiting for her to say something, drive the conversation. Then she'd fall asleep, and Emma watched her mother, who reminded her of the blue screen on the TV when you turned off the DVD.

Her father told her to be patient. *It's just a stage.* But maybe it wasn't. Maybe she'd be this jellied blob of a mother for the rest of Emma's life while Emma did everything.

"Come, look," Caleb called.

In the hall, a giant sign Gracie had made on the computer, eight pieces in all, hung on the wall.

WELCOME HOME—WE LOVE YOU MOMMY!

Caleb's artwork decorated the taped-together papers. Flowers, birds, houses, and hearts circled the words. Flashes of turquoise and yellow smudged the sparrows' breasts, purple outlined the parrot-green houses, and the flowers and hearts were deep red.

Tomorrow her mother would walk in and see this. Emma's throat tightened, remembering her mother's halting voice on the phone yesterday. *Luurve you, Eem.* For two days Emma's father had barked reminders to have everything in its place. Then Aunt Vanessa called: *Keep it perfect, Emma. Make sure Gracie and Caleb shower.* Grandma Anne apologized for not being able to help clean the house. Grandpa

Jake came over to stick money in her hand to *get something for you and the kids.*

Grandma Frances called to ask if her mother needed anything. Anything at all.

As though Emma had some imaginary phone line to the inside of her mother's brain.

CHAPTER 23

Ben

Freezing drizzle coated the windows at six in the morning. Saturday. Maddy-coming-home day.

Ben looked around the pristine bedroom he'd cleaned until two in the morning. Around midnight he began questioning his sanity in refusing his father-in-law's offer to send over a cleaning service.

He stripped off the dirty T-shirt and jeans in which he'd fallen asleep and tossed them in the hamper. Careful to keep the sink clean as he brushed his teeth, he set the shower water as hot as he could take it. He stepped in, and he hit play on the shower CD player. A tinny version of Al Green's syrupy voice poured out. "*I'm still in love with you.*"

Their song—his and Maddy's signal for shower sex.

Lucky mornings, he'd called them.

When was the last time one of them had needed each other right in the middle of some hurried morning? When had he last run his hands over her soapy breasts?

He loved Maddy's breasts—could feel the weight of them in his hands, full, dense, serious. So unlike Elizabeth's pale barely-there chest.

Please, God. Send me a magic spell. Let me exorcise sleeping with Elizabeth.

Jesus, if he could go back and exorcise, he should get rid of the damn accident.

He hadn't driven anywhere near that stretch of the Jamaicaway since the crash. He'd drive ten miles out of his way before going near there. He wanted to move, buy a new house—thousands of miles away.

At least he had a new car. He'd replaced his overpowered Camaro with the quintessential family car: a Honda Accord—which seemed like the right mate for Maddy's Toyota Camry. It had taken weeks for him to realize that the Toyota had been towed away, and he'd been grateful for his father-in-law's offer to pick it up and bring it to their house.

Gratitude had become his new lifestyle. Gratitude to Anne for cooking and taking care of the kids, to Jake for his thick wallet—despite refusing what he could—and thankfulness to his father for keeping on top of the legal problems thrumming in the background.

No matter how confident Ben was that the DA wouldn't dredge up enough to charge him, he had to remember that was law, not math. Two plus two rarely equaled four in the courtroom.

Ben placed his hands on the white tile, feeling the hot water beat on his back, the heat as close to painful as he could take, trying not to imagine the future. Wondering if Maddy would ever be able to drive again.

After a careful and close shave, he dressed in chinos and the pink Brooks Brothers shirt Maddy had bought him last Father's Day. Using care to be quiet, he walked to the study to go over plans. Anne had already cooked a major meal for the homecoming dinner, trying, it seemed, to include any and every dish Maddy had favored since birth: apricot-smothered brisket, turkey with stuffing, fresh-baked challah, farfel kugel, and a salad of bitter greens with sweet pecans and shaved parmesan. Even the famous hundred-step chocolate pie demanded by Anne's catering clients.

Maddy's homecoming had taken on the air of Passover crossed with Thanksgiving and Maddy's birthday all thrown in together. When Ben had tried to tone down the menu, Anne had looked so wounded he'd backed off.

God knew what Jake might buy to mark the occasion. A diamond tiara?

Ben touched his pants pocket, assuring himself that he had the key to his home file cabinet. He'd taken to locking things away when he found that his daughters had begun investigating every corner of his and Maddy's lives. Signs of their snooping were scattered like squirreled nuts. Strands of Gracie's hair curled on his desk. The last document opened on his computer changed without him clicking a button. Doodles of Emma's signature floppy puppy faces decorated the backs of envelopes on Ben's must-do pile.

Ben flipped open his calendar, where Maddy's roster of appointments crowded out his court dates. Speech therapy, occupational therapy, and sessions with the physiatrist, Dr. Paulo, lined his calendar. The neurologist to test her. The surgeon to check his work. Maddy would see Zelda, her social worker and rehab case manager, twice a week. Soon there would be a lifestyle trainer. That was actually the real title. Who went to school to become a lifestyle trainer?

He unlocked the file cabinet and took out the notebook in which he'd three-hole-punched his lists of doctors, drug records, schedules— everything, including the rehab notes Olivia, Kath, Anne, and Vanessa had put together for Maddy's recovery. Despite reading as much as possible—towers of brain injury books were next to his side of the bed along with dusty unread law journals—he never caught up. Cleaning his glasses one more time, he flipped pages, picking out the relevant passages, words he'd highlighted as he had in law school.

Most recovery, Olivia wrote, *takes place in the first six months. However, though improvement takes place at a slower rate in the second six months, this does not mean that it will eventually slow to zero. Ben, take note of this and be patient!!!!*

Oh, yeah, he just loved Olivia's little sidebars. He'd told her last week that though he appreciated her information distillations, she could refrain from underlining. Moreover, he'd wanted to say, yes, Olivia, he knew it didn't all happen in the first six months, but when, and for what, should he be hoping? Despite her promise that it might never slow to zero, when would they know that they'd reached the end? That Maddy's healing had finished and wherever she was, was as good as it got?

He skipped ahead to a note Anne had given him last week, written in her perfect slanted script.

Dear Ben—

These are the symptoms (from that book I told you about) that I've already noticed: Maddy is sensitive to slights and shows a little emotional instability.

She gets headaches and she's spacey. Her lack of insight makes me nervous. Jot down everything you notice so you don't forget when the doctor asks. Watch her.

The dysarthria symptoms I've seen are slurring and speaking softly (almost like whispering), breathiness, speaking very slowly—a changed vocal quality.

Other possible symptoms I've read about are rapid rate of speech w/ mumbling quality (thank G-d, she doesn't have that!); limited tongue, lip, and jaw movement (also, thank G-d, no); abnormal intonation when speaking (a little, but I know it will go away); hoarseness (maybe she has a little?); and drooling or poor control of saliva (thank G-d, no!).

Ben rubbed the back of his neck and steeled himself for the next page. He tried not to hate Anne for writing all this—it looked too bold and ugly, these words slashed on the paper.

Ben, some tips in the book that I think would be helpful are: PATIENCE (Number One most important, Ben). Reduce distractions. Pay attention to Maddy. Watch her for cues and clues

*as she speaks! Be honest and let her know when you have difficulty
understanding her (but only nicely).*

Love,
Anne

She expected so little of him.

Why not? The knowledge that his rashness had caused this sat between him and everyone else in the world. Much more than recklessness. Stupidity. Gross idiocy. Worse, eventually he had to let Maddy
know someday. But not yet. Not until the time was right for such
truth. Right now he wanted to keep their newfound trust. Maddy
needed him, she clung to him; he'd become the center of her universe.

Ben would change. He'd be a better person. He liked the gentle
side he'd found with Maddy.

He fell back in his chair, his arms crossed over his forehead. Maybe
this had all happened for a reason—maybe God was curing him of the
rage that had always been his curse.

Right. God used Maddy to teach him his lessons.

Why not? The God of his youth was nothing if not a mean
bastard—the tote-that-barge, lift-that-bale variety. What would
hurt Ben more than hurting Maddy?

Ben led Maddy and Anne up the walkway. He took a few breaths
before putting his key in the door. Seeing Maddy leaning on Anne as
she stood on their porch, shaking as she waited to walk through their
door, just about killed him. Her fragility—in appearance, in voice, in
action—Jesus Christ. He had to keep superimposing this new Maddy
on top of the woman he'd known for so long. Everything was wrong.
Harshly bright sun spotlighted bristly places on her scalp. Angry red
scars peeked through the wiry strands. Chopped off short hair, where
someone at rehab had tried to even things out, had replaced her
massed curls. Where she'd had tight lean muscles, there was now soft,
almost flabby, gauntness.

"Wait," Maddy whispered as he put the key in the lock.

This soft halting voice—was it permanent? He worried she'd never regain her vigorous tones. He'd give a million dollars to hear her yell at him.

"What is it, sweetheart?" Ben asked.

"Ring. Ring . . . ring."

"You want me to ring the bell?" he asked.

Anne put a light hand on Maddy's back. "This is your home, darling."

Maddy kicked at the dried brown leaves blown on the porch. "No ask."

"Don't ask why?" Ben asked.

Maddy nodded.

"Okay." He took out the key and rang the bell. Maddy slipped her hand into his and gave a squeeze, which he answered with a double squeeze back. Maybe she needed the children to come to her; maybe seeking them seemed too frightening. Maybe she just needed one more minute. Maybe she just wanted to hear the goddamn doorbell.

Maddy held his hand tighter.

They listened to the family thudding, running, crashing toward them.

Caleb pulled the door open with a flourish. "Mommy, Mommy, Mommy." He threw his arms around Maddy's waist. "Mommy. I got you!"

Ben let go of Maddy's hand so she could hug Caleb, and then entered the house, though he kept his hand hovering over her body.

"Mommy!" Gracie squeezed in next to Caleb. Maddy bent and kissed her on top of her head. She sank to her knees, laughing and crying as the three of them folded in to one another.

Emma, off to the side, wiped her hands on a towel. Jake stood next to her, squeezing her shoulder until Ben feared his father-in-law would break off a piece of his daughter's arm. Maddy looked up. "Come. Come . . ." She held out her arms, and Emma dropped the cloth and ran over.

"Did you get our cards?" Caleb asked Maddy.

"Got . . . all," Ben heard her whisper into Emma's hair.

Anne wept. Ben watched his wife and children, the three shades of deep black-brown hair mingling, Emma's braid falling over Gracie's arm.

Ben wanted to fall down on his knees.

Instead, he knelt behind Maddy, supporting her from behind as the children leaned on her. "Let Mommy get up, okay? She's tired—we need to remember that."

"'Kay," Maddy whispered. "'S fine."

"Do you want to see the sign we made, Mommy?" Caleb asked.

Maddy smiled. "Yeh."

Caleb tugged on her to get her up. "Hold on, buddy," Ben said, reaching for Maddy. When Ben had her safely on her feet, he relinquished her to Caleb and Gracie.

"There! Isn't it good?" Caleb pointed at the raggedly taped papers.

"Buuuut . . . ee . . . full." Maddy smiled over their heads at Emma.

"Why are you whispering?" Caleb asked. "Talk regular."

"We talked about this, Caleb," Jake said.

"It's okay, Jake," Ben said. "*We* talked about this—Maddy and I. The kids shouldn't be afraid to say or ask anything. Right, hon?"

Maddy's nod looked uncertain. "You okay?" Ben asked.

"Did I do something wrong?" Caleb asked.

Emma put an arm around Caleb. "You didn't do anything wrong. Mommy's talking slow because she's still a little sick."

"Does it hurt to talk?" Caleb touched his mother's neck with one finger.

"Careful, Caleb," Jake said.

"'S'kay. Nah . . . glass." Maddy bent, took Caleb's hand, and held it to her left temple. "Broke. Here. But. Nah hurt."

"Mommy means she was injured in her head," Ben added. "Her brain. That's where the trouble comes from—the problems—but she's not in pain now."

"How does a brain hurt make her not talk, though?"

"We don't have to discuss this right this second." Anne came over and put her arms around him. "Let's go into the living room, everyone."

Ben wanted to remind everyone again of Maddy's and his wishes— *let the kids ask away!* However, his wife had become public property and he didn't know how to get the control back in his court. Mostly, he worried about Maddy's frightened confusion, so he let Anne lead her out and followed meekly in their wake.

CHAPTER 24

Maddy

Maddy the carapace.

Her mother steered her to the couch, where she lay as though on display. Like in a museum maybe? What was a carapace? Did it mean anything? Words popped into her mind without grounding. Her brain seemed like a half-filled trunk. Where once it was packed with rows of facts and thoughts, now things rolled around, came out of nowhere. Was a carapace a shell?

Maddy the shell displayed for her family.

Did that make any sense?

Her sweet Gracie offered pillows, blankets, books, and food. She worried, worried, worried about her. Gracie, she was her heart.

Caleb, puppy boy, needed calming. *Down, Caleb. Sit, Caleb.* Everyone became so nervous as he asked question after question.

Emma, Emma, watching, guarding, the child of her flesh. *Flesh of my flesh, bone of my bone.* They were too connected. If they stood within reach of each other, their skin sizzled.

Without warning, her mother began placing a pillow behind her back.

"Maa . . . mahm." She wrenched up a smile. No longer reflex, smiling. She had to think it. Put up mouth. Zelda said she had to smile.

"I just want you to be comfortable, darling." Mom blinked away tears that made Maddy want to punch her. She didn't want to make people unhappy simply by being.

"No." *Feels like shit. Feels like a stone.* She reached behind, plucked out the pillow, and threw it on the rug.

"Whatever feels good, hon." Her mother's tremulous voice threw confusion at her. *Be sure, Mom. Act definitive. Stop it.*

Gracie snuggled in close and then stopped, perhaps fearful she'd cause pain. Maddy pulled her in through a tiny motion of her arm.

"Mommy?" Caleb asked.

"Yes."

"Do you still think?"

"That's such a stupid question, Caleb. Of course Mommy thinks. She's recovering from an injury, not retarded." Emma looked at her. "Not that retarded people can't think."

"Nobody needs to talk about anyone being retarded," her father said. His jaw was too tight. Maddy imagined it snapping off.

She put out an arm to Caleb, and he flew to fill up her empty side, sticking out his tongue at Emma in the process. "I . . . think." She took a series of decent rehab-taught breaths. "I will . . . be fine."

"You need to expect to have some good long recuperation time, honey," her mother said.

"Day by day. That's how we'll do it," Ben said.

"Not. So. Long." Fatigue crept over her.

"See! Maddy knows she'll be up and around in no time." Her father gave a thumbs-up signal.

In answer, she lifted her hands over her head. Rock style? *Rock, rock, rock. That's not right. Word, word, word, damn. What the fuck is that word?* She pictured a sweaty beat-up man. *Rock.* "Fuck."

"Shah, shah," her mother crooned, placing a hand on Maddy's head. "See, we can't rush anything. She doesn't know what's up or down yet. It's called impulse control."

"Anne, Maddy is right here. Don't talk about her in the third person." Ben came over to the couch. "Slide over, buddy," he told Caleb.

He reached around their puppy to rest his fingers on her shoulder. All the contact. Awful. Smothering.

"Get off," she whispered—wanting, craving, needing to shout.

Gracie and Caleb jumped off the couch.

"Too much," she said. "Can't . . ." Can't what? What was the word, what word, what word? "Damn . . . damn it."

"Relax, baby." Ben started to put his arm around her and then drew back when she hissed. Everyone stared at her.

"No . . . problem." Watch the amazing pop-up mother. Like those flat sponges suddenly filled with water, the mom-on-her-back rose from the flattened form on the couch. She couldn't even share the joke. *Fuck. Can't talk—can't be funny?* Would she have to learn to mime?

"What? No . . . food?" She watched her mother jump up. Ah, her mother was the original pop-up mom.

"You can have anything you want," her father said. "Look at you, for God's sake. You're skinny as a rail."

"Coma diet." She could tell two-word jokes. No one knew if they were stolen from rehab. "Then . . . prison food."

Now their laughs were too hearty.

"Prison food!" Caleb twirled in a circle, his arms straight out as he spun. "Potatoes fried, potatoes boiled, potatoes with tomatoes."

Everyone laughed. Maddy became dizzier and dizzier watching him. "Fuck . . . potatoes."

What, no laugh?

So tired she could die, she went up for a nap. She heard her sister, Vanessa, Sean, and their kids swim into the house. *Not swim. Swan? Swami?*

Sworm?

"Everyone ready? Ben, want to get the guest of honor?" Her mother's voice drifted up the stairs, through the door, sounding shaky. Because of her, or had bitchy Vanessa already made their mother craaaaaaaazy? And why was her mother calling her a guest? Become half dead and you're demoted from family to company? She heard Ben climb the stairs.

She wanted to stay up in the bedroom. Her eyelids seemed taped shut. Taped shut by fairy sleep angels flying over her head, wearing skirts make of pink crinoline.

"Maddy?"

The bed sagged. Ben.

"Honey? Are you awake? Supper is ready."

She didn't think she could speak. She tried to crack open an eye. He lay next to her, but not touching.

"Maddy?" He brushed away her curls with feather fingers. "Everyone is ready to eat."

So eat. Eat, my fairy subjects.

She heard more footsteps. Not kid feet. Not man feet. Sister feet.

"What's going on?" Vanessa asked. "My mother's waiting. Is she okay?"

Is she okay? Am I deaf, dumb, and blind?

Maddy forced a slit of eye open and saw her sister standing there waiting. For what? Did Vanessa want her to jump out of bed? Give Vanessa a big sloppy hug and kiss? Was she jealous that Maddy had been getting all the attention since the accident?

"Me. Talk . . . to me."

"Whoa! Look who's awake!" Vanessa flopped on the bed. "Don't worry; it didn't insult me when you went to your room the moment we came in." Her sister leaned in and kissed her on the cheek with her shiny red mouth.

"Ick." She wiped off the Vanessa lip glop.

"Ick?" Vanessa lay with her legs straight out; now Vanessa and Ben jailed her. *Bound me? Boundaried?* Maddy the hot dog in the Vanessa-Ben bun. "I missed you."

Vanessa turned so they were almost nose-to-nose.

Missed you, tootsie.

"I . . . Me miss."

"I know, I know. You missed me also." She traced Maddy's hip and thighs. "Look how much weight you lost!"

"Coma . . . diet." A signature line? "Not worth . . ."

Vanessa turned on her back, running her hands over her flat stomach and jutting hip bones. "I don't know. Lose weight. Get away from the kids. Is it actually that terrible?"

"There's a reason Maddy calls you the bad seed," Ben said.

Maddy kicked him as well as she could. "Mean."

"Vanessa knows I'm teasing, right, Ness?" Ben asked.

"I'd never predict what you mean and don't mean, Ben." Vanessa's smile seemed odd. Maddy frowned, unable to follow the conversation.

Caleb charged into the room. "Are we eating? Mom, are you coming?"

Maddy tried to respond to her son, but nothing happened.

"Mommy?" He came over and poked a finger at her arm. "Mommy?"

Stop! He rapped her skin with an iron rod. Poke, poke, poke.

"Stah," she shrieked, needing them to stop.

Caleb shrank, backing into Emma, who'd just come into the room. Would they all leave now? Please leave. "Leave," Maddy said.

"Mommy wants us to leave," Caleb told Emma.

"I heard." Emma wrapped her arms around Caleb.

"She's not upset with you," Ben said. "It's just the recovery. She needs to sleep when she needs to sleep." He put a hand on Caleb's head.

"But she didn't say please or thank you," Caleb said.

Please. Thank you please thank you please.

Morning sun made a pattern on her hand.

Where was she?

Not prison.

Not hospital.

Ben lay next to her.

Home.

She smiled. Touched him.

How strange, sleeping with another person. Did they wake covered with bits of each other? Is that how they become family? Maybe it was just that. That's why they drifted apart when they were separated.

People reconnected with cell matter! If she nestled right up against Gracie, Emma, and Caleb, would they get closer quicker?

Sleeping soothed her. Tired, her thoughts became soup. First morning thoughts were her best.

"What . . . day?" she asked.

Ben opened his eyes, his waking gestures familiar. Rub left, then right eye. Stretch face out with a series of movements she'd copyrighted to him. Jaw in, jaw out, Ben woke his face.

"It's Sunday." He yawned. "Are you okay? Are you hungry? Want to shower first?"

She could only hold on to one question. Yes, she wanted hot water running over her body, but without bars to hold and buttons to push for nurses, she might slip and hit her head and lose more brain. She didn't know how to tell him all these things one word at a time.

"Coffee?" he asked.

"Yes! Coffee."

"Okay, give me five minutes and I'll go down and make it." He turned over, offering his warm back, shoving the pillow under his head. Rain spattered on the windows. The cloudy room felt like a safe cave.

She stayed on her side, watching Ben. What did they used to do on Sunday? She scrunched up her face trying to remember. Envision it, Zelda told her in rehab. If you can't remember, imagine.

Lying in bed with all the kids, watching cartoons on their bedroom television. When they were oh-so-little that even Emma liked being part of the pack.

Hazy thoughts of mornings after angry nights. She and Ben each rolled to the edge of their own side of the bed. Why had they fought?

She squeezed and pressed, trying to remember things Zelda had told her might be gone forever. Her mind had washed away memories. Some might roll back.

She kept asking Ben to tell her *how it happened* until he seemed angry. He didn't want to say it over and over, he told her. Didn't like going to the place where she got hurt. No one liked to tell the accident story. For her it didn't matter. Not really real since she couldn't remember. Just a scary story but *her* scary story, and she wanted to hear it so she could find her way out of the fog.

Once upon a time Maddy and Ben drove on the Jamaicaway. A Ford forced them away from the right spot. The Ford ran into them. She fell out of the car. The end. Oh. Rain fell.

Cold. She turned to Ben's body. She stroked his back, tracing the indented line, the spine, pressing her nose to his shoulder. Taking in Ben—the soap he used. What was the name? Brown soap flecked with gritty bits. His arm smelled like sleep-Ben.

She turned him on his back. Touched him.

"Wait. Let me lock the door," he said, climbing out of bed. "The kids." He walked awkwardly, his erection leading him.

"You . . . fun."

"I'm funny?" he repeated as he climbed back into the bed.

She stood and stripped off her thin white nightgown. "Like. This." She walked toward the door, tipping out her pelvis as though it forced her to swing forward one hip at a time. When she reached the door, she pivoted on one foot to head back to Ben.

Arms out, she walked toward him slowly. He pulled her to him. The length of his stiffness pressed into her stomach. She buried her face in the sweet spot of his neck.

He pulled her close.

His embrace crushed her. His breath smothered.

Off off off.

She needed to get away.

"Stah," she whispered. "Stah. No breathe."

Ben let go. She rolled away. He followed, placing a hand on her hip.

"Can't breathe? You can't breathe, Maddy?"

She shook her head. He jumped up and pulled at her until she sat at the edge of the bed. He patted her back. "It's okay, baby. This is what all the books say: Sometimes you'll want it like crazy, and then you can change your mind in a flash."

"Whah. Do I. Do?" she asked.

"With what? Do with what, Mad? You don't have to do anything. It's okay. It doesn't bother me."

"Not. That!" She stood and looked around. She walked to the bookshelf and grabbed the first book her hand hit. "*Can't read.*"

"You can read, Mad. It's just slow coming back."

"No!" She pulled out volume after volume, throwing them to the floor. "Can't."

She stopped. They stared at each other. "My . . ." She couldn't catch her breath. Her chest pumped up and down. "Life. Whah about. My life?"

CHAPTER 25

Emma

Emma scrubbed at the white gunk stuck on the table, working so hard she thought the wood would crack, determined to erase the lump of solidified sugar adhered to the counter. Did Caleb twirl when he sugared his cereal and then deliberately splatter milk to ensure that the drippings turned to resin? Dried bits of it stuck to the side of the sink. Grandma had attempted to clean the kitchen the previous night, but her father forbade it. Those were his exact stupid words: "I forbid it, Anne. You and Jake have done more than enough for today. Get some sleep."

Once she'd loosened the worst of the crap, she sprayed water over the pile of dishes and pots and started pulling things out to stack in the dishwasher. Clearly her father didn't think that she had done more than enough. Oh, no. Always more for Emma to do. No forbidding Emma against housework!

Caro probably was snuggling into her comforter while Caro's mother readied a bowl of low-fat oatmeal with sliced bananas and pretend brown sugar. Zach's mother no doubt had made whole-wheat apple pancakes for everyone, as his father read the Sunday *New York Times* aloud to her.

She wanted to get out of here. She wanted to run, do cartwheels, leap on and off the balance beam at the community center, or swim a million miles—anything as long as she moved—but if she tried to go anywhere, her father would flip out. Her mother probably wouldn't even know. She'd just stare at her, empty-eyed. Scary puppet eyes that made Emma want to knock on her mother's forehead and ask, *Anyone home?* But then it changed—just as she got used to having a zombie for a mother, the next moment she examined Emma so intently, it was as though her mother possessed X-ray vision.

Emma peeked into the living room to check on Caleb and Gracie. Their whole family had become so frigging creepy. Gracie wrapped herself in her red bathrobe as if it were the Shroud of Turin—that was a Catholic relic, right? At least Gracie's robe was clean. Grandma Frances had told Gracie cleanliness was next to godliness, and if she wanted God to let Mommy come home from rehab, she had to let Emma wash it. Then Grandma Frances gave Gracie the set of ivory rosary beads that she'd been given by her own grandmother. Wait until Mom saw Gracie on the couch, fingering the holy white beads as she read the Sunday comics.

Shivering sadness overcame Emma as she realized that her mother probably wouldn't even notice. Not that any of it mattered. From Emma's point of view, Gracie might as well be fingering jelly beans. Crosses, Stars of David—none of it meant anything except phony promises.

Caleb sat at the other end of the couch, chewing on the top of his knees through his flannel pajama bottoms, racing miniature cars down his legs, stinking like dried-up pee again. His pajamas were clean, but his body still carried the smell from the previous night's bed-wetting. Soon the whole house would smell like Caleb pee. Emma had started sniffing herself before she left the house—afraid that she, all of them, carried the odor.

Her father's footsteps sounded upstairs. The toilet flushed. A lock snapped open. Muffled voices drifted from upstairs. What could they talk about? Her mother barely made sense.

Emma couldn't recognize her mother's tread. Before the coma, her mother flew down the stairs, light and fast. Now she clomped one stair at a time. Like Frankenstein. Her father matched his step to hers, both of them sounding tentative and old. Emma wanted to hear her father's usual impatient hurrying, sounding as though he'd soar if he could.

Her mother looked haunted as she entered the kitchen.

"Good morning, Mom." Emma's attempt to hug her brought an awful gasping sound from her mother, flinching as though Emma were trying to strangle her.

"Mom's feeling a little unstable this morning, honey." Her father's hand hovered above her mother's shoulder. "It's okay, Mad. Let's have breakfast. Then you can have a pill. You'll feel better."

"What's the pill for?" Emma asked.

"Anxiety," her father answered, while her mother gave Emma that chilling smile where her mouth turned up but the rest of her face forgot to follow. Emma tried not to stare at her mother's hair sticking up in all directions.

"'Kay," her mother said.

What did her mother's flat whispery *okay* mean?

Okay, I don't mind Dad answering all the questions?

Okay, I'm going to get better?

Okay, I'm here but gone?

Emma turned to get mugs from the cabinet.

"Look, Mom. Your favorite mug!" Emma held up a red mug with *World's Best Mother* written in clumsy white script.

"Cup," her mother said. "Don't . . . remember."

Grandma Anne had tried to prepare Emma for the way her mother would blurt out whatever was on her mind, but still the words brought a jolt of hurt.

"I made it for you." Emma tried to sound matter-of-fact and mature.

"Mom shouldn't have coffee right now," her father said. "Caffeine can bring on more anxiety, and she just had a bit of a panic attack. I better check with the doctor."

"I . . . decide," her mother said. "Me. Me. Me." With each repetition of *me*, her mother jabbed herself in the chest.

Her father took a box of cereal from the cabinet and shook it. "Honey, it's not a good idea. Let's wait till we talk to the doctor."

Her mother looked as though she were trying to scream *no*, but she only succeeded in making a painful-sounding bark. She tried again, but seemed unable to form the words. Appearing invaded—as though the zombie in her had taken over—she grabbed the sugar bowl and hurled it toward the cabinets. Glass shards and sugar sprayed in a wide arc as it shattered.

"Maddy, baby." Her father rushed to her mother, who sat slamming her hand on the table, sobbing as though her world had imploded.

Her mother stood. "I. Want. Coffee." She glared at Emma and her father.

Emma stared from one to the other. "What should I do, Daddy?" she asked.

"Coffee," her mother repeated in a strangled voice: *cuf . . . eee*.

"Right after you take your pill," her father said.

"Should I get her pills?" Emma asked. "Want me to make some tea? Want chamomile, Mom?"

"For God's sake, Emma," he said. "Can't you just be quiet for a minute?"

CHAPTER 26

Ben

Ben could barely remember normal, that fairy tale from another world, a world where people did things like sleep and smile. Maddy had been home for two weeks, and it seemed that long since he'd slept through an entire night. Or truly smiled.

Normal was for people who hadn't fucked up their families. Normal wasn't for men who raced around in a car built for thugs and assholes.

Tonight he'd have traded ten years of his life for an evening watching the Red Sox, but the devil didn't show up to make the trade, so he stumbled in exhaustion through Caleb peppering him with questions as he tried to get him to sleep.

"What's temporary love syndrome, Daddy?" Caleb asked.

"Temporary love syndrome? Where'd you hear that?"

He could be asleep in less than thirty seconds and say screw it to the hours of tasks still ahead.

"Grandma said it on the phone." Caleb kicked his tucked blanket out, undoing his grandmother's hospital corners. Ben had thought about telling Anne not to bother making Caleb's bed so carefully, but then decided it would sound ungrateful. Only Anne stood between his family and total chaos.

"She said Mommy has temporary love syndrome," Caleb said. "Is Mommy going to fall out of love with us?"

After a confused moment, Ben got it. He put a hand on Caleb's jiggling leg. "No. That could never happen. It's not temporary love syndrome—you heard it wrong. It's temporal lobe syndrome."

He tried to think of a way to explain it to Caleb. "*Temporary* does mean limited. Good work. What Mommy has is temporary, but *temporal lobe* means a part of the brain. Up here." Ben poked his own temple and then Caleb's. "And *syndrome* means a condition—something that is happening in someone's body, or a pattern of things happening that mean there is a condition in place. Like a dirty syndrome would mean someone had a syndrome of not cleaning himself or his stuff."

"Do I have a peeing syndrome?" Caleb asked.

"Sort of, I guess. But you'll be over that soon." Ben pressed a hand into his temples where another tension headache was growing. Maybe he had buried-in-shit syndrome. "Temporal lobe syndrome is the name of Mommy's brain injury. What she hurt when she . . . when she bumped her head."

"Will she get better?"

"Of course. Absolutely."

"All better?"

Ben considered all the things he should say, reassurances mixed with not-too-frightening honesty, and took the lazy way out. "Yes, Caleb. She'll get all better."

He kissed Caleb good night before his son could ask any more questions, turned off the light, and headed downstairs. Gracie's lamp was off—had he even said good night to her?

Anne was in the kitchen, wrapping sandwiches for lunch. He lined up apples on the counter. Granny Smith for him, McIntosh for the kids.

"I can finish up here." The dull knife he'd grabbed hacked more than sliced the apples. Where did Maddy take them for sharpening? Asking Anne meant she'd take care of it within a day, and adding to her workload would be shameful.

"It's okay. I'm just about done. All that's left is putting the right lunch in the right bag." She smiled at him, her grin reminding him of

Maddy's. "Imagine Emma's face if she ended up with Caleb's Fluffer-nutter?"

"You know that we'd be lost without you, right?" This was so true it terrified him.

Her dismissive gesture was classic Anne. "Family. It's what we do."

"Perhaps. In a perfect world." Ben wished he had the ease to give her a spontaneous hug. The sort Maddy would bestow without thought. "I'm grateful it's true in your world."

Anne rested her hands on the counter. "Any news about the case?"

Ben clenched his fist over the dull knife. "The wheels of justice turn slow but grind exceedingly fine, Anne. When it grinds over our way, we'll get it dismissed. Trust me. They haven't a thing to go on. They know that. This case is low on their list. Barely a blip. If, by some stupidity, they charge me, we'll get it dismissed," he repeated. "Trust me."

"That's good, Ben. And that's what you keep telling us. But really, is that the point?" She looked down and wrapped the last sandwich. "I mean, of course it's important that it get dismissed. But either way, eventually you have to tell Maddy what happened. She's going to find out. You can't bury your head in the sand forever."

"Why not?" As though it made a fuck's worth of difference how it happened. What was, was, right? Did they want him drowning in the past or taking care of the future? He'd deal with the case if and when it came up. Burying his head in the sand sounded fine right now. "What is so important about her knowing?"

"This accident didn't come out of the blue. Face it, Ben. Whatever the law says—guilty, not guilty, charged or dismissed—it's not like you were simply driving along like a law-abiding citizen and got smacked in the rear. Right?"

Answers eluded him. He sagged in defeat.

"Look." Anne took the knife from his hand and held it tight. "This is your decision. Jake and I, Vanessa, we all agreed. And we'll keep our promise. But Maddy deserves the truth. From you. About everything."

•   •   •

The moment Anne left, he headed to the study, hoping to read at least the front page of the *Boston Globe* before going to bed. Instead, he found Emma curled in his leather chair, surrounded by books, bobbing her head in time to whatever played through her earphones.

"Isn't it time for bed, honey?" He raised his voice so she'd hear him above her music.

"Not yet." She didn't look up.

"Homework?" When she didn't answer, he tipped her book down, forcing her to look in his eyes.

"*What?*"

He removed her white earplugs. "Don't shout at me. I'm not shouting."

"Right." Now Emma was barely audible.

"What did you say?"

She looked up at her father, tugging her book back up. "I said *right*. As in, you were right. You weren't shouting. I'm agreeing with you."

"Please, no sarcasm. And we need to be quiet so we don't wake Mom."

Emma rolled her eyes. "Don't worry. If there's one thing Mom does really well now, it's sleeping."

"That's enough," Ben said. "If you can't keep a civil tongue in your head, go upstairs."

Emma slammed her book against her knees. "Don't take your junk out on me. You're not the only one picking up all the extra work around here."

"I'm not in the mood for this."

"Oh! Sorry, Dad," she said in singsong. "Is that what you want to hear?"

He wanted to hear *Thanks, Dad. I love you, Dad.* He wanted to sleep for twelve hours. He wanted someone in the house not to need hand-holding and coddling. He wanted Anne to keep her opinions and criticism to herself.

"What I want is to hear a more respectful tone."

"Well, too bad. This house is like a mental hospital. All any of us hear is crazy talk. That's us now." Emma stomped out of the room.

Lacking the energy to be the father who'd make the right point, or even the father who gave a fuck, Ben headed to the glass-fronted cabinet and grabbed a bottle of bourbon. Quick and neat, he tipped the bottle to his lips, swallowing one shot and then another in two gulps. Then he filled half a highball glass. Peace for one night, that's all he wanted. One night to come home, turn on the television, watch the news, read the paper, eat still-hot food, check his mail, and go to bed.

Okay, he'd screwed up. But it was an accident—he hadn't done anything with deliberation. There was no intent. It's not like he drove down the Jamaicaway with a goal of hurting his wife, damn it. A million men drive too fast and don't have accidents. Did he deserve a forever sentence of indentured servitude? He'd become a lifer in a pile of shit. A dull ache throbbed over his eyes. He picked up the paperback thriller he'd started two nights before and then closed it and turned on the television.

Drinking had been stupid—instead of peace, he had a pounding headache.

As he went to the kitchen in search of aspirin and water, he turned off the hall lights and checked the back door. He found the aspirin bottle in the junk drawer, swallowed three, and went upstairs. Opening the bedroom door as quietly as possible, he unbuttoned his shirt and crept to the bed. Maddy slept on her back, arms flung out to either side. Before, she'd always been a side sleeper, rolling herself deep into the covers. Maddy's injury had affected her so profoundly that even her sleeping positions had changed—a small but still unnerving transformation.

He settled carefully on the bed, wearing only boxers, craving Maddy's heat on his skin, but her new starfish position made it difficult to get close. Not wanting to wake her, Ben curved around her body as best he could, one leg hanging over the edge of the bed.

Maddy's chest rose with each quiet breath. Emma was right. Since the accident, Maddy slept as deeply as Caleb and Gracie, as though she'd become a child herself. Before, she'd been the one who woke at the first sign of trouble in the house. His ability to sleep through everything had made her irrationally angry. *I can't believe that you can sleep,* she'd say as she climbed back into bed with a hungry squalling infant Caleb, sometimes with Gracie trailing, clutching Maddy's nightgown in her tiny hand.

He matched his breathing to Maddy's.

In and out.

Each night he went to sleep dreading the morning. *Get better, Maddy. All better.*

"Ben?"

He startled at her voice. "Did I wake you, honey? Sorry."

"I sleep. No. Matter. Day?"

"It's Monday night. Eleven o'clock. Tomorrow Vanessa's coming over." Ben remembered this as he said it. Anne's biggest catering client needed her, and he had a trial, so Vanessa had agreed to drive Maddy to rehab and keep her company until dinner. "We'll get pizza when I get home."

"Yes. Kids?"

"The kids are fine."

She rolled over and rested her head on his shoulder. She smelled sleepy-warm, like a cookie. "I love. You," she said and closed her eyes.

Ben ran down the courtroom steps and jogged to his car. Today he'd won, and Ben loved being a winner. The case had been a small one—but still, he'd mixed it up with Judge Floramo and come out on top. Ben hated Floramo, a bully. Getting one over on him made success all the sweeter. Ben's client, a triple threat, poor, young and pregnant, had been caught shoplifting. Asshole judge thought he could teach her a lesson, and he'd locked her up. Ben had freed her by getting her out on the kind of technicality Floramo was famous for screwing up.

After a record-breaking no-red-lights twelve-minute drive from Dorchester to downtown, Ben found a legal parking spot only a car's length from his office building. What other miracles did the gods have in store for Ben Illica? After bypassing the elevator and tearing up the stairs, he slammed his briefcase on his desk and flexed his shoulders, remembering every smart thing he'd said in court that day.

How long had it been since something had run through his veins besides fear or regret? Holding the copper Lincoln paperweight Maddy gave him for some long-ago birthday, transferring it from hand to hand, he swung his feet up on his desk and picked up the phone to call home. Three rings later Maddy's voice came from the answering machine.

"*You have reached the home of Ben, Maddy, Emma, Gracie, and Caleb. Please leave a message!*"

Hearing his old Maddy was sweet and sad; he'd almost forgotten her real voice, the slight impatience in her husky tone.

Ben checked his watch. Four o'clock. They were probably all at the pond or J.P. Licks. Anne and Vanessa nagged them to go outside all the time, as though Maddy were an infant who needed fresh air.

"Hey, everyone," Ben said to the void of voicemail. "Just checking in. I hit a home run in court today, thought you'd all like to know. I'll call when I'm leaving."

He hung up, disappointed at not reaching anyone.

A soft knock came as he shuffled papers without purpose.

"Come in."

Elizabeth fell into his guest chair. After his house, his kids, and Maddy, Elizabeth seemed too glossy to be real.

"We need to talk," she said.

In the history of the world, did men hate any four words more?

"What's wrong?" he asked.

She sat silent, her face impassive.

"Am I supposed to guess?" Ben forced the words to sound light. Caring. Paternal.

"You're shutting me out. It's like colliding into a wall. My internship is up next week, and I don't want to leave like this. This is bad. For me. For my career." Elizabeth crossed her arms. "Are you angry at me?"

"I'm not, Lissie. How could I be? You were an angel."

"Really?" She clipped off the word. "Then I suppose treating angels like trash is de rigueur in your world?"

Ben dredged for a platitude to ease her out of his office. Meanwhile, he closed the door. He sat on the edge of his desk and cleared his throat, coughing up his fatherly voice. "I know you're hurt. If I hurt you, I'm sorry. Truly sorry."

"I'm not hurt, Ben. I'm livid. Don't get the two confused." Elizabeth crossed her arms. "It's one thing to fall together for a one-night stand. I understand I may have put more on it than you did. But you treat me like something's wrong with me. You avoid me. You never meet my eyes in meetings, in the hall. Why do you choose to be mean?"

She reached for a tissue. This was why men should never have affairs. Why would you want two women's tears? How could any sex be worth that?

There really was no answer but the truth here. "Elizabeth, I fucked up. You're right. I was mean, but trust me, not because of you. It's all me. I couldn't believe what I did." There weren't any rewind buttons in this life. "I'm overwhelmed. My family. Maddy leans on me. She's broken."

"Couldn't you have explained that instead of running away?"

God, how young she was. In her list of men, he had great import. For him, she was his embarrassment.

"I was ashamed. I shouldn't have turned to you as I did. It was wrong. But you . . . I found you impossible to turn from." He didn't even know how much he said was bullshit and how much was true. Elizabeth had been the next step that night. Like the alcohol he overdrank that night, an antidote for pain. A weak man's choice.

Anger and affairs, perhaps they were always the choice of the pathetic.

Elizabeth's posture softened. "Listen. I'm not trying to add to your burdens. I suppose it was inevitable—our ending like this. But you knew I really fell for you hard, didn't you? I'd sworn that I'd never sleep with a married man. We were just so—"

Ben clamped his hand onto hers. "Right," he said. "I know." He tried to think of the perfect words, but nothing close to appropriate came to mind. "Right."

CHAPTER 27

Maddy

"Where do you keep your mint tea?" Vanessa asked. "My stomach's off. Probably from eating white bread. Why do you have that junk in the house?"

Vanessa stood in the living room doorway, her body poking out of the kitchen. Maddy cocked her head. Mint tea? Did they have mint tea? Did she like mint tea? What was it, anyway? She couldn't wrap her mind around the concept, although she could picture mint Life Savers. When they were kids, Vanessa and she would stick their tongues through the Life Saver holes and see whose candy lasted the longest.

Why was her bread junk?

"*Maddy!* Can you hear me?" Vanessa shouted.

"Not. Deaf. Stupid."

"Are you calling yourself stupid, or are you calling me stupid?"

"You. Fucky."

"Fucky. That's a nice way to talk to the sister who's taken care of you all day."

"Taken. Care. Ha."

Vanessa had watched Maddy make lunch. Tuna sandwiches. From

a bowl of already-made tuna left by their mother. But Maddy put it on the bread. With mayonnaise. Vanessa made coffee, and Maddy swirled thick cream into hers. When she tried to pour cream in her sister's coffee, Vanessa shrieked as though it were poison and then looked at Maddy's cup as though she'd lost her mind, reminding Maddy that *before* she'd taken *skim milk* in her coffee. *Skim, Maddy!* Vanessa had repeated it as though trying to cram this important knowledge into Maddy by sheer force.

Ha. As though Maddy wanted to drink sludge.

"You know what?" Vanessa put her hands on her hips. "I think it will do you good to be by yourself for a bit. Emma will be home with the kids any minute, right? I should get Ursula and Melody from the babysitter. You'll be okay, right?"

Maddy nodded. She made a big smile. Lips up! Being alone sounded great. Thank God Vanessa wasn't a worrywart like their mother or Ben.

"Yeah, you'll be fine," Vanessa said. "It will be good for you not to have someone clicking and clucking over you every second."

Before Maddy could answer, Vanessa had already slipped on her ballerina flats. She reached into her huge screechy-green bag and got out a book. "Here," she said, holding it out. "I just finished this— you'll love it. I know it will be difficult, but you should try, right? Push yourself. You need to reacquaint the muscles. I read a theory about that online. Just do a few sentences each day. For fun."

What was her sister talking about?

Maddy stared at the book, not taking it, wondering what her sister wanted her to do. Vanessa shook it a few times, looking at her, peering over the oversized black sunglasses she'd already put on.

"Take it. It's for you." She placed it in Maddy's hands and kissed her on the cheek. "It's fun. A beachy kind of read. You'll enjoy it."

After she walked out, Maddy stood, confused, holding the book in two hands. The cover was bright pink and prison gray. She threw it on the kitchen table, wishing she could really read it. Drink in every word. *Fuck you, Vanessa.* Reacquaint her muscles? Reading for fun had left town. Since the accident she could read perhaps one tortured page at a time, word by word, and by the time she got to the bottom of the page, she'd forgotten the beginning. It was not fun.

Her head hurt. Should she take a pill? Aspirin sometimes helped, but last night she'd taken one of the strong-ass ones. That's what Ben called them. She didn't even know the real name. Ben just gave her a strong-ass when she needed it.

Poor Ben. Needing to take care of everything in the house. Maddy tried to do more when he wasn't home, but her mother hovered every time she turned around. It was like having your shadow sewn to your shirt.

She looked at the clock. Digital. 2:15. She took her little brown notebook out of her pocket. *Twosday, Octobr 26/ Zelda: 11:00. Sista take me. Sista stay till Ben coms home.*

Time had turned into a strange and elastic concept. She'd talked to Zelda about it again today. Maddy had to *learn to use coping mechanisms* as her battered brain healed.

Time management: gone.

Multitasking: gone.

Ben wrote her schedule for the next day before they went to bed. Some schedule. Rehab doctor, and therapist, and bloopy boo, boo hoo, poor you. She wanted to go to work and see Olivia. Too bad.

What did she do at work?

Talk, talk, talk.

Tears filled her to the top and bottom. It happened in a second. In her chest and her throat and her eyes—tears even clogged her legs. Zelda and Dr. Paulo said it's impossible, but they didn't know. She could feel them.

She decided to pick up Gracie and Caleb. Surprising them would be fun! She could do the short, short drive. Or the medium walk. Yes, she would walk. Zelda said she should exercise. She'd get there before Emma arrived to get them. They'd come home like four amigos!

Wait. Ha! If she drove right now, she couldn't miss them! Make sure she did it right! Wait right in front of the school and surprise Ben with how much more she could do. Help him.

She picked up the book Vanessa gave her and threw it again, harder this time.

Normal, Zelda said.

You'll get over it, Ben told her.

"Fuck you," she told the book and them.

She had to get back to work. How could she do that if she couldn't read two pages in a row? Ben kept telling her to calm down; it's a slow process.

Asshole.

Ben. He was the opposite of her—such an organized man. The keys to her car hung off a hook next to the phone. Might as well take the pretty new car, right?

She remembered to put on her shoes, lock the door, and take her pocketbook so she had her driver's license. Ha! She knew what to do. As she hunted for and then gathered the objects she named each one aloud: *Shoes. Jacket. Pocketbook.* Her pride didn't last long. When she got to the car, she couldn't open it.

"*Stop it,*" she yelled when tears came again.

She went through the list like Zelda taught her. Mentally checked everything off. Shoes. License. She'd even remembered to wear a watch so she could keep an eye on the time.

Shit. Keys.

She reached into her pocketbook. There they were! See? Small glitch. Glitchette.

There it was, right outside the garage. No room for any cars inside. *Wait.* Maddy squished her face, trying to think. What did Ben say about that? *Remember?* Something about the mess? He didn't like it?

The question slipped away. She slipped into the car. Shiny tan leather inside, all slithery and slippery. Zelda said she probably wouldn't be scared when she started driving again as she had no memory of the accident and probably never would. Sliced right out of her brain. Like a wedge from a block of cheese.

The key slid in the place. Ha! She'd picked the correct one right off the bat! Now, she looked at the dashboard. So many numbers and dials. Sort it out. That's what Zelda kept telling her.

Don't get overwhelmed. You can sort it out, Maddy. Just slooooooooooooooow down.

Concentrate. Extricate the important information. Another bit from Zelda favorites.

Extricate.

Mitigate.

Concentrate.

Sort.

She turned the light knob on and off. She beeped the horn. Not loudly. Very appropriate.

Appropriate.

Extricate.

Mitigate.

Concentrate.

Sort.

She talked herself through the process. She even remembered to try the windshield wipers—Just in Case It Rained—a move she was especially proud of since sun blasted through the windshield. Extra careful. Just in case.

What else?

Seat belt!

She disengaged the car from park, slid it into D4—four driving, for driving—and readied for her glide down the pebbled driveway. Excellent! She turned up Vanessa's CD and sang along with the Black Eyed Peas: *Whatcha gonna do with all that junk . . . Check it out. Uh, huh. Check it out, uh, huh.*

Plan! Plan before driving!

At the end of the driveway, she would make a left. A short slide to the road, Maddy-honey-girl, then, a right turn. One short baby-sized block, then left on Centre. Voilà! Straight to the school.

She remembered!!!

Ready for takeoff.

She breathed deep, took her foot off the brake, and stepped on the accelerator.

Her breasts bumped the steering wheel. Metal cracked the splintered old wood as she slowly smashed into the closed garage door.

"*No, no, no.*"

The car kept going forward. *Stupido. Wrong way, stupid.* She needed to back out.

Reverse. R for reverse.

No! Hit the thing that stops the car, stupid fuck retard.

Her disobedient foot jammed harder on the wrong pedal. The car strained at the wooden door, splitting it wider, opening up to the garage packed with boxes and summer chairs and grills and three giant teddy bears her father had once bought for the kids. She steered into the bears until the car stopped, or maybe the bears stopped the car. She moved the stick thing into P and took out the key.

She climbed out of the car, walked out through the splintered door, and headed back to the house. So tired.

Climbing the stairs seemed impossible. Instead she went into the living room and fell facedown on the couch. She smelled her family on the cushions, the blanket, and the throw pillows. She buried her nose in them and pulled up the blue-and-white afghan her mother had made all the way up to her neck.

"Mom? Mommy? Are you okay?"

Someone shook her shoulder. She opened gummy eyes. Emma bent over her, looking pale and scared, frightening Maddy.

"Whas wrong?" she asked—her slow painful words not matching her racing heart. "You . . . okay?"

Over her shoulder she saw Caleb and Gracie pressed together, their jackets still on, their eyes wide open.

"Whas wrong?" she repeated, wishing she could shout or scream. Had something happened to Ben? What would she do without Ben?

"Mom, what happened to the car?" Emma asked.

"Car?"

Gracie stepped forward and put a small hand on Maddy's foot, clasping her toes in her fist. "The car is smashed into the garage, Mommy."

"Did Aunt Vanessa do it?" Caleb rocked from foot to foot.

"Where's Aunt Vanessa?" Emma asked.

They were pelting her with their words. "Vanessa went. Home."

"I better call Daddy," Emma said.

"No." She struggled to sit up. "No."

Please, she didn't want Ben racing home and making her into a baby. She strained to remember. What was wrong with the car? Poor Ben. She was sick of Ben looking hangdoggy.

"Show me," she said to Emma.

Caleb took her hand, and they walked to the front door with Emma and Gracie following.

"Put on your shoes, Mommy," Gracie said.

She looked down and flexed her white-socked toes. Where were her shoes? Ben's slippers were sitting face-forward on the shoe mat. She put them on and shuffled out the door.

The vines on the porch were brown and crackled. She could see through them to the driveway.

"No car! Stolen?" she asked.

"No. Look!" Caleb said. He tugged at her hand, pulling her down the porch stairs. She tried not to fall in the flopping slippers. The gaping hole in the garage reminded her of a jack-o'-lantern. Halloween would come soon. She loved Halloween.

"What happened?" Emma asked.

Were these the only words she knew anymore?

"Went wrong. I'm. Make supper."

"Supper?" Emma repeated. "The car— Never mind. We'll order something, Mom. Pizza. When Dad gets home."

"Yeah, pizza with Daddy," Caleb agreed.

So tired, but yes, they should have supper. She could show Ben she didn't need a babysitter.

"I'm cook." She turned and scuffed back to the house.

"I'll make it, Mom," Emma said. "You rest."

Maddy walked past them into the house, straight toward the kitchen, and stopped at the entryway. She put up her hands to block them from following her into the kitchen. "Me. Just me."

"I don't think that's a good idea," Emma said.

She pulled up all her energy and tried to sound like a mother. "No. Just me."

They stared: Emma with slitted eyes, Gracie worried, and Caleb jumping from foot to foot. Yes. This was right! They needed her!

"It's okay." None of them moved. She took a breath. Slow, bringing calmness inside. "This I can do." Ha, slow, but four words. She'd said a four-word sentence! And now she could cook!!

Maddy walked into the kitchen, sensing them still standing there behind her, little statues of uncertainty. She turned around. "Don't call. Daddy."

Now she marched forward, her mind clearing as it eventually did after sleep. Too bad she was always tired. Zelda said that was also normal. According to Zelda, everything was normal. Sleeping eighteen hours a day? Normal! Headaches boinging in and out as frequently as she breathed? Normal! One minute jumping on top of Ben, desperate to screw, the next hour screaming if someone brushed against her?

Normal!

Normal!

Normal!

But she had plans! She would go back to work. She would be alone in her house. And she would cook a fucking supper.

CHAPTER 28

Emma

Emma listened for sounds from the kitchen, terrified that her mother might be lying dead across the kitchen table. *Please call us, Dad.* She shifted on the study's leather couch, hyperalert and ready to run in and rescue her mother.

She felt like the story she'd learned in English class last year. She'd turned into Odysseus, caught between Scylla and Charybdis. Monster number one was her Scylla mother, who'd flip out if Emma called her father, probably pull another nutty with the sugar, or maybe spin her head around till her neck became a choking spiral. Monster number two: her Charybdis father, who would freak on Emma for not calling him. He'd give her one of his interminable lectures, as though she were one of his delinquent clients.

Emma, you have to be responsible, learn to make the proper decisions.

Meanwhile, back in the kitchen, her mother was probably chanting *fuck, fuck, fuck* or *I love you all so much* in her creepy whisper. Her father had promised Emma the cursing was simply a stage.

"Mom will get over it," he'd say. "Don't worry."

Meanwhile, Emma felt as though she couldn't leave the house and she wouldn't dare ask friends over. *Please excuse my mother's swearing;*

she has a slight case of brain-injury cursing. Zach would smile politely while averting his eyes, repulsed by her gross family.

"Emma?" Gracie came and sat on the other end of the couch.

"What?" Emma stared at her book, unwilling to let Gracie's sadness pull her in and pile on top of her own.

"How much time do you think God gives us when we make a promise? To have to keep it, I mean."

"What do you mean? What kind of promise?"

Gracie shrugged and looked at her feet. "I promised God I wouldn't eat any more candy if he made Mommy better. Then Grandpa brought over all that chocolate. And I ate a lot of it."

"I don't think God expects you to keep those sorts of promises," Emma said.

"But what if he does?"

"I think God just wants you to be a good person, Gracie. I don't think God gives a shit if you eat candy—especially so close to Halloween."

"What do you think we're going to do for Halloween?" Gracie asked.

"You and Caleb will go trick-or-treating, like always."

Gracie made figure eights with her bare toe. "But Mommy always takes us."

Emma placed her book in her lap. "So I guess Daddy will take you."

"Then who will hand out the candy?"

Her father loved doing that. Yet another chance for him to be a big shot—holding his hand over the candy bowl, as though debating what the miniature witch or spaceman in front of him deserved. Judge and jury—even with the little kids waiting, holding their decorated brown bags.

"I'll hand out the candy, Gracie. Don't worry." Emma pointedly picked up her math textbook.

"But you and Zach are going to a party. I heard you tell Caro." Gracie started chewing on her thumbnail.

"Don't—that's gross." Emma pulled Gracie's hand away from her mouth. "And don't listen in on my conversations."

"I have to. Otherwise I don't know anything. No one ever talks to me," Gracie said.

"That's not true, Gracie." But her sister was probably right. "No one talks to anyone around here anymore."

"Daddy talks to you."

"Daddy orders me around. That's not talking."

"It's not being invisible. Like I am."

"You're not invisible, sweetie." Emma gave in and closed her book, placing an arm around Gracie's shoulders. "You're the only nice one in the house. Everyone loves you."

Gracie shrugged again. "So what. No one ever talks to me. That's why I have to listen."

Emma opened her mouth, but she couldn't think of what to say.

"Mommy used to talk to me," Gracie said. "And she really listened."

"You can still talk to her, you know."

"It's not the same." Gracie stared straight ahead for a moment. "Emma? Do you think we should tell Mommy? You know. About Daddy going fast. About his maybe making the accident happen?"

Emma's chest tightened at the thought. "If we want to be dead."

"I think people should tell the truth. I think Mommy should know the truth."

Emma closed her eyes. She didn't want any more drama in the house, and she didn't want her father to explode. "Remember what Daddy said? It just takes time. He'll tell her when she's better."

"But what if she doesn't get any better?"

"She will."

"But what if she doesn't?" Gracie's voice broke.

"I don't know. I guess we'll just have to love her like this." Emma tugged Gracie's ponytail. "If you want, Caro and I will take you and Caleb trick-or-treating. And we'll make you costumes."

"I wish Mommy could make me a costume."

"I know, but I don't think she can, sweetie."

"Should we go check on her?" Gracie asked.

Emma hugged her, grateful for her sister giving her some sort of odd permission to go in the kitchen. "Yes. She probably needs our help."

Emma peeked into the living room as they went by. Caleb lay on the rug with yet another electronic game Grandpa had bought him last week, a half-eaten bowl of soggy Frosted Flakes in front of him, which was exactly the kind of cereal their mother never used to let them have. At first, their father had tried to be strict about those things, but now he threw anything they wanted in the shopping cart. Last week he'd bought four boxes of Dove ice cream bars when Gracie asked for them and then let Caleb and Gracie each eat one on the way home, even though Grandma had supper waiting and they were dripping ice cream and chocolate all over the car. Some stupid loyalty kept Emma from taking one, despite dying for the comfort of cracking open the brittle chocolate with her teeth and then reaching the creamy vanilla ice cream.

Emma and Gracie faced a tightly shut door at the kitchen entrance. Emma couldn't remember ever seeing the connecting door between the dining room and kitchen closed. She eased it open, the old hinges creaking.

"Mom?"

Emma stuck her head in, and then pushed the door into the usual position, flush against the kitchen wall. Her mother slept sitting in a kitchen chair, her head resting on her arms on the table. Flour whitened her so-short dark curls. Bowls, measuring cups, sacks of flour and sugar, and mixing spoons covered the table. Butter had fallen to the floor. Eggshells lay in the sink on top of piles of dishes and pots. Vegetable remnants were scattered on the chopping board.

Lumpy batter with pools of liquid sat in a bowl on the counter. Emma crept over and peered in. "What do you think this is?" she whispered to Gracie.

Gracie came over, and Emma tipped the bowl toward her. "It looks sort of like cookie dough," Gracie said.

"Taste it," Emma said.

"Why should I taste it?" Gracie asked.

"Just do it."

Gracie stuck a fingertip in the bowl and put it to her tongue. Emma wondered if she should stop her. It could be poison—what if her mother had mistaken rat poison for sugar? Did they have rat poison in the kitchen? They didn't have any rats, but who knew what might be around.

"What is it?" Emma asked.

"It's like cookie batter that's missing stuff. It tastes crunchy."

Emma opened the drawer and got a teaspoon. She covered the tip in the batter and brought it to her nose—sniffing before tasting. Sweet and buttery, probably okay. She licked the spoon. Undissolved sugar crunched. Lumps of butter coated with flour made the strange texture. An unmixed pool of dark liquid floated on top—it looked like an entire bottle of vanilla.

"Waa?" Her mother lifted her head an inch.

"Mom, what's this?" Emma asked.

Her mother blinked a few times, then got up and shuffled to the counter, still wearing their father's slippers. She looked into the bowl and shook her head.

"Mess." She began crying. "Cookies. Be. A good mother. Shit, shit. Shit."

Emma placed a hand on her mother's back. "It's okay. It tastes good—sort of."

"Tired. Head hurts."

Emma checked the clock. Five thirty. Should she call Kath? Their father would be home any minute.

"I'll get you some aspirin, Mom." Emma turned to Gracie. "Get Caleb," Emma whispered. "We'll clean up before Dad gets home."

CHAPTER 29

Ben

Ben approached his street, loosening his tie with one hand, using the other to make a right. The tie had been choking him for twenty-five minutes, but these days he drove as though listening to Barry Manilow or some such shit, both hands on the wheel as he crept along the road.

If Maddy seemed okay, they'd all go out to dinner. Somewhere local. Bella Luna would be good. Elizabeth had deflated his high, but he'd won a case and still wanted to puff out his chest.

He hoped Maddy was in a decent place. He thought about what she would have done before if he'd been excited over a court victory. Something corny, like having the kids make a banner. She might have stopped on the way home from work and bought a bottle of champagne. Maybe even the good stuff.

Now, even if Maddy could drink, it would be something like Cold Duck. All they could afford was cheap faux shit. Ben tensed up each time he looked at their bank account. Maddy's saved-up sick time had run out ages ago. His father-in-law kept raising the issue of money, and Ben kept putting him off. They were already into Maddy's parents for more than he wanted. When would Ben have to hit the kids' college fund? The emergency fund was already—

What the fuck?

The Camry's back end stuck out of a gaping hole in the garage door. He turned off his car and got out.

"Maddy," he called as he opened the front door. "Emma? Kids? Where is everyone?" He walked down the hall, looking for signs of life, hearing scuffling. He walked through the alcove to the kitchen and found the three kids trying to clean up an unholy mess. Gracie knelt on a chair, washing a huge pot.

"What in God's name is going on?" he asked.

They avoided looking at him. Caleb raised white puffs of dust as he swept debris into the middle of the room. Emma worked on grease smears covering the table.

"Where's your mother? Is she okay? *Look at me,*" he yelled when they didn't answer. "Where's Aunt Vanessa? What happened to the car?"

Even Caleb remained quiet, leaning on the broom until the bristles bent at a ninety-degree angle. Emma squeezed the sponge until Ben thought it would disintegrate in her hands.

"Gracie, what happened?" Ben asked.

She gave a little gasp before responding. "Mommy tried to drive the car. And then she tried to cook."

"But she's okay," Emma said. "She just has a headache. She's sleeping."

Ben worked at not flinging his keys or kicking a chair. Jesus, he wanted the satisfaction of hearing something break. He needed some sort of big crashing sound. He needed a place to hurl this ball of anger.

"How come no one called me? Where's Aunt Vanessa?" He stared from one to another. "Gracie?"

"She left."

"When?"

"I don't know, Daddy." Gracie's voice trembled. "She wasn't here when we got home."

"Don't yell at us—we didn't do anything." Emma pressed her lips together.

"Why didn't you call me? You know better."

"Mommy said not to. She wanted to show you she could do stuff," Gracie said.

"She did a hell of a job, didn't she?" Ben sniffed. "What's burning?"

They looked around. Caleb touched the stove. "It's hot," he said.

"Oh, God. I didn't check it." Emma slumped in the kitchen chair, throwing the sponge on the table, her legs splayed out like a colt.

"Leave it, Caleb!" Scorched food odors overwhelmed Ben when he opened the oven. He lifted out a white casserole dish and placed it on the stovetop.

Dried-out lumps of carrot, shriveled beans, roasted dry pasta. He grabbed a spoon and shifted a shell. The shells had never been boiled, just put in the oven uncooked, although it looked as if maybe milk or some other liquid had been poured over the mess. Desiccated tuna, shriveled celery. Maddy had attempted tuna noodle casserole. Gracie's favorite.

"Daddy?" He felt Gracie's tentative touch on his back. "Are you okay?"

His kids trembled in front of him.

"Sure, baby. I'm just going to check on Mommy. Leave the mess. I'll tackle it later." He got up, dusted off his pants, and started walking out.

"Dad?"

"What, Emma?"

"We heard your message. Congratulations."

Maddy lay facedown on top of the bedspread, barely covered by a small thin afghan. She looked cold, small, as though trying to compress her body. Ben sat beside her, then collapsed and took her hand. Saw the grit caked under her fingernails. Flour dusted her black hair so thoroughly it appeared gray.

"Ben?" She gripped his hand and frowned. "Is okay?"

"It's fine." He reached over and brushed sticky strands of hair from where they covered her eyes. "But baby, do you know what you did?"

"I tried. To cook supper." She rolled over and looked up at the ceiling. "But I screwed."

He waited a minute, trying to remember Zelda's words. Wait. Let her complete a thought. Don't finish it for her.

"I try, Ben. My thoughts jam."

She began crying. Soon the house would be floating in her tears. All their tears. This was their crying season.

"Tried to read. *Joy of Cooking.*"

Hearing her breathe out sentences word by word made him want to join her in crying. He missed his voluble Maddy, her sentences rushing out in waves.

What if she never got any better? What if this was it?

"We appreciate your wanting to cook for us. Really. But honey, it's going to take time."

"Time." She spit the word. "Ha!"

"Patience is harder for you now, which is sad, because you need it now more than ever. But we love you and need you to be safe."

She stared at him with wide frightened eyes. "Hate for me?"

He rubbed her arm. "Never. Roll over. Let me do your back."

She pulled up her T-shirt. Ben unhooked her bra, revealing smooth rosy skin. He drew a large loop with his fingernails, then smaller and smaller concentric loops until he hit the middle, and then started again.

"Do you remember driving, Mad?"

"No. Doctor said. I'd never remember."

"Not the accident, sweetheart. Today. Do you remember driving the car?"

She turned her head toward him, her face scrunched with effort. "Today?"

He nodded. "Today. Can you think hard?"

Her head bobbed with effort and then glee. "I remember!"

"Good. It's good that you remember. However, it's not a good thing to have done. Driving is bad."

Like dealing with a three-year-old. Good. Bad.

Maddy got on her knees, her legs folded beneath her, her face set in a serious expression. "Driving is bad," she said. "Got it."

• • •

Ben couldn't do another thing—not buy pizza, not clear the kitchen enough to put out plates, not even search for paper ones. He simply wanted a clean house and hot food, and he wanted it served by someone other than himself.

They arrived at his in-laws' house dirty and hungry. Maddy slept during the ten-minute car ride from Jamaica Plain to her parents' Brookline home. When Ben parked, Maddy woke.

The kids ran up the driveway, ahead of Ben and Maddy, and barreled into their grandparents' house. Emma flew behind them as though years were washing away and she'd become ten years old again.

Maddy still sat in the car, looking stunned.

"I drove?" she asked for the third time. "I get so stupid now."

Ben took her hand and kissed it. "Hey! Five-word sentence!"

She smiled at him. "Accidental. Car knocked in. Sense."

He rapped his knuckles lightly on her forehead. "Don't try it again."

"Don't leave keys." She pointed to her temple and laughed. "Brain-dead. Remember?"

They got out and followed the kids toward the house, holding hands. Ben couldn't remember the last time they'd done that before the accident. Now it had become their habit. She squeezed, and he squeezed back twice.

"What would I do? Without you?"

"You won't ever have to. No worries, Mad."

He brought her in for a hug. She pressed deep, grinding in, bringing an unwanted erection.

"Whoa." Ben backed up.

"Mmm. Want you." Maddy hooked her fingers into his belt loop, tugging.

"Right. Me too. But we're at your parents', hon."

"So? We go upstairs? Huh?"

He imagined them walking in and heading to Maddy's old bedroom. "I don't think so. Your mother has supper ready. The kids are starving."

"Kids can eat." She reached down and stroked him. "We can screw."

"Maddy . . ." He groaned, feeling her hand wrap around him through his trousers. "Stop. Please." He pulled her hand away. Christ, he'd be hobbling into his in-laws' house.

"*No!*" She ran from him, away from the large Colonial and toward the carriage house. "Catch!"

He stumbled after her, barely able to see in the diffuse light given off by the lavender dusk. "Maddy, wait!"

"Catch," she repeated.

As Ben ducked through the carriage house door, he wondered how her athletic skills could be so intact with her brain so mixed up. Of course he knew it had to do with where her injuries were—not in the brain stem, not in the cerebellum—but what made intellectual sense didn't make emotional sense.

The carriage house smelled of softening cardboard. Anne constantly considered expanding her catering business and moving it out here, but meanwhile, it remained what it had been for years—an unused space, a dusty version of how it had been when Vanessa and Maddy were children. Toys, dolls, paint, and craft supplies peeked out of old boxes. Army cots that Vanessa and Maddy had once used to play house were stored in the back room. That's where Ben found Maddy, sitting cross-legged on the olive-green canvas, grinning, unbuttoning her shirt.

"Maddy. We can't."

She revealed her breasts button by button. He found the revelation of her white cotton bra under his old denim shirt oddly arousing—her breasts exposed gave him an erection stiffer than he'd felt in years.

"Okay. Fast, then." She stopped unbuttoning and reached for the waistband of her jeans.

"Very fast." Quick enough to finish before Jake came out searching for them. Though at the moment, he didn't give a shit.

Ben yanked the pull chain affixed to the ceiling, shutting out the light she'd put on. He knelt at the edge of the cot, testing it for strength first. "You know I love you, right?"

"Yes." Lying back, her arms above her head, shirt half open, and the dim light scarcely revealing her bare thighs. She shimmered.

He fell on her, hungry, needing no beginning; they were ready to finish. Her legs closed around him. Maybe these tsunamis of hunger for him all came from a particular clunk in her temporal lobe, but again, intellect lost against emotion and he chose to believe they'd carved out this newfound desire despite the horror. That this one bit of good came out of the bad and his guilt.

No matter how many times they'd made love since Maddy came home, he couldn't get close enough. Her breasts gave beneath him as he buried his face into her neck, smelling vanilla and sugar from the cookies she'd tried to bake. He pressed her hands above her head, holding back as he felt her building. Her head moved from side to side as she rode out an orgasm.

Sweat dripped from his forehead as he watched her, her eyes wide-open wild. She slowed, and he went faster, deeper, desperate.

Even as he came, sadness enveloped him. Though he'd tried and tried, he couldn't push in deep enough to feel forgiven.

"So good," Maddy said. "Sex. Love it. Love you."

She rose on her knees, nearly tipping over the old cot. Ben steadied them by placing his hand on the cement floor. "Just have good," Maddy said. "Always. Okay?"

"I promise," Ben said. "Just good."

CHAPTER 30

Maddy

Maddy felt sad every minute of every day. A bottomless cold lake of depression threatened to subsume her. Gone was the mania that had brought cookies and driving three weeks before.

Her father tried to fix things in his usual way: money. He gave her a taxi charge account. Ben was upset, though she couldn't grasp why, but he kept quiet as her father performed his little ceremony, first handing Maddy a set of cards he'd made with the cab company's phone number written in large numbers and then giving her instructions. "Just tell them your name," he'd said. "I arranged it. That's all you have to do. Now you have a bit of freedom, but safely."

Plus, they'd programmed a new phone that had only a few numbers coded in. Temporary, Ben promised and her mother swore. They'd return all her friends soon. Right now they didn't want her overwhelmed.

In fact, what she felt was underwhelmed in a bleak nothingness.

She stepped out of the house. The cab company had sent the Russian driver, the one she loved for being silent, for never asking more from her than an address. Emma or Ben wrote out the addresses for where she was going so she didn't have to wheeze them out word by word. Wordlessly, she handed the driver a piece of scrap paper with the rehab address written in Emma's deliberate cursive.

The driver parked in front of the rehab building in a dank end of downtown. All day cabs spit out and then took back the halt and the lame. Getting to Zelda's fifth-floor office required taking an elevator and then navigating corridors endlessly patterned with brown-and-yellow-checked linoleum. Bright blue, green, and red footsteps guided you, but she always forgot what color to follow.

She opened her worn notebook, shuffling the pages until she found her foot-color note—*Zelda: Blew Feet*—and then followed outlines of blue footsteps until she reached the door reading *Outpatient Rehabilitation*. News played on a fuzzy-pictured television hanging from the wall in the outer office. Damaged people—fellow members of the club—slumped in scratched plastic chairs.

Ever-changing cryptic quotations, uplifting poems, and what she supposed were meaningful Biblical references covered the bulletin board outside Zelda's office. Looking for fresh hope, word by word she slowly read:

> *Nothing begins, and nothing ends,*
> *That is not paid with moan . . .*
> —FRANCIS THOMPSON

Thanks, Zelda and Francis Thompson, whoever you are. That sure lifted my spirits. She considered typing up *Abandon Hope, All Ye Who Enter Here* and sticking it on the board.

If only she could remember how to type.

Ha! She'd told herself a joke. The next saying seemed designed to remind her how much she was failing.

> *The ideal man bears the accidents of life with dignity*
> *and grace, making the best of circumstances.*
> —ARISTOTLE

Dignified and graceful. Perhaps that should be her goal.

"Maddy. Come on in." Zelda stuck her head out as she turned from Aristotle to Primo Levi.

> *Sooner or later in life everyone discovers that perfect happiness*
> *is unrealizable, but there are few who stop to consider the*
> *antithesis: that perfect unhappiness is equally unattainable.*

"Just read *Bartlett's*? All week?" Maddy thought of Primo Levi's words. Was this the best she'd have, knowing that she wouldn't always be unhappy? How dark a balm was that?

"You can speak better than that." Zelda stepped aside so Maddy could enter the office. "You're forgetting to take your breaths before you speak. Relax the muscles in your mouth. Send your energy to your mouth."

"Give me. A second. Damn." Ha! She hadn't said *fuck*. She found her way through the piles of books and magazines to the leather chair across from Zelda's cushioned rocker that helped her counselor's sciatica. "Let sit. Before lecture."

"*Let* me *sit*," Zelda said. "You can't take shortcuts when you're speaking. Remember? Verbs. Subjects. You don't want to sound like a refugee your entire life, do you?"

Sometimes Zelda's "just the facts" made Maddy want to kick her, but most of the time she relished being with someone who didn't look at her with pitying cow eyes. Silver strands mixed with red in Zelda's long cape of hair. Half witchy, half model—Maddy thought of Zelda as an occupational therapist of the mind. Rehab called her the adjustment counselor.

"What's on first today?" Zelda asked as she swung her green suede boots up on her desk. Zelda's beautiful clothes hung off her dime-thin body like woven money.

Maddy tugged at the pocket of her tight jeans and pulled out her notebook. Saw her ill-written notations of crap, crap, and more crap. Everything seemed a reminder that she couldn't drive, or work, or cook, or clean, or mend, or sew, or sow. Sex was her sole skill. She gorged on Ben, but that feast only satisfied her for moments.

Eating presented the same pleasure and problem. No matter how many cookies or meatballs she stuffed in, nothing satiated her past the eating. On Sunday, she ate half of Emma's birthday pie and still felt empty. Each week her pants grew tighter, and still she crammed more in her mouth.

"Fat. Getting fatter," she said.

"*I'm getting fatter,*" Zelda corrected.

"No. You look good. Skinny."

"Your sense of humor is intact," Zelda said. "That's good. How lucky that piece of your brain stayed whole."

Lucky funny me!

"Still fat. I am still fat." She said the sentence one halting word at a time.

Zelda tipped her head sideways. "Do you remember that we spoke about this last week?"

Remember, remember, remember.

"Yes," she said. "But still fat."

"You've simply gained normal postcoma weight," Zelda said.

Zelda could be calm. It wasn't her adjustment counselor waist dripping over her waistband.

"You're in a period of adjustment," she continued. "You don't recognize your satiation point. That's normal for you at this moment."

Right. Her normal would be a stuttering fat woman.

"Fine," she said, not wanting to talk about it anymore. "Work. Halloween. Driving. Birthday. Emma's."

"I assume that's your pidgin-English way of presenting topics to talk about. I pick Halloween," Zelda said. "What are you thinking?"

"I told? What happened? Right?"

"Work on breathing as you speak, Maddy." She took a slow breath and relaxed her upper body for demonstration. "Yes, you told me what happened. Is it still a problem?"

Problem? She'd lost motherhood rights, not even able to make costumes for Gracie and Caleb, although at least they hadn't had to wear shiny junk from CVS. Vanessa atoned for leaving her to smash up the garage and burn the house down by manufacturing a nurse uniform for Gracie, complete with a little Florence Nightingale cap and cape. Then she'd made Sean watch the baby and—oh, shit, a blank. Name? Name? Her niece. Vanessa's older daughter. What was her name? It was like a bear. Ursine?

"Maddy?" Zelda recalled her to the moment.

"Vanessa made Caleb . . ." She stopped and took a breath. "A spaceman."

"Right. You told me. However, that's not what bothered you, correct? It was Gracie."

Gracie. Her little heart. Poor baby. Her face fell when Maddy said she planned to go trick-or-treating with her and Ben. She'd covered it with a quick smile, but Maddy saw it. Did Gracie think she'd call people cocksuckers if they gave Gracie hard-candy lollipops instead of chocolate?

"She was embarrassed," Maddy said.

Zelda nodded. "Probably. So what? Who wouldn't be embarrassed if their mother was swearing or shuffling along beside them?"

"I don't shuffle!"

Zelda nodded again. Nodding was Zelda's specialty. "Good. Be glad about that. How lucky you are to have so few physical deficits. Okay, so Gracie would have been embarrassed. She wanted Halloween to be completely about her. Big deal, Maddy. It's normal. You're head-injured." Before continuing, she reached down for a pillow to cushion her bony behind.

"Ah, that's better." Zelda settled into the cushion with a sigh of relief. "Patients are incredibly self-centered when recovering from even a fairly mild brain injury—mild being relative, of course. You think everything is about you. Part of your healing progress is recovering empathy in appropriate ways."

"Empathy? I worry. About kids. Constantly."

"No, Maddy. You constantly worry about how the kids feel about you. That's different."

Had she ever liked Zelda? She hated her. She didn't want to hear that Maddy didn't even want to wake up some days. That she had headaches. That she couldn't drive. That she slept half the day and could barely open a bag of premade salad for lunch.

After grabbing her chart from Zelda's desk, she tried to prove her points by reading aloud in her slow stumbling speech. "Poor memory. Reading difficult. Slowed reactions. Altered sexual behavior. Emotional instability. Sensitive to slights." She stopped. "Why go on? I used to. Write charts like this. Not be the chart."

Zelda reached over and took the chart back. "Stop moping about your deficits. All this will get better."

"How much? How much better?" she asked. "I want. All the way."

"Do you know what Ernest Hemingway said?" she asked.

Maddy didn't bother answering—whatever she said, Zelda would tell her anyway.

" 'The world breaks everyone and afterward many are strong at the broken places.' That's from Hemingway."

Maddy rolled her eyes. "You have sayings. For everything."

"You can be one of those people. Strong at the broken places. You won't be the same. Not ever. But neither will you be this person you feel today."

She took her feet off the desk, rose, and then came over to Maddy's chair, sitting on the ottoman facing her. "There's going to be an entirely new Maddy. You don't know her yet; you're still crying over old Maddy. That's okay, but not for much longer. We're not going to let self-pity arrest your mind."

She imagined Mr. Self-Pity wielding a billy club, shoving her mind in jail. "That another quote?"

"A bastardization. Joyce. I'm feeling show-offy today." She wrapped a hand around Maddy's ankle and squeezed. "Now, let's get back to work."

"Told Emma. She was mean. Made her cry," Maddy said. Zelda shot her a look. "*I* made her cry."

Zelda lowered her glasses a bit. "How did that make you feel?"

"Bad. Horrible." She took a breath and aimed for longer sentences. "She yells at Caleb."

"Is she mean to him?" Zelda asked.

"Yes. But she has. Pressure. Too much." She stopped to gather her thoughts and breathe, just as Zelda preached. "I didn't want to. Make her feel bad."

Emma had tried to wipe away her tears before Maddy could see them. She'd turned away when Maddy tried to hug her. Said she was fine in that way that meant the opposite.

"I say terrible stuff," she said.

"Madeline Illica, listen to all the four-word sentences you just made! Great job!" Zelda grabbed a box of tissues and handed them to her. "Saying things like you said to Emma is yet another effect of traumatic brain injury—call it TBI truth serum. You've lost your filters. Feel it, think it, say it—that's your life at the moment."

"I'm scared," she said.

"What are you scared of?"

She shrugged. "Money. Not enough. Ben. Hating me." She shredded the tissue Zelda had handed her. "Leaving me."

"You're worried about Ben leaving?" Zelda tilted her head. "Has he said something?"

Maddy sat up straight, backing away from Zelda's intensity. "No, no, no. He's wonderful." She tried to form the words properly. "But I'm . . . an albacore."

Zelda looked surprised. "An albacore? Oh! You mean an albatross."

"See. Stupid."

"Self-pity speaking again?"

"Ben won't want me." She gestured at her soft belly, her dented brain. "I know what I am. I'm. I'm . . ." She searched for the right word. "Crappy broken. A crappy broken fat lady. Fuck. Hate shit."

"Maddy, we must get your self-image in line with reality. You can't keep walking this same road."

"How do I. Stop?" she asked. "Saying all crap. In my head?"

"Time. Patience. Retraining." She paused. "There may be times you'll appreciate it, Maddy. You'll be able to say things you never could before."

"Sometimes. I get mad. So mad." She shook her head. "Don't even. Know why."

"Frustration. There's much more inside you than you can possibly say or even cope with knowing. Thus, it becomes soup. But slowly you'll catch up."

"All the way?" she asked.

Zelda laced her fingers and brought them to her chin. "I know you want me to say yes, absolutely yes. But truthfully, I don't know how far you'll go in getting back. This is trial and error to some degree. Some of it will be dumb luck." She rocked toward Maddy and looked her in the eye. "But a large portion is about you—how much work you're willing to do."

CHAPTER 31

Emma

Emma clicked the remote.

Off.

On.

Off.

If her father was home, it would drive him mad. But he wasn't. He'd barely noticed she hadn't gone to school.

Fine.

That's what he said when she told him she had a headache. *Fine.* Fine that she had a headache? Fine that she was staying home? Fine what, Dad?

Clearly, he'd forgotten today was her actual birthday. Her mother didn't even know. Nobody forgot Halloween. Oh, no! That was for the little kids—Aunt Vanessa practically built the Eiffel Tower for them.

Okay then, *fine.* Staying home would be her birthday gift. Not that Sunday's birthday pizza hadn't been simply wonderful. Oh, it was simply terrific! The same pizza they'd have again tonight, because Tuesday was pizza night at the Illicas. Not to mention pizza Thursday. Oh, and absolutely, that crappy supermarket apple pie had been more than enough! And of course she hadn't minded having her great big special birthday pizza celebration on Sunday because today, her real birthday, wasn't convenient. Not with pills for Mom, rehab visits for Mom, and therapist meetings for Mom. Can't squeeze a birthday cake in there—not with needing to make it all about Mom 24-7. Too bad her father hadn't lavished this attention on Mom before he smashed her up.

Nobody had even baked their traditional moka-choka-latta birthday cake, the one her mother had named from the "Lady Marmalade" song. Every birthday her mother sang the song in her off-key voice as she measured flour and sugar, accompanying Patti LaBelle like a backup singer. After stirring and creaming, folding espresso into the chocolate frosting, her mother would play it again and again, turning the volume louder and louder, until Emma, Gracie, and Caleb were drawn to the kitchen.

Sunday night—her so-called early birthday celebration—had been wretched. Gracie bought Emma a biography of Florence Nightingale and a chocolate bar. Caleb drew a crazed house picture with a roof made of cookies and a door made of carrots. Before, her mother would have diagnosed the picture, making up an entire funny story of how it represented the inside of Caleb's mind. Instead, Mom slouched there looking sad-trying-to-look-happy.

Emma's father gave her a card with five twenty-dollar bills.

"Next year," her mother had said.

"Next year what?" Emma supposed she had sounded bitchy since her father had given her a dirty look and answered for her mother.

"Next year we'll go to the fanciest hotel in Boston," her father had said.

"No," Caleb said. "The Swiss Alps!" He and Gracie had recently watched *Heidi* on DVD.

Her mother looked so depressed by the entire thing that Emma spent the rest of the night acting as though everything were fine, wonderful, great—the best birthday in the world! Pie! Pizza! What had Emma expected anyway? Piles of presents while her mother tried to remember the name of the president?

So fine, no big deal.

• • •

Later that afternoon, Emma and Zach sat at one of the tables dotting the plaza by the so-called Pit—the Harvard Square hangout. At four o'clock, kids jammed the place. Emma supposed Zach would rather be almost anywhere else, but she liked it, and anyway, he'd asked where she wanted to go for her birthday. Street poets recited, and dancers spun on the concrete displaying their blazing gymnastics. Three women whose bottom halves were hidden behind a large wooden crate pulled the strings on puppets dressed as soldiers and Middle Eastern children. Emma leaned forward for a better view.

"I told you this was a stupid idea," Zach said. "All anyone here wants is for people to look at them and think how cool they are. So much for being different if all you want is for people to admire your differentness. Do you know what I mean?"

"I think they look pretty cool," Emma said.

"No, you don't. You're just saying that. I can tell." He caught her hand across the white iron table. "Want to eat something?"

She shrugged.

"So what do you want to do? You asked to come here. A bookstore?" He pointed to the Harvard Coop across the street.

"Can't we just stay here and watch?" she asked.

Zach sighed and stretched his legs. Emma wanted to run, race, dance in the middle of the Pit.

The pill she'd swallowed before meeting Zach raced through her.

Now she had five left. She'd counted them out as though they were tiny palace guards, designed for the express purpose of keeping her sadness out of the kingdom. And when they were gone? If she asked Caro for more, it would seem as though she'd moved from needing help as she took care of everyone in her family to being a grubby little addict.

That was it. When they were gone, they were gone.

"Fine," Emma said. "You win. Let's go for a walk."

He smiled, stood, and held out his hand. "Want to walk through the Yard?"

She didn't. Nothing sounded more boring than scuffing through the leaves in Harvard's barren quadrangles. She wanted to go to stores and sift through piles of glittery junk. Smear on nectarine-scented lotions. Taste root-beer-flavored lip gloss. Try on black leather jackets. She should be here with Caro.

"Fine," she repeated.

They walked through Harvard Yard in silence. Intent-looking students hurried by. Gray afternoon light cast gloominess on the sterile-looking quadrangle. Tourists held cameras. Mothers pushed strollers. Professors with briefcases looked important.

"This is depressing," Emma said.

Zach looked at her. "Do you realize the history that's here? I'll probably apply here."

She grabbed his hand and squeezed. "Hug me?"

He pulled her in. The silver birthday bracelet he'd given her caught on her sweater.

Zach's body felt slight against her. She leaned her head against his shoulder—they were almost the same height. A few feet away a kid with a metal-studded face handed money to an emaciated guy with stringy hair covering his eyes.

Pills? Pot? Something worse?

Emma thought of the bottles rattling around her mother's medicine cabinet since the accident. What would it be like tuning out all the time? Did you forget things? Did you disappear? Emma already felt invisible to her family. Had that happened to her mother? Would her whole family disappear soon with all their forgetting?

"Let's go somewhere else," Zach said. "How about my house? We'll have dinner with my parents. They'd love it. My father will even run out and get you a cake."

Emma couldn't think of a worse way to end the day than having a mercy cake. "I should go home."

"You said your grandmother was there, right?" Zach gave her a giant grin. "It's your birthday. Come on."

"Well . . ." Emma pictured herself tied up in knots by his parents. Smiling, yessing, and saying *Oh, this is delicious* while wanting to cry or break a plate. Was that how her mother felt—always saying yes to her father when half the time she meant no?

"I don't want to go to your house," Emma said. "It's my birthday. Take me to the movies, okay?"

Emma kicked at the film of slush in front of her house. Despite the darkness and the sudden icy rain, she'd walked home from the bus stop as slowly as possible. She opened the front door quietly, hoping to avoid facing anyone. She perched at the edge of the hall bench to take off her muddy boots. She tiptoed until she saw her father pacing in the kitchen as he spoke on the phone.

"Sometimes I just don't know how long I can keep this up, Kath," her father complained into the receiver.

Her father must have ticked off Kath because his next words were, "Am I supposed to be punished forever?" After a long pause, he said, "I know. You're right. It's just . . . What the hell. I guess this is my sentence."

Emma slipped farther down the dark hall. The television was on in the living room. It was always on, the heartbeat of their house. She sped up when she heard her father's the-conversation-is-over voice.

"Right, right. Right. I know. I know." Emma recognized her father's growing impatience. "I have to go, Kath."

Her father called her name from the kitchen, preventing her from heading upstairs. Emma backed up and stuck her head in, watching as he placed a greasy-looking plate in the dishwasher.

"Home pretty late, aren't you?" he asked.

"I called. You weren't home. I told you I was having supper at Caro's," she lied. "It's only eight o'clock."

"It's a school night."

Emma didn't say anything to his brilliant observation. She watched him carefully place each dish into the correct slot. It had always bugged her father how haphazardly her mother loaded the dishwasher.

Now he got to put in every dish just how he wanted. *Happy, Dad?*

"What did you have for supper?" he asked.

"Bagels and cream cheese."

"That's it?" He lifted his eyebrows.

"And salad," she lied again.

He grabbed a faded yellow towel and began drying one of Grandma Anne's baking dishes.

"Did you have dessert?" he asked. "Grandma sent over rice pudding. Homemade. With the yellow raisins you like."

Hearing him try so hard made her want to cry, and she was so tired of feeling sorry for people. "No, thanks, Dad." She turned to leave.

"Sit for a minute, Em. I want to talk to you."

Rolling her eyes, she sat, bringing her knees up to her chin and hugging them. "Where's Mom?"

"Resting. She seemed upset, so I gave her a pill," he said. "Honey, why are you always running out?"

"Running out? I'm here all the time! Who takes care of Caleb and Gracie practically every day that Grandma isn't here? Me. Who does almost all the cleaning? Me."

"Mom's doing a lot more than before."

Emma kept her mouth shut. Her mother cleaned and cooked a little more now, but it was slow and painful—painful for Emma anyway. Watching her mother think so hard about where the dust rags were or how to fold sheets. Everything done in baby steps.

"You're hanging out with that boy too much." Her father bent, picking up a Cheerio from the floor.

"'That boy'?" Emma laughed. "News flash, Dad, Zach is the straightest boy in the world. He makes me look insanely wild."

Her father didn't look particularly comforted. Emma read his mind: *They all want the same thing. Don't trust anyone.*

"Nevertheless, I'd like to have you home more," he said.

Emma slumped and toyed with the sugar bowl her father had bought to replace the one her mother broke. This one was plain white, and Emma hated it. Tipping it back and forth, feeling the sugar tilt with each movement, she tried to think of what to say. Her father sat across from her.

"Are you going to answer me?" he said.

"I didn't hear a question, Dad. You just said you'd like me home more. That's a statement."

He took an obvious breath for control. "I don't know if you under-stand. I need you on my side."

Emma rested her head on her knees again. She looked down as she answered him. "It's just too sad here. I hate being home. It's like being punished every second." She thought of throwing her missed real birthday at him, but when she looked up, she couldn't—she wished she'd kept her mouth shut. Looking at him hurt, he seemed so old—like Grandpa Benedikte but without the bravery.

He nodded. Too slowly. "Okay. I get it." He turned back to the dishwasher.

Now she wished she'd never said a word.

Something crashed. Emma looked at the clock.

"Goddamn it!" her father swore from the hall.

Nine thirty. She crouched on the bed, listening.

Emma threw down her Latin book and ran into the hall. Her fa-ther's too-red face looked like an imminent heart attack; his lips were set in a thin line. Her mother came out of their bedroom twisting and untwisting the belt tying her faded bathrobe.

Her father kicked the overturned laundry basket and then punched his fist against the bathroom door.

"Damn it, Maddy, you put dirty clothes away again! I had to take a load of pissy underwear from Caleb's dresser. Don't I do enough with-out having to undo everything you screw up? Do me a favor, okay? If you can't do it right, don't do anything."

"You didn't. Have to . . ." Her mother took deep ragged breaths.

"What? I didn't have to what, Maddy? Clean? Wash?"

"She means you don't have to yell, Dad," Emma said.

"What's wrong?" Gracie ran out of her room in her nightgown, curls flattened on one side of her head, springing wildly on the other.

"Go back to bed," her father barked.

Gracie stiffened into a robot child and stiff-tip-toed to Emma, who pulled her in close.

"Trying. To help." Her mother backed up until she stood against the wall.

Her father slammed scattered clothes back into the basket.

"I'll take care of it, Dad," Emma said. She came forward, holding out her hands.

"No, no, no." He held out his hand to ward her off. "The laundry is too *sad* for you, and of course it's too difficult for your mother. So just like everything else, it becomes my responsibility."

"Dad, I said I'd take care of it."

"And I said go back to your room."

"Stop," her mother begged.

"Stop what?" her father yelled. "Stop taking care of everything? Stop and let you screw things up more? I have to go through every fucking piece of clothing in the house to see which is dirty and which is clean."

"I said I'd do it," Emma said for the third time. She wedged herself between her parents and looked up at her father. "Leave Mom alone; she's trying."

Her mother sank to the floor and wrapped her arms tightly around her legs, her body shaking. Gracie ran to her. "Stop it, Daddy," she said. "You're scaring Mommy."

Emma watched the rage seep out of her father, as though Gracie's words had pulled out a stopper. He brought a hand to his head and ran it repeatedly over his crazed hair. Finally, he stepped over to where Gracie and her mother cowered and knelt before them.

"Mother of God," he said. "Listen, I'm sorry. Christ Almighty. I'm sorry, Mad, okay? You know how I get when my buttons get pushed. Stop crying. Please, okay? No more." His words didn't match his tone. Even as he apologized, he sounded angry.

"You shouldn't talk to Mommy like that," Gracie said.

Her mother lifted her tear-stained face. "It's. Okay. Daddy is. Upset."

Emma thought she would throw up from hating her father, or punch the wall like him, or start throwing everything in the hall down the stairs—the phone table, the laundry basket, Gracie's backpack. She had that whizzy dirty feeling that came in the hours after taking one of Caro's pills.

"You just made a mistake, Mom. Don't apologize for him." Emma turned to her father. "At least she's trying. You're such an idiot, Dad."

"Don't talk to me like that," her father said, his lawyer voice suddenly available to him. "Go to your room. Now." He thrust his finger at her chest. "Go! You too, Gracie. Both of you. Back to sleep. Show over."

Emma didn't move an inch. Her mother and Gracie huddled together as though they lived in a mental institution.

"Don't put this on me!" she yelled. "I'm sick of pretending. I'm not going to make believe everything is fine while you go around making everyone miserable."

"I'm not telling you again, Emma." Her father came toward her, his face tightening.

"You started it, Daddy," Emma screamed. "It's your fault, so don't get mad at anyone else."

"Just get the hell into your room!" her father said. "I can't take another minute of shit from you."

Emma whirled around to face her mother and Gracie, planting her feet wide apart, jamming her hands on her hips, and leaning forward. "It's his fault, Mom. He's the reason you're like this. He drove like a madman in the rain. A maniac. That's what Grandpa said. And they're making a case against him. In court. Reckless driving. Weaving. Driving to endanger. *Endanger*. If he didn't drive like a lunatic, you'd be just fine. Daddy told us not to tell. He made us lie. But it was all his fault."

The sudden silence sounded louder than all the shouting.

Emma ran into her room and slammed the door.

CHAPTER 32

Ben

"Come on, Maddy. Let me in." Ben, hoarse from pleading, put his ear against the locked bedroom door, listening for sounds of life. Soon it would be midnight, but the kids were all awake, huddled in Emma's room, waiting for him to fix everything. Jesus, what the fuck was Maddy doing in there? Was she asleep? Locked in the bathroom with the pill bottles lined up like bullets? How long could he wait for Maddy to open the door on her own?

Anne and Jake could probably get her out.

Christ Almighty, the last thing he wanted to do was call them. They'd drive over in their bathrobes, Jake ready to yank Maddy out of Ben's reach and Anne carrying the eiderdown in which to wrap her.

What the hell was she doing in there?

"Please, Mad. I'm begging you." He closed his eyes and threw his head back in prayer. *Please, let her be okay.* In answer, God led Maddy to throw something against the door. *Thank you, Lord.*

At least he knew she was alive.

He trudged down the stairs to the kitchen and opened the junk drawer. Rusty scissors that barely worked, candle nubs, matchbooks, out-of-date coupons, crusty glue bottles—debris from their lives crammed every inch. He piled it all on the counter, emptying the drawer until he got to a small Tupperware container filled with keys. Copies of their house key, neighbors' keys, Anne and Jake's keys, Vanessa's, Kath's—God forbid any of them couldn't get into the others' space any time they wanted.

Minutes ticked by before he found the original skeleton keys for the house, four of them, all covered with green-black tarnish. The moment he touched them, their sour oxidized scent clung to his fingers.

He ran upstairs and jammed one key after another into the bedroom lock until, finally, the fourth one slid in, the tumbler clicked, and the door swung open. Maddy sat cross-legged on their bed, frantically riffling through *People* magazine. She ripped a page out, crumpled it, and threw the paper to the ground.

"Get out," she screeched as best she could. "Find another. Room."

Ben went to the stuffed chair under the window. Despite his great need to rest, put up his feet, and feel cushions behind his neck, he planted his feet on the floor and his hands on his knees. "How about putting down the magazine and taking a deep breath?" he asked.

Maddy dropped the shredded *People* and picked up *Time*, slamming the magazine repeatedly against the bed in time to her words. "Fuck you. Fuck you. Fuck you."

Then she threw the magazines, one after another.

Ben ducked. She scrambled to the side of the bed and reached for a small glass reading lamp. He lunged and grabbed both her hands.

"Let go," she said.

He held her. "You have to stop throwing things."

In answer, she spit. Her saliva hit his chin. He fought his instinct to hit her, fling her to the floor.

"Maddy . . ." He stopped, not knowing what to say. Would he have to call an ambulance, have them pink-paper her?

"Should I call someone? Do you want Kath? Olivia?" he asked.

Maddy's wrists became limp, and her body folded in. Ben let go, and she curled on her side. He fit his body to hers and tried to hold her tight from behind, but she wriggled away and faced him.

"Why. Did. You. Lie?" She kicked out and landed a sharp blow on his shin.

"Why did I lie?" He winced at his words, remembering Maddy talking about her clients. *When they repeat the question, I know they're lying. It's how they buy time.* Wisdom he'd used in his interviews, his crosses.

"Don't play. Ben. I can't speak. So good. But I can. Think." Maddy sat cross-legged and grabbed a pillow, kneading it until he thought feathers would fly around the room.

He stayed silent—unable to find anything that could be meaningful to say.

"Don't wait. For me. Coward. Say something."

He faced her. "I'm sorry." He searched for other words, better words. "You know it was an accident, right? You have to know that. A horrible, horrible accident."

Maddy hugged the pillow to her chest and rocked.

"I didn't lie. I only didn't tell you because I wanted to protect you." Ben leaned forward and reached for her, trying to touch some part of his wife—her ankle, her toe, anything. She drew away. "They said you wouldn't remember. That maybe you'd never remember. I needed to wait until you healed. I did it because I didn't want to add to your pain. I thought you'd need to trust me a hundred percent—so I could help you a hundred percent."

Tears threatened as he prayed for the comfort of Maddy's arms, wanting the moment to be over.

She jabbed a finger at him. "Who. Are you. Crying for? Me or you?"

"Maybe both of us," he said.

"Fuck you. I didn't have. To be this way, Ben. If. You were good."

Four days later, Ben sat in the living room, turning the pages of the Sunday *Boston Globe* magazine section, registering neither sentences nor pictures. The younger children curled next to him on the couch, Caleb hypnotized by an audiobook coming through his earphones and Gracie lost in reading yet another book with a magic-themed cover. Since the accident, Anne could barely keep up with Gracie's thirst for fantasy worlds.

Emma hid in her room, the best place she could be. Ben didn't want to see her, afraid that he couldn't forgive her, or that even if he could, he'd lash out at her. Grab and shake her.

He was an asshole. She was just a kid. He'd leaned on her too hard in these past months.

Yet he was furious.

Maddy slept. She hadn't spoken one word to him since their battle. If she wanted something, she requested it through her mother or sister. Though she was angry with Anne and Vanessa for going along with Ben's lie, Maddy had to talk to someone. Vanessa would call him at work, ticking off the items Maddy needed: tampons, cranberry juice, some brand of shampoo that was only sold in a far-off store a million miles from their house. He swore Vanessa made up that last request.

Ben didn't know how to react to this nonspeaking Maddy. It felt like she'd died. Before, she'd shown her anger by pecking at him until he got the point. She'd bang around cleaning, cooking, and slamming laundry baskets, and then she'd talk more. Since the accident, Maddy's rage had seemed directed at herself and she'd allowed Ben the great luxury of being her protector.

His shameful truth was this: Ben missed that role.

Only Anne took any pity on him. "Just be patient," Anne had said the previous night, calling to tell him that Maddy and the kids would be eating dinner with her and Jake for the third night in a row. "It would be difficult for anyone to work through this, much less someone struggling with her problems."

"Honestly, Anne, I can't even tell if her speech is improving, it's been so long since we've spoken."

"Every day it gets better, dear. Don't worry," Anne said.

Ben's gloomy little attempt at humor had died on delivery.

It was ironic. After months of wishing for just one day of peace, God had answered his prayers. Night after night he'd come home to an empty house. Now he knew what his grandmother, his wrinkled

Romanian peanut of a grandmother, had meant when she'd warned him, "Careful what you wish, Bennie."

What could he do to atone?

Tonight they were supposed to have dinner with his parents—he'd accepted the invitation weeks ago. He dreaded the evening, whether Maddy went or not.

Gracie leaned on Ben. He rubbed her shoulder before pulling away and slowly folding the paper. "I'm going to wake up Mommy," he said.

"Do you think she wants a muffin?" Gracie asked. "I can go with Emma to J.P. Licks and get the blueberry kind she likes."

"That's okay, sweetie. I have it covered." Ben leaned over and kissed first Gracie and then tried to reach Caleb, who bobbed his head away.

Maddy's need for sleep seemed unending. Dr. Paulo had explained the healing, the normalcy of it all—but Ben couldn't come to grips with how she slept for hours after the rest of them were awake.

He prepared a cup of coffee before going upstairs. Cream mixed with two teaspoons of sugar made it an inviting toasted-almond color—before the accident Maddy had drunk an evil-colored brew, barely lightened with skim milk. He used a mug from the sunshine set he'd bought for her one evening while alone and wandering through Copley Plaza the previous week, a bright yellow with a blazing orange sun. Upstairs, he placed it on the night table, covering it with a book to keep it warm.

Maddy wakened. For a moment he looked into her loving eyes, her you-hold-my-life-in-your-hands eyes—the eyes he'd seen since she'd returned from the rehab. Moments later, her bitter-blame eyes came back.

"Do you want to get up? I brought coffee." He hoped she'd notice the mug. Three matching ones lined a shelf in the kitchen.

She struggled to shake off sleep, retrieving the pink nightgown strap slipping over her shoulder. Her tangled curls, dream-rosy cheeks, and newly rounded face made her look like Gracie. She complained about the weight she'd gained, blaming her inability to judge or control her portions—she'd eat an entire row of Oreos without noticing—but Ben found this plumped-out Maddy endearing. Protecting her seemed more important than ever now that she'd lost the hard muscles she'd had from years of running with Kath.

"Coffee." This was the first word she'd spoken to him since the incident. She said it without inflection. Asking, not demanding. Just a word. He handed the cup to her with as much simplicity.

"We're supposed to go to my parents' tonight," he said.

"I remember. Wrote it down."

"Are we going?"

She took the warm cup in two hands, dipping her head into the steam before sipping, using her bent knees as a table.

"You have to talk to me sometime, Maddy," Ben said when she didn't respond. "Tell me to get lost. To screw myself. Just, please, talk to me."

"How did you. Feel?" she asked. "Then?"

"How did I feel?" Ben clenched and unclenched his fists. "What are you asking? How I felt when I first realized you were hurt? When you were in the hospital?"

"Everything. Tell me it all." The yellow mug shook in her hands. "Give it back. My story. My life."

He cleared his throat, but it still felt like sand. "I wanted to die, but if I did, I wouldn't be there for you. I thought God punished me for being an asshole for so long, but I couldn't fathom why he'd picked on you and not me. Except that nothing in the world could hurt me more than seeing you pay for my sins."

"Lawyer speak." Maddy made a talk-to-the-hand gesture she must have learned from her clients.

Ben wondered what would satisfy her. "I'll make it up to you. I promise." He needed words to calm her, words to show her the pain this also gave him.

"Make it up? *Listen!* What if it stays? Like this?"

"It won't. Dr. Paulo says—"

"Spare. Me." Maddy swallowed more coffee. "Why did you lie? Say it fault. Of other guy?"

"Because it wasn't just me. The other guy was practically . . . Oh,

Jesus, Maddy. That doesn't matter. I lied for you—so you could lean on me without question. I lied for me—so you wouldn't question my ability to take care of you, so you wouldn't have additional stress."

"Asshole." She crossed her legs, looking like Gracie in that position.

"I didn't want you to hate me, baby," he admitted.

"I hate you now. You stole truth. From me," she said. "Already broke me. Why steal more?"

"I screwed up," Ben said. "I wish someone had stopped me." Anne, Vanessa, Olivia, Kath, Jake—they shouldn't have gone along with him.

Maddy snorted and gave a strangled laugh. Ben took the mug from her hand, afraid she'd spill the coffee, break the cup.

"What's so funny?"

She snorted and reached for the coffee. "Who could win. A fight with you?"

He held on to the cup. "Did your sister say that? Olivia? Who?"

"No one. Said it." Maddy slapped her free hand on the bedspread. "I. Am remembering. Before. Stuff is coming. Back. You yelled. Threw stuff. But. I don't remember. Why."

Maddy's words came extra slow this morning—as they did when she took sleeping pills or had headaches.

Or maybe the anxiety of dealing with him caused her sluggish speech.

"Give back. Coffee," she demanded.

Ben handed her the mug. "Look at your coffee. That might be the sole good thing we can find. Before it looked like you were drinking war rations. Now at least—"

"*Coffee?* Accident a gift, Ben? For good coffee?" Maddy slammed the cup on the bedside table, liquid sloshing.

He gingerly placed a hand on her leg. "Now it tastes better. That's all I meant."

"Asshole." Maddy picked up the book Vanessa had foisted on her, threw it at the door, and stared up at their chipped ceiling. "Fucking lawyer."

•　•　•

"More roast?" Ben's mother gestured toward the bloody platter.

He shook his head. "No, thank you." He'd lost his taste for big planks of rare meat, the staple of his mother's family meals.

"Children?" his mother asked, nodding at the plate. "More?"

His kids shook their heads, silent, until Ben's mother shot them a look.

"No, thank you, Grandma," Caleb recited.

His mother smiled, satisfied. She invited little conversation, though she had a soft spot for Gracie, who was pliable like Ben's brother. Andrew had always been his mother's favorite.

"Dear?" Frances asked her husband.

"If you please," the Judge said.

His mother lifted a slice of rare roast and slipped it on her husband's plate without a drip.

Steak knives clicked against bone china. His father cut his meat into even bite-sized pieces, finishing the job of dicing it before allowing himself to eat. They'd spoken little since the accident. Last time Ben had seen him, the Judge had offered money. *Tell me if there is need,* his father said as though speaking of something shameful. Each time they saw each other Ben gave his father the look that meant *any news on my case?* The Judge gave back the smallest lowering of his lids and the briefest left turn of his chin that indicated *nothing yet.*

Yesterday Caleb asked if he would go to jail if they didn't win. Ben promised that wasn't even in the cards.

"What is in the cards?" Caleb had asked.

"Nothing you have to worry about," Ben had answered in typical parental reassurance, even as he saw an entire deck of possibilities— losing his job, Maddy, the kids—not probabilities, sure, but his rationalizing offered no comfort.

"Ketchup?" Maddy asked.

Ben winced, knowing his mother considered ketchup an insult to her cooking.

"Does the meat lack flavor, dear?" his mother asked.

Maddy looked confused. "No. I mean . . . yes?" Maddy's voice rose and squeaked.

"Don't quiz her, Mom. She just wants ketchup." Ben stood. "I'll get it."

He opened the swinging door and went through the small butler's pantry to the kitchen, returning moments later with a bottle of Heinz that he set firmly on the table.

"Anything else?" he asked his wife.

Maddy shook her head and uncapped the bottle. Everyone watched as she tipped it, the large, red pool gathering on the white plate. A bit dripped over the lip as she righted it. As she reached for her linen napkin, she knocked over the bottle. Ketchup oozed on the white tablecloth. Panic showed on her face as she blotted the stain, spreading it further.

"No!" Maddy wailed. "Damn it." She stood and backed away from the table, knocking over her chair.

Ben put his arms around her while Emma righted the chair. "Hey, it's okay, Maddy."

"*No!*" She turned to Ben. "Fuck you. I hate you."

"Now, now," the Judge said. "There's no need to go on like this. Maddy, calm yourself."

"*Fuck you, also!* Hate you too." Maddy lifted her plate with both hands.

The Judge stood and pointed a finger at Maddy. "Put that down. There will be none of that in this house."

"Sit, Dad," Ben said softly. He eased the plate from Maddy's shaking hands and helped her into the chair. "Shh, shh." He touched her back. "You're all right. Everything is all right."

"Don't worry, sweetheart," his mother said. She covered the stain with her own napkin, and then placed her hand over Maddy's. "It's only cloth."

Maddy caressed her own cheek with her mother-in-law's hand. "Thank you."

His mother gave Maddy's curls a brief pat before sitting.

Silence resettled over the table. After finishing the main course, Ben was ready to leave. Dessert wouldn't be more than the usual cup of cherry Jell-O, and he had no desire for the muddy Turkish coffee his father favored. He pushed back his chair.

"Wait," his father said.

"The kids have school tomorrow, Dad. Maddy is exhausted."

Maddy didn't deny it—and if she had, the dark circles under her eyes would have given her away. Ben had to get her out before she hit the wall.

"We can't go yet, Daddy." Gracie smiled in a way he hadn't seen for too long. Impishly.

His mother pushed back her chair. "Just wait one moment, Ben. Gracie and I will be right back. Caleb?" She tipped her head at her grandson, and he rose.

"We have a surprise," Caleb whispered loudly in Ben's ear as he passed his father.

Emma, Maddy, Ben, and the Judge waited without speaking. Emma played with the crystal salt and pepper shakers, switching them left to right, right to left, until Ben wanted to snatch them from her hands. He watched, amazed his father didn't scold her. Instead, the Judge sat with a satisfied almost-smile. Maddy looked tired enough to sleep in her chair.

Caleb swung the door open using his hip, a small boom box in his hand.

"Introducing, Grandma and Gracie. Ta da!"

His mother walked in carrying a silver tray with a cake. "Happy birthday, Emma dear," she said. "I'm sorry we're late."

Gracie, her cheeks matching her pink blouse, came out dancing, lifting first one shoulder, then the other in a rolling motion in time to the song playing from the tape deck.

"*Hey sister, go sister, flow sister,*" Gracie sang as she wiggled toward Emma, swinging her nonexistent hips.

"It's the Christina Aguilera version," Caleb said as if he'd pulled off some major coup.

Ben's mother bobbed her head as she brought the cake to the table. "*Moka-choka-latta,*" she sang in her church voice.

He felt as though the sun had come out, seeing Maddy smile and clap her hands. His chest tightened as she stood and joined Gracie and Caleb, her arms up high, making jazz hands, and bumping hips with Gracie.

"Listen!" Caleb announced as the tape segued into Patti LaBelle. "Now it's the other one!"

Maddy slipped into the slightly different beat without a pause. Emma rose and stood across from her mother. They lifted their hands in unison, singing, "*Gittche, gittche ya ya,*" and for one moment, Ben let himself believe everything would be okay.

Everyone fell asleep on the ride home as Ben drove cautiously, slowly. After parking, he scooped up Caleb and lifted him into a modified fireman's carry. Gracie and Emma walked ahead, holding their mother's hand until they reached the door. After giving Maddy a quick hug, Emma opened the door with her key, leaving it open for Ben.

Gracie stumbled upstairs. Ben didn't bother waking Caleb enough to wash up, just made him pee and let him collapse on his bed. After, Ben tapped on Emma's door.

"What?"

Ben's fatigue fought with knowing he should connect with his daughter. Exhaustion won the battle. "Good night, sweetheart," Ben said through the door.

In their room, Maddy slept with Gracie curled around her. On any given night recently, he'd find one of the kids in here, even Emma, who'd pretend she'd fallen asleep watching TV, leaving him to the couch again.

"Gracie," he whispered. "Come on, sweet peach. Let's go to your room."

Ben led her down the hall to her bedroom and tucked her in. Sleepy-warm, she pulled him in for one more kiss. "Stay, Daddy."

"I have to go to bed, peach."

"No. I mean really stay. We need you."

On some level, Maddy used to say, kids always knew when things were wrong. *It doesn't matter if we fight quietly, Ben. Kids watch their parents as if we're the most important TV show in the world, and they never take their eyes off the screen when there's trouble.*

"I'm not going anywhere." Ben swore to himself that he would make good on this promise.

Back in their bedroom, he turned off the television and light, took off his jeans and sweatshirt, and climbed into bed, nestling into Maddy's back. Asleep, she seemed to forget her fury, wriggling closer, until their parts matched and he felt her old flannel nightgown against his legs. Fabric so familiar and worn, so soft and thin, touching it was almost like stroking her skin. He ran his hand over the curve of her hip, waist to thigh and back again. Her softness seemed vulnerable, like her. How had he ever treated such fragile creatures as his wife, his children, with such abandon?

Maddy hummed in the back of her throat as he slipped his hand under the cloth and rubbed the lowest part of her back, the top rise of her buttocks. He kneaded the flesh at her waist. Pulling, tugging, he got her nightgown up until she lifted her arms and he could pull off the soft flannel and run his hands over her sleep-hot flesh.

She lay back, letting him cover her. Their rhythm was familiar, exciting. He clutched and held on. "Things are clearer now," he whispered. "Maybe too clear."

"What's clear?" She rested her fingertips on his shoulder.

"How much I love you and need you. I think I need you more than you need me. I don't like feeling this way . . ."

He waited for her to answer, to console him as she'd always done, whether he deserved it or not.

Maddy pushed him off and went to the bathroom, leaving him with his confession hanging out. She came back wrapped in a robe. Even in the dark room, Ben saw her solemn expression. She touched the blanket where it covered his knee.

"I don't want you anymore. I want to be alone."

CHAPTER 33

Maddy

Maddy woke alone and cold. Surprised to be on Ben's side of the bed. It had been eleven days since he'd left. She missed his scent. She missed his hand on her back. She missed leaning against him through the night.

The clock read 9:30, though the dreary December light made it seem earlier. Like dawn. Staying under the covers was the only thing she wanted.

A thud of emptiness had followed Ben's absence. Her mother was now here every minute. Having her parents virtually living there drove her crazy, but she was afraid to be alone with her heartbroken children. Gracie had keened like a grieving war widow, bent over double, as Ben made promises that weren't his to make: *It's only for a little while, cupcake. You'll hardly know I'm gone. I'll be back before you know it.*

Maddy's parents were there to witness Ben leaving. Her father with his arms crossed. Her mother almost crying. Emma suffered Ben's kiss on her cheek. Caleb clutched at Ben's leg until Maddy's father pulled him away.

When Ben kissed her—on her forehead, on her mouth—his lips burned against her cold ones.

Every third day he came to take the kids to dinner. Tonight they were going to talk. Alone. Maddy and Ben. In a restaurant. He'd asked her as though for a date.

"Maddy? Are you up?" Her mother peeked in, and then opened the door all the way. She placed a cup of coffee on the nightstand.

"Thanks, Mom." She picked up the mug and took a sip, wincing at the taste. Her mother kept bringing coffee as she used to drink it— bleak with skim milk.

"Sorry, honey." She smacked her hand to her forehead. "I keep forgetting to buy cream."

"And sugar, Mom. I take sugar." She took another sip and wrinkled her nose. "This tastes disgusting."

"Golly, sure can count on you for straight shooting," her mother said.

"Joke?" she asked. "Are you mad?"

"Of course I'm not mad," she said. "Who doesn't like to be told she makes awful coffee?"

"And you. A. Caterer," she said. Ah! Another joke.

"Are you okay?" Her mother wore her intolerable poor-Maddy face. "Don't you miss him, honey? Aren't you lonely?"

"How could I. Be lonely? When you and Dad. Won't go away."

Her mother sat at the edge of the bed and touched Maddy's forehead as though checking for a fever. She batted away her mother's hand. "That's not the same as a husband. You should rethink this. I know you're angry, but honey, how can you possibly manage without him?"

Maddy crossed her legs and sat up straight. "Are you tired. Of us? Don't want to help?"

"No, no. I just—I just don't want you doing the wrong thing."

"Should worry more about. Ben doing. The wrong thing." She pulled off the covers and stood. "Driving crazy. Yelling. You going to work?"

"I have to make ten dozen muffins for a Hadassah meeting in Framingham." Her mother gave her a sudden hard hug. "You know how much Daddy and I love you and how much we love being here with you and the kids. We just want everything to work out."

When Maddy came out of the shower, her mother was gone. Finally, she was alone. Her mother's constant harping on Ben's innocence drove Maddy nuttier than she already was. "It's not like he *tried* to hurt you," her mother repeated nightly, her emphasis so thick it resounded like a scream. Having help came with a price tag. "It was an accident" had become the mantra Maddy had to swallow with every one of her mother's home-cooked meals. "The case will be dropped—Benedikte will take care of it."

Accident. Accident. Accident. Everyone kept reminding her it was an accident. Especially Ben. *I'm sorry, I'm sorry,* he'd say every night when he called. *Must you grind me to dust for an accident?*

How could they all call reckless driving an accident?

Driving to endanger.

That sounded purposeful to her. She'd never think he meant to hurt her. That wasn't the point. But an accident? When someone drove so fast that the car skidded out of control? That wasn't an accident. That was rashness. That was believing you were above the laws of nature. What if one of the kids had been in her seat? What if Gracie or Caleb or Emma had been thrown out and smashed? If he killed one of them, would he whine that he was innocent?

Maddy ransacked her closet, searching for something decent to wear. Who cared that she had nowhere to go? She was tired of looking ugly, tired of crying, tired of being mad and sad. A blouse that didn't gap, pants that closed—that's all she wanted. .

Shirts. Dresses. Jackets. She rejected one after another. Small and limp with disuse, they belonged to someone else.

Somewhere was a remembered white shirt she thought might match a shapeless black shift she'd discovered in her closet, probably left from early on in one of her pregnancies. Tugging open every drawer brought nothing. She searched Ben's closet but couldn't find the blouse hanging anywhere.

Maybe it only existed in her mind.

She dragged a yellow step stool up from the kitchen, placing it carefully in front of her closet, moving aside anything that could trip her before she reached for the high shelves where there were boxes and stacks of put-away clothes. *Pride goeth before a fall,* she reminded herself. Her chest swelled with pleasure at her own careful planning. Then she grew proud at remembering a quotation worthy of Zelda's door.

As she stretched toward an old pile of sweaters, three large flowered hatboxes toppled over, their contents falling across the closet floor and onto the bedroom carpet.

She climbed off the stool. Carefully. Receiving blankets, stiff rolls of ribbon, miniature hotel sewing kits, and unmatched socks spilled from the boxes. Her housekeeping skills: ineptitude on parade. She tried to gather the items into piles that made sense—throw out, keep, and give away. Removable shoulder pads. Cards from long-forgotten Mother's Day celebrations. She sniffed a tiny bottle of body lotion from the Marriott Hotel, and then quickly pulled away from the rancid dead-flower odor, wondering why she'd kept all this crap.

A brown flannel bag for shoes sat by her knee. She undid the drawstring, and plastic pill bottles spilled out. Her hands shook as she picked them up one by one, reading:

- *Ambien. Take as needed.*
- *Lorazepam. May cause dizziness.*
- *Valium. Use care when driving or operating machinery.*
- *Klonopin. May cause drowsiness.*
- *Xanax. Alcohol may intensify this effect.*
- *Lunesta. Vicodin. Percocet. Librium—*

Her stash. Some bottles more than ten years old—pills she'd squirreled away for years. She'd forgotten. A bottle rattled in her hand as she shook it. She opened it up, curious. The cap was childproof, but opening it wasn't too difficult. Opening it filled her with a joy, her skill! Until it turned to disgust.

Joy at opening a pill bottle hardly seemed an event to celebrate.

Pouring the entire bottle into her hand felt like possibility. Would these make her feel better? End the sadness and anger? Make her decisions?

She shoved the bottles back in the fabric bag, threw on an old beige turtleneck and jumper, and ran from the bedroom, escaping to the hall where she pulled on boots, grabbed her cell phone, and slammed out of the house.

November wind cut through the back of her wool coat. She buried her bare hands in the too-small pockets and walked in the direction of Centre Street. Instead of making the inevitable right toward the local stores and restaurants, she turned in the direction she thought would lead to downtown, thinking that maybe she'd walk to Ben's office.

A hat would have been smart. *Fifty percent of body heat is lost through the head.* Real or invented knowledge? Facts returned daily, but she never knew if they had any basis in reality.

Perhaps being bareheaded was good. Fresh cold air would wake up more memories and skills. Walking, air, and a frozen head could become her prescription.

How long since she'd lived without reliance on pills? Had it stopped when head met asphalt?

How long since she'd felt safe? After she woke, everything was messy and scary. Before, she'd imagined her life was safe and whole, but now she had no idea who she'd been. How scared was that former Maddy?

One long-ago snowy night, Ben had slipped an engagement ring on her finger. The diamond had overwhelmed her—so perfect. Brilliant. Valuable. At the moment of joy she'd thought, come the Nazis, she could sew the ring in the hem of her coat and trade it for freedom. Food. In Ben she was sure she had a man who would take up guns and fight. Her Raoul Wallenberg. Her hero.

Why had she needed pills for protection from her hero?

The wind died. She unbuttoned her coat and slowed her pace. This was the longest she'd walked since the accident. At Northeastern University her legs trembled. She feared that she'd collapse. After resting for a moment on a bench, she crossed Huntington Avenue, a broad street bisected by trolley tracks, and wandered into a Store 24, hoping to find rescue, something to quell fatigue.

In her wallet she discovered ten twenty-dollar bills. Ben. He worried that she'd leave the house without money, so bills appeared as though she possessed a money genie.

Wandering through the aisle of the crowded store, she ran her fingers over boxes of Trix. *Trix are for kids!* She pushed at the plastic wrapping of Oscar Mayer bologna, hearing the meat jingle in her head. Legions of water bottles lined up in the cooler. She grabbed one and brought it to the front of the store.

When her turn came to pay, she placed the bottle on the metal counter crowded with a million other things she could buy. Key chains. Lollipops. Slim Jims. She held out a pile of bills to a frowning man with skin reminiscent of malaria. Was her money dirty? Did most people pay some other way? Should she have said something?

"I need. Change," she said.

"Where are you from, huh?" He shook his head. "You shouldn't be so trusting, miss."

She kept her hands out, palms up. "I need help."

He picked out a limp twenty-dollar bill and handed back a fistful of change and smaller bills. "You're lucky you met me and not the night guy."

Gratitude overwhelmed her as she nodded with thanks at her lucky, lucky malaria man.

Clutching the money, she walked to the closest trolley stop, the one that would take her back in the direction from where she'd come. She would go to work. To Olivia. Minutes later, a trolley pulled in and she boarded, realizing too late that her cold water still sat on the Store 24 counter.

Holding out the change in her hand, she asked the trolley driver, "Could you take? What you need? And tell me. How to get. To Beth Israel. Hospital?"

"Lady, don't you have a Charlie Card?"

"Card?" Did you have to identify yourself now to get on the T? She remembered 9/11. Rules had become strict. Scary. She shuddered.

"Where's your T-Pass? Don't you know what I'm talking about?"

The driver shook his head, so skinny the uniform bagging on his chest billowed out with his movements. "Never mind."

He waved away her money and directed her to a handicapped seat across from him and said he'd tell her exactly which stop to get off, warning her that after she got off she'd have to walk many blocks to get to the hospital.

Maddy fell into the bucketed seat, proud that somehow she'd made it this far.

The place where she once spent every day didn't seem welcoming. Brookline Avenue looked desolate, despite the people hurrying back and forth between the sterile brick buildings. Didn't the world allow curves on buildings anymore?

She stood in front of the hospital where she worked and where the ambulance had brought her after the accident. Her only memories were from before, when she'd rush from the house with sopping wet hair to get the kids to school on time. Family always trumped vanity.

Now she could spend all day drying her hair.

The entry to the hospital seemed familiar and not. She waited for some inbred sense to lead her in the right direction toward her office, but nothing came. She opened her book and searched for Olivia's number.

"Come get me. In the lobby," Maddy begged Olivia.

Drained, she curled up in a blue foam chair until Olivia appeared, all juicy bright in buttery yellow. Maddy drank her in as though she were sacramental wine.

"Hey, you," Olivia said, putting out a hand to pull Maddy up.

"Hey, you." She smiled and stared at Olivia. "Skinny. Pretty."

Olivia ran her hands along her hips. "A few pounds fell off. A miracle, huh?"

"Truly miracle," she said. "Never thought possible."

Olivia hugged her tightly. Laughing.

"I love you," Maddy burst out.

"I love you too, honey."

In the elevator, she stroked the shoulder of Olivia's blouse, so smooth and soft, like baby skin. "Do you miss me?"

"Almost as much as I miss my morning jelly donut. They tried to put someone new in your office. Just till you came back," she said. "But I ran right over to human resources and banged a file big as my ass right on Steve Reilly's desk, telling him to watch out before I called in the Americans with Disabilities Act."

"My desk? They want my desk?" Why did they want to take her desk?

"Don't worry. It's nothing."

The office seemed neater than Maddy remembered. Olivia used to accuse her of being a slob. Had Olivia cleaned her desk? It looked so blank. She fidgeted with a stapler labeled *Madeline Greene Illica* in green ink. Why had she marked her office possessions? Could the hospital be rife with supply thieves?

Olivia leaned back on the arms of her chair. Their desks were close enough to shake hands while they talked on the phone if they so wished.

"Want to work." *Use pronouns,* Maddy heard Zelda chiding.

Olivia placed her elbows on her desk and rested her chin in her hand. "Now?"

"I need it."

"Are you bored?" she asked.

"No, not bored." Bored had become a foreign concept. Entire days slipped away while she tried to understand the world: like who first thought of eating garlic?

"I'm scared."

"What are you scared of?"

She shrugged. "Money. Not enough. Ben and I over." She ran her fingers over a Red Sox pencil cup that she didn't remember. "Maybe he won't want. To come back. If I let him."

Maddy would understand if Ben didn't come back—carrying other people's burdens wears a person out. Clients' pain had worn her out before. Sometimes she'd felt crippled by the anguish she swallowed. Like turkey drippings that were too rich to eat on a regular diet.

Olivia rolled her eyes. "Come on. He's begging to come home. You told me. Kath told me. Your mother told me. It'll probably be tomorrow's headlines in the *Globe*."

"It could happen. Shit. We work in a hospital. Happens all the time. Remember Cigarette-Face?"

Cigarette-Face was Joe, a client whose wife had been dying of liver cancer. He resembled a stubbed-out cigarette, but inside was a hero who sat with his wife, reading to her eight hours a day. Joe slept in a chair by her bed and fed her as though it were his honor. Once a week he came to Maddy's office to weep because he didn't want to cry in front of his wife. That was all he needed– someone to hear his suffering.

"What are you talking about, Maddy?" Olivia asked. "First of all, you asked Ben to leave. He's dying to come back. And Joe stayed with his wife. He was our saint."

"Right. Exactly. I don't think. Ben's like that."

If Olivia didn't want her at the office, she didn't let on. She gave Maddy a pile of folders and told her to catch up on cases. Ha! Another joke. She shuffled papers while Olivia saw clients down the hall, jumping up from her desk like an excited puppy each time Olivia returned.

And then she told Maddy it was group day. The Wednesday Blues Club.

"Please. Let me come," she begged.

Olivia shocked her by saying, "Okay. Might as well. They never stop asking about you. Do you remember the last time you were with them?"

Maddy squeezed her eyes shut, trying to picture it. After a few moments, she sighed. "No."

They pulled on their coats and headed toward Olivia's battered car. "Right before your accident."

• • • •

As they drove the roads leading to Dorchester, Olivia filled the silence, passing on hospital gossip and commenting on the landscape.

"Look at that!" She pointed to an empty lot heaped with rubbish. Twisted shopping carts strewn among bare mattresses held garbage. A naked one-legged doll, her white skin potent against a torn black Hefty bag, lay on her back. "You gonna see that in Beacon Hill? No way! But here, big effing deal. Why shouldn't these people have to look at shit all day, right?"

"Emma. She's the one." She'd tried to keep this a secret from Olivia—knowing how angry her friend would get at Ben for putting Emma in that position. "Told me. About the accident. About the charge. About Ben." Maddy's words slid out in a TBI truth serum torrent.

"Jesus, what the hell. I didn't know she was the one who told you. She must be a wreck. How is she handling it?"

"Forget it. Don't want to talk. About it." *How was Emma handling it?* Another way Maddy failed each day.

"Emma will need a lot of guidance," Olivia said. "No one's paying enough attention to her. Certainly not Ben. And you can't. Let me help you." Olivia hit her horn as the driver in front of her braked for a yellow light. "Emma needs it."

"Don't. Tell me. What we need. Just be my friend. The group. Everyone still there?"

"Listen, up, Maddy. Maybe this isn't such a good idea. So much has happened, and now Emma."

Maddy grabbed a tissue from Olivia's ambitiously organized dash drawer. "Going to work. Not going to cry. Stop."

Olivia pressed her lips together and then pretended to smile. "Fine. I'll stop. For now."

After they parked and walked three blocks, Maddy became calmer. Zelda had said going back to work would be like putting on a suit that you remembered as comfortable but now didn't quite fit anymore. Therefore, you had to tailor it. She reflexively reached for her pocketbook, ready to pop an Ativan—the Ativan Dr. Paulo prescribed—but stopped. She'd be fine. Just fine.

• • •

The room where the Wednesday Blues met hadn't changed; it still had dingy beige linoleum, a circle of dented metal chairs, and the smell of a basement too often flooded.

After ten minutes of hugging her, the Wednesday women got past the excitement of Maddy's appearance and went back to talking about themselves. Almost nothing seemed different except Maddy. She met the one new woman, Jasmine, a well-curved girl with a loud mouth who reminded her a little of her sister at that age—if at seventeen Vanessa had been pregnant and worn a swirl of purple and yellow faded punches as eye shadow.

"My baby came this weekend. It's the second time in a row they gave me unsupervised visits," Kendra said. Her braids shook with excitement as she spoke, wiggling and tapping her foot. "And she cried like they were tearing off her arms when that bitch social worker took her back. No offense, Olivia, Maddy."

"None taken," Olivia said. "How did it feel when she cried?"

"It felt good." Kendra crossed her arms. "Because she knows I'm her mama, and she should be with me. She knows that."

"So what does that make you feel?" Olivia asked.

"I just told you." Kendra looked so young that Maddy thought the girl might stick her tongue out.

"No," Olivia said. "I mean how did it feel knowing that your situation made your baby upset?"

"It's not like I wanted her sad, if that's what you're trying to say. Can't I be glad that she knows who I am? She remembers me. I was happy. Is that so wrong?" Kendra tightened her eyes into stubborn slits.

"Yeah. It's wrong." Sabine curled her hands into fists. Still so thin that she seemed raw, Sabine hadn't changed. "It was you being so fucked-up that put her there."

"Don't start on me, Sabine."

"I'm not starting on you." Sabine remained unruffled. "I'm telling you what is. You put the tears in your child's eyes, not the social workers and not the crackhead who beat you up. 'Cause you stayed with him just like he was, didn't you? Did you even think about what he might do to your baby?"

"Fuck you," Kendra said. "You know what Olivia and Maddy say— we stay because we love them, not because they're mean."

"Fuck me, but you know it's true. Just like it's true I gave my baby away." Sabine wrapped her arms around her thin chest and hugged herself tight.

Maddy struggled to remember Sabine's story. A child of rape. Mother who hated her for that rape. Then drugs. As Sabine's final punishment for her life, the state took away her baby.

"Go easy, Sabine. Self-responsibility doesn't mean we control the world. Leaving is difficult," Olivia said.

"I have an announcement," Moira broke in.

Moira. Our mother of cookies.

"What?" Maddy asked. The group turned to her as though the table had spoken. "I can speak. You know."

Nervous laughter swept the room.

"I left Ed," Moira said in her soft brogue. "Yesterday. That's why I didn't bring anything today." She spread her arms as though indicating the lack of cookies.

"Wow, Mama. Why'dja let me go on and on when you have that news?" Kendra, who always sat next to Moira, grabbed the older woman's hand.

Maddy leaned in, eager to hear. "Why? Did. You leave him?"

"You," Moira said. "You helped me decide."

"Maddy hasn't even been here in a hundred years." Amber whined as though Maddy had been on a shopping spree. Her stringy blond hair looked oilier than ever.

"Moira has the floor, ladies," Olivia said.

The women shuffled their feet and sat up straighter. Only Sabine didn't seem affected by Olivia's mild rebuke.

"Did you know I went to see you in the hospital, Maddy?" Moira asked.

"I don't remember." Maddy hated that Moira had watched her while she lay unconscious.

"I didn't stay but a moment." Moira twisted her hands. "But it made me think how you worked so hard, to help us and all, and yet that's how you were rewarded? With a coma? What would my reward be? What medal would I get for letting Ed beat the crap out of me and for convincing myself God must have a plan? For telling myself I was protecting my children?"

No one answered. Olivia opened her mouth to speak, but Moira held out a hand. "Please. Let me finish."

She picked up her cup of tea and took a long swallow, the group watching as though Moira were the brand-new movie.

"It's ended up being too simple." She held her chapped hands to her lips as though praying. "He scared me, sure, but even more, Mother of God, I was terrified of opening my goddamn mouth. Excuse me."

"Just say it," Sabine said. "Spit out that crap you been eating."

Moira's smile lit up the face that must have been lovely before old bruises and lines set in so deep. "I said to myself, stop worrying about him killing you. You're murdering yourself. All he has to do is finish the job. I'd been praying to God, not realizing that all that time God *was* helping, I just didn't recognize his hand. He'd sent me you all—I just hadn't been listening. All these years, it was like the Bible says, I've been a prisoner of hope."

Ben waited at a table by the huge glass windows, already seated when Maddy arrived at the Top of the Hub restaurant. She'd been ferried by the cab service. Ben had picked this touristy special-occasion place as though they were celebrating something.

"I have something important to tell you," he'd said when asking her to join him for dinner.

As she walked toward the table, she placed a hand over her racing heart. They were fifty-two stories up, perched at the top of the Prudential building. Beyond the glass-walled restaurant, filled with what seemed like acres of white linen, Boston flashed like a carpet of fireflies.

Ben stood and pulled her chair out, beating the maître d' to the job. For a moment, Maddy believed she could start new. She wanted to twirl in the flashes of lights and feel sparks ignite right inside her heart. Ben and Maddy sat, sending freshly minted stares across the gap of not seeing each other every day.

Ben's grin was huge. "I have good news. My father called today. It's all going to be okay. The other driver? He was legally drunk. They can't charge me. And I would think he'll be—"

Maddy stared at him, her twinkly twirling feelings gone.

"I know this all means very little to you. You are still . . . hurt. And it was my fault."

She remained silent.

"I want to come home, Maddy." Ben reached for her hands as though their reunion were preordained. She pulled away.

"What has changed?" she asked.

"I'm not . . . There's no criminal charges. No charges at all. It wasn't my fault. That other guy? The one driving the Ford. It was him."

"Really?"

"The lawyer just called."

"Oh. That's why you look. So happy?" She grabbed a slice of bread from the basket the waiter had placed on the table. And two pats of butter. "What did *you* do?"

"What do you mean?"

"Nothing? You did nothing?" She buttered the bread thickly. Tried not to scream. He didn't answer. "Well? What, Ben? All him?"

He put a hand on the edge of the table, the white cloth wrinkling under his hand. "I probably drove too fast."

"Probably. Yeah. Probably." She dropped the bread on her plate. "Guess. What I found. In our room?" She didn't wait for him to an-swer. "A bag of pills."

"Pills? Emma's? Emma has pills?"

"*My* pills!" She spoke too fiercely, using too much air, forced to then stop and take a breath, unable to speak for a moment. "Ones I took. To live. With you."

Ben deflated as if she'd popped him. He opened his mouth to speak, and nothing came out. Had he known about the bottles?

"Collecting pills. My old hobby. I remembered. That. Knowing. They were there. Made me feel. Safe."

She wished she could speak better, faster. Hurl out words to tell him all her memories were flowing back—how each bottle of Ambien or Vicodin offered the promise that she could handle anything. Knowing that even on nights the cruelest Ben came home, she'd be okay. Pills offered sweet promises and dreams of forgetting.

"Did you know?" she asked.

"I don't think so." His words were slow. Maybe he couldn't process now. His own personal traumatic injury of the soul.

Maddy worked to look as intent as she could, not knowing if she any longer had the ability to intimidate.

"Maybe I did—a little," he admitted. "I guess I thought your job caused you stress. Your clients. The kids."

"They numbed me. From you."

"That was before. We can start over." He captured her hands. "I've been thinking. About you. The kids. Me. We can change everything. It won't be like before. I know I have . . . culpability. But I will make it up to you."

"This isn't a triumph. Movie. Ben." She frowned at him as she freed her hands. "Not Lifetime channel. Before? Before was humiliation. Not tragedy. It was just you. Your temper. Being mean. Impatient."

Silence fell as the busboy filled their heavy amber glasses with ice water.

"First a string. Of small failures. And big. Damaged us," she continued. "You always late. Yelling. Throwing things. Sometimes worse. All just a moment. I thought.

"And now this." Maddy held out her hands and swept them in front of her, indicating to him what he'd done.

"Maddy. Please. Forgive me. At least consider it."

She remembered forgiving him. So many times.

The time he'd shattered her grandmother's crystal bird—grabbing it off the shelf in the middle of his rage.

When they'd had to replace the kitchen counter because he'd pounded it so hard it cracked.

Emma running into the living room. Eight years old. Crying hard enough to make Maddy's throat hurt just to hear her. Ben on her heels. Screaming so loud his neck veins jumped like worms. Because Emma broke his pen. Not his heirloom watch. Not his computer. His pen.

Barking at her, blaming her, shaking the stupid pen.

She remembered this as they sat in the starry restaurant up so high.

"I gave you years," she said. "Years of chance. Nothing changes. Just. Gets worse. Look at me."

"Everything is different. I've changed."

"Zelda's door has sayings. I told you. I copied this one. Thought it was about me. But now I know the truth. I wrote it to remind me. About you. Subconscious. Maybe." She slid a piece of paper across the white tablecloth. Ben's face fell as he read it.

> *There are two things a person should never be angry*
> *at, what they can help and what they cannot.*
> —PLATO

"I think you have at least. Twenty-two things. You shouldn't be angry about. Every day."

CHAPTER 34

Emma

Emma dreaded breakfast. Going out to restaurants for ordinary meals seemed like just one more punishment for having your parents living apart. Weren't dinners with Dad hideous enough without expanding these horrors to the morning? Both her parents had become mental.

That her father blamed her for everything was so obvious. Why shouldn't he? Who else was to blame? And now, the case had been dropped. Dad was right. Her mother had never needed to know.

So good work, Emma. You broke up your parents' marriage. And now your mother is somewhere between Frankenstein and a member of the walking dead.

She looked out the window, watching for her father's car. The moment he appeared, she planned to drag Caleb and Gracie out. Emma couldn't take seeing her father stare at her mother, all big-eyed pathetic-looking, while her mother practically spat at him.

Her father treated Emma as though she had explosives strapped to her chest. He'd probably never be normal with her again.

It had been another zombie-Mom morning at the Illicas. Grandma Anne arrived before anyone woke. She made supper at seven a.m., and then sandwiches for school, then vacuumed, packed lunch boxes, and ironed a blouse for Gracie. At some point Mom wandered into the living room with a handful of cookies, lay on the couch, and turned on the TV—breaking two of her previously adamant rules from before.

No television with breakfast!

No sweets before lunch!

There he was, pulling into the driveway.

"Gracie. Caleb. Come on, Daddy's here," she yelled.

Grandma Anne came to the door, wiping her hands on a towel tucked in her waistband. "For goodness' sake, let your father come in, sweetheart, so I can give him a cup of coffee and a muffin."

Gracie and Caleb skidded into the hall in their socks. "Put on your shoes," Emma said before answering her grandmother. "We have to hurry, Grandma. Dad has to get to work."

Grandma sent a stern glance her way—stern for Grandma anyway. "Aren't you going to say good-bye to Mommy?"

"I did," Gracie said.

"Me too." Caleb grabbed his lunch box. "I want to see Daddy."

"Bye, Mom," Emma yelled toward the living room as she opened the front door. The little kids sped out toward their father, leaning against the car with his arms folded.

"Can we have Dunkin' Donuts chocolate donuts?" Caleb asked their father as he ran to the car. "Can I have chocolate milk?"

"No. And yes," her father said. "You can't learn anything on donut fuel."

"Emma let me have a Little Debbie cake. Before breakfast!" Caleb said.

"Jesus . . ." Her father stopped before saying more. He opened the back door for Gracie. Emma challenged him by lifting her eyebrows—just a tiny bit though—while keeping the rest of her face blank.

"Then I guess I'll save a little money on your breakfast." He kissed Caleb and Gracie, and then looked at Emma. She came forward, allowed a brief hug, and walked around the car to get into the front passenger seat.

"Nope. I got room," Caleb said.

"How about Sorella's?" her father asked.

"Cornmeal pancakes!" Gracie blew a kiss at their father. "I love Sorella's. Oh, thank you, Daddy."

Emma thought she'd puke watching this little lovefest.

"Sorella's it is." Her father looked back at the house once more before backing down the driveway.

The restaurant was almost full, not that it was hard to fill such a tiny space. Emma didn't know how they even fit in as many tables as they had. The cooks worked right out in the open, squeezed into some midget kitchen. Her father and mother thought it was cool—their word, never hers; she thought it was gross, the word and the place. Who wanted to see people sweat over the frying eggs you were going to eat?

Gracie and Caleb attacked their pancakes, and her father dug right into his bacon and eggs. Emma didn't even want her cereal; she just dipped her spoon in and out of the bowl so her father wouldn't get annoyed.

"So," her father said. "What's up in school today? All your homework done?"

"I have a spelling test," Caleb said. "Want to test me? Cold. C-O-L-D. Smart. S-M-A-R-T."

"Excellent—seems like you were studying last night. S-T-U-D-Y-I-N-G." Her father gestured to the waitress for more coffee.

"Witch. W-I-T-C-H. Emma tested me."

"Good job. Both of you." Her father's forced grin seemed as phony as the Saks salesclerk's smile had been when Emma and Sammi tried on hats last weekend.

She gave her cereal another stir.

"I had to write a story using compound sentences with subjects and predicates." Gracie poured additional syrup on top of her already drowning cornmeal pancakes. "Do you know what subjects and predicates are?"

"Hmm," her father said. "The subject is the what, and the predicate tells something about the subject? Like me saying *brilliant Gracie*? You are the subject and brilliant is the predicate."

"Are you and Mommy getting divorced?" Caleb asked.

Her father placed his fork on his plate. "I hope not," he said.

"Then don't," Caleb said. "If you hope it."

"It's not that simple," her father said.

Emma couldn't catch her breath.

"Why? Just come home." Caleb stabbed the bit of egg left on his plate.

"'Cause Mommy is part of it," Gracie said. "That's why it's not simple. She makes the decision, also."

"Does Mommy want a divorce?" Caleb asked.

"I don't think Mommy *wants* a divorce—but Mommy's not happy."

"Is she still mad at you? For driving so fast?"

"It's complicated, Caleb," her father said. "It's not just that she's angry, she's also . . . Well, I guess she's angry."

"Are you being punished for being bad?" Caleb took a much too huge forkful of pancakes and shoved them in his mouth. Pancake mush practically fell out of his mouth, and nobody was there to stop him.

Emma squirmed. *Shut up, Caleb.* She didn't want to hear her father get angry; she didn't want to hear him be maudlin. She was sick of both her parents, period.

"I'm just not sure, Caleb." Her father picked up his fork again and sighed.

All her parents did anymore was say *I don't know* and look sad. Emma couldn't decide which of the two made her want to kill them more.

After school Emma found she couldn't bear to get on the bus to come home. Paralyzed or traumatized or simply sick of it all, it didn't matter. She simply couldn't.

She walked down Louis Pasteur Avenue and then followed the Fenway to Brookline Avenue. A few blocks away there was a movie theater that played enough films to keep her there until midnight if she wanted.

She wanted.

• • •

Emma may as well have walked in with cowbells tied to her neck when she tried to sneak into the house at nine o'clock that night. Gracie greeted her at the door, opening it before Emma even had her key out.

"Daddy's going to kill you," Gracie whispered. "Where were you?"

"*Emma?*" her father shouted from the living room. "Get in here. *Now!*"

"Dad's here?" Emma asked.

"Grandma called him. Because you didn't show up to get us. He called Aunt Vanessa, Kath, even Olivia. All your friends. And the police!" Gracie walked down the hall, holding Emma's arm as she talked. "The police wouldn't do anything for twenty-four hours. Daddy was really mad 'cause Sammi and Caro weren't home and because he didn't have your boyfriend's phone number."

Emma shrugged her shoulders. "I doubt he even remembers Zach's name."

She entered the living room. Her father sat in an upright dining room chair, tapping his foot on the floor. Grandma Anne and Grandpa Jake flanked her mother on the couch. Her grandfather jumped up when he saw her.

"Thank God you're safe." Grandpa Jake hugged her until it hurt.

"Were you being held captive somewhere?" her father asked. "Kidnapped? If not, start getting ready to live in the four walls of your room for a long time."

"Whoa. Calm down." Grandpa Jake kept a hand on Emma's shoulder. "Let her sit and get her breath."

"Get her story straight, more like it." Her father strode over and gripped Emma.

"I said to calm down." Grandpa kept his protective stance as Emma tried to edge toward him.

"This is my business, Jake. My family." Her father tugged at Emma. "Get over in that chair, Emma. Now."

She shrugged off her father and sat in the upholstered chair to which he pointed.

"Take a breath, everyone," Grandma said. "She's home. She's safe."

Her father ignored Grandma and bent over Emma, thrusting a finger at her face. "Do you have a clue what you did to your mother? To Caleb and Gracie—who waited and waited until they had to walk home by themselves?" Stale coffee breath assaulted her with each word.

"But they were okay, thank God," Grandma said.

"Jesus, Anne." Emma's father slammed the wall. "That's not the point. Anything could have happened. Anything."

"But it. Didn't." Her mother came over to where Emma sat and ran a hand over Emma's thick braid. "At least Gracie knew. The way. Home."

"That's not the point, Maddy!" her father yelled.

"Nobody even knows I'm alive anyway, not unless I'm doing something for them." Emma banged the textbooks she still held against her knees. "One time I'm not the perfect daughter. One damn time. Who do you think has been taking care of Caleb and Gracie and the house and everything else in the world since the accident?"

"Don't you think we appreciate you?" Her grandmother looked so sad.

Emma shook her head. "Oh, Grandma, I'm not talking about you," she said. She tried not to cry as she watched her father's chest heave in and out.

"Emma, we're a family," her father said. "There are certain things you can't ever forget. Most important, you can't terrify us."

"You're so blind, Dad," Emma said. "We're not a family anymore. Mom's body is here, but that's all. And you left."

"We are a family. Don't ever talk like that. And that is certainly not true of your mother. Jesus. No matter how angry you are, you can't ever say things like that. It's not true. Your mother is getting better every single day." Her father ran his hands through his hair, as though trying to present his argument correctly. "Like it or not, you're older. I depend on you. You let me down."

"I let you down?" Emma lost all control and began sobbing as though she were a little girl. "I went to the movies by myself. That's where I was. Because I couldn't be here and I had nowhere to be. I let you down? You let the whole family down, Dad. Over and over."

"And you disappointed me, Emma. Didn't you?" Her father's words punched a hole in Emma's chest. "I told you not to talk about the accident—to leave it to me. Telling your mother about it was my job. Now look where we are."

"Stop." Her mother got off the couch and reached for Emma's father. He pulled away, holding his arms out as though telling everyone to back off.

"You just didn't know when to shut up," he said to Emma. "You couldn't wait—you couldn't listen. Everything had to be about you."

"No, you're talking about yourself!" Emma's breath came in staccato bursts. "You're always scaring everyone. Everyone has to do everything your way. Now everyone hates you, and you can't take it."

Her father came toward her. Their eyes met. Emma's muscles locked as she waited, but she continued. "I'm not afraid of you anymore."

Her father closed his eyes. He took a breath that seemed to go on forever. He looked around and then stepped forward, kneeling at Emma's knees, touching one of her hands with the lightest of pressure. "It was all me. You are so right," he whispered. "I'm so sorry. Don't you know why I was so angry when you didn't come home? I would die if anything happened to you."

Emma bowed her head. Tears blotched her jeans.

"Nothing was your fault. I know that. Oh, baby, don't you know how sorry I am?" her father continued. "That I hurt your mother. That I hurt you. Your sister and your brother. I'm sorry—I have no other words."

Emma felt the pressure to help him—give him a break—but she couldn't do it. She couldn't say a word.

"Say something," Gracie begged. "Daddy wants to fix it. Listen to him. Do something."

Grandma Anne walked over and kissed the top of Emma's head. "Forgiveness can make you feel better, Emma."

Everyone stared at her, waiting for her to do something. God, she was only fifteen. What did they want from her?

Her mother watched as though waiting for Emma to unravel the world.

I'm only fifteen, Mom!

She ran upstairs.

Now she wanted pills to take away her energy. Put her to sleep.

She slipped into her parents' bathroom and opened her mother's cabinet.

CHAPTER 35

Ben

Ben slid the Holiday Inn security card into the metal slot on his room door with more ease and familiarity than he wanted, and then waited for the flash of the green light to give him entry. He should call home and check on Maddy and the kids. If Emma answered the phone, she'd have to talk to him.

Last night had been the worst since the frenzy that had brought him here, not that tonight was going to be any feather in his cap.

Months of watching G-rated movies and eating crap faced him. His life would soon be an endless reel of malls, museums, and Mc-Donald's and pizza like every other divorced father he knew. And as depressing as that imagined future was, it was way too optimistic since it presumed that Emma would go anywhere with him after last night.

He threw his jacket on the second bed, which had become his open-air closet. Heaps of crap that the maid tried to make into neat piles threatened to take over. Tomorrow he'd have to throw all his clothes in his car and bring them to that place that charged by the pound. He couldn't do laundry at his parents'—they didn't even know Maddy had thrown him out.

He undid his tie and unbuttoned his shirt, exchanging it for a sweater, staring at himself in the mirror as he switched clothes. The baby-blue crewneck he chose was one of Maddy's favorites. She always said he looked sexy in that color. Made her want to jump his bones, she'd said. He used to laugh, but inside he'd felt his heart take over his chest. She knew that, didn't she? How goddamned happy she'd made him?

Why should I know that, Ben?

Jesus, the bathroom. The poor maid couldn't perform miracles, not with his razor, cologne, deodorant, comb, brush, aspirin, and all his other shit cluttering the microscopic sink. Zita, the weekday maid—in the weeks since he'd been here he'd come to know the weekday and weekend maids—did the best she could, even lining his toiletries up in size order, for Christ's sake. She was a good woman—good but unlucky, stuck at sixty cleaning up after idiots like him. Ben overtipped each week, his small attempt to make up for Zita's lousy deal in life.

Icy streets made it difficult to navigate as he walked out of the hotel to search for supper. Ben had gone home to shovel when it snowed three days before, and then become irrationally incensed when he saw it already clean—too clean to have been done by Emma. Jake had probably sent some of his guys to shovel—the best shovelers in Boston.

Ben walked along Beacon Street, looking for whichever restaurant seemed least filled with children or wives. He wandered around, vaguely attracted by a deli until he looked through the window and saw Anne's doppelganger eating falafel.

Finally, in Kenmore Square, he found a McDonald's filled with college students and seniors. Ben stood on line behind a crumpled old couple appearing as though they were dining out on their Social Security. They each ordered a small hamburger. No McNothing—just a shriveled burger on a bun. One small fries to share. A small carton of chocolate milk for each of them. Ben wanted to buy them each a McMansion of a meal—a giant burger, extra-large fries, apple McPies, shakes—anything their hearts desired.

He should.

Then the couple got their small white bag and the moment passed. As penance, Ben ordered a Filet-O-Fish. His least favorite McMeal.

He sat alone, picking a seat facing the window. Friday night couples passed him on Commonwealth Avenue. He thought about what his family was doing. Finishing supper. Anne and Jake were, he supposed, ensconced in his house with his children and his wife. Watching his TV.

After crumpling his greasy bag and leftover fries and throwing the garbage in the trash, Ben walked half an hour to Brookline Booksmith, relishing the cold wind as another notch in his penance. He cruised the aisles, looking for something distracting, rejecting one thriller and mystery after another. Anxiety prickled when he recognized the names of authors that Maddy liked—books that she couldn't read anymore.

He left the fiction section for biographies. If he couldn't divert himself, he could at least look to others for help—men and women who'd fought wars, cancer, droughts, and floods. What had he ever done that had been great? Slipping down the aisles, he made his way to the self-help area, scanning the sections:

Gambling
Drugs
Eating
Sex
Alcohol
Anxiety
Panic

Compulsions for all.

He knelt to read the titles in the area labeled anger management:

Beyond Anger
Free from Anger
No More Anger
Stopping Anger

As though buying porn, Ben grabbed every volume, too embarrassed to be seen choosing. Zita could have the extras. Maybe she had an asshole husband.

He took the armload to the counter and added Lindt chocolate balls, bittersweet for Maddy, milk chocolate for himself. He stuck the candy in his pocket. Then he headed back to the Holiday Inn to read and eat chocolate.

Shit.

Forget being nicer to women, soon he'd be one.

The strings of the bookstore bag dug into his hands. Sharp wind cut harder than before as he walked back to the hotel. Tree branches whipped around. His cheeks burned red and cold from the brewing storm when he finally reached the entrance.

Ben headed to the lower lobby level, which doubled as a bar, seeking a couch, a soft chair—somewhere private enough to slip one of the books out of the bag and ease his mind with a bourbon.

He'd just removed his coat and sat in a club chair when he heard his name.

Elizabeth stood a few feet away.

It took a moment for him to compute: Elizabeth. Here. Books. Bourbon.

"I've been waiting for you," she said.

"Waiting?" Ben gripped the top of the book bag. "Why?"

"I wanted to see you." Elizabeth wore well-worn jeans. A thin sweater skimmed over her fine-boned body. Her hair fell loose along her back. She looked like a college kid.

Anger rushed in. He needed to read. He needed to call his kids and say good night. Elizabeth? Not needed. He hadn't seen her since she'd left a month ago, a leave-taking he'd celebrated by having a beer with his slice of pizza that night, toasting to a hope that the next time he saw her she'd be married.

He snuck a peek at her finger. No miracle diamond sparkled.

"I heard you moved out," Elizabeth said.

Ben remained quiet.

"I stayed in touch with Aaron," she said. "He told me you were staying here."

Aaron fell off his favored-lawyer list.

"He said you and Maddy had separated." Elizabeth lowered herself into the chair angled next to him. "I've been thinking about you."

Dear Jesus, she had an unfinished crush going on. Sometimes he thought beautiful women had the hardest time with rejection, as though it somehow lowered their net worth. The world couldn't be right until the proper order was restored. They left men, not the other way around.

"You did everything you could, didn't you? For your wife." Elizabeth leaned over and placed a light hand on his knee. He felt her heat through his trousers, the sensation physically pleasurable despite himself. It had been too long since he'd been touched. "You were a hero. I know that."

Ben thought of the ugly lies he'd told her about Maddy. The way he'd shoved both of them under the bus: Maddy and Elizabeth. "You shouldn't be here."

"You're right. But I think about you. And when Aaron said . . ." Elizabeth pulled back, her face crumpling.

Fuck. "Come with me." He held out his hand, desperate to get her out of the lobby before her sobs started. Before they were noticed. This hotel was in Brookline—not that far from his in-laws. With each step, Ben imagined someone seeing them. Pictured that someone whispering to his mother-in-law: *Guess who I saw in the Holiday Inn with a beautiful young woman? She was crying,* they'd say with hand-wringing relish.

Not that Elizabeth was that beautiful—but she was beautiful enough.

Once they were in his room, she went to use his bathroom and he sat on the edge of the bed, covering his knees with his sweat-nervous hands.

Elizabeth came out and glanced around. She gave a shy smile, her incipient tears miraculously gone, and sat next to him on the bed, tucking one leg up and to the side. Ben locked himself in an upright military stance.

"I'm not comfortable having you here," he said.

"You're separated." Elizabeth put a hand on the mattress and inclined toward him.

"It's just a temporary break."

"I've thought about you. You taught me so much. Being with you, talking, everything, it meant more to me than I think you knew."

Yes, she wasn't that beautiful, but she was that desirable with that soft sweater falling over her breasts.

"I'm getting back together with Maddy." Ben remembered the taste of Elizabeth's lipstick.

"I don't know why I miss you so much." Elizabeth rested her head on his shoulder, a clean expensive scent drifted from her hair. He ran a hand over it, the glossy sheen, so different from Maddy's curls. She lifted her face to him, all yearning admiration. She thought he was Mr. Fucking Wonderful. In her fantasy, she'd made him some kind of prince.

"Sometimes I think I love you, Ben."

"You don't. You don't even know who I am."

"I know the important things. How smart you are. What you do for people like B-bird. You were probably the first person who actually helped him—look at the difference you made in his life."

B-bird. Out on bail with yet another continuance as the case got weaker for the prosecution and witnesses dried up. Did Elizabeth think getting one more murderer to stay on the streets was some fucking crowning achievement for Ben?

"Getting him free isn't the same as making a difference. Maybe being locked up was the right thing." The world ran on rules; Elizabeth should know this.

Now she sat up a bit straighter, looking less soft sweater and more pressed shirt.

"He's a fatherless boy who grew up in the projects," Elizabeth said. "His mother has been an alcoholic most of her life. He had his first drink at seven. When did he ever have a chance?"

"That's sad—not a reason to get away with murder."

"This doesn't sound like you," she said.

"Maybe I'm having a crisis of faith," he said. "Or maybe I'm just having a crisis. Come on. I'll take you home."

• • •

He dropped Elizabeth in front of her brownstone. Then he headed home.

"Welcome to the Jungle" blared out of the CD player as he drove past Northeastern University on Huntington Avenue. Guns N' Roses—that's what he needed, no matter what anyone said.

Fucking Elizabeth.

Fucking world.

Fucking him.

He thanked God for letting him stop, for helping him push Elizabeth away. Ah, yes, God. Thank you for keeping me from fucking Elizabeth.

He turned and passed the gas station on the corner of South Huntington and Tremont.

In his torrent of need, he'd driven toward home. Toward Maddy. He pushed the button for home on his cell and got Maddy's voice inviting him to leave a message. He wanted to go there—see her right now.

The Volvo in front of him cut him off from the right, squeezing in next to him, trying to beat the trolley at South Huntington Avenue. Ben pounded on his horn until he wanted to give himself the finger. He turned up the CD volume, drove two more blocks, and then stopped, his chest hurting. He parked across from Angell Memorial Animal Hospital. A rescue shelter. He tried to appreciate the satire as he turned off the ignition, and then tried to slow his breathing before he stroked out.

He reached into his coat pocket, looking for the package of Tums he'd taken to carrying, and pulled out the bag of Lindt chocolate. Inside was the assortment of chocolate he'd chosen for himself and Maddy—flattened, squashed.

CHAPTER 36

Maddy

Eighteen days had passed since Ben left.

Maddy knew because she'd marked the date in her journal and today she'd counted—brushing away corn muffin crumbs from the page as she finished saying each number out loud. Then she returned to the list of chores left by her mother, who wrote them in huge letters on the blackboard her father had hung in the kitchen just days after Ben moved out.

The phone rang as she sat folding socks after first matching them up—part of her mother's rehabilitation plan. Sock therapy.

"Maddy, I heard something. Something not good." Her sister's shout invaded her brain like an assault.

"I'm not deaf, Vanessa. Keep telling you." Her sister thought she couldn't hear; her mother considered her blind, someone who needed lists written in foot-high letters. When they weren't shouting or miming, they treated her as though she were dust in the corner—annoying but inevitably still there day after day.

"I'm in the car—can't talk long. The light's about to change, and I promised Sean I'd stop talking when I was driving. Guess what?"

"What?" She held a sock up to the window. Black and navy were hard to tell apart. Was this her brain, or had it always been hard to see these shades?

"When I took Ursula to nursery school, I ran into cousin Gail. She got so fat!"

Vanessa sounded happy. She hated cousin Gail.

"Gail said she saw Ben last week. Dropping a *young woman*—actually she said *girl*—off in the Fenway. By Northeastern. You remember that Gail teaches there?"

"Ben? A girl? Who?"

"Gail didn't know who, stupid!" She laughed. "Oops, sorry. Anyway, she said the girl was blond and pretty. Long straight hair. Have to go. Green light."

"Wait. What time. Did she see. Ben?"

"I don't know—ten? Maybe nine?"

Vanessa hung up. When her mother's footsteps alerted her approach, barely knowing why, Maddy ran into the bathroom and slammed the door.

"Sweetheart? Are you all right?" her mother called.

"Nothing. Is ever right." Why couldn't she keep her mouth shut? "Leave me. Alone."

Her mother knocked on the bathroom door. When Maddy didn't answer, she knocked again. "Should I call Dad?"

So intensely did she want to curse at her mother that she knew she must be getting better because she didn't let out a single *fuck you* or *cocksucker*.

"Mom. Go home. Please. I need. Time. By myself."

"I'm not leaving until you tell me what's wrong, Maddy!"

Are you stupid? Deaf? Blind to me? I want to be alone. That's why I'm in the bathroom.

She bit the corner of the towel.

The next knock sounded tentative. Tapping, really. As though she thought Maddy had turned into a rabid animal. She splashed cold water on her face and the back of her neck. Then she opened the bathroom door and announced, "Maybe Ben. Slept with someone."

"Don't be crazy—of course he didn't!" Her mother shook her head so hard Maddy waited for it to fly off. "Is that why you were hiding in the bathroom? Don't be ridiculous. He wouldn't. I know it."

"You don't. Know. Vanessa called." She repeated Vanessa's words, one halting almost-sentence at a time.

"So he drove someone home." Her mother patted Maddy, forgetting, as they all did, that since the accident she hated being touched when she was upset.

"Ben loves sex." She threw the words with as much passion as possible—needing to convince her mother and stop the constant Ben campaign.

Her mother rolled her eyes as though Maddy were thirteen. "He's not an animal. Stop building castles in the sky. Your imagination has the best of you. As though you don't have enough problems."

Maddy balled her fists to keep from sticking up her middle finger—proud at her control—and walked away to call Kath.

Searching for something to concentrate on other than hating Ben, Maddy stared at the back of the cabdriver's neck, mottled with age, bristly little hairs coming out of his skin. She didn't want to hate the driver. Rage already rented too much space in her brain.

Kath waited in the lobby of the high school where she worked as the director of student services. The yellow brick building exuded an exhausted, day-is-over, three o'clock feel, smelling of overamped teenagers, winter coats, and dirty mops. She barely had time to cry before Kath hustled her out and into her car.

"Where are we going?" It took four tries, but Maddy finally buckled her seat belt.

"For a walk." Kath shot out of the parking space and made a U-turn.

"Where?"

"You'll see," she said.

They sped toward whatever destination Kath had in mind. Cars flew by on Storrow Drive. Fast and furious. Had Ben driven faster than any of them?

"Why would he?" Maddy banged her fist against her knee. "How long?"

"We don't know anything yet." Kath pulled into a small parking area off Soldiers Field Road. "Come with me. You need a chance to let go."

She led Maddy to a path by the side of the Charles River, a desolate weedy section she didn't recognize.

"No one is ever here during the week. You can yell and cry and say any damn thing you want."

"I can't yell. Not enough. Breath. Remember?"

"See, that's just not fair," Kath said. She took her hand and squeezed. "If you can't yell, swear as much as you want—fuck Zelda's no-dirty-words exercises."

"I hate him. Want. To kill. Plunge. A knife. Into his. Fucking heart. Twist it. Stomp him. Fuck. Hate him." She wanted to howl. Bands of tension cinched her chest. "Scream for me, Kath."

Kath put her hands on her bony hips and screamed loud enough for the veins in her skinny neck to stand out. "Ben Illica is a goddamn moron. He's the supreme asshole of the United States of America! Ben Illica is a useless stupid prick!" She turned to Maddy. "Good?"

She nodded. "Good."

They walked in silence, Kath watching her closely. For signs of what? Maddy wondered. Throwing herself in the river?

"He cheated already. Lying. He cheated me out of truth. What he was like. Our life. What it had. Become."

"Maybe he felt so evil he couldn't face up," Kath said.

"Ben never ran away. From anything," she said.

"Ben never got into a rage so big it caused physical damage before."

"Making excuses? For him?" She tripped over a branch and grabbed Kath's arm. "Shit. Can't even walk."

"No. Trying to make sure you don't go over the deep end." Kath gripped her arm. "And you may not beat yourself up. Or become a professional victim."

Maddy tried to order the words pouring through her mind. "He was mean. Before. And the other night. He scared us all."

"I know you're tired of hearing the word *accident* and that he's sorry. He's trying to do better—I know this. I don't know if that's enough, but really. Can you live alone now? Honestly."

"Listen to me! I spent years. Pushing it all. Down. And then. This. And now. Is he feeling so sorry for himself. That he found a blond. Comfort doll?"

Maddy tried to think what she might have said to herself if she were Kath being honest. Kath not worrying about Maddy taking care of herself and the children. *He's always been a schmuck. What did you expect from him after all these years? He's always been a selfish prick.*

It wasn't as though the signs weren't there from almost the beginning.

Not the very beginning, of course—when things were all starry with sex and glitter, you hid things like the tendency toward martyrdom you'd picked up at your mother's breast and sudden furies you'd learned from your father.

One minute Ben would be rubbing knots from her neck, the next exploding over something she said. Sometimes the never knowing seemed the worst.

Truth rolled in like acid. Remembering how on guard she'd been every time the door opened and Ben walked in. He never reached for control. Lashing out seemed so much easier. Did all men have that in their toolbox? Was Ben so much out of line? That's what always tripped her up, not knowing what was normal in relationships. So many women acted differently around their husbands, a bit guarded, laughing nervously, watching for their husbands' reactions before they formed their own opinions.

She knew other women who put on an emotional apron when their men were nearby, just like her. But did that make it normal? Okay?

Even during Maddy's pregnancies, Ben allowed his reactions to override her vulnerability. Carrying Caleb had been the worst. July was the cruelest month to be pregnant. You'd think August might be harder—but Maddy didn't think so. August in Boston sometimes brought the relief of cool nights.

During July she was in her eighth month—too early to hope for the relief of delivery, so bloated that two-year-old Gracie and seven-year-old Emma made designs by indenting her swollen calves. She'd lurched between stuffing herself with butter-slathered saltines and living on cucumbers to rid herself of the water weight induced by her carb cravings.

Sweaty wood had slipped under her hand as she gripped the banister, slowly struggling down the stairs, holding Gracie's hand. Emma bumped into her from behind with every step.

Maddy still remembered the sink filled with plates and silverware, everything coated with chicken grease.

The baby had kicked as though planning an escape straight through her flesh.

"Em—why don't you get the pot and the cereal?" Emma strutted with self-importance when faced with chores. She also insisted on oatmeal with berries whatever the humidity level.

Maddy brewed coffee, craving the one guilt-ridden cup she allowed herself. Emma measured oats, reading the directions aloud, and mixed them into the cold water. Once the coffee brewed, Maddy took over, standing on her eight-month swollen feet, stirring the oatmeal until it thickened, then turning off the burner and putting bowls on the table.

"Mommy has to go to the bathroom," she'd said as she lined up juice glasses. Mommy had to go to the bathroom every second of every minute. "Watch Gracie, okay? Don't take your eyes off her."

Gracie's unusually sweet and placid nature made it easy to entrust her to Emma, but still Maddy left the bathroom door open—modesty being yet one more casualty of motherhood. She took advantage of her moment of alone time to study her ragged cuticles. They crept up to cover her nail bed more each day. Nail polish was verboten during pregnancy. Of course she could buff and file, but really, at a certain point, who cared? It wasn't as though she and Ben were holding hands these days. Who would she buff for? The UPS guy holding out his thingie for her signature?

Seconds after she left the bathroom, murderous screams exploded through the air. One hand under her giant belly, she ran over the slippery oak floor to her babies. Spilled oatmeal steamed on the floor;

Emma, sobbing, tried to hold a hysterical Gracie.

"Ben!" Maddy screamed from the kitchen. "I need you. *Now!*"

He skidded into the kitchen, his tie looped loosely around his neck. "What's wrong? What happened?"

Gracie shrieked, arching her back, trying to shake off the ice cube Maddy rubbed on her angry red arm.

"She burned herself," Emma whispered before hiding behind Maddy.

"Jesus!" Ben threw out the word as he came toward them.

"Hold her arm under the cold water," Maddy said. "I can't hold her up."

Ben lifted Gracie and brought her to the sink, slamming the previous night's dirty dishes from the basin to the counter, shattering a bowl in the process. An accident, Maddy prayed.

Gracie screamed, trying to pull away as Ben forced her tiny arm under the streaming icy water. "*What happened?*" he shouted over Gracie's shrieks.

Maddy stroked Gracie's leg, whispering *shah, shah* in a futile attempt to calm her. "I think she grabbed the oatmeal pot handle and spilled it over."

"You think? You *think*, Maddy? Where were you?"

"The stove wasn't on." She bent over the sink, watching him spray the water on Gracie's tender flesh, her heart turning as welts rose. "How is she?"

Ben took Gracie's arm away from the faucet for a moment, inspecting the damaged skin, and then placed it back under the water. "Bright red. Let's pray she doesn't end up with scars. Were you watching her?"

"I needed to pee," she said.

"You left her alone with hot cereal on the stove?" Ben asked.

Emma pressed closer.

"Please. No inquisition." Maddy worked to keep her voice from shaking.

Gracie cried, twisting, trying to get free of Ben's iron grip.

"Stay still," he bellowed.

"Don't yell, Ben, you're scaring her."

"I'd better start to scare someone around here. What's going to happen when you're watching three children?"

She tipped back her face, keeping to the vow she'd made two days earlier: *I need to learn fear control. I think that's how I let Ben win. Showing my weakness feeds something in him.*

Gracie's chest shook with sobs; snot bubbled from her nose. Maddy took her arm from the water for a moment. It was still red, but no blisters rose.

"Give her to me," Maddy said. "I can hold the ice on her now." She sat in the kitchen rocker and held her arms out. She took a deep breath and caught Ben's eyes straight on. "You need to calm down. Right now."

Sometimes she wondered if Ben loved his anger more than he loved his family. Given the choice between biting back a rant and the relief of bellowing, he'd release his steamy rage every time.

Maddy pushed away the memory. The present had enough pain without her grasping for more.

"I need to pick up my kids," Kath said. "Come with me. Have supper with us. I don't want you home alone."

Being with Kath's unscrewed-up family sounded unbearable.

"I can't."

"How about I drop you off with Olivia?"

She wrapped Maddy's scarf tighter around her neck, as though Maddy were one of her daughters. Poor Kath. She needed to fix, to help. All the shrinks, guidance counselors, social workers, and nurses, they were all obsessed with the halt and the lame. Had that been her?

"Want to go home," she said.

Traffic was heavy. She gave in to sleep as Kath drove, barely finding the strength to kiss her good-bye as she pulled up to her house.

"Maddy?"

Ben knelt next to the sofa where she'd been sleeping.

"Maddy? Honey?"

An afghan that hadn't been there before now covered her.

"You've been asleep awhile," Ben said.

"What time is it?" she croaked.

"Six thirty," Ben said. "I came to get the kids for supper, but they weren't here. Your mother took them to her house. She left a note."

Anne the matchmaker. Maddy chewed on her rising anger.

"Are you hungry? When I saw you sleeping, I made soup. Mushroom barley. I used the recipe from that vegetarian cookbook you like."

Mushrooms. A cure for what ailed them. Is that what he thought? Soup would solve their problems?

Ben reached over and brushed hair off her face. Despite everything, his touch still soothed her. He leaned over and kissed her forehead.

She held up seven fingers, praying for him to hold up three. *Thirty percent, Ben. Come on. Tell me you stayed in the right group.*

"Ben," she asked. "Who did you sleep with??"

When he didn't answer, her stomach juices curdled and rose to her throat.

"Someone. Saw you. With a woman."

Yes or no, Ben.

"Did you sleep with her?"

His hands remained at his sides. She waited. He stared. She stared back. She tucked her thumbs under rigid fingers. She willed him to show three fingers.

Please. Tell me that you're not a complete asshole, Ben.

Slowly, finally Ben nodded yes, looking as though the effort exhausted him. *Yes,* he nodded. *Yes, I slept with her.*

"Who. Who. Who?" she asked as though who mattered. As if that were the point.

"Elizabeth," he said. "Elizabeth Fullerton. My intern from this summer."

Elizabeth. Elizabeth the whore. She nodded. Maddy remembered her from some picnic. Memorial Day? A moneyed do-gooder type. Straight hair falling around her horsey bitch face.

"She came to my hotel yesterday, but I didn't sleep with her. I didn't touch her. I drove her home. It only happened once. Before. While you were—" Ben stopped, closed his eyes, and shook his head. Then he resumed. "In the hospital. Yesterday she came to try to get me—but I wouldn't."

"Want medal?" she asked.

"She had a crush on me."

Who cares, Ben? "Sounds like her crush. Had great success."

"She just showed up yesterday. Out of nowhere. And I told her she had to go. I drove her home. That's all."

"*Who cares?*" She screamed as well as she could ever scream now. "Who the fuck cares? Yesterday? Shut up, Ben. Why? Why sleep with her? How. Could. You?" Waves of rage made everything inside her tumble, knocking her heart into her guts. How could such hatred stay inside a body? She waited to erupt in boiling pus-filled hives of anger.

Ben dropped his head into his hands, scraping deep furrows through his thick hair. Gray strands she'd never seen before shot through the brown. "It's nothing. It meant absolutely nothing. I was scared. About you, Maddy. She—she was just there. I was tired. I was depressed. I was worried. The kids needed so much. You. You might not make it. Seeing you lying there had me terrified. Doing what I did, it was like having ten shots of bourbon. Trying to drown out the pain."

"Depressed? Scared? Drink. Rip things up. Cry to. A. Goddamned priest." She pulled the afghan off. "You should have. Drunk the bourbon."

"I didn't look for her. It just happened."

Right. She jumped on top of him—Supergirl, able to leap tall penises in a matter of seconds. How could he sleep with that shiny, shiny girl while she slept like the dead?

"Things never. Just happen, Ben. Get. Out."

"Maddy. I'm telling you the truth."

"Do you think. Truth is a free pass? Old truth?"

CHAPTER 37

Emma

Audubon Circle looked like an expanse of suburban gardens crossed with the stuffiness of Beacon Hill. Before meeting Zach, she hadn't known this Boston neighborhood existed. Emma walked by glowing houses, incandescent rooms visible through open drapes that revealed giant china cabinets and dining room tables the size of cars. Sculpted bushes outlined generous lawns.

Where would her father live if he never came back? Two nights before, at yet another McDonald's dinner, he'd hinted that he was looking for an apartment. "It's been a month, kids," he'd said. Gracie wept so horribly that he'd backtracked—talking about options as though their family were some stupid corporation.

A brass lion's head stared out at her from the middle of Zach's glossy red door. Running her tongue over her teeth, she searched for stray bits of popcorn from the bowl she'd shared with Gracie that afternoon. Then she'd popped her last pill, wanting to be fun and smiley for Zach's family.

She lifted the heavy door knocker once.

At least tonight she wouldn't have to sit through another depressing dinner with her father, acting as if everything were normal and he wasn't looking for an apartment and living in a hotel, and leaving them.

"Emma!" Zach's mother greeted her as though she'd recently cured world hunger.

"Hello, Mrs. . . . I mean, Dr. Epstein."

"Please, I told you last time—it's Shoshanna—there's no doctor here tonight. Give me your coat, dear."

Emma wished she'd worn something better than her grimy down jacket with the feathers poking out, not to mention the pilled sweater underneath. All of her clothes were limp with being overworn. Her bras were getting too small. She'd heard Mom talking to Kath about money, and now she was frightened to ask for anything.

At least Emma could still squeeze into her clothes. Poor Gracie was busting out of her skirts, and her brother's stomach showed from above his T-shirt every time he moved.

Zach's mother reminded Emma of Grandma Frances's good china, all muted and expensive-looking. When Zach's twin sisters, Gabrielle and Alana, walked in, wearing their cashmere sweaters and candy-pink lipstick, Emma wanted to turn, leave, and never come back. The sisters, miniature perfect, appeared to be female versions of Zach. Three Epstein females smiled with Zach's magazine-perfect grin.

"Welcome!" Gabrielle swung a college-girl version of Dr. Epstein's perfectly layered bob. "Happy Chanukah!"

"Happy Chanukah," Emma repeated. She didn't know they'd be making such a big fuss. For God's sake, it was already like the third or fourth night. If it weren't for Zach, she'd have totally forgotten it was Chanukah. This year the holiday fell weeks before Christmas—that's probably why nobody in her family even noticed the holiday.

Last December her mother's holiday display had driven Grandma Frances a bit insane, but the rest of them loved the mixed-up display. Her father had hugged her like she'd hit a home run when he saw the mantel lined with religious decorations of the holidays—a bright red cross; a silver Star of David; a green, red, and black kinara; a flaming star and crescent; a saffron-colored Ganesha; a black-and-white yin-yang; and a golden Buddha—all intertwined with twinkling white lights.

Plus, they had a Christmas tree and a menorah.

Emma followed the sisters Epstein into the living room, where Zach and his father were playing chess. Grandma Anne had been right; she should have brought a box of candy or something.

Zach looked up. "Hi."

"Emma, so glad you could make it." Mr. Epstein rose from one of three velvety couches making a giant chocolate-colored U.

Vacuum cleaner lines showed in the pale cream rug covering half the living room. There wasn't a television anywhere in the room. In her house, TV had become the living room shrine.

"Sit," Mrs. Epstein said. "Have a cracker. Some cheese." Zach's mother held out a white plate with crackers, cheese, and grapes. Fanned out on the shiny living room table were tiny blue-and-white napkins. Cloth.

"No, thank you," Emma said.

Instead of pushing it at her again, as Grandma Anne or her mother would have—*Come on, take something. At least try it!*—Zach's mother simply put down the plate.

"You must be happy school vacation is almost here," Mr. Epstein said.

"Oh, yes. Very happy." Her words fell in a heap at her feet. Brilliant conversation she was making. Had Zach lost his power of speech? "It gives me a chance to catch up. On my reading."

Catch up on watching SpongeBob *with Caleb was more like it.*

"Do you celebrate Chanukah?" Alana asked.

"Umm. Usually at my grandmother's house." Emma picked at the edge of her sweater. "She made potato pancakes last night." That was a big fat lie.

"Do you light candles?" Gabrielle fingered the silver Tiffany bean hanging from the faceted chain circling her neck.

"Remember what I told you?" Zach asked. "About her mother?"

"We light them. Always." Emma sent Zach a *shut up* look. "Especially now."

"Zach mentioned you were Jewish," Mrs. Epstein said in a phony-sounding not-that-it-matters voice.

"Half," Emma said. "I'm half Jewish."

"Who's Jewish? Your mother or your father?" Alana asked.

"My mother." Emma hadn't realized Zach's sisters were religious fanatics. She took a chunk of cheese and put it on a cracker, placing a tiny napkin under it. Every little crumb would show on this couch. Velvet. Why would anyone make a couch velvet? And who was stupid enough to buy one?

"That makes you Jewish," Gabrielle said as though giving Emma first prize in the Judaism contest. "It comes through the mother."

Emma stuffed another cracker in her mouth, not having a clue what to say, wanting to say something sarcastic and stupid that would get her thrown out.

Really? Do tiny dreidels float through the mother's umbilical cord?

Zach's mother leaned forward and patted Emma's knee. "Let's give Emma a break from the Epstein third degree. How *is* your mother, dear?"

Emma nodded, blinking back sudden tears. She wanted to be on the couch with her mother and Gracie, even if Gracie did have a disgusting snuffling cold. Her father had taken Caleb to a basketball game. Mom and Gracie were watching *A Christmas Story* and *Bad Santa*. Her mother said they might as well get ready for the kind of Christmas they were probably going to have—screwy as her brain. It had been funny the way she said it. The Epstein family would probably choke on their kosher cheese and crackers if they knew her family celebrated Christmas.

"My mother's fine." Even if that was a lie, her mother did seem much stronger lately.

"It's difficult when families go through these tragedies," Mr. Epstein said. "So often it's the children who are forgotten."

Zach sent his father a warning look. She could imagine what he'd told his family. *Poor Emma with her messed-up family.* Then they'd all gazed at each other in gratitude for their perfect non-messed-up home.

"I'm lucky," Emma said. "We have a great family. Super close—in fact, my mother's accident brought us even closer."

• • •

"What was wrong with you?" Emma asked the moment she and Zach left the house. She zipped her coat to her chin as they walked to the bus. "You hardly said one word."

"Because my family wants to get to know you. They already know me." He put his arm around her shoulders.

"You mean they want to see if I'm good enough for their precious son." Emma batted him away. She stopped in front of the bus stop, watching her breath float away in cold winter puffs. "Your family is wrapped too tight." She stamped her feet from the cold. "It's not like we're engaged or something. That was like an inquisition."

Bands of pressure went across her stomach. She felt like throwing up. Last time she took the pills the same thing happened.

What if she'd poisoned herself?

"They were only trying to talk to you. You turned into a mummy."

"That's your family's idea of talking? *How are your grades, Emma? Are you thinking about colleges yet?*" she mimicked. "It was a second degree to see if I deserved to be your girlfriend."

"My parents care about me," Zach said.

"And mine don't?" Emma jammed her mittened hands into her pockets to keep from throwing something, anything. She took a deep breath, trying to calm the pulsing from her stomach cramps, the nausea.

"You're the one who's always complaining about how your dad doesn't even know what you're doing."

"That's because my mother almost died, idiot." Her chest burned with hating him. "My father worried about me all the time before this, and even now he'd never have been rude to you. Nobody at my house would quiz you about being Jewish."

Zach put a hand on her shoulder. "Relax, okay? I was upset at how stuck-up you were acting, but I'm not mad at you anymore."

"Stuck-up?" Emma lifted her puffed-up jacketed arms and pounded the air. "News flash. I didn't do anything wrong."

Zach's drawn-out sigh made it seem as though she were dating some old man.

"Okay, I'm sorry. Can we drop it?"

"Just go home," she said.

"I'm riding home with you. That's it."

They rode the bus in near silence. Emma pressed her forehead against the dirty window each time Zach tried to talk, the cold glass comforting against her hot skin. Taking shallow breaths helped with the cramping.

When the bus arrived at Emma's stop, Zach followed her off and took her hand.

"Let's go for a walk," he said, his voice indicating his interest went beyond walking.

"I don't want to," Emma said. "Go home."

"Come on," he begged. "Just for a while."

Zach no longer looked cute, but like one more person in this world who needed something from her. He squeezed her hand as she tried to pull away.

"Don't ruin the whole night," he said.

Without answering him, Emma slipped her hand out of her mitten, leaving Zach holding the empty blue wool, and ran the block to her house.

Once inside, she slammed her backpack on the hall table, tore off her jacket, and stomped into the living room. Gracie and her mother sprawled on the couch, her mother resting her hand on Gracie's ankle.

Afraid that she'd throw up right then and there, she ran into the small hall bathroom, landing on her knees in front of the toilet just in time. Everything she'd eaten at Zach's came out in waves. Her hands shook as she tried to grab the towel from the rack.

"Here." Her mother stood in the open doorway holding a half-full glass. "And here," she added, handing the towel to Emma.

"What's that?" Emma croaked out, pointing her chin at the glass.

"Coke."

"We don't have Coke," Emma said.

"I've always kept some in the basement. Hidden. For when one of us. Got sick. Drink a little. It helps with nausea. Or if you. Throw up again. You'll need something in your. Stomach."

Emma took the chilled glass. Smashed ice floated in the Coke.

That's what her mother had always done when any of them got sick—smashed ice in a plastic bag so they had the soothing feel of ice chips in the medicinal soda. She glanced at her mother's hand to make sure she hadn't bashed a finger or something, but they all looked intact.

She pulled herself away from the toilet and sat cross-legged on the cool tile. Her mother leaned over and flushed away the horror that had been the Epstein dinner. She wet a washcloth, sank beside Emma, and took her hands. Scratchy hot fabric soothed away the awful bits of sick on her hands and face. Her mother's touch brought forth a bout of tears.

"Do you feel any. Better? Bad food? Maybe a stomach flu?" Her mother held her damp hand. "Should I call Daddy?"

"No!" Emma wrapped her arms around her mother. "Please don't tell Daddy!"

"Okay. Tell me. What's wrong?"

Emma spoke into her mother's robe. "I did something bad. Very bad."

Her mother said nothing, just stroked Emma's hair from her forehead in a soothing rhythm, reminding her of . . . of her mother.

"I . . . Caro gave me . . . I didn't feel like I could do everything. And Caro gave me pills."

"What kind?"

"Legal ones. She had a prescription. Ritalin."

Her mother nodded. "So many kids. Get that pill. It's stupid." She took a breath. "Though not as stupid. As her giving it. To you. And you taking them."

"I know it was wrong, Mom. And they made me feel awful." Emma sat up and looked into her mother's eyes. "Well, not every one felt awful. Some made me feel good."

"That's very, very scary. For you. And for me."

"Once I felt so bad I took one of your pills. One of your 'relaxing' pills."

"More scary." Her mother put a hand to her chest. "We need to make this. Stop. Now. I have to talk. To Daddy."

"Please, please. Don't tell Daddy right away, okay?" Emma clutched her mother's hands. "I swear to God that I won't do it anymore. It was stupid. I know. There was just . . . I was so—"

"Overwhelmed. There was too much work. For you. I know, baby. I know."

"Will you?"

"Tell Daddy?" Her mother shook her head. "Not right now. But I can't make forever. Promises. We have to talk. A lot."

"I know." Emma smiled. "I'd like that."

"Come to the couch. And bring a brush."

"So. Besides your upset. Stomach. Bad night?" her mother asked as she settled next to Gracie. "Emma had a bad something. Maybe Zach's mother's cooking."

"Zach is an idiot." Emma sat on the floor in front of her mother and unplaited her braid.

"What did he do?"

"Oh, I can't even describe it. His parents are so . . ." She grimaced. "His father even grilled me about my grades!"

"Poor Emma," Gracie said.

"And they asked me things about being Jewish!" Emma added. She shook out her long hair, spreading it over her shoulders.

"Like what?"

Emma put the brush in her mother's hand and leaned back. "Like who was Jewish—you or Daddy. And like they gave me some big prize by saying that since you're Jewish, I'm Jewish."

Calmness enveloped her as her mother brushed her hair. For the first time since the accident, Emma felt almost happy.

"That's why I'm. Glad. I married Daddy."

"Because he's not Jewish?" Gracie asked.

"No. Because it didn't matter. Like that. Like Zach's family. Like just being born. One way. Makes you special. Or better."

"Is that why you never took us to temple?" Emma asked. "Or had us bar mitzvahed?"

"Bat mitvah. For a girl." Emma turned and saw her mother's sweet smile. "I got. Lots of presents. It felt like. I was being welcomed. Into a club. Where only some people. Could join. I never liked that."

"You didn't like being Jewish?" Gracie asked.

"That's not it. I love it. Especially the food." Her mother rubbed Emma's temples in soothing circles. "But people fight. Religion. Makes people mean. Or lonely. Like they're not. In the club. Or their club. Is wrong."

Her mother took a breath after the long speech. She bent over and kissed the top of Emma's head and then continued. "So Daddy and I never. Joined. Anything. Maybe. We were wrong. Did you miss it?"

Emma wasn't sure, but she didn't want to hurt her mother. "It was fine."

Gracie fingered the angel on her collar. "Should I take this off?"

"No!" her mother said. "In fact, I think. I want one. Prayers can be answered. But they should never. Be called. To hurt. As though. You have. The only answer."

"What do you think the answer is, Mom?" Being able to ask her mother for guidance made Emma want to hug the world.

Her mother answered with slow surety. "Your deeds. An open heart."

"Oh, I really love you, Mom." Emma reached up and took her mother's hands. "God, Zach wasn't even embarrassed by his parents."

Emma paused. "Mom? Do you think Daddy hates me?"

"Daddy loves you."

"But he blames me, right?"

"For what?"

"For telling you. And making him move out."

Her mother squeezed her hand. "Emma. I told Daddy to leave."

"Because of what I said. Because I said he was so mad that he hurt you." Emma slid back down and tugged her mother's hand back to her hair, hungry for her touch.

"No. Because of what. He did. Because he didn't tell." Her mother reached for Emma's hand. "You told the truth. That's good."

"But now you and Daddy are getting a divorce." Tears thickened Gracie's already cold-clogged voice. "I don't want that."

"I know," her mother said.

"Daddy would come back if you said so," Gracie said. "Please let him come back."

Emma wanted to beg right along with Gracie.

Baruch Atah Adonai, Eloheinu Melech Ha'Olam, please bring my father home.

CHAPTER 38

Ben

Maddy, Emma, and Gracie were curled up together, asleep on the couch, when Ben returned with Caleb from the Celtics game. The eleven o'clock news showed a raging fire in East Boston.

"Why is everyone sleeping?" Caleb asked.

"Shh. It's late, that's why," Ben whispered to his son. "Come on, buddy. Bedtime."

"I'm up," Maddy said softly.

"Mommy!" Caleb ran to the couch. "Did we wake you up?"

"Ouch. You got me in the stomach, idiot," Emma yelled.

Caleb dove between Emma and Maddy until Emma finally said, "I give up," and slid to the floor, dragging a pillow with her.

"Guess what? The Celtics won! Daddy bought me food and candy, and Uncle Andrew got me this." He waved a green hat in front of Maddy's face. "He said since he didn't have a son, I could be his onray son so he had someone to go to games with. What's onray? Is it like X-ray? Can he see through me?"

"Uncle Andrew meant honorary, stupid," Emma said.

"Don't call him stupid," Maddy said.

Caleb stuck his tongue out at Emma. "I'm not stupid. I'm brain-injured."

Ben watching for Maddy's reaction.

"You're not brain-injured." Maddy tickled Caleb's stomach. "You're tummy-injured. Because Daddy. Put so much. Junk in there."

Emma groaned. "Mom, don't encourage him."

"Why not? He's special." Maddy showered Caleb's face with kisses.

"Special needs, maybe," Emma said. "Probably caught it from Mom."

Ben caught Emma's eyes and laughed. His chest tightened when she smiled back. He turned to Maddy, trying to share the moment, but she wouldn't look at him.

"We should. All go to sleep," she said. "Emma? Help the kids into bed?"

"I can do it myself," Gracie mumbled, her eyes closed.

Emma tugged at Gracie's arm until she stumbled up; she put out her other hand toward Caleb.

"Daddy? Will you come up and kiss us?" Gracie asked.

"Right up, sweet pea." The air turned sour the moment the kids left. "Did Emma have a good time at Zach's house?" Ben asked. "We should probably invite him over here now, right?" He walked around the room, picking up books, a doll, a sweatshirt.

"There's no 'we.'" Maddy walked over and took everything from his arms and dumped it on the couch. "Leave that stuff. Go kiss Gracie. And Emma. She needs you."

Ben wasn't surprised when he found Gracie's room empty. He opened the door to his bedroom—Maddy's bedroom—and saw his younger daughter sprawled across the cover. Everything in the room looked spotless. Perfect. Anne's touch was all over the house. He despised it.

"You have to go to your bed, sweet pea," Ben said.

He led her toward her own bed. "Emma thinks you hate her," she murmured as he bent to kiss her. "She told Mommy."

Ben took an afghan from the foot of the bed and tucked it around her. "I love Emma very much. And you. And Caleb."

"Do you love Mommy?"

"I loved Mommy before I ever loved anyone else in the world."

"But you loved Grandma and Grandpa Illica first, right?"

Ben paused. He screwed his kids up enough. "Sure. I meant in the falling-in-love romantic way."

"Do you still love Mommy that way?"

He bent over and kissed her. "More than ever."

In the hall, a light came from Emma's room. "Honey," he called softly through the door.

"What?" Her tone was neutral.

"Can I come in?" Ben pushed the door and peeked in. Emma sat on the floor, her laptop on her knees. "What are you doing?"

She shrugged. "Nothing."

"How was your night with Zach's parents?"

Her scowl told him not so good. She shrugged again, her eyes still on the computer. "He's an idiot. I think I'm breaking up with him. Maybe I already did."

"Are you upset?" he asked.

"Only a little about him." Emma turned and looked sadder than she'd been in her whole life. "A lot about us. Everything is my fault."

He sat beside her. "Nothing is your fault. I told you that."

"You had to leave because of me."

"That's not true, Em." Ben clutched her hand. "I was wrong. I should have told your mother how the accident happened. And then I got so mad . . . you were forced into telling her."

It was true. He'd made his daughter begin to uncover his sins, and then he made sure Maddy found out the rest all by herself. What a coward he'd turned out to be.

Emma threw her arms around his neck. "I'm sorry, Daddy."

"You have nothing to be sorry for."

"I'm sorry you're not here."

Ben squeezed her hand. "Me too," he said.

• • •

Ben wondered if the waitress thought he was pathetic, sitting at the table in Zaftigs restaurant for so long. He'd finished his eggs, bacon, home fries, and fruit, drunk four cups of coffee, read every article in the *Boston Globe* and *New York Times*, and it was still only ten a.m. He could think of no way to fill the empty day ahead of him except by going to work. Hey, he could work in jeans—that almost made the day festive, right?

Driving downtown, he detoured to see his father—a sudden decision, which he confirmed as a good decision when he got a parking spot only five houses from his parents' brick townhouse. They lived in a particularly dense antique street in Beacon Hill, a neighborhood noted for gaslights, brick sidewalks, and old money.

"What are you doing here?" his father asked when he opened the door.

"Are you going to ask me in?" Ben asked.

"Your mother's not here," said the Judge.

"I know." Saturday morning. Choir practice.

His father stepped away—reluctantly, it seemed—giving him room to enter.

"There's coffee in the kitchen," his father said. "I'm seated in the library."

Ben filled a cup and carried it carefully. When he entered the study, his father seemed to have forgotten Ben's presence. Finally, he looked up, neatly folded the *New York Times* along its original crease line, and placed it on top of an inlaid side table.

"What brings you here?" the Judge asked.

Ben stared into his father's eyes. "Maddy's kicked me out."

"Because of the accident?"

"And other things."

"Such as?"

Ben examined the pattern in the Oriental rug, counting the numbers of boxes within boxes.

"Don't want to say?" His father lifted his white china cup, took a sip, and set it down with a sigh. "I'm limited to one a day now. Can you believe it? It hardly seems worthwhile to wake up. Sometimes, when your mother isn't looking, I sneak an extra one. Of course, who am I fooling? So who did you sleep with?"

"*Who* doesn't matter. It was back when Maddy was in the hospital."

"Do you love her?"

"The girl? Don't be ridiculous." Ben leaned his elbows on the leather arms of the club chair and steepled his fingers. "I need help."

"I can't remember the last time I heard you admit that."

"Don't make this any harder for me than it is," Ben said.

"Why shouldn't it be hard for you? You did a damn foolish thing." His father stood and began pacing. "I did many stupid things in my day, but I was always loyal to your mother."

Sarcastic remarks almost slipped from Ben, but he caught himself. His father should be proud of his faithfulness. Ben wanted that for his parents.

"Anyway, this is about much more than that," his father said. "Your behavior throughout your marriage has been abominable. All that yelling and screaming."

Ben stared at his father as though seeing an apparition.

"Did you think we didn't notice? Your family is our family." The Judge placed his large hands on his knees. "It shamed us."

Ben formed words to lash out and then swallowed them. "How come you never stopped me?"

"How come you never stopped yourself?" His father's face sagged. "Perhaps you blamed me? Perhaps we made our home too restricted, too silent, and once you had freedom you took it too far. Or perhaps you simply caught that penchant for anger from your grandfather."

"Grandpa Charlie?"

"You knew him when he became mellow. Your mother grew up with glasses whizzing past her head. When I proposed, she made me promise to always keep myself in check."

Ben thought of the quiet cool house in which he was raised— apparently it was a haven for his mother.

"You always had a temper. Remember how we fined you each time you raised your voice? I wish we'd gotten it all out of you. You loved the sound of your own loudness."

Awareness chilled him, thinking of the relief brought on by his tirades.

"What are you planning?"

"I'm trying to get her to forgive me. I think she still loves me."

"Love. You say it as though it solves everything."

"Doesn't it?"

His father fixed his eyes on Ben. "If you're out of the house, you better start thinking about a lawyer, Ben." He gave a bark of a laugh. "Another one."

Ben drew himself up. "We're nowhere near that level of acrimony."

"Her father will hire her one in a New York minute." His father snapped his fingers. "A sharpie, that's for sure. They'll take every cent you have."

"Back up, Dad."

"Don't be a fool—wouldn't you give the same advice to Caleb, if you were in my shoes?"

"If I were in your shoes, I'd wonder why Caleb had screwed up so royally and how to help him get his family back."

His father stopped pacing. "If you can get your wife back, fine and dandy, although she probably deserves far better than you. Nevertheless, you'd best start worrying about protecting what's yours. Without a lawyer, your bank account will become a leaky faucet. And don't tell me you can do it yourself—because in that case you'll have the stupidest lawyer of all."

What had Ben been thinking, coming here for help? How sad that even after turning forty, he still thought that somehow his father held wisdom that Ben himself lacked.

On Sunday, Ben woke early, made a crummy cup of coffee in his hotel room, laced up his sneakers, and drove to Jamaica Pond before breakfast. The boathouse, the bathrooms, everything was locked up. The cracked cement fountain was dry, the water turned off for the winter. The pure blue morning light depressed him. Gray clouds would afford some cover, some comfort.

An elderly man approached, so bundled Ben knew his age only by his gait. A large collie bounded past. Two women deep in conversation came toward him. Like lovers, they only had eyes for each other. One woman listened, rewrapping a fleecy pink scarf around her neck as she nodded and laughed. The other almost skipped as she related what must be good news. Scarf woman hugged her friend and shrieked with delight.

"July twenty-second—I can't believe it!"

What couldn't she believe? A baby? A wedding? Europe? Whatever it was, she seemed thrilled.

They seemed like best friends. Ben always thought he and Maddy were best friends. Yes, they fought. His fault, no doubt. But he wouldn't dream of leaving her—not before, not after, not now. *This is for life, Mad,* he'd said when he gave her the engagement ring. *Not pretend forever.* He'd meant it. Richer, poorer, better, worse, sickness, health. Hadn't he proved his commitment—done his part? Time for her to keep up her end of the bargain.

Running now, Ben stripped off his gloves. What was she thinking? Who'd take care of her and the kids? She could barely read. Was she planning to move back with her parents and let Anne and Jake raise his children? Over his dead body.

His footsteps matched the hammering in his temples. Despite chastising his father, he thought of smart lawyers, ways around this. He could have Maddy declared incompetent, be appointed her guardian ad litem.

Ben stopped, placing his hands on his knees as he tried to catch his breath, tried to figure out how to grab back his life as it slipped through his fingers.

He wanted his best friend back. He needed her.

She needed him, for God's sake.

•   •   •

"I went to my father. For advice," Ben told Maddy as she unpacked the groceries he'd brought. He'd gone from the pond to Whole Foods, buying every expensive organic piece of produce he thought Maddy might like. Runny cheese. Crackers thick with seeds. Canned goods branded with smiling fish and vegetables. He hoped his own smile appeared endearing and not the grimace it felt like.

Maddy sat on the floor in front of the cabinet where they kept the cans, pulling them out and then putting them back, using some system that Ben didn't understand and Maddy wouldn't remember tomorrow.

"Impressive. Or stupid. Not sure. Don't care." She measured cans of chickpeas and string beans next to each other.

"Nothing my father said was the least bit helpful," Ben pressed on. "Yet somehow he helped simply by being him."

Maddy looked over at him. "Stop being devious. Say what you want. To say."

He knelt next to her. "Maybe I'm more like my father than I ever knew. It's always about me, right? All the time. Even when you were hurt, I still worried about me. I think I'm finally getting a clue."

She held a can of wild salmon, waiting. The floor gleamed.

"But I realized today—just now, as I ran at the pond—that it's about you. You were hurt. You were the one damaged, and it's your life that's . . ." He stopped.

"You're just finding out. Now?"

"Of course not. But finally, it's in my bones. And I know that you need me. I can help." He ran a hand over his cheek. "You still love me."

"I don't even know. Anymore. Anyway, I'm too busy. Learning how to live."

"But—"

"It will hurt. To say good-bye. Of course. But it must end."

"No. There's no must. We're meant to be together."

"We were meant to be safe. With each other." She built a tower of tuna cans.

He dropped to Maddy and took her hand. She didn't pull it away, just let it remain limp in his. "I know I've been awful. But I can be a good man." He stared into her eyes, trying to will her back to him by force.

"Too late." Maddy pulled away and stood. "Maybe you have to love. A bad man. To learn to love a good man. Maybe. You've just been. My bad man. For too long."

"I care about you. More than I care about anything."

"Care?" Maddy looked down at where he crouched. She grabbed her omnipresent notebook from the counter, riffled through the pages, and then stabbed her finger at the paper. "Listen: *The ideal man. Bears the accidents of life with. Dignity and grace. Making the best of circumstances.* That's Aristotle. I copied it. From Zelda's office. I so wanted to be. Dignified and graceful. But now I know. How could I? I didn't have an accident. Of life. It was. An accident of marriage."

CHAPTER 39

Maddy

Maddy pulled four plates and glasses from the kitchen cabinet. She bent to get napkins from below, pushing aside the stack of organic tuna Ben had brought two weeks before, evoking all over again the annoyance she'd felt as he spread the Whole Foods wares before her as though presenting offerings to some domestic goddess who had never been Maddy.

Maybe it was supposed to be like this: just the kids and her. *Bashert,* her grandfather would say. Meant to be.

Ben had begged her to go to his Christmas party that evening. He promised *she* wouldn't be there, but why would she take the word of a man who cheated? Why trust a woman who'd jump a man while his wife was in a coma? She'd probably be there ready to grab Ben as though he were an appetizer—her personal plate of pigs in blankets.

And then there were his coworkers. Did he think she could stand being under the glare of their concern? She'd dealt with this each time she visited her own workplace, her weekly acclimation visits as she worked toward someday getting back there on a regular basis. Coworkers took her hand and asked their poor-Maddy questions with big cow-pity eyes. *How are you? Really. Are you feeling better?* All the while searching her face for fresh kill for the gossip bank. Scanning for brain damage.

So what do you think? Ben's office buddies would ask each other after talking to her, holding little plastic glasses of crappy wine in their hands and eating even crappier cheese and crackers as they examined her for signs of intelligent life.

No, thanks.

Tonight Maddy planned to devote herself to conquering a major recovery objective, making dinner by herself. Notes outlined the steps she'd take, an assignment from Zelda. She'd planned the menu with her mother—something nutritious the kids would like. Nothing that required perfect timing. Maddy needed to begin with food that was patient.

Cooking supper plan:
Turkey meatloaf. Honeyed carrot pennies. Baked potatoes.
Get recipes from mother.
Start cooking three pm to eat at six.

This would be her first night making supper completely alone since the bad night.

There'd be no Ben listening from the other room for the sound of flames crackling; no Gracie at the kitchen table, pretending to do homework as she tracked Maddy's every move; no Caleb bouncing between watching television and studying his mother. Emma wouldn't monitor her like a miniature nanny.

Maddy's father had taken the kids out Christmas shopping—no doubt buying entire sections of Target and Macy's to make them happy. He'd wanted her to come, but she'd declined. Stores overwhelmed her these days. When she'd let him drag her the month before to pick out a Chanukah present for her mother, she'd barely made it through the afternoon. Clothes, jewelry, purses, sizes, colors, types, departments, negotiating, people pushing. Too multimedia, Zelda said. Maddy would opt out of consuming for now. Saving money for when she became post-Ben poor was an excellent idea anyway.

After she said no to joining them shopping, her father wanted to bring dinner back—*you don't have to keep pushing yourself,* he'd said—and eat with them, but she'd said no to that also, telling him to just drop the kids off and not to come in when he did. Tonight was for Maddy and the kids.

She'd weathered his hurt tone.

Get over yourself, Dad.

For the third, maybe fourth time, Maddy checked the list of ingredients. Her mother had typed the recipe in an extra-large font—once again treating her as though she'd been blinded rather than become a slow reader. As though one disability begat another. Her mother still had a hard time realizing bigger didn't help, and shouting instructions didn't make them any more intelligible.

"Just be patient, for God's sake," Maddy kept telling her mother. "Let me do it my way. Who cares?"

Damn. The recipe wasn't making sense.

Carrots, butter, honey—these things were supposed to go together? She crumpled the paper and threw it on the floor.

Then she picked it up.

Boo hoo. Poor Maddy.

She willed herself to snap out of it.

Poor victimized Maddy.

People didn't just want to pet pathetic victims—they also wanted to kick them. Crying gave away her power, and God knows she had little enough clout left.

She smoothed the recipe paper, trying to erase the wrinkles, and then she read it in her usual welcome-to-the-slow-class way.

After peeling and then laying out the carrots in straight lines, she sliced them into discs. She needed hours to cook because no one trusted her to use the food processor—including herself—and she had a need these days to make everything equal. Quite different from before, when she'd smack the knife into vegetables at random angles and lengths, rushing them toward the pot.

She tipped the plate of carrot discs over the pot and slid them into the bubbling mix of butter, honey, water, and brown sugar. *NOT TOO*

MUCH SUGAR, her mother had written, shouting even through the paper. *YOU'RE NOT MAKING DESSERT!!!!*

Using an old wooden spoon, Maddy made gentle strokes through the liquid. At moments, being slow bestowed a beatific aura upon her. As though she were a nun. An instant became pure unto itself. Now, when she hugged Gracie, she was doing nothing but embracing, not mentally beginning the next step, not pulling away from her daughter so she could fold the laundry.

Of course, now she had another problem. Transitions. She could stay in that embrace for a year. Zelda promised it would come together. Like a recipe. Her brainpan had to reduce it to the right brew; she was making reasoning essence, Maddy reduction.

Ketchup, breadcrumbs, and an egg folded into the ground meat to become a slick thick blend. She stirred in dry onion soup mix. Then she remembered to turn back to the stove and stir the carrots again. They'd almost begun sticking—but that was okay. She'd almost burned food plenty of times before the accident.

Two hours later, when she heard the door open, she hurried to the hall to greet the kids. "Okay, you guys. Into the living room. No arguments. It's almost ready."

Emma looked uncertain, Gracie worried, and Caleb hungry.

"Really. It's all fine. No more than five minutes."

"Here," Caleb said. He handed her a white bag with a spot of grease, meanwhile hiding something behind his back. "From Grandpa."

"You look pretty, Mommy," Gracie said.

Maddy took the bag from Caleb and then twirled in the garnet-red silky dress Vanessa had given her. "For a special night," her sister had said. Maddy couldn't imagine a more wonderful occasion than this dinner.

She threw kisses and returned to the dining room. Gently, carefully, she lit candles, filled glasses with ice and sparkling water, and hit the dimmer switch. It looked normal, like something she might have done before.

Better. She didn't think she'd lit candles for a long time.

Once more she smiled. And then knotted her brow.

Something was wrong.

She looked around. Nothing was out of place. Lemon oil scented the air along with cinnamon candles.

What was incorrect? An odd energy tilted her balance in the wrong direction. She walked the perimeter of the room, stopping, staring, four times, until the lack of equilibrium clicked into place.

Where there once were two gleaming cobalt wedding glasses, deep blue veined with twists of gold, now there was one. Had one of the kids broken the missing glass?

That seemed so unlikely.

Her mother would know. Meanwhile, forget that. At least she'd figured out the problem of what was lost. She could hear Zelda lecturing her: *Concentrate on the good.*

On the table went the covered meatloaf dish. The dish of sweet carrots. The potatoes. Butter. Sour cream.

She walked out to the hallway and called for the kids. "Dinner!" She wanted to say it over and over.

Dinner!

Dinner!

Dinner!

She straightened a plate of croissants—ones that had been in the bag delivered by Caleb. Not part of her menu, but what the heck. She'd never been an extremist.

Not that she remembered.

The kids ran in as a pack, as though they'd been biting their nails out in the living room, waiting to see if she'd burn the house down.

"It looks beautiful, Mommy! Like a picture," Caleb said.

"You did a great job." Emma's hug felt like a kid's embrace again. Gracie came up with her hands behind her back. "Here." She thrust a large bouquet of yellow freesia at Maddy. "From us. Grandpa didn't pick them out—we did."

"And we paid for them," Caleb said. "Well, mainly Emma. From her camp money. But I gave a dollar that Grandpa gave me last week."

"Me too," Gracie said.

Delicate perfume rose from the flowers, and she inhaled. "My favorites."

"That's what I said! I picked them out!" Caleb said. "I win."

"We all win." She hugged her son. "We all win."

"Not all of us. Daddy isn't here," Gracie said.

"He's at the party, remember? He had to go," Emma said. "For work. He could have come for dinner if we wanted, right, Mom?"

"Sure, sweetheart." Feeling magnanimous and having the power to bestow wishes in the candlelight warmed her. "Who's ready to eat?"

Emma helped bring in the dishes and placed them on the trivets Maddy had miraculously remembered to put on the table.

She ladled out carrots and cut slices of meatloaf. The kids forked up potatoes.

"Mmm. Delicious, Mom—really, really great," Gracie said.

"I did. A good job. Right?" She took a forkful of the vegetables and nodded for compliments.

"Right!" Gracie said.

Each bite they took gave her more pleasure. "More?" she asked when they'd scraped their plates.

"Daddy!" Caleb yelled.

She turned and saw Ben behind her, a finger up to his lips.

"Surprise, Maddy." He put one hand on her shoulder, and with the other presented a wrapped bouquet. "Merry two-days-before-Christmas."

"Flowers." She didn't take them. "The kids beat you."

"Big deal, Mom," Emma said. "Dad's are probably prettier. Open them."

She unwrapped what were, no doubt, a true dozen red roses, Ben's go-to gift. Instead, she found a rolled-up scroll of heavy embossed paper tied with a riot of colored raffia.

"Open it, Mom," Gracie begged.

Their frenetically happy tension induced a sudden desire to leave, turn on the television, go to sleep.

Her unsteady hands plucked at the knot until the bright pieces of straw let go. Then, using both hands, she tried to unroll the large sheet of watercolor paper.

Ben moved her plate and glass, brushed off crumbs, and removed the silverware, making room.

"I made it!" Caleb yelled. "See, Mommy. I drew it all."

Caleb's Chagall-like portrait had them floating in the air. Maddy wore a white dress, gold stars dotting the fabric. They were crossed, Ben's body bisected by hers. His white suit made him appear part cowboy, part preacher. Silver moons peppered his clothes. Surrounding them were smaller portraits of Emma and Gracie and a self-portrait of Caleb, who hung over her shoulder as she examined the picture.

"It's lovely." She took Caleb's face between her hands and lifted it up toward her own. "Thank you, honey."

"It was Daddy's idea. He said you'd like a family picture for Christmas. Gracie traced the letters. We're going to frame it!"

"It's just beautiful." She smiled and held back from punching Ben.

"And there's this." The envelope Ben handed her felt like his mother's expensive stationery. "Go upstairs and read it. Please. The kids and I will clean up. And then we'll have dessert. Your mom told me what you made. I brought ice cream for them."

He had to gild the lily, couldn't leave her brownies alone. And she hadn't made them; her mother had. Maddy had never baked before. Did Ben think she was going to start now?

She pinched her lips together so she wouldn't scream and swear. Then she climbed the stairs.

Her hands shook as she read the letter one excruciating word at a time.

Maddy,

I read some books. The kind I usually dismiss because I think I am too good and smart for them—Angry Men, Couples Needing Books to Make Their Marriage Work, Men Who Women Should Leave. *You know the type.*

*I want to fix everything. I want to make it all better, or at least
a lot better. I want to be with you while you heal.*

I want you to like me again.

I.
I.
I.

Every sentence began with a plea about him. She crumpled up
the letter and threw it away without finishing his argument for taking
him back, afraid his words would drown her. Bury her in bullshit.

The bedroom door opened. Ben held out a cup of tea.

This husband who wanted to heal her, make it all better, this particular husband didn't even give her time to finish the letter if that's
what she wanted. He didn't even remember how long it took her to
read these days.

He didn't even knock.

"You always have. So many words," she said. "I wish I did."

Ben set the cup on the night table and lowered himself into the
rocking chair. "Maddy. I understand. Finally. Please. I can't breathe
without you."

"You're breathing, Ben."

"I'm not being dramatic. I honestly don't have a clue what I'll do
without you and the kids."

"The kids will still be. Your kids."

He sat forward. "Not in the same way. I want to wake up and go to
sleep in the same house as them."

"See. Still about you. *You. You. You.*"

"Right. You're right. I'll work on it. The anger. The self-pity. Everything. And you'll concentrate on healing." He stopped. "Am I asking
too much?"

She thought about it, trying to find the words, the words that he'd
taken from her. Wondering if she'd always be thinking about what she
couldn't do or say.

"Ben. What happened to the glass?"

"The glass?" A befuddled expression came over him. He tipped his head to the side as though to better receive her words.

"Our wedding glasses. The blue ones. There's only one now. Where's the other?"

He pressed his lips together as though keeping words from her.

"Tell me."

He rocked forward and pulled at his wedding ring. The way he avoided her eyes told her part of the truth without a word. She wasn't surprised when he spoke.

"I broke it. I was angry. And I threw it at the wall."

"Were you angry at me?"

"No. I was angry at what happened to you."

"And in this anger about me . . . Missing me. Worrying about me." She had to stop and catch her breath, holding up a hand to prevent Ben from interrupting. "Did you think about me? Me coming home? Me loving those glasses? Me looking for them?"

"I guess I was only thinking about me." He put his hands out, palms up, as though offering himself on a platter of shame. "I hated myself the moment I did it. It was wrong. I have no excuse. Nothing to offer but apologies. I'm so sorry."

It was just a glass. No more, right?

But it wasn't replaceable. Those glasses witnessed their marriage.

Freud took aim, and the pair was irretrievably broken in half. Ben had smashed it in a moment of anger. Heartbroken anger, she was certain, but nonetheless anger that took precedence over all else at the moment. Even as he mourned her, he'd broken off yet another piece of them. She'd been crushed in absentia.

"I've changed," he said. "You'll see."

"You want. Forgiveness. That's never too much to ask. Of course. I can forgive you." She stopped to breathe, putting a finger to Ben's lips to keep him quiet. After a moment she continued. "Otherwise. I won't. Live right. Not with. Anger. Weighing on me. Renting all that space. In my head. But. Can I live with you?"

"Because of . . . ?"

"No. Yes. Maybe. All of it. The sex with her, it was for you, I know. Soothing. Like candy. You were a baby." Maddy paused, desperate to form truthful words. "But. You're not. A baby. You're a man who didn't try hard enough."

"It will never happen again—never." Ben grabbed her hand. His touch smothered her, made her feel as though her hand were dying. She swore she could feel *him* now on her flesh—as though he were spreading his molecules on her. She pulled away, wiping her hand on the blanket. Wanting to wash off his touch.

"I know I wasn't perfect," Maddy said. "But you snapped our hearts. I can't forget. What you're capable. Of. Such rage. That you. Forget everyone. But yourself." Her sentences were getting shorter, worse, as though Ben's pressure, his pounding need to return, pushed her backward. If she let him come home, maybe everyone would get better except for her.

Ben straightened. His face contorted with the effort of being calm—of not arguing.

"*Was.*" He insisted. "It's what I *was* capable of."

She laced her fingers. "If you had. Paralyzed someone. A stranger. Or ruined. Someone else's mind. What then? You'd still have broken our family. Two families."

"Is that why you don't want me back? Because of what might have been?"

"No, Ben. Because I don't want. To wait every night," she said. "Wondering about how. My night. Will be. Your moods. I don't want them. Ruling our world." She unfolded her legs, cramped from the cross-legged position. "My world. I can't. I won't. Protect anyone, including me, from you. Not anymore."

They remained silent. Ben turned away from her as she lay back against the pillows. She heard his wrenching ugly sobs.

"I'm sorry," he said, his words muffled. "For what I did to you."

"I know. That I do know."

Did she have the courage to struggle with this, with him, while also making the enormous efforts she'd need to recover? If she were alone, with her mother and father, would it be easier?

Her children, she knew what they wanted.

How about me?

What do I want?

She closed her eyes and prayed for wisdom.

Ben touched her shoulder. Traces of his father showed in the crepelike skin around the corners of his eyes. When she rested her hand on his chest, she saw her mother's fingers.

Maddy didn't want to lose this family.

But she couldn't serve any more tears for supper.

She needed to learn how to live her life.

"Get help, Ben," she said. "Go find someone. A therapist. A friend. A group. I can't do it for you. I can't social-work you anymore."

So quiet it barely sounded like him, he asked, "Can I come home if I prove myself?"

He looked so sad. Ben needed her to say yes; he wanted her to wrap him up with a big flourish of a bow. The temptation was so strong she almost choked on the *yes!* Tried to get it out from her heart. A *yes!* to make him happy. A *yes!* to make the children happy.

Yes! to make everyone around them think happily ever after.

She could soothe a world of people with her yes.

"I can't imagine what will happen if we're not together. To you. To us," Ben said. "It frightens me."

"What do you think will happen if I said no?"

Ben pulled back a bit, as though warding himself against the inevitable. "We'd lose hope. The kids. Me. And you, Maddy. Wouldn't you lose hope for what we could be? Hope that we could bring back the best of us?"

Could Ben comprehend how faraway worry about "us" seemed at this time? Concentrating on retrieving even a tiny bit of "her" consumed Maddy. How could she worry about her marriage? She didn't know who "her" would be in the future. Explaining this seemed impossible.

But maybe that's what she owed him. The kids. Trying to teach him.

"Ben. I need to find me now. Not *us*." She had to explain in a way that promised nothing. "I need to do that alone. Well, alone with the kids. Listen. Perhaps *maybe* is possible. Maybe is the only thing about us I can imagine."

She saw Ben's hope surge. She sensed his gathering strength.

"But no more," she warned. "Don't ask any. More of me than that. I'm not asking. For patience. Or time. I'm saying the door. Isn't nailed shut. That's all."

"That's plenty. Thank you."

"It's not time for thanks. The thing of it is this. Maybe I don't know how. To give up on someone I love. But if I need to, I can learn."

"You won't have to. I'll prove myself."

She pulled back away, avoiding his touch as he reached out. "I don't know."

"What does that mean?" Ben, Ben, her lawyer word-mincer, he wanted certainty. A gift she no longer had to offer. Not now. Maybe never.

"Find an apartment. Fix yourself. I hate you as much as I love you. Maybe I have for a long time. I don't want that anymore."

Ben stood and nodded. "I will become your good man. You'll see."

She didn't know if he could manage goodness.

She didn't know if offering hope was a mistake.

She didn't know if Ben could keep his promise.

And she didn't know if she'd be sorry when she woke up alone tomorrow.

However, she'd told the truth, something that once had seemed so impossible. After telling the truth, you couldn't, you didn't, take it back.

The past had already happened. Using hope and courage, they constructed their solid present. And perhaps, just maybe, now there was a chance of shaping an honorable and loving future.

All of them.

ACKNOWLEDGMENTS

Many people supported me in writing *Accidents of Marriage*, but none more than my husband, Jeff Rand, who holds my heart.

Stéphanie Abou has been my wise, warm, and determined partner from the beginning, as has everyone at Foundry Literary + Media. Atria Books is everything you want a publisher to be. Judith Curr's wisdom and love of books is always apparent and I thank her for allowing me a place in the Atria fold. Greer Hendricks is my dream-come-true editor, and I am forever grateful to be working with her. Sarah Cantin makes everything about publishing happier, easier, and better. Elaine Broeder and Lisa Sciambra define indefatigability and goodness. Kimberly Goldstein and Mary Beth Constant performed miracles with my mountains of errors.

Nancy MacDonald is a rock, improving everything she touches. Rose Daniels built a website that makes me grateful for her every day.

Ginny Deluca provides faith when my own is lacking; Melisse Shapiro keeps me safe from bad choices (by letting me say them all aloud). My life would be lacking a center without them. My beloved writing group—Nichole Bernier, Kathy Crowley, Juliette Fay, and Liz Moore are four of the wisest, warmest (and when need be, strictest) women in the world.

To my circle of cherished and trusted writer friends—bless our virtual water fountain: my dearly loved Chris Abouzeid, Ann Bauer,

Robin Black, Jenna Blum, Dell Smith, Becky Tuch, and Julie Wu—you are all way beyond talented and loving.

Heartfelt thanks to the Grub Street Writer's Center of Boston, especially Eve Bridburg, Chris Castellani, Whitney Scharer, and Sonya Larson, for bringing us all together and making dreams come true. Real-life hugs to everyone in the fabulous online Fiction Writer's Co-op, with a special shout-out to Cathy Buchanan for putting us all together.

Thank you Nina Lev for listening to me agonize, and Kris Alden for telling me which authors I should be reading and sharing them.

My deep love and thanks belong to my family, including the sisters of my heart, Diane Butkus and Susan Knight. I bask in the love of my cousin, Sherri Danny, sisters-in-law, Nicole Todini and Jean Rand; and my brother-in-law, Bruce Rand. And Mom, you are always with me.

Those who own my heart, who offer comfort, joy, and understanding: my sister (and best friend), Jill Meyers; my children and my granddaughter: Becca Wolfson, Sara, Jason, and Nora Hoots, thank you all for being so sweet and funny, and, again, the love of my life, Jeff Rand.

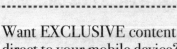